Sam Frances is a British crime thriller author from Tyne and Wear. She writes stories that combine her love of sardonic characters with her background in policing and lives in London with her partner and their wolf pack of pets.

When not writing (or daydreaming about writing or listening to writing podcasts), she can usually be found no more than 9–10 metres from a block of cheese, either in deep conversation with one of her cats, or playing a musical instrument poorly.

You can find her on Instagram and X @SamFranWriter. *One By One*, the second book in the DS Alice Washington series, is her second novel.

Also by Sam Frances

ALL EYES ON YOU

ONE BY ONE

Sam Frances

ACCENT

First published in 2025 by Headline Accent
An imprint of HEADLINE PUBLISHING GROUP

2

Cataloguing in Publication Data is available from the British Library

Paperback ISBN 978 1 0354 1844 2

Typeset in Sabon by CC Book Production

Printed and bound in Great Britain by Clays Ltd, Elcograf S.p.A.

MIX
Paper | Supporting
responsible forestry
FSC
www.fsc.org
FSC® C104740

Headline's policy is to use papers that are natural, renewable and
recyclable products and made from wood grown in well-managed forests
and other controlled sources. The logging and manufacturing processes
are expected to conform to the environmental regulations
of the country of origin.

HEADLINE PUBLISHING GROUP
An Hachette UK Company
Carmelite House
50 Victoria Embankment
London EC4Y 0DZ

The authorised representative in the EEA is Hachette Ireland,
8 Castlecourt Centre, Dublin 15, D15 XTP3, Ireland
(email: info@hbgi.ie)

www.headline.co.uk
www.hachette.co.uk

For my dad,
who'll always be a rock star to me
no matter how badly he plays guitar.

Prologue

Dolls: small models of human figures, made to look real with all the right parts. Bodies and arms and legs with pretty little heads.

I see you, your big doll eyes almost lifelike. Almost, but not quite. You've fooled them all, but not me, never me. My eyes are real. I see what you really are. You put on your show, but I remember. Never forget, never forget.

Now it's time. Time for everyone else to see.

Play nice now, like a good little toy. But I will make them see. So many ways to get this done. And it must be done, it's the only way. But how best to bend you, break you? So easy to snap you, to beat that pretty little face until the porcelain cracks. Or would one small pull of my finger on a trigger be all it takes? A simple muscle contraction setting everything in motion as the cylinder rotates and churns inside the chamber. The inner mechanics invisible to the outside world before my shots are fired, bang, bang, bang, bang. Or would a blade be more apt? Sharp and slick as I slice you, proving you are more than flesh-coloured plastic, filled with bone and tissue and fat and blood and lies.

1

And then I remember, the choice is mine, no longer yours to own. Whatever I decide is how this will end. I am in control.

This is the only way. The only option left to get what I want. To make it stop.

And it will stop. When I say so. It will all be over soon.

1

I wasn't sure which part of my predicament was worse: being late dialling into my Teams call, the sight of Roy's arse crack escaping his trousers as he fannied around under the desk trying to connect me to the internet, or – the pièce de résistance – the fact I'd be joining the thing with tampons up my nostrils to quell the nosebleed I'd been gifted in custody by a detainee with more flailing limbs than an octopus on crack. Or maybe it was the lingering sensation of the other shot I'd taken to the face in the process. Rubbing my cheek raw with paper towels had removed the globule of spit that had crawled down the side of my face like a fat snail, but not the memory of it.

I love my job, I love my job, I love my job.

Nausea swelled as Roy's waistband slipped another inch down his pasty buttocks. 'Jesus, Roy,' I said through the tampon strings tickling my lips. 'Pull your pants up! When we get connected, the last thing everyone at headquarters wants to see is what you had for breakfast.' The only silver lining was that at least he was rolling around under there in his normal work attire and not the neon-yellow Lycra onesie he'd adopted since taking up cycling which made him look like a radioactive sausage.

Roy banged his head on the underside of the desk as he reached for another loose wire. 'Christ's sake!' he said. 'Haven't had any bleedin' breakfast yet.' More grunting followed, and finally my laptop connected.

'Yes! I'm in, you're a star. Now off you go.'

A mound of grey, wiry hair appeared by the edge of the desk as Roy climbed out from under it, standing and straightening his clothes. 'You sure you don't want to sort your face out first?'

'I'm fine,' I said, waving him away. The look he liked to dish out after everything that happened last year took over his face, the *come on, we don't do bottling stuff up any more, remember?* one that reminded me of a concerned uncle. Though it had started to lean more on the side of patronising ever since him and Trudy had moved in together and began their 'fifty-six is the new twenty-six' health kick and Roy seemed to be seriously considering adding 'Zen Master' to the Detective Constable title in his email signature. 'Worry less about my face and more about that fraud job you need to update so I can do the supervisor's review later.'

The transformation from uncle to teenage son who'd been asked to bring the used glasses and mugs down from his bedroom by his mother happened instantaneously.

'Sarge,' he said in begrudging affirmation, before trudging out of the Inspector's office and pulling the door closed behind him.

The meeting host let me in from the virtual lobby and squares spread across my screen. I didn't recognise most of the faces in them. The one I did know was mid-sentence, pausing as I appeared amongst the throng.

'Thanks for joining us, Alice, eventually,' DS Bret Seaborn said, emphasising the last word in an unusual break from that monotonous voice of his. I hadn't missed it since he'd left us for a job in the intelligence bureau up at HQ.

Oh, do piss off, Bret, I wanted to say, but given any appearance of professionalism on my part was currently hanging by a literal tampon thread, I resisted the urge to make it worse. 'Morning, everyone, DS Alice Washington, Fortbridge CID, dialling in on behalf of DI Jane Josephs who's on leave. Apologies for the tardiness – I had a, shall we say, *incident* in custody that delayed me. Please, carry on.'

Confused looks stared back as Bret cleared his throat and returned to the agenda. 'All right, so, as I was saying, Detective Superintendent Scott won't be joining us so you're stuck with me as chair.'

I scanned the faces on the screen. There'd been a few names on the invite list I'd recognised, but none of them were on the call. Practically everyone had sent a deputy. A deputy deputy, in some cases. Clearly Fortbridge Rocks music festival wasn't at the top of anyone's priority list. I ground my teeth, reminding myself why I'd volunteered for this in the first place. Being too busy covering for Jane gave me a valid excuse for a few more weeks to avoid the Chief Constable's request to join her new project. The dread of what I'd say when that time was up bubbled in my stomach, but I forced the thought away as Bret started talking again.

'If we can go around the virtual room for a run-through of Op Skunk,' he said, running his hand through his neatly cut light brown hair. 'As we're only two weeks away, I'm sure your plans are watertight.'

I'd never been involved in policing Fortbridge Rocks before, but I'd heard enough to know the operation name was the perfect moniker for the stinker in Wessex Constabulary's annual events calendar. Whoever doled it out clearly knew what they were doing, getting a sliver of revenge on the poor man's Glastonbury for sucking resources from the emergency services every August. Nothing but a bunch of pissed teenagers from surrounding towns and villages giving themselves alcohol poisoning or getting off their tits on weed before engaging in feeble punch-ups over who had the best forehead-sweeping emo fringe.

My name was called and I un-muted myself before talking them through the local bronze plans for CID and the neighbourhood policing teams.

Bret nodded curtly when I was done. 'All noted, thanks. And you're covering the SAG while DI Josephs is away, yes?'

I suppressed the eye roll that came on at the very mention of the Safety Advisory Group. The last gathering of all the organisations with skin in the game for making sure this thing ran smoothly resulted in a near brawl after Mavis Mulberry – who took her role as community representative so seriously you'd think she'd been appointed Secretary-General of the UN – insisted the organisers make the bands sign agreements promising not to sing about devil worship so as not to corrupt the village youths. 'All covered. I've got the joys of a site visit tomorrow afternoon.'

Bret moved on. 'Katie, can you update us on the comms plan, please?'

I zoned out as the Digital Media Manager gave an overview of the messaging they'd be putting out over the course of the two-day-long festival and fell into a daydream as Bret moved on to the ops planning team to give their update on resourcing.

'Great, thanks, Samir,' Bret said. 'OK, my turn with the latest from both the Super and the intel side.' He cleared his throat. 'The festival is graded low risk, but there are a couple of things to be mindful of. Number one being the anticipated county lines contingent, some mid-level nominals potentially travelling down from Liverpool. Merseyside have a job running this week that'll hopefully nip it in the bud, but something we're keeping an eye on. Number two, the latest Met Office update is a heatwave.'

There'd have been an audible groan if not for the fact that everyone bar Bret was on mute. The last couple of weeks hadn't been heatwave levels of hot, but warm enough for me to regret the impromptu decision at the start of summer to have my French bob redone, my do now far too short to tie back without three quarters of it immediately falling back down around my face, leaving me with a mass of hairgrips as my only defence against the building humidity that made me look more like a frizzy-headed LEGO woman than a Parisian fashionista. And we'd already seen spikes in the reporting data. In my nine years of experience, heatwaves and party atmospheres usually resulted in massive over-consumption of alcohol, and crime and aggression going through the roof.

'And last but by no means least,' Bret continued, 'I don't need to remind anyone of the sentiment towards policing at the moment.' I certainly didn't need the reminder, given my face could be used as Exhibit A of public feeling towards the service. The throbbing of the bruised cartilage in my nose intensified as if it could hear him. Bret carried on solemnly, '. . . and the Stanmore sentencing due later today will no doubt add to it.'

He paused, giving us all a moment to gather ourselves as a policing collective and ride out the gut punch DI Ian Stanmore's name delivered to the very core of why most of us got out of bed in the morning. He may have worked for a different police force, but that didn't matter. What he'd done had affected every single one of us. Because he hadn't just taken advantage of his position of trust; he'd deliberately forged himself the career pathway that would get him closest to the most vulnerable in society. He'd set trust in the police back at least fifty years, and was one of the reasons I was reluctant to take the Chief up on her offer to be included in the cohort of female officers being shipped around the county, participating in Op Unite, the name assigned to her new roadshows. It wasn't that I didn't think they were well intentioned, but I couldn't shake the notion that it felt the opposite of empowering. More like being a gymkhana show pony trotted out with the aim of convincing more women to sign up to the job at a time when I was struggling to sell it to myself, let alone anyone else.

I love my job, I love my job, I love my job, I told myself again, hoping the repetition would cement the words as fact. Being a police officer had been who I was ever since the first time I'd seen Dad in his uniform, when I'd sneak his warrant card out of his pocket and present it to fake suspects in the mirror. It was all I had. All I'd wanted. I'd had no qualms about being married to the job. But in the last few months, this marriage felt more like an abusive one. One that sucker-punched me in places the bruises wouldn't show every time I begged it to be better. And after what I'd gone through last year, and everything happening now – every day another headline, another misconduct case, another officer exposed for exploiting the power it was a privilege to be given – I wasn't so sure what I wanted any more. I let out a deep sigh and the tampon in my left nostril broke free, plopping on to the desk like a sad, bloodied tadpole.

Bret's voice pulled me from my pity party. 'Sorry, folks, give me one second . . .' He muted himself but his lips carried on moving as he talked to someone over the top of his computer. He carried on for another thirty seconds or so until he came back to us. 'OK, seems like there's another factor to consider. We have ourselves a surprise headline act at the festival, and the team monitoring the intel picture for the county lines job have picked up some death threats made towards them.'

'Who's the band?' I asked.

Bret paused. 'That's the interesting part. It's The Dolls.'

'What, *The* Dolls?' someone queried.

'The one and only,' Bret said.

'I thought they'd split up after all that business?' another voice chipped in.

'They did,' I interjected, 'and I'd hardly call their last lead singer getting murdered live on stage "business".' The call went silent and a wave of unease crawled across my skin. If their reputation was anything to go by, The Dolls had turned our soft event into a red-hot ball of fire.

2

By the time I came back into the CID office, Roy was at his desk dipping carrot sticks into what looked like home-made hummus. 'You not sick of this rabbit food malarkey yet?' I said, slumping into my chair opposite.

'This stuff's magic,' he said. 'I dunno what Trudy puts in it, kicks you right up the arse.'

I'd had quite enough of Roy's arse already. And as happy as I was that he'd found someone new after his self-inflicted divorce, it was still jarring to see him in the healthy regimen Trudy had instilled. I almost missed the overbearing smell of his usual foot-long salami sub with all the trimmings. But I couldn't deny he seemed better for it: the excess fat that used to hang over the top of his belt was flattening, and the only time he had a reddened face these days was post-exercise. The flush of enlarged blood vessels that used to simmer beneath the surface of his cheeks and across his nose from overconsumption of whisky had disappeared. He really was quite the new man. A Roy 2.0. Last year had taught him that this was the only life we got, so better damn well make the most of it. And he had. With Trudy. With

11

everything. Jealousy prickled my skin. Because what exactly had I achieved? Sure, there was therapy, an undeniable step in the right direction. But nothing else had changed and I still lived a lifestyle akin to Macaulay Culkin at the start of *Home Alone* – you know, before he got his shit together.

'Here,' Roy said, holding one hand towards me and gesturing at my nose with the other, 'think you need a change-over.' He unfurled his fingers, two new tampons sitting in his palm.

I took them and resisted the instinct to shove them up my sleeve, a muscle memory reaction finely honed during most women's teenage years when you had to treat dealing with your period like a stealth-trained SAS operative. 'I think it might finally be done bleeding now, but thanks. And wow, eating hummus *and* being on hand with fresh sanitary products for your female colleagues? Who even are you, Roy?'

'No need to be giving me a *Blue Peter* badge just yet – I only asked the cleaner to get them from the ladies' loo. Seriously though, you sure you don't wanna go down to the hospital and get it checked out? Could be broken.' He leant closer and squinted, surveying the damage.

I tapped the bridge of my nose. It was painful, but nothing felt out of place. 'Stop fussing, it just needs a bit of ice.' Roy rolled his eyes before sticking his finger in the hummus pot and scooping the last bit out like a child polishing off the remnants of a cake mix bowl. 'Anyway, you'll never guess—' My update on the festival briefing was rudely interrupted by the ringing phone on my desk. 'Hold that thought.' I reached for the ancient handset, knocking over a cold, half-drunk mug of coffee in the process. 'Oh, shitting hell . . . urgh, sorry, DS Washington,' I said into the mouthpiece, attempting to mop up the spill with a wad of Post-it notes.

'That's quite the telephone manner you've got there,' the caller said.

Distracted by my attempt to stop the expanding brown pool from soaking into every scrap of paper on my desk, it took a second to recognise Bret's voice. Excellent. A bashed-up face, soggy paperwork *and* one-on-one time with Viscount Serious Seaborn III. Which of God's favourite kittens did I kick this morning? 'Reserved especially for you. What d'you need?'

'How's your face? Saw what happened on the log.'

'Oh . . . erm . . .' Was that concern I was hearing? Had *I, Robot* malfunctioned? I'd glimpsed normal human behaviour in Bret on my return to work last year, though I hadn't been convinced his commentary about it being nice to see me back wasn't just to further cement himself as Jane's golden boy rather than because he'd actually meant it. 'It's fine. Nothing broken, I don't think.'

'Good.' He cleared his throat. 'You'll still have to fill in a work-related violence submission, though. We'll need to include it in the dailies for the SMT morning briefing tomorrow.'

Of course all he was bothered about was making sure I followed standard operating procedures. At ease, Geppetto, the wooden man hasn't become a real boy just yet. 'You're calling to chase up paperwork? They not got enough for you to do up there?'

'More than enough, thanks, that's why I'm calling. I've had a look, and no reports have come in from the band about the threats, so chances are we've picked them up before they have. They'll need the heads up, especially with the festival being mentioned specifically, and seems as though you're leading locally . . .'

He didn't need to finish by officially doling out the task. The festival was on my patch. My circus, my monkeys. 'Right, do we know where they're staying?'

'No,' Bret said, 'but they're represented by a company called All Star Talent Management – they should be able to tell you.'

I wrote the name on my hand given I'd rendered all the paper on my desk useless. 'Got it. And the threats themselves, what do they say?'

'You can see for yourself,' Bret said. 'They've been posted in the comments section on the announcement about them headlining the festival.'

'Right, and how long before we can expect to hear if there's any useful profile information associated with the account sending them?'

A sigh came down the line. 'I've got half the team on holiday at the minute and a backlog as long as my arm, so it'll probably be next week now.'

'Next *week*?'

'It's social media, people say weird shit all the time. D'you know how many requests we have to wade through for

14

hate speech, threats, doxing-related harassment? You name it, we've got it in the queue. Anyway, nine times out of ten these keyboard warriors are all bark no bite.'

He was probably right. Death threats on social media happened every day. This was likely just some nutter in their pants posting to give themselves a cheap thrill. But with the band's history, something told me not to take any chances. 'Let's hope so. Anything else?'

'Nope.'

I said a speedy goodbye and hung up before he could bleat on about work-related violence paperwork again.

'Who was that?' Roy asked.

I updated him on the festival, The Dolls and the threats as I cleaned my desk with some tissues.

'My Laurie loved them,' Roy said, his face softening in the way it did when he spoke about his daughter or his whippet. 'She always had them on. Mind you, they didn't half have some angry lyrics – had me worried there for a while. Can't say I cared too much for the songs, but that singer had a crackin' pair of lungs on her, like Freddie Mercury and Janis Joplin had a baby, just a dot of a thing an' all.'

Apart from having a few of their biggest hits on my workout playlist, I hadn't known much about The Dolls until the death of their lead singer, Ris Angelini. Hadn't followed the band's stratospheric rise to fame after their launch off the back of *So You Think You Can Rock?*, the reality TV show behind their creation. Ris and I had been the same age at the time of her murder, but my twenty-first year on this earth was clearly worlds apart from hers. While she'd been setting venues on metaphorical fire across the UK with her frontwoman performances, I'd done nothing but train like I was being conscripted to some war-torn country since I'd finished university that spring, using Wessex Constabulary's recruitment freeze as an opportunity to get myself in peak physical condition before starting basic training. But there'd been no missing the news about her death, especially not when it happened in such dramatic fashion in my own back yard, in front of thousands of adoring fans at Swindon's Big Top Ballroom, and especially with Dad's division running the investigation.

I googled THE DOLLS FORTBRIDGE ROCKS. Most of the links directed me to the big announcement on their social media pages alongside a picture of the band, including Ris. 'That's weird, they're using an old stock photo. You'd think they'd have at least stumped up for a new one, trading standards and all that jazz.'

Roy shrugged. 'From what I remember, they weren't exactly the best of friends. Not surprising, really – chucking a load of kids into a competition like that, piling on the pressure with a million-pound record deal and then setting them off on a tour of sex, drugs and rock and roll. Recipe for disaster.'

I clicked on the main announcement post and skimmed through the caption. Roy got up and stood behind me, reading over my shoulder.

'Christ alive, has it really been a whole decade?' he said, clearly reading their explanation that the comeback was to mark the ten-year anniversary of Ris's death.

16

'Commemorative my arse,' he continued, 'sounds like code for "all the money's run out". Why the comeback at their age? Bit too old for all this angsty teen stuff, ain't they?'

I baulked. 'Oi, they're the same age as me. Mick Jagger's still going and he's, what, eighty?'

'He can give it a rest an' all as far as I'm concerned, get a bleedin' allotment like a normal pensioner.'

I carried on reading. No replacement for Ris had been announced. And they were apparently putting their differences aside to pay tribute to their dear friend. Roy let out a 'Pfft' from behind me.

'*Dear friend?* Are they taking the piss? I remember Laurie and her mates got into a right barney over them. Laurie was "Team Ris" and her mate was "Team-whatever-the-hell-the-others-were-called", and they fought over it like cats and dogs. I'm telling you, they're doing this to make a few quid.'

'Do I detect a hint of cynicism there, Roy? I thought you'd *cleansed* yourself of that kind of talk these days.' He'd tried to avoid his usual diatribes since Trudy had given him a *Psychology Today* article debunking the myth that venting was a beneficial cathartic release.

'Not cynical,' he said, rolling up his shirtsleeves, 'just calling things like I see 'em.'

'Can you call them from somewhere else, please? I'm trying to concentrate.'

'All right, all right. You wanna cuppa?'

'If you mean an actual cuppa, yes, but if you mean that green shit you made me last time, then absolutely not.'

'Fine,' Roy said, 'but don't come crying to me when you get heart palpitations before you hit fifty.'

'Noted.' I leant closer to my computer screen to read the rest of the post commentary, scrolling through the responses.

> **@Astronomighty**
> THE STARZ ALIGN 🔭🔭🔭
> **@EmoChicadee**
> OMGOMGOMGOMGOMGOMGOMGOMGOMG THEY
> ARE BACK BABY – LOOOOOSING MY MIND!!!

I landed on the threat about halfway down the list of comments.

> **@Riot_GRRRL_til_you_DIE**
> ONE DOLL DOWN FOUR TO GO. DEE DEE HAD IT RIGHT.
> SEE YOU ON STAGE. PICK U OFF 1 BY 1 BANG BANG
> BANG BANG ⚰️ ⚰️ ⚰️ ⚰️ ⚰️

A chill ran down my spine at the Dee Dee reference. There was no need for a surname to know who they were talking about: Ris's so-called best friend and killer, Dee Dee Nolan. The hairs on my arms rose like an army of tiny cobras reacting to their charmer's music. I had a bad feeling about this. The reminder that Ris's murder had been the ultimate betrayal by someone purporting to be her friend sent a flash of Tess through my mind. No matter how hard I tried to dismiss the memory, I couldn't help but look at the desk where she used to sit, her chair empty after budget cuts meant HQ hadn't stumped up for a replacement researcher. What Tess had done in no way amounted to murder, but the line she'd crossed was one our friendship would never come back from.

I forced her from my mind, occupying myself for the rest of the afternoon with trying to get hold of the band's agent. After leaving messages with half the staff at their talent management company, I called it a day, a sense of foreboding sitting heavy in my stomach like an undigested meal. I needed a distraction. 'Fancy a drink over the road before you head off?' I asked Roy. 'And yes, I'll allow you to get a low-calorie soft drink.'

'Can't tonight, me and Trudy have got our couples yoga class,' he said, throwing his rucksack over his shoulder.

'Course you have. Never mind, I'll, erm, ask someone else.' I scrolled through my phone as if it would magically find me someone to hang out with, when in all honesty, since losing Tess, there was only really one other person for me to call.

3

My relationship with Dad had improved over the last year, but we still hadn't mastered the art of hugging with ease, our arms moving around each other like two people struggling to untangle a bag of wire coat hangers as we attempted our greeting. The Chinese takeaway I was holding didn't help matters.

Dad gestured at my nose as we pulled apart. 'What you done to your face?'

If I told him what had happened, he'd come out of retirement before I could finish my sentence and establish a national taskforce to take down the elbow thrower. 'Just bashed it.'

'Right.' He scratched the side of his head. 'I didn't know you were coming, kid.'

'Thought I'd surprise you with a bit of company.' *Yeah, this is totally for his benefit, nothing to do with you being a complete Billy no-mates.* 'A visit from your daughter *and* Norton Abbot's finest spring rolls? Big day for you, eh?'

'Yeah, er ...' Dad winced as plates chinked together behind him.

I peered over his shoulder in the direction of the noise. 'Sounds like you've already got company.'

'Kinda, yeah.' He rubbed his brow. 'I was going to—'

Before he had the chance to finish, his next-door neighbour, Irma Constance, appeared in the kitchen doorway, adorned in a bold orange and yellow print maxi dress that only someone with her dark brown skin could pull off.

'Alice! Hello, darling, we didn't know you were coming.' Material billowed around her legs as she glided across the living room. She nudged Dad out the way and planted a kiss on each of my cheeks before hugging me. My body stiffened. I'd only met Irma a handful of times and none of them had involved this level of physical contact. Maybe she was drunk.

'Looking lovely as always,' I said as she released me. 'What are you doing here?'

She skimmed her hand across her afro which was trimmed shorter than last time I'd seen her, now a mere dusting of silver coating the top and sides of her head. 'Having dinner, of course, what else?'

Since when did Irma and Dad have dinner? He usually pretended not to notice the not-so-subtle hints she dropped trying to wangle an invite to join us when she 'just happened' to be coming out her front door at the very moment that I was pulling up outside their row of terraced cottages. Looks bounced between us for what was only a few seconds but felt like forever before it dawned on me: this wasn't a driveway ambush. She was already here. I was the one who wasn't supposed to be. Her words replayed.

We didn't know you were coming. 'Oh!' I thought and said simultaneously.

Irma slapped Dad on the shoulder. 'You didn't tell her, did you?'

Dad scuffed his shoe across the carpet like a scolded child, clearly still feeling he was doing something wrong, despite Mum having been gone eight years. 'Hadn't gotten around to it yet, no.' His cheeks flushed. 'Irma and me, we've, er, well . . .'

'Oh, Jesus, Mary and Joseph, Mick,' Irma interjected, 'we'll be getting birthday letters from the King before you get your words out.' She turned to me, tilting her head to one side. 'Me and your dad are . . . well, I don't know what people call it these days – shacking up?'

Dad pinched the bridge of his nose. 'Bloody hell, Irm, don't beat around the bush, will ya?'

'Alice is a grown woman, no need to sugar-coat things.'

I liked Irma and had encouraged Dad to move on, but I'd need more than sugar to erase the thought of them doing anything akin to *shacking*. I jumped in before she could carry on talking, 'Wow! Keep the details to yourself, but that's great, I'm really happy for you both.'

Dad blushed harder as Irma linked her arm with his.

The only thing I had to link arms with was the plastic handle of the takeaway bag digging into the crook of my elbow, and the feeling of being a third wheel was suddenly stronger than the aroma of Szechuan chicken wafting up from it. 'Let me get out of your hair. I've completely gate-crashed.'

They lurched forward in unison and grabbed an arm each.

'Don't be daft,' Dad said. 'You're here now, might as well stay for dinner – Irma's made loads.'

As much as I liked Chinese food, whatever Irma was cooking smelt ten times better. And I should make an effort to get to know her properly if the two of them were going to be spending more time together. 'Only if you're sure.'

Irma pulled me through to the kitchen. 'Sit,' she said, pointing to the dining table before returning to whatever she'd left bubbling on the hob.

She'd already started making her mark, with plates and glasses laid out on colourful placemats rather than plonked directly on to the tabletop. Maybe the place would start looking homely if she kept this up. I sat down as Dad added another place setting before relieving me of the bag of takeaway and putting it in the fridge.

'Here we go.' He grabbed a bottle of wine and poured out three glasses before Irma placed a large, steaming pot of what looked like a beef stew on to a metal trivet in the middle of the table.

'Dig in!' Irma proclaimed before we all served ourselves.

I scoffed mouthfuls of velvety chunks of meat before following up with a hunk of buttery bread like a carbohydrate chaser shot. Dad and Irma's eyes bored into me, their food barely touched. 'What?' I said, the question muffled by the bread filling my right cheek.

'You'd think you'd not eaten in months, like a bloody gannet,' Dad said. 'You looking after yourself properly?'

I swallowed. 'Course, just busy with work and stuff, the usual.' *And stuff.* Who was I kidding?

Dad took a swig of his wine and gave Irma a knowing look before turning back to me. 'Not too busy, I hope?'

He never missed an opportunity to remind me of the agreement we'd made last year after our Hallmark movie moment: my promise not to let work take over my life in the way he felt his policing career had clouded his before retiring when Mum got ill. 'The joys of Fortbridge Rocks festival planning. Jane's on holiday, so I'm covering a lot of her stuff.'

'It's no bother that one, is it? Wasn't in my day,' Dad said. He'd been the divisional commander for the south of the county before taking over as Chief Superintendent of the Major Crime Unit. His experience of the festival would have been a literal walk in the park compared to some of the big jobs he'd led at headquarters.

'Not quite as straightforward this year.' I filled him in on the situation with The Dolls.

Dad shook his head. 'That's a blast from the past. Tough one, that. Poor kids, on all sides – even the lass who did it. I'm not condoning it, obviously, but you couldn't call what she had a childhood. Very sad all round.'

'That wasn't your job though, was it?' I asked.

'Not directly, but it was my team's, ultimately. Gordy Scott picked it up, took on most of the SIO jobs around that time. I, er, well . . . wasn't at my best. It was when your mum was diagnosed, so . . .' It didn't matter that Dad had retired as fast as possible after they'd found Mum's cancer; he'd never forgive himself for them only having two years of proper time together before she died. 'Anyway,' he continued, 'open and shut investigation, really, just left Gordy and the team to get on with it.'

Gordy Scott must have thought he'd hit gold having a murder with thousands of witnesses *and* a confession land on his desk.

'Wait,' Irma said, 'is this the singer that got pushed, just before the show at that place in town?'

I nodded. 'That's the one.'

She tutted. 'What a thing to do, and they were friends, weren't they?'

'Supposed to be,' I replied, 'but I wouldn't say shoving someone off a forty-foot stage roof qualified them as besties.'

'They'd definitely *been* best mates,' Dad interjected, 'that's what was so sad about it. They had all these photos in the papers of the two of them together as little 'uns.'

I vaguely recalled the images: Dee Dee and Ris arm in arm, holding musical instruments, probably no older than eight or nine. 'Clearly something went wrong to go from BFFs to murderer and victim.'

Irma shuddered. 'Horrible business. Can I suggest a new house rule of no talking shop at the dinner table?' she said, glancing back and forth between me and Dad.

My inner child wanted to role-play an American teen drama, dramatically swiping my plate off the table and yelling, 'You're not my real mom!', but then I remembered I was thirty-one and Irma was quite right that all this talk of death and betrayal was kind of a buzz kill.

Dad and I shrugged in agreement.

'Good,' she said, clapping her hands together. 'We were thinking of having a barbecue at some point over the next few weeks, weren't we, Mick? Make the most of this nice weather.'

'Uh-huh,' Dad said. Irma stared at him as if waiting for him to carry on. 'What?' he asked. Her eyes widened, willing him to say something. 'Oh, yeah, erm, if there's anyone you wanted to bring along, kid, that'd be OK.'

'Maybe a nice eligible bachelor?' Irma said, throwing me a wink.

Oh God. She'd been seeing Dad for barely two minutes and all of a sudden she was acting like Cilla bloody Black. I'd rather go back to talking about death and betrayal.

'Or just a mate,' Dad said swiftly, possibly sensing my hesitation. 'I haven't gotten to the part in therapy yet where they teach you how to avoid murdering any bloke who so much as sniffs the general air space in the vicinity of your daughter.'

It was surprising enough that *I* had taken the leap towards therapy; it boggled my mind that Dad had too. And not just to Irma's therapy garden, to *actual* therapy. With a person. Now that I thought about it, that was probably what made him realise he deserved some happiness, allowing Irma into his life. First Roy, now Dad. How on earth was I being out-therapied by a Baby Boomer and a Gen X-er? I appreciated his support with the deflection, but there was also something embarrassing about the fact he felt the need to do it.

I shrugged a 'maybe' and stuffed more bread in my mouth before changing the subject. The only person I could think to invite was Roy, and he'd no doubt be too busy doing something ridiculous with Trudy like taking a class that taught you how to make tofu not taste like crap.

Jesus Christ, you've got to get yourself some fucking friends!

4

It had gone ten by the time I pulled on to my driveway. The sun had long since set into the valley behind Myrtle Cottage, but the heat it had pumped out all day lingered in the heavy night air. There was no ginger furball in sight on the doorstep. No wail of feline fury telling me the master of the manor's evening meal was hours overdue. He was probably still out courting that pretty calico stray that hung around the farmer's fields out back. Great – even the damn cat had a more active social life than me.

I threw my bag on to the kitchen island, turned on the TV and poured myself some water. The large patio door had outdone itself in absorbing every ounce of the sun's rays and turned the room into an oven. I glugged down two glasses of water then leant back against the counter, letting out a deep sigh and rolling the empty glass, still cold from the water, back and forth across my forehead.

I'd thought a lot about my predicament on the thirty-mile drive back from Norton Abbot. The idea of trying to make new friends in my thirties seemed excruciating. But at some point, I was going to have to accept that lone wolf was a term less applied to strong, independent women and more to school shooters and terrorists. I needed to ease myself in. Find a hobby. Even my therapist had said the same thing. 'Aggressive Time Management', she'd called it when she'd told me to block out at least an hour every week to do something for no other reason than because I wanted to. Of course I'd dismissed it at the time, not expecting to get *homework* from going to therapy. I'd prepared myself for pouring my heart out, offloading all the years of tension, thinking I'd get my very own Robin Williams/Matt Damon 'It's not your fault' *Good Will Hunting* moment, when she'd get up, hug all my issues away, anoint me successfully 'therapised' and send me on my jolly way.

But alas . . .

The bottom of the glass caught the bridge of my nose, hitting the exact spot where I'd been smacked earlier. 'Ow, shit!' I yelped, putting the glass down and checking my reflection in the stainless-steel microwave door. By some miracle, the only visible damage to my nose so far was a small bruise flowering in the middle of it. Leaning closer, I scanned the pale thin skin under my eyes. No sign of any shiners. I went to the freezer and rummaged in the drawers for something to use as a makeshift ice pack, a box of Birds Eye Potato Waffles being the best I could do.

Wrapped in a tea towel, I pressed the cold surface against my nose, a chill running down my spine as I turned around. It wasn't the ice burning my face that had caused the reaction, but the sight of the gaunt face of DI Ian Stanmore staring back at me from the BBC News at Ten, trying and failing to hide from the camera flashes as he'd entered court earlier that afternoon. Rage bubbled faster than Irma's stew had on the hob. I jabbed at the power button on the remote before the headline banner about his sentencing outcome ran across the screen. I'd heard more than enough about that piece of shit, and my love of the job was already precarious at best. Finding out he'd probably got nowhere near what he deserved risked cutting me loose completely.

I spun at the *tick-tick-tick* noise coming from the patio door. 'At least I've still got you, eh,' I said as Vince pawed at the glass, his yellow eyes wide at the audacity of it not already being open after I should have sensed him coming and rolled out a miniature red carpet leading directly to his food bowl. I let him in, the bell on his royal-blue collar jangling as he ignored me and trotted across the kitchen. 'Oi, twat bag, nice to see you too. And yes, thanks, I've had a spiffing day, you?' He stared blankly and licked his lips, clearly wanting nothing more from me than his supper. I fulfilled His Lordship's wishes before grabbing my laptop and going upstairs.

The bedroom curtains had been closed all day, going some way to keeping it cooler than downstairs, but it was still stuffy. I pushed open the window, then changed into the most lightweight pyjamas I could find before climbing into bed, pressing the box of waffles against my nose with one hand while logging in to my computer with the other.

Surely there was *something* outside of work that would entertain me for a measly hour a week. I opened Google and went to type into the search bar, but instead my fingers hovered over the keys. *Come on, you must be interested in something! Even the Unabomber had a hobby – hiking in the wilderness, the man couldn't get enough of it!* I chewed my bottom lip. The only thing that came to mind was my knack for making unusual food combinations work, which was less of an interest and more a necessity given I rarely had proper food in the house.

I gave up looking for something specific and typed THINGS TO DO FORTBRIDGE instead. Most of the links were either showcasing the famous iron bridge that tourists loved to photograph, or directing towards the Fortbridge Rocks website. I went to the second page and scanned more links. 'Crocheting, no, Wessex Rotary Club, no, Fortbridge in Bloom gardening group, no. Pig racing? Absolutely not. Ooh, wait, hello,' I said as an advert for a new kickboxing studio on the industrial estate popped up. That sounded more like it. Group exercise wasn't usually my bag – my hand–eye coordination being questionable to say the least – but this looked like a proper martial arts studio, not the aerobics version of combat-meets-dance I'd failed at before. I booked myself in for a class the following night. A Friday. Perfect. Fingers crossed the other attendees would also be fellow anti-social bastards with no plans who just wanted to kick things and get their pent-up aggression out in silence. *Bliss.*

'There we go, a changed woman already,' I said to Vince as he joined me on the bed, curling up by my foot. At least I'd done *something*. Taken a step. Maybe I'd make a friend. And maybe I wouldn't. But either way I'd learn how to roundhouse-kick people in the head. Silver linings and all that.

I was about to close my laptop and go to sleep when curiosity got the better of me and I did another search, this time on The Dolls. Images flooded the screen, mostly of the band but interspersed with shots of Dee Dee. There was nothing recent; all the images of her were either from around the time of her arrest or from previous years hanging out with the band.

Dee Dee had a similar look in all the photographs: hair so dark brown it looked black, almost always in the same half-up, half-down style, the top pulled taut away from her round, pale face, the bottom long and thin, hanging down to her waist. Her head was tilted down in most of the images following her arrest, like she was trying to avoid the camera, with small, hooded eyes peering up through thick eyebrows. She looked like any other emo-leaning teenage girl at that age, not a killer. But if I'd learned anything from my time in the job, people were good at hiding things, and the ones capable of committing heinous crimes rarely looked like gargoyles; they looked like everyday people.

I clicked on one of the old news articles.

The Western Herald, 18 February 2014

MURDERER DOROTHY NOLAN 'SHOWED NO REMORSE' AFTER KILLING FORMER BEST FRIEND AND ROCK SENSATION, COURT HEARS

A woman who murdered former best friend and lead singer of rock band The Dolls by pushing her from the stage roof at the Big Top Ballroom 'showed no remorse and immediately fled the scene', a judge has said, as the killer was handed a life sentence.

Dorothy 'Dee Dee' Nolan, 21, from Swindon, pleaded guilty to the September 2013 murder of Marissa 'Ris' Angelini, 21, in December.

At today's sentencing hearing, as Lord Highland gave the killer a life sentence and ordered that Nolan must serve at least 15 years behind bars, the judge said the murderer committed 'a cold and wicked crime' when she lured Miss Angelini to the stage roof before pushing her off in front of thousands of fans who were left 'traumatised' after witnessing the incident as they waited to watch the band perform. 'As a result of your jealousy-fuelled actions, a young woman with her whole life and exciting career ahead of her is dead, leaving her family, friends and fans devastated.'

The only positive thing Lord Highland had to say about Dee Dee was that she'd pleaded guilty, but whether that was for her own benefit to get a few years knocked off her sentence, or to avoid putting the Angelini family through the added ordeal of a trial, was anyone's guess.

I re-read the judge's words, wondering what must have gone through the crowd's minds in those initial moments before they realised what had happened. I'd read something at the time about a witness who'd said they thought it was a stunt at first, like Ozzy Osbourne chowing down on a bat or Jimi Hendrix setting fire to a guitar. And never mind the audience who saw her fall, her body broken and limp on the stage, but what must the rest of the band have gone through when they saw her lying there? According to reports, they'd heard the audience's screams but hadn't come out of their dressing rooms at first, mistaking the wails of terror for excitement and anticipation about their imminent arrival on stage.

Jesus.

Clicking back to the main search results, I scrolled through the other headlines, a mixture of mainstream news reporting the facts of the crime and its aftermath as well as random opinion pieces claiming to have personal insight into the case even though most of the so-called authors had probably never even met Dee Dee or the band.

LIFE AFTER RIS: WHERE ARE THE DOLLS NOW?

FRIEND OR FOE: WHO IS DEE DEE NOLAN?

DOLLS SLAYER WON'T SEEK APPEAL

RISING STAR: THE LIFE AND DEATH OF RIS ANGELINI

QUEEN OF THE DOLLS TO QUEEN OF THE MEAN GIRLS: WHEN GOOD GIRLS GO BAD

My eyes were drawn to the last one, expecting the girl who'd gone bad to be a refence to Dee Dee, but as I opened it, it was clear it wasn't. It was about Ris. 'Bloody hell, do these people have no shame?' I skimmed the article, which couldn't have taken a more victim-blaming angle if it tried. The scathing piece relished how fame had allegedly changed Ris. How she'd gone from some kind of Mary Sue to Elvira. A quiet, A* student catapulted to fame, spending the first year of her time in the band staying behind for hours after shows signing autographs and taking photos with fans, a stark difference to the last couple of months, hiding behind thick black sunglasses and huge security guards to keep crowds at bay once their US tour was announced, apparently now too good for the people who'd helped her get famous in the first place. It was a dick move, but it hardly warranted Dee Dee's actions.

I closed the article and read the rest of the search results. Of course the tabloids pulled out all the stops to win the award for most salacious headline, but the one that caught my eye was a link to a video. The now mostly defrosted box of waffles slipped from my hand as I read the title.

THE DEE DEE DOLLS (DOCUMENTARY) – 2019: WATCH NOW!

'What the hell?' I opened it and read the synopsis. The stars of the show seemed to be a rather troubling online community of young girls who clearly agreed with the twattish article suggesting Ris got what she deserved, and had appointed Dee Dee as the leader of some queen bee emo cult. An online community with an axe to grind against The Dolls – could this have something to do with the threats? Was one of these idiots posing as @Riot_GRRRL_til_you_DIE?

35

I pulled up the first episode and was about to hit play when my phone buzzed from the bedside table.

A red alert shone out from my work email app as I picked it up. I paused for a moment. Surely it could wait until I was back on duty tomorrow. If it was urgent, someone would have called. My finger hovered over the screen before I remembered I'd literally spent the last half-hour reading articles about the band and was about to watch a bloody documentary all about Dee Dee. Who was I kidding? When it came to being a cop, there was no such thing as off duty.

I tapped my finger against the screen and my mailbox sprang to life, an email from All Star Talent Management sitting at the top of it containing the contact details for the band. I typed out a message to Roy.

Band are staying at Aurora House, that old farm and mill in Cherry Falls Woods they've turned into a dumb wellness retreat thing. Take your best yoga pants you ride at dawn.

Little bubbles pulsed across the screen telling me Roy was replying.

Maybe I could teach them a thing or two about what REAL music sounds like while I'm there. Not half bad on the old six string back in my day you know.

I was about to reply, advising him it wasn't the wisest choice for a middle-aged man with no discernible musical background to start giving lectures to a younger,

36

predominantly female group who, from what I'd read, had amassed three top fives and two number one songs in their first year, broken the record for fastest-selling debut rock single ever and toured thirty-six sold-out dates across ten cities, but I stopped myself. Given they had a song called 'Cop Killa', I wasn't expecting them to be the most welcoming bunch, and I could do without the admin that would be associated with Roy getting his head caved in with a guitar.

Meet at station first. I'll come with.

5

Kit climbed the grand stairway of Aurora House with as much nonchalance as she could muster in case anyone was watching. She scanned the name plates on the other bedrooms she passed along the way – Raven, Dormouse, Dragonfly and Grasshopper – before reaching the one she'd been assigned at the end of the hallway: Mockingbird. She hadn't thought anything of it at first, but now she tensed every time she looked at the sign, unable to shake the feeling that being associated with a bird known for its mimicry would shine a spotlight on her own imitation, alert everyone to her deception.

Closing the bedroom door behind her, she locked it, finally able to unclench. But the release wasn't enough. She needed more. Something to truly separate herself from the person she was outside this room, the person she *had* to be in front of the others. She wasn't sure whether it was the heat – because of course she got the room with the faulty air con – or the desire to rid herself of the day, but her clothes were choking her. She yanked them off, T-shirt, bra, jeans, knickers, socks, all tossed into a crumpled pile in the corner of the room.

She double-checked the door was locked. Now wasn't the time for uninvited guests. Aside from the fact she was bollock naked, there was work to do. *Real* work. Work that actually mattered for once in her life. She knelt on the floor, the plush carpet cushioning the bone beneath her skin, and checked for what felt like the millionth time that the spare keys for every door in this place she'd managed to sneak out from the office cabinet were where she'd hidden them, between the bed slats and the mattress. One of the keys stabbed her fingertip and the tightness in her chest dissipated. Still there. Ready and waiting to do their job when she needed them to.

Leaving the keys, she slid her suitcase out from the gap under the bed and unzipped it before rummaging through the only items she possessed in the world. She pulled out the baggy old Motörhead T-shirt she always slept in, the one that reminded her of better times, even though the once-familiar smell that had done its best to cling to the fabric had finally been lost after all these years, no matter how much she avoided washing it. Pulling it over her head, she hugged it to her body for a second before climbing on to the king-size bed. It was too hot to get under the covers, so she lay legs and arms akimbo on top of the duvet, only now realising how exhausted she was. How much energy the pretence was draining from her.

She stared at the ceiling light, its supposedly trendy spiked limbs hanging like the sword of Damocles. Taunting her. Mocking her like the room's namesake. But she could do this. She'd already done better than expected. Struck the perfect balance of being knowledgeable and interested in the band without fawning over them. Ever the professional. Just the right amount of ego-rubbing for them to feel at ease around her. It hadn't been hard. Everyone in this place was far too distracted thinking about themselves to notice much about anyone else. And it wasn't like it had come from nowhere, the act she'd played. She *had* been a fan of the band back then. Right up to the moment her life changed for ever, until nothing and no one mattered to her any more. The memories flooded her mind and she gripped the duvet as she recalled the scream that had erupted from her almost of its own accord. The sight of limbs at unnatural angles she hadn't been able to tear her eyes away from.

The images and sounds fought her as she pushed them away, sucked them down and locked them back in their box somewhere deep inside her. *Turn the lock, throw away the key, turn the lock, throw away the key.* Now wasn't the time. She had to focus. Keep this up until she'd done what was needed. Before anyone realised why she was really there.

6

I'd grown used to negotiating country lanes during my three years in Fortbridge, but I was still on constant alert for rabbits, voles or kamikaze pheasants shooting out in front of me from the cover of the surrounding fields at any given moment. I stared ahead at the narrow road leading to Cherry Fall Woods on the southern edge of the Wessex border and updated Roy on the gist of the weird documentary.

Dee Dee had been put on a pedestal by a subset of teenage girls who saw Ris's murder as their version of David and Goliath, or as one girl referred to it, 'the takedown of Stacys for Beckys everywhere', which, after some googling, I'd discovered was incel language for 'conventionally attractive women' and 'average women' respectively. They talked like they were in some morbid version of *Mean Girls* where Regina George died when the bus hit her and everyone was absolutely thrilled about it. It was bizarre. No wonder those who'd taken part hadn't shown their faces, just shadows and actor's voices explaining their membership to the disturbing fan club.

'Absolutely crackers. What is the world coming to, eh?' Roy said. He gulped the last of his green smoothie and let out a loud 'ahh' from the passenger seat like he'd had a sip of cold, bubbly cider instead of something that looked like it had been dredged from the River Fort.

'Says the man drinking whatever the hell *that* is voluntarily. Is that an actual breakfast choice or a cry for help?' I asked.

He screwed the lid on to the empty bottle and shoved it into the rucksack by his feet. 'Trudy can make anything taste nice.'

I restrained the eye roll. 'She can't hear you, you know. Blink twice if you want me to stop off at a farm shop and get you some bacon.'

We approached a T-junction at the end of the lane marked with a sign so dilapidated and covered in moss that if you didn't know where you were going you'd have to pick a direction and hope for the best. I didn't need to check the satnav's red line; I could see the woods off to my left. 'Wipe the liquid spinach off your chin, we'll be at Aurora House any minute now.'

I turned left then took a sharp right into the woods down an even narrower lane carved out between high mud banks, embedded tree roots breaching the soil either side of us like varicose veins.

'How come they can afford this place?' Roy said. 'They fell off the face of the earth after the murder, but they must be doing something right – can't be cheap.'

'Tabby Falstead seems to be the only one who's stayed

in the limelight,' I said, recalling a summary of what I'd read in the *where are they now* article, 'and I'm not sure how to explain what she does – some sort of influencer by the looks of it. Em Drummond tried to go solo but that went nowhere. The last Nush Chandra had been seen was working at a checkout in a supermarket back home in Gateshead, and Ryan Hope was almost unrecognisable, gone full farmer Giles with his own land in North Devon. I doubt they're paying for it themselves, anyway. It'll be their record company, surely, especially as they've booked the whole place out in the run-up to the festival.'

The car bounced in and out of a huge pothole and Roy braced himself against the dashboard. 'Maybe they should put some of that money into fixing this road.'

'I'm sure they'll get right on that after they've spent God knows how much helping the band *reconnect*, which sounds like a billion-pound project in itself. I know you were saying they didn't get on, but Jesus, one of the things I read last night said Ris punched Tabby at one point. So let's hope they can keep the peace until the festival, because if this threat turns out to be more than just trash-talking on the internet, we're gonna have enough on our plate trying to stop someone on the outside going for them; we sure as shit haven't got the resources to stop them killing each other.'

'Seems to be part of their "brand", though,' Roy said, emphasising the air-quoted word like it was a profanity. 'That's what it's all about these days, shouty, yelly, angry guitar stuff, a bit gimmicky if you ask me. I know my

43

music.' He folded his arms high across his chest. 'And that ain't rock.'

I smirked at the fact that no matter how many smoothies he drank or egg white omelettes he ate, he'd never quite shake off classic Roy.

A large wooden sign for Aurora House appeared and I flicked on the indicator. Driving through the open wooden gates, the main building came into view, set back from a large pond. I followed the driveway curving around it, shielding my eyes as the sun's rays refracted, shooting out in all directions from the water's surface and reflecting off the floor-to-roof window panes of the renovated farmhouse-turned-retreat.

Pulling up beneath an overhanging willow tree to keep the car in shade, I accepted the likelihood of returning to a shit-spattered bonnet courtesy of the birds nestling along the branches. With the state of my clapped-out Volvo, it might actually be an improvement.

'Right, let's rock and roll,' Roy said, completely unironically, as we opened our doors simultaneously and got out.

Bright sunlight poured through the domed glass roof of Aurora House's atrium-style hallway, the air saturated with the overpowering scent of massage oils and burnt incense, all three of these factors an assault on my senses.

'Smells like the Body Shop ate Lush and then puked up in here,' Roy said, dipping his fingertips into a small fountain in the shape of Buddha.

'I thought you were into this stuff now.' I tried to breathe through my mouth. 'Lavender for the heart, turmeric for the . . . whatever the hell turmeric is supposed to do other than stain everything in your kitchen the colour of a muddy puddle.'

'Not all at the same bleedin' time though.' Roy pulled a crumpled hanky from his trouser pocket and blew his nose so hard I worried he'd give himself a hernia.

Rubber-soled shoes squeaked against the white marbled floor and a woman appeared in the doorway to our right. Dressed in a bright orange two-piece suit with a white shirt underneath, she looked like a giant traffic cone, *giant* being the operative word given the way she filled the space. She was at least six feet tall, even in flats.

The woman stopped abruptly at the sight of us, folding her arms across her chest. 'Er, 'scuse me, can I help you?'

I was so distracted by her pillar-box-red hair, cut into a bob so sharp I'd risk losing a finger if I reached out and touched it, that it took me a second to get my words out. 'Hi, yes, sorry, we did ring the bell but no one answered.'

She interrupted before I had a chance to finish my introduction, 'And you took that as an invitation to swan right on in, did ya?' In two large strides she was practically on top of us. 'Place is closed, so I suggest you—'

'We're police,' I managed to squeeze in before she told us where to go. 'DS Alice Washington and DC Roy Briar, Fortbridge CID.'

Her eyes narrowed and she looked us up and down. 'Let's see some ID.' We pulled out our warrant cards, which she examined like she was preparing to buy black market diamonds in exchange for her life savings. 'OK.' Her body language and tone softened somewhat, though there was still an edge to her. "Scuse my caution, but people'll try anything to get close to the band. So, what's the problem?'

'Sorry, and you are?' I tried not to trip over my words, distracted by the fact this woman's gravitas levels could give the radiation readings in late eighties Chernobyl a run for their money.

She stuck out her hand. 'Sherrie Pearce. Band Manager.' Her grip was impressively firm and I swear Roy stifled a whimper when it was his turn.

'Right, good, we'll need to speak to you too, as well as the band, about Fortbridge Rocks. Are they here? It would be best to explain all together.'

'They're in the studio.' She looked at her watch. 'They're due a break now, anyway. Tabby had 'em all up at the crack of dawn doing some sun salutation bollocks, 'scuse the French.' She nodded towards a spiral staircase leading to a lower floor from the back of the hallway. 'Come with me.'

We followed her towards the stairs. 'So, this place has its own music studio?' I asked.

She nodded. 'State of the art, got everything, indoor pool and spa, flotation therapy pods, painting room, library, any kind of mumbo jumbo creative stuff you can think of. It's gonna make a mint when it opens properly.'

I wondered if this could be a back-up option in my quest for a hobby. Unfortunately, I was a sizeable way away from being a millionaire and there was no way this refurbishment had been done for the good of the community, clearly aimed at rich out-of-towners from London wanting to connect with nature without having to travel far or lose any daily luxuries. God, I sounded like Roy slagging off the city folk.

Sherrie marched us along a corridor lined with black-and-white framed artwork. The further we got, the more chlorine, presumably from the pool, replaced the incense smells and the louder a sound thudded as if the building had a heart-beat. Stopping in front of a set of heavy-looking double doors, Sherrie braced herself then pushed them open. The suction seal holding them closed broke and the booming of a bass drum coupled with the intermittent screech of an electric guitar poured out.

The music stuttered to a halt, everyone in the studio turning to look at us. For a second, the scene resembled a Polaroid. The type you might see on an iconic album cover: band members dotted around the room against a backdrop of instruments hanging from racks on the red velvet-padded walls or propped up against them. The Dolls looked like they'd barely aged in the ten years since Ris's death, still resembling the photos I'd seen of them in their late teens and early twenties.

Tabby Falstead was behind a microphone stand, her long legs appearing almost too thin to hold the weight of her slight body and the glittery bass guitar hanging on a silver strap around her neck. To her left stood Em Drummond, fiddling with knobs on a more classic-looking guitar with a neon-yellow pick clenched between her teeth. From the photos I'd seen, Em and Tabby had similar builds, but you'd never know it, given the bagginess of Em's combat trousers and long-sleeved top. Along the back wall, Nush Chandra sat behind a sapphire-blue drum kit, bare brown knees poking out through large rips in her light grey jeans.

I ticked the members off one by one on my mental checklist, before noticing there was someone I didn't recognise perched on a stool in the corner with a notepad and pen resting on her lap. A somewhat stocky woman, or girl – I couldn't quite pin down her age through the dark, heavy make-up and the fact she was dressed in a style that meant she could be seventeen or a thirty-something trying to relive her punk youth. A cream T-shirt peeked out from underneath her black dungarees that were only done up over one shoulder, their three-quarter length exposing a large tattoo running up the side of her calf. She avoided my gaze, eyes fixed on her fingers as she fiddled with the frazzled ends of her long black hair that was clearly a dye job, the blue-black tones misaligned with the natural rosy hue of her arms. I was still appraising her when Sherrie broke the silence.

'Ladies, this is Detective Sergeant . . . er, remind me?'

'DS Alice Washington.' I introduced Roy before Sherrie went around the room introducing the band, annoyingly missing the one person we didn't already know.

I looked over towards the stranger on the stool. 'And you are?'

She opened her mouth to speak but Sherrie beat her to it, 'Sorry, forgot you were there, love – like a little mouse in the corner, that one. This is Kit.'

Kit's fidgeting moved from her hair to the small hooped

piercing on her lower lip. She nodded, but added nothing to what Sherrie had said.

I closed the gap between us, reaching out my hand, momentarily distracted by the glinting charm hanging off the black choker around her neck, a small silver letter K. 'Ah, I get it, K for Kit.'

She stopped twiddling her piercing long enough to shake my hand, with a look of derision. 'What?'

I pointed to her jewellery. 'Your necklace.'

'Oh right, yeah, whatever.'

I got the overwhelming feeling I'd said something wrong, but couldn't for the life of me figure out what. 'So, are you a new band member, or . . .?'

'No,' she said, her voice taking a more neutral tone. 'Freelance journalist. I'm doing a piece on the band, covering their reunion, a behind-the-music kinda thing.'

'What for?' Roy said from behind me. '*Rolling Stone*? *NME*?'

Her face impassive, she replied, '*Louder* magazine.'

'Right,' he said, 'not heard of that one.'

The corners of her mouth moved, but I'd hardly call it a smile. 'Not surprised. It focusses specifically on women in rock, a lot of people overlook it.'

She turned her attention back to me, and now that I could see her more clearly, I guessed she was in her early twenties. There was something about her tone, and now that I noticed it, the vibe of the whole room, that reminded me of sixth form college, and suddenly I was filled with the need to earn approval from a bunch of people I didn't even know. I snapped myself out of it. My job was to inform the band about the threat, not relive my school days trying and failing to get the trendy girls to think I was cool.

Sherrie cleared her throat. 'Can we get this show on the road? They've got a lot to get through today.'

'Of course.' I turned back to the others. Kit's disapproving gaze stayed on me, sliding down my face – much like the spittle of the bloke in custody yesterday. A realisation hit me, a thankful distraction from the repulsive memory. There was a band member missing. 'Will Ryan Hope be joining us?'

One of them scoffed but I missed who the noise came from.

Sherrie shook her head. 'No, he's not part of the reunion.'

'Think we've heard enough from men's voices to last a lifetime, don't you?' muttered Em, her words muffled by the guitar pick.

Roy interjected, 'He was a guitarist though, wasn't he, not a singer?'

Everyone except me and Sherrie glared at him. He drew the corners of his mouth down and widened his eyes, a 'crikey' in mime form. Maybe it was safer if I took the lead on the rest of the conversation. 'OK, why don't we take a seat then,' I said, gesturing towards four leather sofas set around a glass coffee table.

'What about the floor bags instead?' Tabby suggested, twirling one of her long blonde curls around her finger. 'They're, like, *really*, really great for posture, and it's good, you know, to be closer to the earth.'

Em pulled the pick from her mouth. 'Oh my days, Tabs, give it a rest. This is a music studio, not a fucking ashram.' She bit down on the pick again like it was some sort of adult dummy.

Tabby opened her mouth as if to protest, but didn't say anything else. I wondered if she'd had enough experience trying to get Em to do something she didn't want to do and knew the mission was pointless. Em Drummond didn't strike me as someone who liked to follow orders.

This was clearly going to be anything but fun.

7

Nush, Em and Tabby sat together on the sofa, Kit hovering behind them as Sherrie occupied one of the single chairs. I pulled the tablet from my bag and brought up a screenshot of the threat. 'I presume you haven't seen this?'

They all leant in to read it.

Nush was the first to speak, tightening the dark ponytail that sat atop her head like a pineapple. 'Nowt new there, marra. We've heard every single way random gadgies wanna bang us, kill us, do all sortsa shit. Some of them get canny inventive like, gotta give props where props are due.' The sing-song tone of her North East accent diminished the seriousness of her words and made it sound like she was telling a children's bedtime story. 'And not really sure how worried to be here, a mean, this divvy cannit even count. "One doll down, four to go." There's only three of us. Unless they're including her?' She looked back over her shoulder towards Kit.

Sherrie shook her head. 'How could they? No one knows she's here. No one knows any of you are here, except your lot,' she said, pointing at me and Roy. 'The agency wouldn't dish that information out to just anyone, believe me – I've got them under strict instructions to keep schtum.'

Kit scoffed. 'The agency might not, but what about the police? Now they know where you are, everyone will.'

'We're not going to advertise the fact you're staying here,' I said, trying to keep my tone professional despite Kit's snippy attitude, 'and I'd suggest you don't either. Keep a low profile, avoid putting pictures on social media, that sort of thing. You'd be amazed what people can work out about locations from uploaded photos.'

Nush, Em and Sherrie all looked at Tabby.

'What?' Tabby said.

'Nee way you can gan two weeks without deein' an Insta live, like,' Nush said to her. 'You'll shrivel up faster than a nun's fanny without ya regular dose of attention.' She slapped the inside of her arm like a drug addict desperate to find a vein.

'Urgh! That's, like, *so* gross,' Tabby said, as if Nush was a younger sibling who'd picked their nose and wiped a fresh snot on her lululemons. 'Not to mention, like, *totally* misogynistic. I'm not stupid enough to broadcast where we are.'

Em made a 'yeah, right' noise that sounded like she was stifling a sneeze before Tabby elbowed her in the ribs.

Sherrie snapped her fingers then held her hand up like she was trying to get the attention of a pack of rambunctious puppies in a dog park rather than three adult women. 'Oi, this is serious, pay attention.'

I nodded a thank you at Sherrie. 'Like I said, if you could dial back any social media posting, and in terms of the numbers in the threats, I'm presuming they've included Ryan in the count. It wasn't mentioned in any of the publicity I saw that he wasn't part of the reunion. We'll need to give him the heads up, too. Just because he won't be at the festival, doesn't mean he couldn't still be targeted. Do you have contact details for him?'

Em, Tabby and Nush all shook their heads but Sherrie nodded. 'I've got his email.'

I handed her the tablet and she pulled out her phone to retrieve the address, then typed it into my notes.

'Thank you,' I said. 'So this username, Riot_GRRRL_til_you_DIE, does that mean anything to you?'

Em rolled her eyes, and Tabby looked at me like I'd picked up the wrong piece of cutlery in an expensive restaurant.

'*Riot grrrl*?' Tabby said. 'You've never heard of *Riot grrrl*?'

Em's smirk distracted me from answering. 'She's a pi—'... copper, what the fuck does she know about underground feminist punk movements?'

There was no mistaking that Em knew exactly what she was doing with her fake slip of the tongue. My neck prickled. For some reason, the insult I'd heard and let wash over me more times than I could remember seemed to hit harder now.

Sherrie stood and thrust her hands into her trouser pockets, the movement so smooth it was clear she'd had a lot of practice extending her role as band manager to include side duties of referee. 'Em, keep a lid on the aggro, yeah? They're just doing their job.'

Em held her palms up in what I guessed was in no way

54

a genuine gesture of apology before slouching back against the cushions.

'Right,' I said, trying to ignore the flush on my face, 'it would be helpful for us to know if you've received any other concerning communications, or if there's anyone who might hold a grudge. Anyone you've had issues with that might suggest this is a credible threat?'

Nush laughed. 'How long ya got, pet? We weren't exactly the most popular bairns in the industry playground back then. And I doubt much's changed, like. Social media's gettin' worse and worse these days, I've never seen nowt like it.'

Em chimed in again, her voice less bitter, like she was resigned to telling a tale as old as time. 'We're women with opinions, we ain't the most popular, full stop. Can't have a shit without someone commenting on it. Have the audacity to suggest women should be treated just like any man? Death threat. Suggest women should have autonomy over their own bodies? Double death threat with a cherry on top.'

'Aye,' Nush said, nudging Em's arm, 'remember when I said custard creams were the supreme biscuit on Twitter back in the day and some bourbon-basher said they were ganna set the tour bus on fire? People are mental, man.'

'What about the documentary, *The Dee Dee Dolls*?' I asked. 'Have you had any contact from anyone involved in it?'

Sherrie tutted. 'Bunch of nutters. Funnily enough, our invite to appear must've got lost in the post.'

'What's that got to do with any of this?' Em said.

'Oh my God,' Tabby said, 'you don't, like, think it's one of them threatening us, do you? Those girls are, like, *so* freaky.'

Em stood up and scratched at the zigzag pattern freshly shorn into her undercut. 'Nothing I'm sure a bit of aura cleansing wouldn't sort, eh Tabs? They're just a bunch of stupid kids, what exactly do they think they're gonna do? This is a waste of time.' She stood on the sofa and Kit stepped to one side as Em swung a leg up to climb over it. 'Can we get back to the music? It's not like you're even gonna catch anyone for this, even if it's a real threat, and don't you have more important things to do like root out the shit in your own ranks?'

'Em,' Tabby said in a condescending tone, 'remember what we agreed, about your negativity.'

'I didn't agree Jack shit, mate,' Em said, making her way to her guitar.

Tabby turned back to me. 'Ignore her, she's always like this when Mercury's in retrograde.'

'Mercury'll be getting shoved up your—'

'Em!' Sherrie yelled, cutting her response to Tabby short.

There was no point telling Em to come back. I raised my voice so she could still hear me. 'We can try and trace profiles on social media. Obviously there are ways people can get around it, but a request's been submitted. In the meantime, anything else worries you, anything at all, please let us know. And to be on the safe side, you may want to think about the security set-up here. We came straight in through the gate and walked right in. It would be good to keep those gates and the front door locked.' I looked to Sherrie. 'What's their personal security situation?'

'I've got a baseball bat upstairs, that do ya?' she said with a wry smile. 'We've got our own security team, they're on their way. They were supposed to get in last night with the rest of us but got delayed; they're due anytime now. They'll work shifts keeping an eye on things here in the run-up, then the whole gang'll be there to cover the festival itself. Good blokes, they worked with the band before, most of them anyway. And—'

Sherrie's sentence was cut short as something thudded behind the sofa. Everyone turned to look at Kit who'd squatted down to pick up the notebook she'd dropped. 'Sorry,' she said, hugging the pad of paper across her chest.

Shaking her head at the interruption, Sherrie continued, 'What was I saying? Oh, and I'm sure this lot'll be fine with me until then. I worked the doors in Camden back in the late eighties, which you might think is worlds apart from the music biz, but I'll have you know it prepared me pretty damn well for dealing with record execs.' I didn't doubt for a second that if any physical threats presented themselves before the security team arrived, Sherrie could probably deal with them with one arm tied behind her back. Upside down. Blindfolded.

We finished up with the band before Sherrie showed us out.

Roy spoke for the first time since his earlier gaffe as we hovered by the front door. 'So, is Ryan Hope as, erm ... interesting as the rest of them?'

SAM FRANCES

Sherrie waved a dismissive hand. 'He's no bother. Not one for the spotlight like them lot. I could see from day one it weren't right for him, tried telling the producers on the show when he got picked, but . . .' She shrugged a *what can you do*. 'He's a good kid, go easy on him. They were close, him and Ris. He didn't take it well when she . . . you know.'

Some of the articles I'd read had suggested a relationship between them, but they'd always denied it. I took the opportunity to get some facts. 'Close as in more than friends?'

'No, no,' she said. 'Not for the lack of trying on his part, mind you – nothing inappropriate, just a bit of a lovesick puppy, you know? They were kids, they went through a lot together. Things kids shouldn't have to go through, and I protected them the best I could but, well, they weren't the easiest bunch in the world, even before Dee Dee went all psycho on us. I tried with that girl and all, I really did. But it's no wonder she ended up like that, being dragged up the way she was.'

I thought back to what Dad had said about Dee Dee's lack of childhood. 'What exactly did Dee Dee's mother do to her, when she was a kid?' I asked.

'Pfft, nothing, that's the point – pretty much left the poor thing to fend for herself. Always too busy trying to get her next fix with whatever bloke she had on the go to give a shit about Dee Dee. D'you know, I heard she hasn't even visited her in prison, not once in ten years. Even *I* went, and I was fuming with her, but I still wanted to give her a chance, you know, to explain herself. But Judith? Nah, she didn't give a shit. I dunno, supposed to be unconditional,

58

ain't it, a mother's love. Mind, going to see her means facing up to reality, accepting a bit of the blame for raising such a messed-up kid, and nothing's ever Judith's fault, of course. Always had some excuse, typical junkie. Anyway, enough of me ranting, I better get back before the handbags start flying.'

I didn't envy Sherrie's task of keeping the band in check. I'd stick to thugs and criminals, thank you very much. 'Sure,' I said, 'thanks for your time, and remember, anything concerning, anything at all, please let us know straight away.'

Sherrie saluted in response and closed the door behind us, locking mechanisms inside the thick wood clunking shut.

'What a delightful bunch,' Roy said.

'Quite the charmers, aren't they? The Dolls and Mavis Mulberry all in one day. What did I do to deserve that?'

'What's Mavis Mulberry got to do with the price of fish?'

'I've got to go to the SAG meeting now, remember? They're doing a festival site visit.' I unlocked the car and climbed in, the vehicle bouncing on its creaking suspension as Roy flopped in beside me.

'How come they've got you doing that and not one of the NPT lot?'

I hadn't told Roy I'd put myself forward to cover the festival planning to get out of the Chief's roadshows. We may have gotten better at being honest, but that didn't mean I had the energy to walk him through every monthly existential crisis – that's what I paid my therapist damn good money for. 'I'll have you know it's a very specialist job, battling over logistics about Portaloo placement and other exciting things like making sure they're equipped to deal with a load of drunk, sunburnt teenagers.'

'Waste of CID time if you ask me,' Roy said.

My phone vibrated and I eased it out of my jeans pocket. 'DS Washington.' My chest tightened as I took in the words from the control room. 'Fuck's sake,' I said as they hung up.

'What's wrong?' Roy said.

'We need to get to the festival site, now.'

Roy grabbed the handle above the passenger window as I slammed my foot on the accelerator and left a trail of gravel dust in our wake, speeding towards the gates.

8

Everywhere I look there are snakes. In the grass, in the walls, in the swamps you call home.

How don't they see you? Your diamond-scaled back slithering, golds and browns and greens glinting in the spotlight. You have everyone hypnotised, eyes fixed on your hissing, flicking two-forked tongue, blind to the serpentine of destruction in your wake. They sit there and watch, doing nothing to help. How does no one see? No one sees but me.

Maybe it's because you don't bite like the others. Their little black eyes, shards of onyx glaring before they strike. Teeth sinking into the skin, leaving puncture marks for everyone to see as they inject their poison, filling to the brim.

Not you.

You do not strike. You are slow and steady as you coil your body around my neck, tighter and tighter. Choking, squeezing until only one drop of life is left before you release.

Only for a second.

Before you squeeze again. Squeeze, release. Squeeze,

release. *Squeeze, squeeze, squeeze until every last drop of me is gone.*

That's what you do.

Maybe it's time I follow your lead. Put on a show the only way I know how, as I sever your snake head and watch what's left of you writhe.

9

Half of the festival site in the middle of Kestrel Park was cordoned off by the time Roy and I arrived. Eddie Lumsdale was doing a better job of manning it than he'd been known to on previous occasions, probably a result of learning the importance of forensics preservation the Crime Scene Manager Bernie McGovern way, or as I liked to call it, the fuck-around-and-find-out technique. His work ethic had improved after last year's mishap, but I was pretty sure Jane hadn't totally dismissed the idea of updating his job title from PCSO to PCSOWHCBA, i.e. providing support to the policing community *When He Could Be Arsed.*

'Afternoon, Sarge,' Eddie said, adjusting the peaked cap that swamped his small head so much he could barely see out from under it. Sometimes I wondered why he didn't bite the bullet and opt for a cadet's uniform. At twenty-five, you'd think if he was going to grow into this one it would have happened by now.

I nodded. 'What we got?'

Eddie rehashed what we'd been told on the phone with

the dramatic flair of a West End auditionee. Another threat left for the band, this time in the form of actual dolls, intercepted by the unsuspecting members of the SAG on their arrival for the site visit.

'Bernie's down there now,' Eddie said. 'He's still taking photos so you can see them in situ. They're well creepy, and I don't like dolls at the best of times.'

I wondered if that was because he was jealous of their stature but kept the comment to myself as Eddie's scrawny arm pointed in the direction of the primary crime scene.

We headed off across the field, parched yellow grass crunching beneath our feet as we zigzagged between the Portakabins, scaffolding and flatbed trucks littering the site. The main stage came into view, Bernie doing his best David Bailey impression kneeling down with his camera. 'We all right to come down, Bern?' I yelled. He didn't reply or look back, just waved us over, keeping his eyes fixed on the digital screen of his viewfinder. I followed the angle of the lens and the hairs on my arms stood up. Four large dolls hung from the scaffolding that made up the roof of the stage, with a fifth piece of rope hanging next to them, but with nothing attached to it.

Bernie stopped pressing buttons. 'Oof, it's hotter than a witch's tit out here,' he said, wiping his forearm across his wrinkled brow before swatting at a fly that had landed on the side of his face. I listened carefully for his next words to assess his mood, which could usually be accurately gauged by the strength of his Scottish accent. He didn't say anything else, and the fact that his motion to dislodge the fly wasn't accompanied by a cry of 'Get tae fuck' indicated he was probably too hot to be angry.

'Isn't the term *colder than a witch's tit*?' I asked.

'A menopausal witch, then. Do *not* tell my Pam I said that – she'll make inferences that'll put me even more in her bad books.'

'How've they managed to get *you* down here?' I said. 'Didn't think you got out of bed for anything less than murder.'

'Me and my Pam should be on a beach in Tenerife right now sipping piña coladas, I'll have you know,' he said in a resigned tone. 'She's no' happy, but I've got two of my lot off sick – one away on a course and another on restricted duties – so it's me or nothing.'

I wasn't complaining. With over thirty years on the job, Bernie was one of the most experienced crime scene examiners in the country. If there was something to find here, I'd bet my life on him finding it. 'What we dealing with?'

'They're bringing me a ladder to get a better look.'

He held out a box of latex gloves. Roy and I took a pair each and pulled them on before walking across, but we didn't need to get that close before we could see it – a knife sticking out of the chest of one of the dolls.

'Bern,' I said, not taking my eyes off the hanging miniature bodies. 'Get that big old boot of yours up someone's arse and tell them to hurry up with that ladder, will you?'

I left Bernie to finish bagging and tagging and sent Roy off on a mission to speak to everyone on site about any witnesses or CCTV opportunities. I had my own mission to complete as I made my way back to Aurora House.

'Twice in one day, Sergeant?' Sherrie said as she answered the gate intercom. 'To what do we owe the pleasure?'

She let me in and was waiting outside the front door as I pulled up, a hulk of a man I didn't recognise standing beside her. Sherrie introduced him as Manu Tuala, the band's head of security, before taking me to the large kitchen diner where the band and Kit were having lunch.

I outlined what Bernie had recovered. Four dolls made up to depict a different method of death, each with one of the band member's names drawn across the forehead in black marker. The doll with the knife through its neck was marked up as Em. The one marked Ryan had a slash wound and red string hanging from its stomach. Tabby's had what looked like a bullet wound in the chest. The only one that didn't have any obvious injuries depicted was the one branded with Nush's name, but it was covered in what I could safely assume was faeces from the smell. 'We've also recovered five pieces of orange baling twine used to hang them up, probably the same type that gets used on most farms around here, one nine-centimetre-blade paring knife, and a note tucked into the clothing of one of the dolls,' I explained.

'What did it say?' Sherrie asked.

I hadn't needed to take a picture of it; I remembered it verbatim. '"Five ways to die. Five, four, three, two, one, dead."'

Nush scrunched up her nose. 'I don't get it.'

66

Em stared at her. 'You a moron or something? Five of us, five deaths. It's not exactly rocket science.'

'Nah man, I get *that* bit, I'm not a fuckin' divvy, but what does my one mean? Everyone else's is obvious. The fifth string with no doll equals Ris is already dead, Ryan's is getting its guts spilled.' She pointed at Em and Tabby respectively, 'You're getting stabbed, you're getting shot. What does mine mean? That I'm ganna shit mesel to death? What kinda way to go is that, man?'

Em scoffed. 'Are you for real? Your proposed method of murder not quite meeting your standards?'

'Wey, it's yet another thing where I get the shitty end of the deal, isn't it? I mean, like, *literally*.'

'Oh my days,' Em said, 'if you start going on about that again, I swear to God—'

'Girls,' Sherrie said, her voice cutting through the bickering, 'I don't think we've got time for this, yeah? Let's listen to what needs doing.' She nodded at me to continue.

Someone calling a group of grown women 'girls' would usually get my back up, but since this lot acted more like a bunch of teenagers than thirty-year-olds, I gave Sherrie a pass. 'So, yeah, there may be some forensic opportunities for us to explore.'

Nush piped up again, 'Surely you'll catch the nutter from my one. There'll be DNA in the shit, won't there?'

'It's a possibility, but from my experience you don't tend to get great results from faeces. For one thing, the bacteria degrades the DNA.'

Nush pulled a face as if I'd brought the soiled doll into

67

the room with me. '*Experience?* How many people do shits at crime scenes, like?'

'You'd be amazed,' I said. 'Anyway, what I really wanted to discuss with you was, and I know this won't be easy, but we have to think about the fact this person has managed to access the site. Before, when things were online, this could have been anyone, maybe not necessarily someone in the country, but now, whoever is making these threats has been here, and they could come back for the festival.'

'What you saying?' Sherrie said.

'That you might want to consider cancelling the performance.'

'Why should they have to do that?' Sherrie said. 'Bow down to whoever's doing this? Isn't that exactly what this loser wants?'

'No!' Tabby said, her chair scraping across the tiled floor as she pushed to her feet. 'This is our performance, our time. We can't cancel, we have a platform and important things to say!'

Nush rolled her eyes. 'Chill ya boots, man, we're singing songs, not freeing Nelson fuckin' Mandela.'

Em scoffed and folded her arms across her chest. 'You're being harsh there, mate. She has got important things to say, like get fifty percent off at ASOS through my affiliate link TABBY123.'

'Hilarious,' Tabby replied, dropping back into her chair, 'except the joke's on you because I only work with sustainable clothing brands actually, sooo . . .'

'Aye,' Nush chimed in, 'the sorta clothes you promote

had better last till the day I crap mesel to death. A hundred quid for a plain white T? Pure joke that, man.'

'Look,' Tabby said, flipping her fishtail plait over her shoulder, 'what I'm saying is, there's no such thing as bad news. No publicity is bad publicity, you know?'

'That's right,' Em said. 'There's only one thing worse than being slagged off, and that's not being talked about at all, yeah? I bet you're loving every second of this.'

'Of course I'm not,' Tabby said, 'but when life gives you lemons—'

'I swear to God,' Em said, pinching the top of her nose, 'if one more positivity cliché comes out your mouth, I will find a bag of lemons, pelt them off your head and smother you in the sack they came in.'

'Well, *I'm* doing the show,' Tabby said, hand to her chest like she was volunteering as tribute in *The Hunger Games*, 'no matter what you two do. And it's not like this kind of stuff doesn't happen all the time. Suzanne Vega wore a bulletproof vest on stage at Glasto in 'eighty-nine. And Taylor Swift has had horrendous death threats, and a stalker, most female artists have, and you don't see them cowering in a room somewhere – no, they're out there, night after night. They don their armour and keep going, like soldiers.'

Em clapped her hands sarcastically. 'Ahhh, I see where this is going. You've surpassed yourself there, making a fashion statement out of a death threat. Who's gonna do a brand partnership with you on that one? The fucking NRA?'

Tabby ignored her and continued, 'It's not just about us,

we can't let our fans down. And we've got Manu and his team. I mean, look at the size of him,' she said, gesturing at the man mountain standing quietly by the door to the back lawn.

She wasn't wrong. The guy made Sherrie look petite. He had a good five or six inches on her, and with his matching cream combat trousers and vest top he looked like a fridge-freezer.

I decided it was time for me to step in. 'Look, if Miss Swift was performing at Fortbridge Rocks I'd be giving her the same advice, but for now she's outside of my jurisdiction. You, on the other hand, I can try to help. And I'm sure the team here'll do a great job, but the threats mention shooting, and being big and physically strong doesn't make the slightest bit of difference when a bullet rips through you at hundreds of miles per hour.'

A few seconds of silence followed, presumably because everyone was taking in the reality of what could happen before Em spoke.

'Nah, we're doing it, we'll be fine.'

I wasn't convinced she actually believed that, and I wondered if she just wanted to voice opposition to anything that came out of my mouth, her own little 'Fuck you' to the badge.

'Tabs can get some of those mudgrass shots she used to try and force down our necks before every gig, eh, Tabs, remember those? What were they for again? I lose track with you, our chakras, our aura, what?' Em reached over and slapped Tabby's thigh.

'They were *wheat*grass, actually,' Tabby said. 'And sorry for trying to boost your energy levels!'

Em shrugged. 'Fucking tasted like mud.'

'How would you know? You wouldn't even drink them,' Tabby said.

'I'll stick to sambuca, ta. Unless you find me a pre-show shot that makes me bulletproof, now that'd be a pyramid scheme I could get on board with.'

'Oh, fuck off, Em,' Tabby snapped.

Em brought a hand to her chest in exaggerated surprise. 'I thought swearing was bad for your spirit?'

Sherrie let out a deep sigh before intervening. 'We get it, all right, it's a risk. But that's how it is these days, I'm afraid, the price you pay for being in the spotlight. And they're gonna be doing bag checks and whatnot on the door. Manu can bring some more boys in, up the security, both here and at the festival, can't you?'

His mouth formed the shape of a 'yeah' but I barely heard anything. I got the impression Manu was more a man of action than words.

Sherrie turned her attention back to me. 'And you've still got two weeks to find whoever's doing this, unless I find them first, of course, which quite frankly I don't think you want, Sergeant, unless you want a dead body on your hands.'

'I'll pretend I didn't hear that,' I said.

'You pretend what you want, darlin', I'll do what it takes to protect my girls, and you can take that to the bank.'

We finished up and Sherrie walked me to the door.

71

'Give me strength, I didn't have kids for a bloody reason,' she said.

'I get this is difficult for them. Mustn't be easy being in the public eye at the moment.'

Sherrie shrugged. 'Never has been, to tell you the truth. I've been in the business thirty years, this is nothing new. There's always been nutters – just new formats for them to do it in is all. State of the world, isn't it? You've gotta make the best of it.'

I sighed, not sure if what Sherrie had said was an example of optimism or whether the acceptance was just depressing. My phone interrupted me having to pick one. 'I better get that.'

Sherrie nodded and closed the door.

'Any luck?' I said, answering Roy's call.

'Nada. The site manager said they're still securing the perimeter, and temporary CCTV installations haven't gone in yet, so anyone can get on site at the minute without too much difficulty. The dolls weren't there when everyone left last night, and none of the site workers had been down that end yet this morning, so no one spotted it until the SAG lot got there. No one's seen anyone hanging around who wasn't meant to be there yesterday or today, so it's likely it happened overnight or first thing this morning.'

'Or could be someone with legitimate access to the site. You got details of the crew?'

'Yeah, most of them, just need the ones not working today.'

'Good, get them checked. And now we know this isn't

some random keyboard warrior, I think we've got some visits to make. Get an address for Dee Dee's mother, and speak to that bloke you know in the prison liaison team. We're going to see Dee Dee.'

'You think she could be threatening them from a prison cell?' Roy said.

'Unlikely, but she's mentioned in that first message, and Ris's body count is included too. Maybe someone's contacted her, thinking they're doing her a favour in some warped way, carrying on her legacy or something.'

'What, like one of those weirdo kids in the documentary?'

'Could be. Do some digging with the production company, see if they have any personal info for the talking heads they can give us.'

'On it,' Roy said.

'And get on to Ryan Hope,' I added. 'Now things have escalated, I want us to go see him in person.'

'Go all the way to Devon?' Roy said. 'Can't we just ask locals to speak to him?'

I opened the car door and slid into the driver's seat. 'In theory, yes, but I can't say I'm feeling the most trusting of people I don't know right now, and cops don't get a free pass.'

'Fine,' Roy said grudgingly, 'but no stopping at some greasy service station on the way there, I'm bringing a packed lunch.'

I rolled my eyes as I stuck my key in the ignition.

10

Forty minutes after picking Roy up from Kestrel Park, I pulled off the A-road towards Dee Dee's childhood home, still occupied by her mother. Everyone in Wessex Constabulary knew the Beacon Hill estate, where violence, criminal damage and anti-social behaviour jobs were ten a penny, with little prospect for improvement given gangs handed out weapons and drugs like Haribos to underprivileged kids barely out of nappies. Even the weather warned us off as we hit the roundabout leading on to it, the sky darkening for the first time in weeks with thick cloud. I'd have been thankful for the respite from the sun, but if anything it felt even stuffier, the air pregnant with water vapour.

'Christ almighty.' I wasn't sure whether Roy was referring to the burnt-out terraced house or the front yard full of overflowing rubbish bags and stained mattresses. 'What a shit hole.'

Fenmore House loomed over us, one of four brutalist residential tower blocks sat at each corner of the square estate like pillars framing a boxing ring; an apt design, given kids here seemed to fight their way up, rather than be brought up. A bunch of face mask-clad teenagers caught my eye in the rear-view mirror as I pulled into the car park, hanging around outside an unbranded corner shop, its windows blocked out by sun-bleached posters.

'Hello,' Roy said as I brought the car to a stop, 'we've got ourselves a welcome party.'

We were in an unmarked vehicle with no uniforms on, but to these kids we might as well have been wearing sirens on our heads; they'd probably sensed us coming from the motorway. I double-checked the car was locked before we made our way towards the yellowing PVC doors at the entrance to the flats. 'Judith Nolan lives on the eleventh floor, what are the chances the lift works?' I said, my gaze scanning the front of the dated building.

Roy looked at his new Apple Watch. 'No harm walking up, get some extra steps in.'

'Urgh, bring back the old Roy who drove the half a mile to the chippy, I say.'

The lift worked, but it stank of urine. I held my breath until we hit the external walkway leading to Judith's flat, making our way past blasting TVs and music seeping through open windows before we stopped outside 11F. I rapped my knuckles on the chipped red panel and it didn't take long for a bolt to clunk before the door inched open, a woman I knew to be in her late forties but looked a good decade older standing in the narrow gap. Her small sunken eyes, the spitting image of Dee Dee's, flitted back and forth between us.

'Yeah?' she said.

'Judith Nolan?' I asked, holding up my warrant card.

She pawed at the fringe swept across her shiny forehead, a patchy bleached-blonde bird's nest that refused to flatten. 'That's me.'

I made introductions, before nodding over her shoulder. 'Mind if we come in?'

There was no panic. No fraught look taking over her face like most people when met with an unexpected knock from the old bill, indicative of the fact it was probably a regular occurrence around here. She stood back and pulled the door wider.

'What d'you want?' Judith said, sniffing and wiping her nose with the back of her hand as we followed her down the short, dark hallway into a living room. 'If you're looking for Darren, he don't live here no more. Kicked him out months ago. Dunno where you'll find him now – scrounging off some other mug, I'll bet.'

A veil of lingering cigarette smoke wrapped me up like a spider web. 'We're not here for Darren.'

She gestured towards a two-seater sofa that had seen better days but was the only proper seating, except for a rusted deck chair. There wasn't much space for anything else in the small room itself or the gloomy kitchenette to the back of it. I sank into the sofa cushions, the filling and springs having given up the ghost of maintaining any sort of tension. Roy took the more sensible option of remaining standing.

Judith leant back against the buzzing fridge and folded her arms. 'Well?'

'We're investigating some death threats that have been

made towards the remaining band members of The Dolls,'
I said. 'Nush Chandra, Tabby F—'

'I know their names.' Tension fanned across her jaw.
'What's that gotta do with me?'

I shuffled into a more dignified seating position. 'The
threats have been made anonymously. We're speaking to
anyone who might have a problem with the band, and given
the history with your family, it probably won't surprise you
to hear your name came up.'

A half-hearted scoff came from her mouth. 'So they
remember it now? Seemed to forget quick enough when I
tried to talk to them after what happened.'

'What did you try to talk to them about?' I asked.

Judith looked at me as if I'd asked the silliest question in
the world. 'About what really went on. I wanted to know
what they'd done to my girl. I might not've been the best
mother in the world, but I know my own daughter, and
the Dee Dee that left this flat to go swanning off on tour
with them was no killer.'

I felt for parents of criminals sometimes. Not for
those who were the main reasons for their little darlings
embarking on a life of crime in the first place, but for the
ones who believed their offspring had diamonds shining
out their arses and couldn't fathom even the suggestion
they'd do anything wrong. As I scanned the flat, which
didn't look like the best place for a lizard to grow up, let
alone a child, I wasn't sure which camp Judith fell into.
Roy had outlined Judith's various dalliances with the law
throughout Dee Dee's childhood on the drive over. With the

number of drug-related offences, I wondered how well she actually knew her daughter given it was a miracle she was never taken into care. 'From what I understand, Dee Dee gave quite a thorough explanation for what she did,' I said.

Judith shook her head vehemently. 'Don't believe a word of it! They said in the papers she was jealous of Ris. *Jealous!* Of what? My Dee Dee was ten times better than anyone in that band! The only reason she didn't get picked was because they said she didn't have the right "look", like we don't know what that means. Just because she wasn't crack-head skinny like the rest of them. Here,' she said, fumbling in her pocket and pulling out her phone, 'look at this.' She scrolled down and then turned it towards me and Roy.

A grainy video began to play of Dee Dee. It looked like it must have been taken around the same time as the photographs of her and Ris as kids that Dad had reminded me of. Someone – presumably Judith – had filmed the footage through a partially open door. Dee Dee seemed oblivious, her eyes focussed on the strings of a guitar balanced on her lap as she plucked them with her right hand, the left moving effortlessly around the neck of the instrument. Her big toe stuck out through a hole in her worn pink sock, tapping against the leg of the stool she was perched on as she counted herself in and started singing. Her voice was powerful but delicate, like it might break at any moment, but never did. She hit the final note, looking up into the camera. 'Mum! Go away!' she shrieked, putting the guitar on the thin mattress of a small single bed before slamming the door closed, the video coming to an abrupt halt.

Judith's eyes filled with tears. Maybe she hadn't been quite as neglectful as Sherrie had made out; she'd gotten Dee Dee a guitar at least, showed an interest in her music. One of the tears escaped and trickled down her nose. 'What's she have to be jealous of? My Dee Dee's got a beautiful voice, like a young Mama Cass. She wrote that herself, you know, was always writing songs, her and Ris. I used to laugh – they were always so serious, like a pair of fishwives, old before their time, but my Dee Dee was always the talented one. Those lyrics, does she sound like a murderer to you?'

There was no denying the song was beautiful, and for Dee Dee to have composed it at such a young age was impressive. But if I listed all the talented people in the world who'd done horrific things, we'd be there all day. 'It's a lovely song, but we're not here to talk about Dee Dee or what she did.'

'She didn't do nothing, I'm telling you, it's a cover-up or something.'

I'd lost count of the number of times I'd dealt with parents, spouses and children of the people I'd nicked over the years, adamant I'd gotten the wrong person. Reasoning with them about the overwhelming evidence never usually got me anywhere. 'Have you sent any messages to the band, Judith?'

She shook her head. 'You think I've got them on speed dial or something? I ain't even got their phone numbers.'

'What about their social media accounts, have you interacted with those?' I asked.

Judith held her phone out and swiped through her small

list of apps before shoving it into my palm. 'Here, look for yourself. I don't do social media, and I ain't got no other devices. Dunno if you've noticed,' she said, holding out her arm to show off the room, 'it ain't exactly PC World in here. Darren took anything worth selling.'

It was only now I noticed the room didn't have a TV, just an empty rectangle a lighter shade of cream than the wall around it and holes in the plasterboard where one had been mounted at some point. 'D'you mind if my colleague has a look around to verify that?' I asked.

'Be my guest.'

I nodded at Roy and he turned, making his way to the first door off the hallway.

'Look,' she said, shifting her weight from one foot to the other. 'I'm being honest here, *grudge* doesn't come close to describing how I feel about those people. They took advantage of my girl, knew her and Ris wouldn't want to be apart when they were going on tour, gave her some fancy job title, Band Operations Technician or something, but she was their lackey. And they know what really happened, when Ris was killed, they must do. And they've left my Dee Dee in that cell all this time. They're the ones who want locking up, not my girl. Believe me, if I wanted to threaten them, I wouldn't be a coward about it on the internet, I'd do it to their faces,' she said, breaking into a hacking cough. She turned her back to me, spluttering into a hastily grabbed tea towel.

'Do you need some water?' I asked.

She paused for a second, then balled up the towel and

threw it into the sink. 'I'm fine, just one of them summer flu things.'

Whether Judith realised it or not, her little rant only added further credence to the core of Dee Dee's confession: that her and Ris's friendship had soured when Ris was selected for the band and Dee Dee wasn't, even though Ris hadn't wanted to audition in the first place, only doing so after one of the production team saw her helping Dee Dee practise in the waiting room. That fact had really stuck in the craw of *The Dee Dee Dolls* participants.

I tried to pull the conversation back on track before Judith managed to catch her breath and kick off again. 'Where were you last night?'

'I work nights down at the care home. I was there nine till nine, got back here this morning just before ten.'

Roy emerged from the hallway and shook his head, suggesting he'd found nothing of note. I was surprised he hadn't come back with a tin-foil hat in his hand given the theories Judith had been spouting. I pushed myself off the sofa, indicating it was time we got out of there. Judith might be sourer than a bottle of vinegar, but I didn't think she was the one behind the threats. 'That's all we need for now. Thanks for your time.'

She carried on as if I hadn't said a word, 'If someone's threatening them, maybe it's because someone knows what they did.'

I paused. 'What do you mean?'

'Have you not been listening? To my Dee Dee! Framed her for something she didn't do.'

I'd resisted the urge to bite back enough already, I couldn't hold it in any longer. 'The band didn't put Dee Dee up on that stage roof, Judith, they didn't put the crowd of people there watching what happened, and they weren't even there when she confessed to what she did. So what are you suggesting they did do, exactly?'

Her lips wobbled, eyes refilling with tears. 'I don't know, I just know my Dee Dee, and she wouldn't do that. She's a good girl and she might as well be dead too. I haven't seen her in ten years, won't even let me visit.'

From what Sherrie had said, I'd assumed Judith hadn't bothered to visit her daughter, but the expression on her face suggested otherwise. It didn't take an expert in psychology to figure out what was going on here. And she may have been decades too late, still avoiding responsibility like her life depended on it, but her desire to make amends, in her own way, couldn't be denied. I felt myself caving under the weight of her pain and regret. 'Who won't let you visit? The prison?'

She shook her head. 'No, Dee Dee. I've lost track of the amount of times I've asked to be put on her visitor list. Says no every time. I've tried sending letters. They all come back unopened.'

'I'm sorry.' I didn't know if it was a good idea or not, but something told me to throw this woman a bone. 'We'll be visiting Dee Dee as part of the investigation; is there anything you'd like me to tell her?'

Judith straightened as if she'd been shocked by some dodgy wiring. 'You'd do that?'

I nodded.

She swallowed hard, her eyes flitting about as if she'd been asked to give a speech in front of thousands of people with no notice. 'Tell her ... tell her I've turned my life around, got myself a job, and I ain't touched anything, you know, *chemical* in years, and, and ... tell her I love her and I'll do anything to get her out of there. Whatever it takes.'

There hadn't been any recent drug-related offences against Judith's name from what I could remember of the list Roy summarised. But that didn't mean she was telling the truth about getting her shit together, and there was no way Dee Dee was coming out of prison anytime soon. Still, it was hard to ignore the pleading look on her prematurely wrinkled face. 'OK,' I said, making for the door.

The lift smelt even worse than it had on the way up, as if someone had been caught short again in the time we'd been in Judith's flat.

'You going soft or something?' Roy said.

'What d'you mean?'

'Passing notes from Looney Tunes.'

'It's not like I'm sneaking her in up my jumper for a visit; just passing on a basic message, and I don't think trying not to be too judgemental is the same as being soft. You never know what people have gone through, do you? I mean, your life can't exactly be going swimmingly if you live here and get pregnant at sixteen like Judith did.'

'You're too nice. She's off her rocker.'

'It's called compassion. Maybe you should try a scoop in your smoothie along with your protein powder.'

'So we ruling her out then?' he asked.

I stopped holding my breath as we exited the lift. 'There's clearly no love lost there, but I think she's telling the truth, that she wouldn't hide behind anonymous threats. Let's see what Dee Dee has to say for herself.'

We emerged from the reception as the group of kids we'd seen on our way in scarpered in several directions from the car park. 'Oh, for fuck's sake,' I said, taking in what they'd left behind, the word PIGZ scrawled along the side of my car in black spray paint.

11

'Little bastards,' I snapped, taking my anger out on the mouse, clicking harder and harder with each graffiti photo of my car I uploaded to the system.

'What happened to your *compassion*?' Roy asked from his desk.

'Used it all up on Judith. They should be thankful the paint was still wet enough to come off in the carwash, otherwise me calling them "bastards" would be the least of their worries.' I hit the enter key like it had insulted me, submitting my report. 'A waste of time that'll be. I bet you fifty quid none of the CCTV around there works and no one saw a bloody thing, and local uniform won't thank me for giving them paperwork to do and messing up their detection rates.'

'Careful,' Roy said, leaning back in his chair, 'you're starting to sound like me. You're too young to be a cynical old timer – still got another twenty years to moan yet. Pace yourself.'

I massaged my scalp. 'Dunno what you mean, nothing but sunny dispositions over here.'

'In that case, you OK if I knock off ten minutes early so I can go with Trudy to pick her sister up from the station? That prison visit request's gone in, and I'm waiting on a contact number for Ryan Hope. I'll keep my phone on in case they call back. And I'll get on to the documentary stuff first thing tomorrow.'

Eddie's pea head popped out from behind a computer on the other side of the office. 'Documentary? What documentary?'

'*The Dee Dee Dolls*,' I said. 'Some wackos who worship the ground Dee Dee Nolan walks on.'

'Want me to watch it for you? Report back?' he offered.

Whether Eddie was genuinely trying to be helpful or if he just wanted an excuse to watch TV and call it work was anyone's guess. 'I've already watched it. What we're after now is tracking down someone at the production company, see if we can get IDs on the talking heads who were on it.'

'My uncle works in TV, want me to ask him? He's pretty well connected.'

In the three years I'd known Eddie, I'd learned it was best to keep him occupied. And the insight he'd provided last year in my big stalking job hadn't proved a total washout. He might be a lazy sod when it came to business as usual, but for anything to do with celebrities, it was safe to say Eddie would be all over it. Ask him to recite parts of the Police Reform Act and he'd struggle, but he could list every single Big Brother winner and runner-up in chronological order without pausing for breath. 'You do that, Eddie, thanks. There you go, Roy, one less task for you. Get yourself off, I'll be doing the same in a second.'

A grin spread across Eddie's face as he pulled his phone from his pocket and went into the hallway, presumably to call his uncle.

Roy threw his rucksack over his shoulder. 'Right, see you tomorrow,' he said. 'We're taking Trudy's sister to that new vegan place, Plants and Plates or something, they call it. Have a good one.'

He'd given up asking about my social life, and I didn't bother telling him that, for once, I had plans tonight with my kickboxing class. Why rock the status quo?

The business park housing the kickboxing place was sandwiched between a veterinary hospital and a garden centre. I scanned the units, disappointed not to see a McDonald's. I'd be starving after this, and all I had in the house was a microwave meal that would barely serve as an appetiser.

Most of the people streaming in through the front door to the studio were kids and teenagers. Oh bollocks, had I accidentally strayed into a children's lesson? I followed the line into reception, praying the adults were already inside. There were a few grown-ups, clustered together in friendship groups, clearly regular attendees chatting about what they'd been up to since the last session. Where were all my anti-social brethren? The ones content with kicking people in the head without the small talk? I tutted before going to the counter to pay.

The young woman behind the till gave me a first-timer form to fill in. 'D'you have a pen?' I asked.

She nodded over my shoulder. 'Only got the one, you'll have to get it from that gentleman when he's finished.'

I turned to see a man in a light-grey T-shirt hunched over, using an orange plastic chair as a table to fill in his form. The defined muscles in his right shoulder flexed under the thin material as he lifted his arm away from the paper, shaking the pen, presumably to loosen the ink before he tried writing again. He scribbled on the page before putting the pen between flat palms, rolling it back and forth like he was some wild camper trying to start a fire with sticks. I wasn't sure if it was the thought of flames or the lumberjack-ish nature of the act, but there was definitely a sensation of sorts somewhere in the depths of my stomach. *Oh, hello loins, nice to see you haven't completely shrivelled up and died in there.*

My eyes were still fixed on the man's lightly tanned forearms as he stood and turned around. I almost choked on my own saliva as I clocked his face.

'You got another pen back there, this one isn't—' Bret stopped talking as he saw me. *Nice going, loins!* He tapped the pen on his palm. 'What are you doing out here?'

His tone made it sound like I was somewhere I shouldn't be. 'Hoping to punch and kick things. What are *you* doing here?'

'The same thing, I guess.'

Before either of us had time to say anything else, a man

approached, one of the instructors, I presumed, given he was wearing a vest with the studio's logo emblazoned across it. He placed a hand on each of our shoulders.

'Hello, hello!' he said. 'You must be my newbies. You two together?'

I went to say no but Bret beat me to it.

'God no, we hardly know each other,' he said, taking a step back from me as if to prove his point, which wasn't exactly wrong, despite the fact we'd worked in the same office for over two years before he'd moved jobs, but there was no need for him to be acting like I had some contagious disease.

The man removed his hands and clapped them together. 'No problem, my friends, no problem at all. You're the only ones here for the first time so you can work together,' he said, in a tone that suggested he was doing us a favour.

'I'd rather work on my own actually,' I said, making sure Bret knew I didn't want to be associated with him just as much as he didn't with me. 'Give me a bag or one of them rubber dummy figure things and I'll be good to go.'

'That's not how we do things, I'm afraid,' the instructor said through a toothy smile. 'We go in pairs, helps the kids socialise. The first half is partner drills, then we finish with bag work.'

'You really should advertise this as a kids' class,' I couldn't help but bark back, clawing at some semblance of dignity.

'It's not. Just, erm, no offence, but most adults are busy Friday nights so ...' Touché amigo, touché. I let out a sigh, a mixture of frustration and embarrassment. 'Let's get warmed up, shall we?' the man said, sweeping his arm towards the open double doors beside us.

He turned and walked into the hall without giving us time to object. I wanted to bolt in the other direction, swallow the sunk cost of the class, go home and pretend this never happened. But I'd driven all the way out here, and why should Bret have all the punchy fun? Neither of us had won our previous head-to-head when we'd gone for the MCU sergeant's position last year, me pulling out to focus on my mental health, him getting pipped to the post by his counterpart golden child Celeste Augustus, but now he was up at HQ and I was still in Fortbridge, it felt like he'd taken a step ahead while I languished in career purgatory. I'd be damned if he got one up on me in yet another set of stakes. And with any luck, maybe an opportunity would arise to kick him in the kidney with impunity. Maybe this wouldn't turn out to be such a dud of a night after all. I held my arm up and pointed in the direction the instructor had gone. 'After you, then.'

Bret's chest rose and fell exaggeratedly before he stooped to pick up his kit bag. 'This is not the Friday night I had planned,' he said, walking in ahead of me.

'Now *that*, we can agree on.'

The warm-up was painless enough, running laps around the large square of interlocking black and red foam mats in the centre of the hall, followed by dynamic stretches and some shadow boxing as one big group to show the new people the basic punches and kicks. Bret and I walked in silence to our first doubles station like we were being sent to his and hers matching gallows. The first activity involved sitting opposite each other with the tips of our toes touching, taking it in turns to pass a weighted ball between us as we did sit-ups. As much as I wanted to launch the ball at his head, I decided somewhere around the third set that if we were going to have to do this then I'd at least make the most of it. 'Anything come back on that profile threatening The Dolls yet?'

He paused mid sit-up. 'I told you it'd likely be next week.'

'No harm in asking. You never know when—'

'Can we not?' Bret said, interrupting me.

'Not what?'

'Talk about work.' He pushed the ball towards me, a little harder this time.

'What's wrong with talking about work?' I said. 'It's not like we've got anything else in common.' I had no idea if that was true. I didn't know what Bret's interests were, aside from wearing hideous hunter-green woollen jumpers with elbow patches and being condescending.

The instructor blew his whistle, indicating it was time to move on to the next station, which for us was hitting opposite sides of a punchbag. I stood and rammed my hands into a pair of white and blue boxing gloves, BO-tinged air puffing out as I displaced it.

Bret got to the bag first and started pounding. 'There's nothing wrong with talking about work *at* work. But right now, it's my night off. And if it's all the same to you, I'd like to focus on what we're doing. Neither of us came here for a chat.'

He was right, but my desire to argue with him took control of my mouth like a dentist's anaesthetic as I pummelled my side of the bag. 'My bad, I forgot socialising wasn't your thing.'

'Just because I don't socialise with people from work doesn't mean I don't socialise. And I dunno where you get off being judgemental about it, you're hardly a social butterfly.'

I flung every ounce of my weight into the next punch. Was that a dig about Tess or was I being overly sensitive to friend-related jabs at the moment? I wasn't sure, but that didn't stop the anger rushing me like I'd been dropped into a pot of boiling water. 'What is your problem?'

'I don't have a problem,' he said, eyes fixed on the spot of the bag he was hitting, 'unless I count you going on about work when I'm trying to relax.'

'Sor-ry,' I said, my punches perfectly coordinating with my sarcastic apology, 'I'll tell whoever's planning on trying to kill the band at the festival to press pause until you're back on duty, shouldn't be a problem.'

He opened his mouth, presumably to defend himself, but was interrupted by the instructor's whistle.

We took the break in our conversation as an opportunity to end it, doing the rest of the drills in a huffed silence, and I left before the cool-down, checking my phone as I got into the car. I had a few new emails and a text from Roy.

Got address and phone number 4 R HOPE. Tried calling no answer.

I typed out a response.

Let's go down tmrw AM. Pick you up at 9. NO hardboiled eggs in
the car this time!!

Moving on to my emails, the first was from the kickboxing studio somehow already waiting for me, asking
for feedback on my first – and what I'd already decided
would be my last – session. I deleted it and almost did the
same with the next one, which was some spam advertising
a dating app when I paused, finger hovering over the trash
icon on the screen.

While my inept loins clearly needed recalibrating after
completely misdirecting their attention earlier, I couldn't
deny the little spark of something I'd felt before realising
it was Bret I was looking at hadn't been *so* terrible. And
while I had more than enough experience of what happens
when you let the wrong people in, it wasn't like I could keep
the door closed for ever. Dating apps couldn't be that bad,
could they? Not the wild, wild west they were when they
started out, and it seemed to be how most people met these
days. Even if I didn't meet anyone, I'd overheard a couple
of mess room conversations that made some of the profiles
on there sound like excellent comedy value if nothing else.

I opened the email from WeMatch, clicking on the
CREATE PROFILE link. The questions started easy enough,
asking for my name. There we go, completed. Absolutely
nailing the dating game already. Second question: occu-
pation. *Bollocks.* Normally I wouldn't care about writing

'Police Officer'. Some people avoided it, more for safety reasons than anything to do with pride in their career, putting something vague like 'Emergency Services' or 'Public Sector Worker', but I'd never understood how that would play out. What would you even talk about on a first date if you couldn't mention this all-encompassing job that infiltrated every part of your life? I put 'POLICE' anyway and filled in the rest of the questions before saving and submitting.

'There,' I said, feeling rather smug with myself, 'that wasn't so hard.' I set some basic filters and scrolled through the first ten profiles it suggested, clicking the WeMatch button on one that looked relatively normal, and by that I mean his profile picture wasn't an image of him riding an elephant topless with a bow and arrow strapped to his back with a dead ferret in each hand. The competition wasn't exactly stiff. Now I supposed I'd have to wait. See if Jake expressed a shared interest then see how long it took him to do something weird if we made a connection, like ask me to send him photos with baby carrots stuck between my toes.

I dropped my phone into the centre console, turned the radio up loud and drove out of the industrial estate, flipping off Bret's car like the mature adult I was as I passed it.

12

It was almost midnight by the time Kit broke free from the grip of Aurora House. She hadn't had a moment to herself all day, not with the police officers visiting, then the security team finally rocking up, all topped off with that sergeant coming back for a fucking encore.

The booming of her heart had mirrored the pounding kick drum as she'd sat through band practice, so loud in her ears she couldn't hear herself think. And she needed to think. Hard. Figure out what she was going to do if the look on Manu's face when they were introduced, the one he'd held for a second too long, was more than a mere demonstration of the enhanced observation skills required to do his job as he'd taken in every detail around him. 'Fuck,' she said, mentally kicking herself for not even considering that any of the old security team might be brought in. She marched across the manicured lawn towards the surrounding woods, getting as far away as possible from the glow emanating from the windows of the retreat as if it were powerful enough to shine a spotlight on to her features, helping Manu to see something, make him realise he recognised her.

Crossing the treeline, she let the darkness swallow her whole. No one could see her now. Not Manu, not Sherrie, not the band. The thought calmed her a little. Most people felt the opposite of calm hidden away in the dark. But Kit wasn't most people. She'd learned a long time ago that the very worst things didn't happen under the dark, dark cover of a dark, dark wood. They happened in people's homes, tucked away behind the four walls and roof that were supposed to keep them safe. They happened in open view of onlookers with cameras. She allowed herself a moment to breathe, to listen to the voice in her head telling her that surely Manu would have said something if he'd recognised her, reassuring herself she'd changed her appearance so much since then, there was no way he could have.

She turned, making sure no one had followed her, before pulling a pre-made rollie from behind her ear and lighting it. The smoke burned the back of her throat, wafer-thin Rizla paper crackling as the amber glow ate its way towards her lips. Sucking again, harder this time, she thought of her other problem, the one she couldn't dismiss as easily: the police. She paced back and forth between two tree stumps, trying to expend some of the nervous energy coursing through her like she'd been injected with something. She couldn't make the call sounding like this. She needed to at least pretend to be calm and in control.

'Shit,' she hissed, before slumping on to the ground and leaning back against one of the stumps. Since when did the police have time to go trawling social media looking for stuff to investigate? Trust her to be operating in the one police force in the country who were being proactive. She'd had enough experience with cops to last a lifetime, and doing anything outside the bare minimum seemed to be considered luxury service. If only the officers from her past had been as diligent, instead of putting the first two and two they came across together and coming up with a thousand.

The first time they'd come to the house, to make the arrest, she'd been sat in pretty much the same position she was now: leaning back against the inside of the open doorframe at the front of their small terraced house on a hot, sticky summer's evening, just like tonight. Legs outstretched, she'd basked in the sun, swivelling her position every now and then like a human sundial following the warmth of the rays as they'd moved across the front steps. She hadn't heard the two men approach, 'Four Kicks' by Kings of Leon blasting through the headphones that might as well have been glued to her ears, the officers' presence announced by their shadows extinguishing the sunshine. They'd both looked roughly the same age as her dad, similar height and builds too, but in her memory they were gargantuan, the perspective distorted as they towered over her, one asking her name as the other eyeballed her bare leg from the chipped nail polish on her toes all the way up to the hem of her shorts.

Thinking about that was doing nothing to calm her down, riling her up even more if anything. She pushed the thought away before taking another long drag of her rollie. This was all going to be fine. It had to be. Manu hadn't recognised her. And as for the police, looking for current threats on social media was one thing, and sure, they'd have done some basic checks on anyone associated with the band, of course they would. But they wouldn't dig that deep, would they? Worry simmered in her stomach despite the attempted pep talk. How far back would they check? To the time before she was Kit Ashton? Did they even check if people had changed their names? She punched the ground, sending a blast of pain across her knuckles. If she'd messed this all up now, she'd never forgive herself.

Pulling her burner phone out of her pocket, she dialled the only number stored in it. It went straight to voicemail, like they'd planned. 'Call me back. We've got a problem,' she said. 'A big fucking problem.'

13

After Saturday traffic turned a three-hour drive into one of almost five hours, we finally made it to Ryan Hope's small farm in Lynton on North Devon's Exmoor coast. Waiting at the breakfast bar in the rustic kitchen while our host made us drinks, I side-eyed Roy on the next stool over. He was completely oblivious to the fact I'd been mere seconds away from snapping off the indicator wand and stabbing him with it to get him to stop singing along to every track Gold FM had to offer all the way here.

'Beautiful place you've got,' Roy said as Ryan placed two mugs in front of us.

Unlike the others, he looked completely different to the young man in the photos from the band's heyday. His strawberry-blond hair was about four inches longer, scraggy with a natural kink compared to the slicked-back quiff he'd sported before, a gingery-brown beard adding weight to what had once been a slim, pale baby face. His body had bulked out too, almost twice the width. Farmer's carries clearly got their name for a reason in the muscle-building stakes.

Ryan nodded and dropped a sweetener into his own drink. 'It's pretty special. Not far off ten years we've had it now.'

I'd read somewhere Ryan was from Edinburgh, having attended the same first round of auditions for the show as Nush in Newcastle, but he didn't sound Scottish unless you paid very close attention to certain words.

'So you've lived here since you left the band, then?' I asked.

He picked up his mug and leant against the Belfast sink behind him. 'Yeah, the label did their best to get us to carry on as a foursome, but we split pretty quickly. I wasn't sad to be leaving. I live a very different life now. Sometimes I look back at all that stuff and it's like I'm watching someone else. Even before everything that happened.'

'It must have been a lot to deal with,' I said as Roy slurped his drink.

'Doesn't sound like things are any less lively for The Dolls now if I've got police knocking on my door asking about them.'

I talked him through the threats, the shock visible on his face when I told him about the doll marked up with his name. He took a moment to collect himself before answering my question about whether he'd received any similar communications.

'No, nothing,' he said. 'Quiet as usual around here, except for the tourists taking over the place, but that happens every summer, especially hot ones like this. How have the others taken it?'

'They seem pretty thick-skinned,' I said in an attempt at diplomacy.

He gave a nostalgic sigh. 'That the polite version? Haven't spoken to them in ten years but sounds like they haven't changed much.'

'Really?' I said. 'You haven't spoken to them at all?'

Ryan shook his head.

'That must've been difficult. I know you weren't exactly close, but being thrown together like that, living out of each other's pockets, sounds pretty intense. You'd assume it'd leave you with at least some sort of bond, no?' Now that I thought about it, there were parallels to the intakes who went through police training together. Thrown into a new and challenging experience. Sharing good times, bad times, pretty bloody horrific times once you got out on the job during your probation, puppy-walked around to every suspicious death in your sector to get you used to seeing dead bodies. And I hadn't stayed in touch with a single person I came up with, so maybe I should be less judgemental.

'We did get on,' Ryan said. 'Really well, at the beginning. Those first few months and starting the tour, we had such a laugh. I was worried, being the only guy, but it was honestly great, until . . . well, you can probably guess how it goes in that industry. Egos grow, that sort of thing.' He wrapped his hands tighter around his mug but didn't take a drink, like it was more an act of comfort than thirst. 'I was already thinking of leaving. Everything was a bit of a whirlwind that last month or so with me and Leigh – my wife – we met towards the end there and she got pregnant with my little girl really quickly. We found out not long after Ris . . . you know . . . and then there was the whole investigation, it was a lot. I loved the music, still do, got myself a little studio set up in one of the outbuildings, but I just play for me. The rest of it? Not my bag.'

Roy chuckled. 'Getting off your face on drugs and throwing television sets out of hotel windows not do it for you, then?'

'Nah, that wasn't us,' Ryan said. 'Might be a struggle to believe if you've read about us in the papers, but we were a chilled bunch. Beers and a few spliffs was about as far as it went. We all had our issues – what people that age don't? – but nothing compared to what the paparazzi would have everyone believe. And the tabloids seemed to know what we were doing before we did half the time. It just—' He put his mug down beside him on the wooden worktop. 'Sorry, I'm not exactly being helpful here, moaning about the past, but I'm sure you can see why I prefer this version of my life – easy, simple, no cameras stuck in my face every time I leave the house.'

'It must've been so intrusive,' I said. 'I saw some of the headlines, I'm sorry you had to go through that.'

'Is what it is, I suppose,' he said with a shrug of his broad shoulders. 'And I appreciate you taking the time to come here, but I haven't received anything, and I really don't see how I can help you identify who might be behind it, so is that everything? Leigh'll be back soon. She won't want me getting dragged into all their drama again and I don't want to scare her with all this,' he said, his eyes widening as he spoke.

It was understandable that Ryan wouldn't want to freak his wife out, but why did he seem nervous at the mere prospect of her finding us here? 'Of course, we won't take up too much more of your time.'

I was about to go through some security tips when boots crunched on gravel outside, a barking spaniel sprinting towards us as the back door banged open.

'Ry, can you—' The woman – Leigh, I presumed – noticed me and Roy and paused in the doorway. She had a similar look to Ris, a classically pretty face framed by long brown feathered hair messily pinned back at both temples with silver clips. 'Who's this? What's going on?' Panic flooded her face. 'Where's Georgie? What's happened?'

Ryan held his palms up placatingly. 'Georgie's fine, she's playing at next door's. This has nothing to do with her, not even with us really.'

Her shoulders dropped as the panic evaporated, a look of mild concern remaining on her lightly tanned face. Ryan introduced us and filled her in on the reason for our trip, omitting the specifics of the hanging dolls. She sat down on a cushioned window seat by the door and crossed her legs.

'I knew it,' Leigh said, 'didn't I say? Didn't I tell you the second we found out they were doing this reunion there'd be trouble? It's like it follows them around.' She looked from Ryan to me. 'And you've had a wasted trip. Ry's had nothing to do with them since the day he left the band, and they didn't even have the decency to give him a heads up, even though they had the cheek to leave him in the promo pictures! I don't know who they think they are.'

I looked to Ryan. 'They didn't ask if you wanted to take part?'

'No,' he said, 'but that's not surprising. They'd have known exactly what I'd say – not that I think they'd be falling over themselves to have me back anyway. It's a different time now. Back then, I think the label thought adding a man to the group gave it a bit of credibility. I'm not saying that's right – Em's a far better guitarist than I'll ever be – it's just how it was. But now, well, female rage is fashionable, isn't it, and the execs aren't stupid. If there's one thing they do know, it's what sells. Anyway,' he said, clapping his hands together, 'don't get me started. I could go on for hours about how commerciality ruined the music business, but I'm sure you've got more important things to do.' He looked from me to Leigh. 'I was about to see the officers out, so . . .'

Roy and I followed Ryan outside. He stopped to close the door behind us. 'Sorry about that. She didn't have the best time of it when she got with me; the tabloids gave her so much stick, had all sorts of gossip printed about us, some true, most not so true. Everyone seemed to be obsessed with the idea of me and Ris getting together, us being the next Stevie Nicks and Lindsey Buckingham or something, but then when it all kicked off and I left the band, the stories changed to more Lennon and Yoko, if you get what I mean, like the murder wasn't enough of a reason for us to split, they still dragged Leigh into it.'

I thought back to what Sherrie said about Ryan and Ris. 'So nothing ever happened between you and Ris then, romantically?'

'No, I mean it's not a secret that I, you know, *liked* her. We connected. She wasn't into all the stuff that went alongside the music, like me. I think she only joined the band because she knew it would make her mum and Dee Dee happy, which turned out to be quite ironic, I suppose. Anyway, I told her how I felt one night, but she didn't feel the same. And I'm no creep, I was cool with that, made peace with it and we were good friends afterwards, for a bit anyway.' He stopped talking but his face suggested there was more to say.

I took a punt. 'But?'

'Nothing. I know it's been ages but part of me still feels that disappointment in her. I really didn't think she'd let it all get to her, the fame; she seemed, I dunno, different. She was pleased for me when I met Leigh, at first, but then a couple of weeks later she turned up at my room in the middle of the night, completely pissed off her face, I practically had to fight her off. I didn't know what'd come over her, but then when I thought about it, it was obvious what she was doing, and it was cruel, to like, test me or something because I'd found someone else. That was when she changed, when the US tour got announced, it was like a switch flipped and she was a different person. We didn't speak much in those last few weeks, before—'

The three of us flinched as Leigh banged on the kitchen window and waved him back inside. We said our goodbyes and got into the car, Ryan opening, closing, and hopefully locking the gates behind us.

I pulled on to the single-track road, the car thrumming as it passed over a large cattle grid. 'Interesting vibe between the two of them, no? Especially from her,' I said.

'Interesting like how?' Roy replied, pulling a protein bar out of his rucksack.

'I dunno.' I flipped the visor down to shield my eyes from the glare, struggling to see as the sun flickered through the leaves of the overhanging trees, casting a mottled effect across the road ahead. 'He seemed a little desperate to get us out of there before she came back. Why the fuss?'

Roy swallowed his first bite of what looked like two pieces of cardboard held together with some sort of sugar-free caramel substitute. 'You may be experienced in the art of being a detective, but you've still got a lot to learn about keeping the other half happy. Believe me, I learned the hard way. Happy wife, happy life. And I'm not surprised she doesn't want him dragged back into all that. Show me a woman who'd trust her husband going on a rock tour with a bunch of good-looking women and I'll show you a bleedin' liar.'

I took one hand off the steering wheel and pressed a finger into the middle of my chin, feigning a look of confusion. 'Hmm, wonder what could possibly give her cause for concern, since I don't think there's a rock star in history who hasn't been caught cheating on his wife at some point or other.'

Roy opened his mouth, presumably in an attempt to

mount a defence, but closed it when he clearly couldn't think of a single example to prove me wrong. 'Fair enough. Still, the things we do for love, eh?'

What the hell would I know? I hadn't whiffed anything close to love in the last six years. 'Quite.'

Roy gobbled down the rest of his snack and scrunched up the empty wrapper. We were passing through the main street, tourists lining the pavements either side of us, when his phone beeped. He pulled it out and peered at the screen. 'Got an email from Eddie here,' he said. 'He's done some digging on that production company. Only a small outfit, apparently, went bust not long after making the documentary; he's trying to track down the names of anyone involved. And the prison liaison team have been on for me; we can go see Dee Dee Nolan Tuesday.'

'Good, I—' My phone buzzed in the centre console where I'd chucked it. 'Well, well, aren't we popular today.'

'Want me to get it?' Roy said.

'Who is it?'

He picked it up and grimaced as he looked at the caller ID shining out from the screen. 'It's the boss, I thought she was meant to be on her jollies until Monday?'

'Urgh, she is, which means I doubt she's ringing with good news. You better answer it, put her on speaker.'

Roy fumbled with the touch screen and then acted like my very own human hands-free phone holder. 'Ma'am?'

'Alice? What's going on, what's that noise?' Jane said.

'You're on speaker, I'm in the car with Roy. Aren't you still meant to be in Scotland?'

'I *am* still in Scotland,' Jane said, 'not that anyone from HQ seems to have paid attention to that fact – six missed calls I've had from them so far this morning.'

'Why, what's happened?'

'Does the name Judith Nolan sound familiar?' Jane said in a way that told me she was already positive it did.

Oh fuck.

14

Two rest days later, the last thing I felt was *rested*. I'd spent a significant part of my time off trying to find out what the hell Judith was playing at with her little stunt. After several ignored phone calls and two unsuccessful visits to her flat, I was still practically frothing at the mouth as I pulled into the visitor car park at HMP Westbury. '. . . and talk about throwing us under the bus,' I said to Roy as we got out the car. 'Which part of our conversation could *possibly* have made her think we agreed with her? At no stage did we come remotely close to saying "Yes, Judith, please do write a letter to the Chief Constable and demand Dee Dee's case is reopened, put me and DC Briar down as your most ardent supporters, and for the love of all things holy please *do* hand-deliver it to HQ, you know how much the Chief loves a personal touch" – I mean, what the actual fuck?'

Roy nestled his scratched sunglasses on top of his head. 'Heard what she wanted to, I s'pose – amount of drugs that woman's taken over the years she's probably got a brain more shrivelled than a walnut. Anyway, stewing over it won't change anything, Trudy says the only thing worth stewing over is a good ratatouille.'

I rolled my eyes and followed him towards the entrance. It was probably a good thing Trudy was encouraging Roy to let things go, but it did concern me that almost every sentence out his mouth these days started with the words *Trudy says*. I thought back to the pop of colour Irma had imparted on Dad's place. Were they about to head down the same road? Morphing into one another? I made a mental note to be on the lookout for matching David and Victoria Beckham couple's outfits circa the late nineties. If that was what it took to make a relationship work, then maybe I should rethink my flirtation with WeMatch. I hadn't had a reciprocating 'like' from Jake anyway, so it wasn't as if I'd be missing out on much. I kept my opinion to myself and followed Roy inside the prison.

We made our way through security relatively quickly, apart from Roy's debate with the guy manning the bag check after he confiscated his ginger shot.

'How's anyone gonna use a health drink as a bleedin' weapon?' he said as he followed me and the prison officer escorting us to see Dee Dee down the hallway, sans ginger.

'You'd be amazed what people can fashion in here,' the prison officer said, keys jangling on her trousers. 'Table leg batons, anything heavy in a sock; someone even made a bow and arrow out of a toothbrush, some toothpicks and their own hair once – it was quite impressive, to be fair.'

I couldn't help but chime in, 'Shot of ginger to the eyeballs? That shit would burn.'

Roy harumphed and I barely held my laugh in.

The woman showed us into a small room with a table and three chairs, about the same size as our interview rooms back at the station. Same bland grey chipped paint. Same black rubber panic strip running around the room about halfway up the wall like the ring of a barrel. I sat down and Roy plonked himself next to me, still mumbling about his bloody ginger.

Two or three minutes later, he finally shut up as the door opened and Dee Dee Nolan shuffled in. I examined her face. Like Ryan, Dee Dee didn't look the same as her earlier photos. Not frozen in time like Em, Nush and Tabby. In fact, she'd aged more than the decade she'd been in there. Her hair was still long and dark brown in the same half up, half down do, but the weight loss to her face was dramatic. Cheekbones that weren't visible before cast dark shadows either side of her mouth, eye sockets even deeper set in her head.

Roy and I introduced ourselves, but Dee Dee didn't say anything when we'd finished, just sat down in front of us and looked at the table. She tugged her long-sleeved top further down her hands so the edges tucked over her thumbs like fingerless gloves, an odd move given we might as well have been sitting in a sauna.

'Thanks for seeing us,' I said.

Dee Dee nodded, her face without expression. 'Why are you here?' she asked in a quiet voice.

'We're investigating some threats made towards The Dolls. Do you know anything about that?'

Her eyes flicked up for a second before returning to the table. 'No.'

'We thought, given your history with the band . . .'

Dee Dee pursed her thin, almost colourless lips. 'Like you said. *History*.' She lifted her gaze along with her chin. Normally, I'd take such a gesture as a sign of defiance, but her face suggested something else, though I wasn't sure what.

'The threats make reference to you,' I said. 'How you "had it right" with what you did to Ris. Maybe someone looking to finish what you started? Do you have any idea who might want to do that?'

She stared at me, her eyes deep enough to house a thousand emotions, Dad's old detective motto jumping into my head as I peered into them. *Eyes are the window to the soul, kid, give people away every time.* But I wasn't getting anything from Dee Dee's, not yet.

'I didn't *start* anything,' she said. 'I did what I did. That was the end of it. Anything anyone else does has nothing to do with me.'

I don't know what I'd expected of her. More menacing, perhaps? Something that might make me feel she could snap at any moment, in the way that you have sometimes with seemingly calm criminals? Because it's true what they say: the lairy people aren't the ones you need to worry about, the lower tier thugs kicking off in the custody suite, letting everyone know how tough they are. They can be a handful – the small bruise still visible on the bridge of my nose attested to that – but the ones you really needed to watch were the quiet ones. Because they're the ones secretly plotting, finding out where you live and which route your kids take to school.

I rested my elbows on the table, inching my upper body forwards, closing the gap between us in the hope it would help me see a way through the shield that seemed to be deflecting my radar. 'Do you have any contact with anyone outside of prison, Dee Dee?'

'No.'

'What, no one?' I asked.

She shook her head.

'Not even any of your superfans, *The Dee Dee Dolls* from the documentary?'

Her mouth crinkled. Was she holding in a smile? A grimace? I couldn't tell. 'I didn't have anything to do with that.'

'Do you have access to social media?'

She frowned. 'We're not allowed.'

'This isn't our first day on the job,' I said. 'Just because something isn't allowed in prison, doesn't mean it isn't *in* prison.' I'd heard women's prisons were worse for smuggling contraband, more orifices to hide stuff in, though I really didn't want to think about the logistics of that right now, or ever, for that matter.

'Search my cell if you want,' she said. 'I haven't got nothing I shouldn't. Not worth it, I'd lose my job in the kitchen and the music lessons they let me do.'

Roy interjected, 'You gave up everything to kill your friend, what's the difference?'

She swallowed hard but her face remained blank, eyes

staring between our heads rather than looking directly at either of us.

'I don't want to talk about that,' she said, her voice calm. 'It's not relevant.'

'I'm afraid I disagree,' I said. 'I'm more than aware of the case and the reason you gave for killing Ris. You said the two of you were best friends, practically sisters, until she joined the band and it changed her. *They* changed her, souring your relationship. So you can understand why there might be a question about you harbouring a grudge towards the others, can't you? What I don't get is why you would do something about it now, after all these years. Is it because they're getting back together? Does that bring everything back up?'

She waited a few seconds before answering. 'I wouldn't know about that, because I haven't made any threats.'

'Can you think of anyone who might have? What about your mum? She seems to have a pretty radical theory that the band know something they aren't telling about the night you killed Ris, something they're covering up and making you take the blame for. That sounds like a good basis for a grudge to me,' I said.

Dee Dee's eyes locked with mine, the tension fanning out from her jaw at the mention of her mother. 'She *what*?'

Anger – and something else I couldn't put my finger on – flashed across her face as I told her about Judith's letter. I didn't have to worry about what her eyes were telling me any more, her fists doing all the talking as they clenched when I suggested that maybe making the threats could be a warped way of Judith trying to finally do something for her daughter.

'Judith Nolan does things for one person and one person only, and that's Judith Nolan,' Dee Dee said. 'Always has, always will. You can't trust a word that woman says.'

I honestly didn't think Judith was the one behind the threats, but talking about her seemed to be the only thing that got Dee Dee animated enough to say more than a few words to us. 'Maybe she's changed,' I said. 'She wanted us to tell you she's turned her life around, got herself a job, says she's off the drugs. Maybe she thinks she's doing this for you?'

Dee Dee shook her head and folded her arms across her chest. 'She's never done a thing for me in my life. Don't see why she'd start now.'

'She bought you a guitar as a kid,' I said, not that I thought that made up for the rest of Judith's lack of parenting skills. 'She must have had her moments.'

A huge grin spread across Dee Dee's face in a way that made me shift uncomfortably in my seat before she laughed. 'Mother dearest tell you that, did she?'

'No, but she asked us to let you know she loves you, and that she'll do anything to make things right with you. Whatever it takes.'

Her face hardened again as if the shield that had been unplugged momentarily had been reconnected at its source. 'If making stupid threats is what she thinks is the right thing to do, then that's got nothing to do with me. And as we're passing messages, you can take her one. Tell her to keep me out of whatever the hell she is or isn't doing. She wants to make this right? Tell her to go back in time and *not* sell that guitar because she needed to pay her dealer. And you can remind her that it wasn't even hers to sell; Ris's mum bought me that, not her. And while she's at it, she can get back everything else I had that she sold. She can do all that then we're golden.'

Dee Dee slumped back into her chair like the rant had physically exhausted her, the rest of our questions going unanswered.

'Nothing of interest in there,' said the prison officer who'd searched Dee Dee's cell, the same one who'd escorted us in earlier and was now walking us back out. 'Not a lot of anything, really. Our Dee Dee's a bit anal when it comes to her living space, doesn't have much in terms of personal effects, just a few toiletries and some books from the library.'

I'd scanned the bare walls of Dee Dee's cell before we'd left the wing. Not like the others we'd passed on the way out, most of them adorned with a collage of family photos and letters from home. 'Is she not allowed that stuff or does she choose not to have it?'

The woman shrugged. 'She can have things if she wants. Not sure what she'd put up there though, truth be told. I don't think she's got any friends or family.'

Did Roy just eyeball me as she said that or had I imagined it? What was this, my very own version of *A Christmas Carol*? Dee Dee giving a stellar performance as The Ghost of Christmas Yet to Come if my life took an unexpected turn and I managed to get myself locked up? I coughed the thought away before turning my attention back to our escort. 'Technically, she has her mum, but they don't get on – she's tried to contact her several times but had no response. Does she really have *no* visitors?' I asked.

'Not social ones. I've been here the whole time she has, for my sins. I was at Brompton before – that place is a hellhole – ended up here when I missed out on a job up in Hamsley.'

I interrupted before the woman verbalised her whole CV. 'What do you mean, not social?'

'They all get medical and legal people showing up every once in a while, but no one comes just to see her. There's plenty of requests, mind, gets more letters than *Points of View*, that one.'

Roy and I exchanged a questioning glance. 'And she accepts the letters?' I asked.

'Ninety-nine percent of them, no.' She unlocked the door in front of us, shooed us through and locked it again behind her. 'She gets bagsful, but she only accepts from a couple of people.'

'Who?' I asked.

'Back in the day she was always writing to that girl's mum, the one she pushed, but the woman never wrote back. We had to stop letting her send them in the end, we were getting complaints. Not that I blame her, mind you. Someone did that to one of my babies then sent me a letter asking for forgiveness? Woo! They'd get more than forgiveness, I tell you, you'd find me behind bars with the rest of them. I'd—'

I got the impression another tangent was coming so I got in ahead of it. 'You said she accepted them from a couple of people, who else?'

'Yeah, yeah, used to get them every few months back when she was first in here. I'd forgotten about them, to be honest, they'd died off in the last few years, but now you mention it I'm sure she had one a month or so ago. I remember 'cause it was around the same time that *WHAM!* documentary come on Netflix, did you watch it? Most people like George Michael, don't they, but it's all about Andrew Ridgeley for me, I think he's—'

Roy and I exchanged glances. 'No, didn't see that one,' I said before she had the chance to act out the entire director's cut. 'You were saying, who else did she receive letters from?'

'Someone called Rose. I remember, see, I was gonna call my second Rose if it was a girl, but I had a little lad. Guess what I called him?' she said, eyes wide with excitement.

I pulled my lips back between my teeth and bit down, trying to hide my frustration. 'Was it Andrew by any chance?'

She looked like she'd won the lottery. 'Yes! My little Andrew, Andy Pandy Pudding and Pie, he's a sweetheart, bless him. Need to find him a friend called George now – how cute would that be?'

Wow. My widened eyes clearly communicated to Roy that my patience with this conversation was wearing thinner than a catwalk model and he chipped in, 'Do you have a surname for this Rose?' he said.

'Dunno,' the guard responded, as if we'd asked her what

118

she was having for dinner tonight instead of something that might light a fire under our investigation.

'And they wrote to her recently,' he said in follow-up, 'out of the blue?'

'Yeah, like I said, it was when—'

I was officially done with the *WHAM!* chat and butted back in, 'What did it say?'

The prison officer pulled open the last door, bringing us back into the main security check area. 'You think we've got time to read every letter that gets sent in here? We do a dip and skim. Dip sample, skim-read.'

'Did you dip and skim Dee Dee's last letter?' I asked.

'Yeah, but there was nothing exciting in there, just asking how she is, hoping she was doing OK, asking for a favour, that sorta thing.'

I waited for her to carry on, but she didn't. In her defence, she was probably waiting for me to interrupt her again. 'What favour?' I prompted.

'Didn't say, just asked if she could do something again for her, "one last time".'

My spine prickled. 'Did she reply?'

'I think so.'

'And would that have been checked, for any inappropriate content, her asking someone to make threats for her?'

'Outgoing mail is checked for anything unsuitable, and I'd call sending out a threat *unsuitable*.'

Theories formed in my mind. 'What if she used a code or something?'

A hearty 'Ha!' fired from the woman's mouth as if

punched from her stomach. 'This ain't *The Da Vinci Code*, love. Why don't I take you back through and you can ask her yourself?'

I processed for a second before declining the offer. I didn't want to alert Dee Dee to what we'd discovered on this walk-and-talk, especially as I was sure we'd get no answers from her now she'd clammed up after discussing her mother. 'No, that won't be necessary, for now, thank you.'

We made our way outside, Roy singing the chorus of 'Wake Me Up Before You Go-Go' and shaking the ginger shot which he'd been thrilled to be reunited with as we walked across the car park. I glared at him.

'What?' he said.

'If you break into "Careless Whisper" I'll run you over with my car.'

'Good song that,' Roy said before opening the small bottle and downing the contents.

'Not good enough to make it your whole personality like that one back there,' I said. 'I really don't get it, this obsession people have with celebrities. It's just the opposite end of the spectrum to the bloody *Dee Dee Dolls*. Why get so caught up in people you don't even know?' I opened the car door, a wall of heat hitting me. 'And what are the chances that the letters showing up after years and just before the threats started is a coincidence?' I asked.

'Slim to none,' Roy said as he slumped into the passenger seat, sweat immediately beading on his brow.

'And who the fuck is Rose?'

15

'Rose?' Sherrie said down the phone. 'Can't say anything comes to mind. Gimme a sec, I'll ask the girls.'

I could hear her talking but couldn't work out what she was saying as I rolled my chair closer to the whirring fan perched on the end of mine and Roy's bank of desks. I'd been in the office almost twenty minutes since the car ride back from the prison but was still doing a sterling impression of an overcooked rotisserie chicken. I dragged the fan closer. Roy had gone straight back out to take a witness statement for another job so there was no need for me to share it. The cool air rushed over my face as Sherrie returned on the line.

'Not ringing any bells here. Can I ask why?' she said.

'It's something we're following up on. We've spoken to Dee Dee to see if she's been in contact with anyone, or if she's had any concerning correspondence sent to her, and the prison officer said there are only two people she's exchanged letters with since she's been in there, someone called Rose, and Ris's mother.'

'Dee Dee's been writing to *Santina*?' Sherrie barked. I

pulled the phone away from my ear so she didn't deafen me. 'She not done enough to that poor woman already?'

'Don't worry,' I said, 'she doesn't any more, the prison put a stop to it.'

'Too right, should never've been allowed in the first place. What could she possibly have to say to the woman?'

I shrugged as if Sherrie could see me. 'Trying to apologise, apparently.'

Sherrie scoffed. 'Losing Ris broke her, and if that wasn't enough, it was like she lost two kids that day. She was more of a mother to Dee Dee than Judith ever was, not that it was hard to be. And don't get me started on the battle I had with the label fighting Santina's corner. They thought just because she moved back to her family in Italy they could wash their hands of her, keep their grubby mitts on Ris's cut of the band's profits. Well, not on my watch. I made sure she got what she was due, still do. I look after my girls, Sergeant, to the very end. And I'll do it in whatever way it takes if you lot can't, don't you forget it.'

I didn't need to be able to see Sherrie to know she was probably jabbing a perfectly polished fingernail at me down the phone. I also really didn't need the reminder that if we didn't track down whoever was making the threats, Sherrie would, in a way that would likely end with her joining Dee Dee in a prison cell.

'You've made that quite clear. Don't worry, we'll keep you posted, OK . . . yep . . . bye.'

Hanging up the phone, I stuck my face as close as possible to the fan, pressing the button taking it to its highest setting and praying the thing would do me a favour and blow my head clean off.

According to the news bulletin I heard on my drive home that evening, the heatwave hadn't yet reached its peak. How was that possible?

Inside Myrtle Cottage, I opened all the living room windows before going upstairs to change into shorts and a vest, though when I came back down the mugginess had barely dissipated. Flopping on to the sofa, I closed my eyes and let the events of the last few days play out in my head: Judith, Ryan, Dee Dee, The Dolls and their miniature counterparts hanging from the main stage roof. There hadn't been even the mildest breeze at the scene, but for some reason in my imagination the figures swung slowly from side to side, in unison. God, I could use my own breeze right now. And one of those magic watches to stop time so I could figure this all out before the festival. I had eleven days, almost to the hour, because clearly the band cancelling their performance wasn't on the cards. And while I wanted them to for practical reasons, part of me admired their aplomb and was glad they weren't letting this person take away their control over what they did and how they did it.

There was nothing that annoyed me more than victims being expected to change their lives and behaviours because of the actions of others. I wasn't sure how many more times I could listen to the same old crime prevention advice doled out, usually to women, about not walking alone at night, not wearing headphones and all the other allegedly 'handy' tips communicated through every possible medium time and time again after a notable incident. I wasn't stupid; I understood why it was done. It was easier telling law-abiding citizens to change rather than trying to get the bad people to do so. But I couldn't get too high and mighty about it – I'd been the one asking them to cancel. No one had told me to do that.

Em's snarky comment from last week about the supposed incompatibility of being a feminist and a cop played on my mind no matter how much I tried to push it out. I always wanted to do a good job on any investigation, make sure I did everything I could to keep people safe, but this case felt like more than that. It shrouded me in an overwhelming need to prove myself, as if redeeming the reputation of the entire policing profession rested firmly on my tired shoulders, and even the slightest misstep would sever any chance of these women ever having faith in the system again.

No pressure!

The eerie scene at Kestrel Park had confirmed something I'd already suspected: this wasn't just some internet troll. These threats were personal. Made with intent, by someone who'd slipped in and out of the festival grounds unnoticed. Roy had submitted the details of the site crew to the intel bureau, but with their workload and this being the middle of the holidays, I didn't hold out much hope for a speedy turnaround. I was running out of lines of enquiry faster than the beads of sweat trickling down the side of my face.

I opened YouTube on my phone and typed SO YOU THINK YOU CAN ROCK TV SHOW HIGHLIGHTS into

124

the search bar in the hope that learning more about the band might spark something. The first link I clicked was montage footage of the band going back to their respective friends and families to reveal the big news they'd made it into the band. Nush was first up, immediately engulfed in the arms of an older woman I presumed was her mother, their features practically identical. The only real difference was the colour of their skin, the woman's a pinkish white contrasting against Nush's light brown complexion from what must be her dad's South Asian heritage. A raft of other family and friends followed, running out the front door of Nush's run-down terraced house to join the hug, all crying happy tears, while what looked like most of the occupants of the rest of the street watched on, clapping, cheering and holding up hand-painted congratulatory banners.

For Ryan, the hugs were replaced with back slaps and subtle nods of pride from his dad and older brothers. Tabby had fewer people there to congratulate her, but that wasn't surprising given her house looked like you needed to be some sort of high-ranking diplomat or have a peerage to be granted access to the palatial Falstead grounds.

Something fluttered in my chest as it got to Ris's clip, a woman I presumed was Ris's mother and Dee Dee, both looking nervous as they held hands, sitting patiently on a sofa inside a small living room similar in layout to Judith's flat. They'd lived on the same estate, and from what I'd read, Judith and Santina had similar predicaments: both from working-class backgrounds, getting pregnant young, the fathers not sticking around. But clearly that's where their approach to life and parenting bifurcated. The flat on the screen was like a shoebox, working with the same limitations as Judith's, but the simple and clean décor made it look much more like a home and less like a squat than the Nolan residence.

The door in the footage opened and Ris walked in, slender hands cupping her mouth, only half hiding a nervous smile. It was obvious before she said anything that she'd made it. Instinctively, my eyes jumped to Dee Dee's face instead of Ris or Santina's. Could I see it? The forced smile disguising those first sprouting seeds of jealousy? No matter how hard I looked, there was no trace of negativity. Only yelps of delight and claps and jumping, lots of jumping, Dee Dee acting as if she'd been told the place in the band was her own. There was a stark contrast in what I was looking at versus the Dee Dee I'd met that morning. I was distracted from my thoughts by the programme voiceover explaining there wasn't a video for Em, because she'd refused to film one. It filled me with at least a little reassurance that her difficult attitude wasn't just aimed at me.

An alert popped up along the top of my phone screen as I was about to watch more videos of the band, a notification from the dating app. The fact that my gut reaction was more *urgh* than *OMG!* at the interruption told me everything I needed to know before I even opened it. Jake had returned the favour of clicking the WeMatch button on my profile. His 'get the ball rolling' message was fine, a completely normal 'Hi. How's your day been?' But I knew as soon as I read it this had been a mistake. I didn't have the energy or the desire to enter into digital small talk right now, I needed to focus. Instead of replying, I deleted my profile and went back to watching clips of the band.

I wasn't sure what time I fell asleep on the sofa, but it was just after eleven the next morning when the shrill ring of my phone from the coffee table woke me. 'H'lo?' I said, wiping drool from the side of my cheek and sitting upright.

'Alice, it's Jane. Have you seen the news this morning?'

'No, I've only just woken up, I'm not on until two.'

'Turn the TV on then get yourself into the office. We've got some damage to control.' She hung up before I could respond.

I dragged myself up, scanning surfaces for the remote, finally finding it shoved down the back of a cushion. I turned on the TV. 'Oh, you are having my fucking life!' I yelled, taking in what was on the screen. Vince glared at me from his spot in the middle of the rug for waking him.

My phone rang again, Roy this time. 'Yes, I know, I'm watching it,' I said. 'Get on to that site manager. I want to know how the hell that happened.'

16

Jane was sat on her precious yellow sofa as Roy and I walked into her office, with a pile of papers in her lap and a pen in her hand. With reading glasses perched halfway down her nose, you could mistake her for a teacher marking homework rather than a detective inspector catching up on what was probably some new force strategy or the latest performance figures. She slid the glasses off and let them fall against her chest, held in place by the thin silver chain they were attached to around her neck.

Her mood dictated where she let you sit. Everyday inter-actions and general bollockings meant you were pointed to the bum cheek-numbing plastic chairs. Something that required tact or an attempt at compassion on her part allowed you to be invited to sit on the sofa. Roy and I hov-ered in anticipation before she nodded towards the chairs.

Shit sticks.

We assumed our positions. There was definitely about to be a dressing-down, but something felt different. Her expres-sion would in no way be described as soft – which I wasn't even sure was physically possible given her pronounced bone structure – but it certainly wasn't as pursed as usual. Maybe she was still partially in holiday mode. She hadn't said a word by the time we'd sat down, just stared at us as her thin fingers drummed the paperwork in her lap. She continued to stare as we squirmed, before getting up and walking to the small TV mounted on the wall in the corner of the room. Turning on the news, she let the voiceover do the talking for her.

'Well?' she finally said, arms folded as her gaze moved back and forth between us, the movement jiggling the grey-streaked black strand of hair forced across her forehead by a cowlick.

'In our defence,' I said, 'there's not much we could've done about the video. Roy's spoken to the site manager and it was one of the ops staff; they recorded it while he was on the phone to the police calling it in. We hadn't even arrived, never mind gotten to the stage of getting people out of the crime scene.'

'*People?*' Jane's eyebrows jumped so high it was like they were trying to form an alliance with her hairline. 'From what I can see, it doesn't seem like *people* were the problem. You've got half the cast of Old MacDonald tampering with evidence there!'

In any other situation, this would be funny. I'd been the first to share *Hot Fuzz* memes when a pair of angry swans ran into the village pub during the Saturday night rush and made all the clientele flee the place like it was being attacked by marauding terrorists. But I wasn't sure how humorous anyone would find my pleas of *Forgive me, Your Honour, a goat ate the evidence* if this case ended up in court and I had to explain that there *had* been a fifth doll at the crime scene – left on the stage, presumably to represent Ris having already fallen to her death – but that some bellend thought it was a better idea to film and broadcast the thing being chewed on and carried off by Billy Goats Gruff rather than try and preserve it.

Jane sat back down, not on the sofa this time, but on the fancy ergonomic chair behind her desk. She steepled her fingers and rested her chin on them before letting out a long, deep breath.

'Public confidence in us at the minute couldn't be lower if it tried,' she said. 'The last thing we need is video evidence of police incompetence being played on a loop.' I opened my mouth to protest again, but Jane held up a 'shh' finger. 'Don't start, Alice, *I* know this all happened before you got there, but they don't care. Look at that headline.' She pointed at the banner on the bottom of the TV screen.

GOATS NOT KIDDING AROUND AS FORTBRIDGE ROCKS CRIME SCENE DESTROYED.

'It was hardly "destroyed",' Roy interjected. 'Bernie recovered ninety percent of it.'

'Well,' Jane said, 'you want to hope we get some kind of forensic lead on the items that *were* recovered. Roy, follow up with Bernie on that, please, see if they've got any good news for us. Alice, you're coming to HQ with me.'

'HQ?' I said. 'Why?'

She stood and shoved her phone into her expensive-looking handbag before hooking it over her forearm. 'I've got a meeting with the comms team, and Mr Scott wants to see you.'

'What for? Surely he knows this isn't our fault, ma'am?'

'He doesn't want to see you about this palaver, that job rolled down the hill to me. He wants to speak to you about this Nolan woman and the Chief.'

God's sake, Judith! 'What's she done now?'

Jane nodded towards the door. 'Let's go see, shall we? I'll drive.'

After a warning served with a side of finger wagging not to do or say anything to Gordy Scott that would make the situation worse, Jane and I parted ways outside the lift on the seventh floor of HQ. She headed to the east side of the building to the communications office while I made my way to the west wing.

I shivered, the thin shirt I'd gone for to stay cool in the almost thirty-degree heat outside doing bugger all to stave off the freezing cold air blasting from the ceiling vents. Rubbing my arms to flatten the goosebumps, I wandered in what seemed like the right direction before asking a frazzled-looking DC for directions to Gordy's office. He nodded towards the back of the large open-plan floor crammed so tightly with desks it looked like the corporate equivalent of where you might house battery hens.

'Don't worry, he's not as scary as everyone says, not *really*,' the DC said.

131

It took me a second to realise he'd mistaken my goose-bumps for fear of Gordy Scott. There was no time to explain myself. I nodded a 'thanks' and walked through the narrow pathway between the desks, bleeps of radios and ringing phones coming from either side of me like little trumpets announcing my arrival. There was a different feel to these types of offices compared to smaller places like Fortbridge, an electricity in the air. Like anything could happen at any minute. I'd been so desperate to get up here into the Major Crime Unit for most of my career, my future all mapped out, being right at the centre of that fizz of activity after getting my sergeant's experience in Fortbridge. And I could kid myself that was still what I wanted. But the thought of reigniting my ambition for it right now, with the way things were, felt more like trying to light a sodden match, not even the semblance of a spark as the head crumbled against the rough surface of the striking pad.

But if this isn't who you are any more, then who the hell are you?

I ignored the pessimistic voice as I reached the back of the room, turned left down a small corridor and stood outside the corner office. There was no sign of a three-headed dog guarding the gates of hell. No flames. Just a bog-standard door with a gold-coloured plaque on it that read DETECTIVE SUPERINTENDENT GORDON SCOTT. From what I could remember, having seen him in passing before, his full name matched his appearance more than the nickname did. 'Gordy' sounded fun and whimsical, and I had the distinct impression that was not the experience I was about to have.

Pulling my shoulders back and jutting out my chin, I knocked. I waited for a 'yeah' or 'come in', but didn't get either. I knocked again. Still nothing. He knew we were coming straight over. Maybe he'd been pulled on to something else? I was about to leave when I heard the *bing bong* of the Windows start-up tune coming from inside. I knocked again. Louder this time.

'Yeah,' came a voice. I pushed open the door to see Gordy sat behind a large wooden desk. 'Three times, eh? Must be an emergency,' he said, quieter than I'd expected. With his barrel chest and thick neck, I presumed he'd have a more stentorian tone.

'Sorry, sir?'

'Some of the senior management team have an open-door policy; I prefer a three-knock policy. People knock once for any old shite. Twice means there's an actual problem, but not enough that halfway through waiting for me to answer they realise they can sort it out themselves without a guvnor hand-holding them. But three knocks means it must be something only I can deal with. It's a very effective method of time management.' He grinned, a movement which exposed his crooked teeth and made his eyes shrink to tiny black pinholes as his bulbous cheeks pushed up into them. 'So, I'm presuming what you have to say is an emergency of some sort, no?'

'Not an emergency, sir, more a response. You asked to

see me, DS Washington from Fortbridge CID.' I held out a
hand for him to shake but he stayed sitting behind his desk.

'Ahhh, Mick's girl,' he said.

I made myself reply with a forced smile instead of the
words pulsing behind my lips. *That's me. Daughter of man.
Not an officer in my own right with almost a decade of
experience under my belt, but you crack on, sir.*

'Alison, isn't it?' He finally lifted from his chair enough
to reach out and shake my hand, though still didn't properly stand up. His palm was clammy and rough, the gold
wedding band that looked about two sizes too small for
him digging into my finger.

'Alice,' I corrected.

'Alice, yes. Take a seat.' He pulled open the top drawer
of his desk and took something out of it as I sat down.
'Here.' The small white envelope he tossed cleared the desk
and landed in my lap.

'What's this?' I picked it up and flipped it over, realising
as soon as I saw the words FREE DEE DEE scrawled across
the front of it in thick red pen.

'Open it,' Gordy said, 'read for yourself.'

I pulled the piece of paper out from inside and read
the letter Judith had hand-delivered to HQ. It was mostly
misspelled and the second half was difficult to read as it
looked like the pen she'd used to write it had started running out, but her point was clear: Dee Dee was innocent
and the case into Ris's murder must be reopened.

'Want to explain the little shout-out for you and one of
your DCs?' Gordy asked.

'I honestly don't know what she's talking about, sir. We spoke to her about the threats, but we didn't indulge her theory about Dee Dee in any way.'

'Mm-hmm.' He leant over and plucked the letter from between my fingers before refolding it and running his thumb and forefinger back and forth, reinforcing the crease in the middle of the page. 'So you didn't pass messages between Judith and Dee Dee, then, when you visited her in prison?'

How the hell did he know we'd been to see Dee Dee? Surely superintendents were far too busy to keep tabs on that kind of stuff. 'I just told her Judith wanted to make things right between them and about how she's trying to turn her life around.'

'And you were visiting Dee Dee becaaaause . . .'

'About the threats. One theory is that someone may think they're doing this for Dee Dee. She's got a really weird fan base, I wanted to see—'

'And did that get you anywhere?' he said, cutting me off.

'Not yet, but we're still looking into it.'

He paused for a second, tapping the letter on the desk. 'Lucky for you this only got as far as me and not the Chief. Same as Judith's visit this morning when she turned up here demanding to know what we were doing with her letter, and filling me in on your plans for a trip out to HMP Westbury.'

'Judith came *here*?' I said. At least he hadn't been keeping tabs on me, but what was she playing at? Was the woman trying to get herself sectioned?

'She did indeed, and I'd prefer it if that didn't happen

again. So I suggest you have a word with your new bestie, OK? Tell her to get it through her thick head that her daughter is a murderer. End of. The job's got enough shit on its hands at the minute; the last thing we need is a ridiculous miscarriage of justice accusation lobbied at us. She comes back here again for a little sit-in, I'll have her forcibly removed.'

Was that really why he'd called me all the way up here? To get me to ask Judith to relax? 'I'll speak to her. Anything else, sir?'

'No. Just remember, Alice, the service has enough embarrassment to deal with right now, let's do our best not to add to it.' He gestured towards his computer screen. 'Now if you don't mind, I've got a call to dial into.'

'Right, yes, sir.'

I mulled over what an absolute waste of time that was as I walked out of Gordy's office. He could have passed that message on over the phone via Jane, yet he'd made me come all the way up here. Why did I get the feeling this was some kind of power play? But for what purpose? I walked down the hallway, mumbling to myself as I tried to figure out what he was up to, bouncing off firm pecs as I rounded the corner.

'Woah there!' came a familiar voice. I didn't need to look up to confirm who it was, the hideous hunter-green woollen jumper with the elbow patches giving its owner away. 'What are you doing up here?' Bret asked.

'Had a meeting with the Super.'

His eyes narrowed. 'Right, everything OK?'

136

Oh, so *now* he wanted to chat work. Well, he could stick his feigned interest up his arse as far as I was concerned. 'Yeah, fine. I've gotta shoot, so ...' I moved to swerve around him.

'You'll probably want to stop in and see Warren on your way out,' Bret said. 'He might have something back for you on that social media profile request.' He nodded towards the frazzled-looking DC I'd spoken to on the way in. 'You're welcome.'

The 'thanks' I owed wouldn't come out, so I said nothing and went over to the man's desk. 'Warren?'

The DC flinched, wiping the side of his mouth as he looked up from a stack of papers like I'd woken him from a deep sleep. To say he looked like he'd been dragged through a hedge backwards would have been a compliment. 'Yeah?'

'I hear you might have something for me.' I introduced myself and gave him the reference number from the email I'd received to confirm the request had gone in.

He swigged from a neon-green can of a jumbo-sized energy drink and rubbed his face, clicking various tabs on his computer screen before typing in the number.

'Rough night?' I asked.

'Could say that,' he said, not taking his eyes off the screen as he searched through his emails. 'Newborn life.'

'Right, congratulations.'

'RIP more like – how long can a person actually go without sleep? Surely I'm on my way out. Ah, there it is.' He opened the response and pointed his finger towards it. 'No joy, unfortunately.'

I leant over his shoulder and read it, noticing the error as soon as I looked at it. 'The username, it's not spelt like that.'

He squinted and looked closer. 'What?' He pulled up the request form that'd gone in. 'Shit, sorry, I must have typed it out wrong, I mean, who spells "girl" with three Rs anyway, it's bloody stupid.'

It took every ounce of willpower I had not to smack him over the head with his keyboard.

Another mistake, another *embarrassing* mistake, was the last thing I needed.

17

What else to call you if not a tumour? That's what you are to me. An abnormal mass. Growing cells hijacking my blood and oxygen. Spreading and spreading, always multiplying, buried deep beneath the surface. Simmering. Waiting. Before you bubble and blister and split my skin. Everyone else oblivious as you eat me alive from the inside out.

You must be cut away with a surgeon's knife, sharp enough to make the separation clear. No longer will I let you feast on me, eat me, consume and devour me.

I will cut you away and feel nothing.

I will not cry. I will not be sad.

It is no more than you deserve for what you have taken from me.

Now I will take from you, everything you hold dear.

139

18

By the time we got back to Fortbridge, I was still boiling with anger despite the superior air con in Jane's car having chilled me to the bone. New daddy DC was resubmitting the social media intel request as a priority, correctly this time, but only God knew how long we'd be waiting for a result. And our attempt at doorstepping Judith about the letters on our way back had been a waste of time, achieving nothing but glares from nosey neighbours who clearly relished telling us she was at work.

Jane dropped me off in the station car park and left to pick her son up from his afternoon club. I sat on the wall, letting the sun bring me up to temperature. Leaning my head back and closing my eyes, an orangey-yellow kaleidoscope danced across the inside of my eyelids as light forced its way through the thin skin. I took a deep breath, only able to let half of it out before glass smashed somewhere behind me. 'What the fuck?' I followed the sound to the bins where Terry, the station clerk, was holding a sledgehammer and wearing a welding mask, shards of glass and plastic strewn around his feet.

'What the hell are you doing?' I asked.

Terry lifted the mask, squinting at the sun as sweat dripped from his rounded chin. 'Disposals, Sarge,' he panted.

'Disposing of what, exactly?'

Terry turned and pointed to a shopping trolley behind him filled with computer screens. 'All these have been in the property store for donkey's years, older than my kids, some of 'em. No use to the Hi-Tech lot. They've been signed off to be destroyed, and I can't put 'em in the bin as is, some skip divers'll have 'em away. Got to render them unsalvageable first.'

'Right.' My mind wandered back to frustrations at not being able to revisit kickboxing and the loss of an opportunity to get a much-needed release from hitting things. 'Can I have a go?'

Terry handed me the sledgehammer and mask. 'Fill yer boots. I'm about to keel over anyway.'

I took the sledgehammer but left the mask, not fancying dousing myself in Terry's sweaty juices. Wrapping my fingers around the tool's handle, I braced, pausing as a memory forced its way into my mind. Me and Tess at that stupid axe-throwing restaurant she'd insisted on going to for her birthday. I'd tried to talk her out of it, made the best case I could for just eating our burger and chips in peace, but it had been a laugh in the end. I'd actually enjoyed being taught how to throw the axe properly. Tess's words on the way home that night lingered in my mind, *See, told you I know you better than you know yourself!* I gripped the handle tighter, reminding myself that after what she'd done I'd never be able to reciprocate the sentiment, before swinging the hammer over my head, lining up my target and smashing it down, bending my knees to get the full swing. The screen cracked like an egg and satisfaction oozed from me like a runny yolk. I felt strong. Powerful. And most importantly, in control.

'Fun, in't it?' Terry said.

'It *really* is.' I prepared myself for the next swing.

The relief I'd garnered spending the next fifteen minutes smashing shit up lasted the walk up to the CID office then withered as Eddie and Roy took it in turns to share updates with me on the investigation.

'The people who ran that production company are more elusive than bloomin' Banksy,' Eddie said. 'I'll keep trying though.'

'And I ain't got much better news for you,' Roy followed up. 'Bernie's been on – they've got that missing doll; some bloke found it on his land a couple of fields over, called it in when he saw the crime scene footage on the news. They've recovered it but there's no way we're getting anything off it except goat spit. He says the whole face has practically been chewed off, even eaten its bleedin' eyes!'

I pictured the dolls hanging from the stage, my imagination replacing all of them with eyeless versions, and a shiver ran the length of my spine. 'Probably no point even putting it in the lab then, I guess?'

Roy shook his head. 'Already been rejected.'

'Anything of use off the other four?' I asked.

'Not yet,' Roy said. 'DNA screening lab's been backed

142

up all weekend with a stabbing. Bernie's gonna get them in for us this afternoon – should know if they've got any prints in the next few days, won't get DNA results back until next week at the earliest.'

'But the festival's next week.'

Roy shrugged. 'He knows, but they're up to their eyeballs over there, no pun intended.'

I rubbed my temples. People's lives potentially on the line and I've got livestock chowing down on evidence and delays caused by under-resourced departments and bloody spelling mistakes. It really was a wonder how any crimes got solved.

I love my job, I love my job, I love my job.

It was only when Roy said 'What?' that I realised I'd been mumbling the affirmation out loud. 'Nothing . . . right . . . OK, I know we haven't got much to work with, but let's stay on top of this. Eddie, keep at the production company, and Roy, chase up checks on the festival site workers, yeah?'

'I had an idea, Sarge,' Eddie said, his hand raised like a kid in class asking permission from the teacher to keep talking.

'Go on,' I said.

He brimmed with excitement at the green light. 'The TV show the band were on, I used to love it, me, my mum, dad and sister, we all used to watch it every Saturday, like religiously, we'd all put our PJs on and get fish and chips and—' I circled my hand in a 'get on with it' motion before he went into detail about which individual condiment each of them opted for and what they had for dessert. 'It was like watching a soap opera, there was always someone kicking off when they didn't make it to the next round. There was a girl who threw a guitar at a judge once! And I was thinking, maybe it's worth looking at some of those, see if anyone holds a grudge. Them re-forming might have brought up all those feelings of rejection again, you never know.'

I clicked my fingers and pointed at him. 'Get on it.' It could very well have been another attempt on his part to watch TV on work time, but I decided to give him the benefit of the doubt.

He grinned, obviously very proud of himself. 'I liked the singing and that, but the best bit was all the drama. That's why Em Drummond was my favourite – she was always kicking off, it was great. She even got arrested during the live shows.'

I looked at Roy. 'You didn't tell me any of the band had a record.'

'Nothing exciting,' Roy said. 'Couple of shoplifting offences from her teenage years before the band, probably more to rebel against her parents than anything, and two for drunk and disorderly. She ain't exactly Courtney Love.'

Something churned in my stomach and I logged on to PNC. 'Emily – Drummond,' I said aloud before typing in her date of birth and hitting send. I looked at the year of both D&D arrests. The first must have been when she was on the TV show, the second during their time on tour. I opened the records and read the details, my unsettled feeling quashed as I did. Roy was right, there was nothing to write home about, though the name she'd given when arrested for the first time at least provided some mild entertainment. Dick Van Dyke. And the ridiculous thing about PNC was that no matter how obvious it was that a person was giving a fake name, it still got recorded as an alias. I'd seen some good ones in my time. Too many Mickey Mouses to count, at least three Harry Belafonte's, two Whoopi Goldbergs and an Englebert Humperdinck.

I could do with a laugh so I navigated to her alias page. It was annoying that someone had to waste time inputting this—

My finger twitched above the keyboard as I saw the name given for the latter D&D.

Rose.

I opened the record and read the detail. She'd been arrested outside a pub in Stoke Newington with someone else, the pair giving their details to police as Rose West and Myra Hindley. Who in their right mind would think it was funny to give police the names of two of the most heinous serial killers when they were being arrested? 'What is wrong with these people?' I said, switching over to the other linked arrest record.

The second I saw it I froze.

It had taken me to the PNC record of Dee Dee Nolan. Dee Dee and Em. Myra and Rose.

Roy must have spotted the look on my face as the mug he was bringing to his mouth stopped inches from his lips. 'What's wrong?' he said.

'Down whatever's in that cup. We're paying Em Drummond a visit.'

'Why?' Roy said.

'Because I want to know why she didn't tell us she's been writing to Dee Dee in prison.'

Theories swirled as I drove us out to Aurora House, and continued to bounce around my mind as I jabbed at the buzzer by the gate. Once. Twice. Three times. No answer. I rang it again.

'Wait,' Roy said, grabbing my forearm to stop me pressing the buzzer a fourth time. 'D'you hear that?'

I held my breath and strained my ears, not that I had to strain too hard to hear the noise being carried in through the open car window. It was the unmistakeable sound of screaming, and it was coming from Aurora House.

19

We couldn't just stand there waiting for response to turn up – God knows how long it would take anyone to get out here to the sticks. Roy spoke to control as I stepped back and sized up the gate. The architects of Aurora House had gone for aesthetics over a secure anti-climb design and it was only a couple of feet taller than me. I strode to the other side of the road, giving myself as much space as possible.

'What the hell are you doing?' Roy said.

I ignored him, keeping my focus on the gate as I ran at the solid wood panelling and jumped, hooking an arm over the top of it. The corner dug into the crook of my armpit as I gripped, squeezing my body against it and swinging one leg up on to the top, before dragging the other up to meet it. I rolled my body over, dropping on to the other side, hitting the ground with a grunt.

'You all right?' Roy yelled. Instead of answering I paused, listening for more screaming, but all I could hear was Roy. 'Sarge? Sarge!'

I lurched towards the button to release the gate, Roy stumbling through the gap as it parted. 'Come on!' I said,

147

turning and running down the driveway winding around the pond.

'Hello, police!' I yelled as I reached the entrance and banged on the front door. 'Open up.' There was no response, no sign of activity.

Roy tapped me on the shoulder and nodded off to our right. 'I'll try the back.'

'No, you stay here, keep knocking, I'll go.'

Staying close to the wall, I made my way around the side of the house, passing the glass door leading into the kitchen diner. There was no one inside as I peered through the window. I carried on until I was alongside the large conservatory extension that, from what I could remember, housed the yoga studio. There were voices now, raised, and someone was crying.

I rounded the side of the building to see Tabby wrapped in Sherrie's arms, face pressed against her, shoulders heaving. Kit and Nush stood either side of them, stroking one of Tabby's arms each. Em stood off to the edge of the patio scuffing her boot through the gravel in the flower bed lining it.

'It's all right, it's all right, shh, shh, shh, there's no one there,' Sherrie whispered into the top of Tabby's flowing curls. 'It's all—' She stopped, her body stiffening, head lifting as if she'd caught my scent in the air before spinning towards me. 'Oh my—' She let go of Tabby and put one hand to her chest. 'What in the Lord's name are you doing here?'

'We heard screaming,' I said, walking towards them. 'Is everything OK?'

Roy appeared by my shoulder. 'What's going on, everyone all right?' he asked.

Tabby wiped her face with the back of her hand but mascara-tinged tears continued to fall, cutting a streak through the blusher coating her cheeks. 'There was someone out there, in the woods, like, *watching* me!'

'What, just now? Where exactly, can you show me?' I said.

She pointed to the woods at the back of the retreat. 'There, in the middle.'

I turned, following the direction of her finger to see Manu and two other men I presumed were part of his security team trudging towards us from the treeline, shaking their heads.

'See, there's fuck all there,' Em said. 'You sure you didn't have a mirror with you, Tabs? Shit yourself at the sight of your own reflection again?'

'I'm telling you, there was someone! I saw them!' Tabby insisted.

I looked at Roy and nodded in the direction Manu and his team were coming from. 'Go check, will you?' He walked off and I turned my attention back to Tabby. 'Who did you see? Can you describe them for me? Was it just one person?'

She held her loose hair away from her face. 'I don't know. I, well, I more like *sensed* them, I guess, than saw them. I'm like, *really* well attuned to nature and my environment . . .'

'Fuck's sake,' Em whispered to herself before Tabby carried on.

149

'And I definitely heard them, I heard footsteps in the undergrowth.'

'It was probably a deer or something, you idiot,' Em said.

Tabby glared at her. 'It *wasn't* a deer. It was far too heavy sounding to be a deer. It was a person, I'm one hundred percent sure.'

'All right,' Em said, 'it was a fat deer, then. There's no one out there, I'm telling you.'

I looked around at the others. 'Did anyone else see anything?'

Kit, Nush and Sherrie all shook their heads.

'I didn't think nowt of it at first, when I heard screaming,' Nush said, looking at Tabby. 'I thought ya were deein' that spiritual thing again, ya nar, where ya scream into the woods.'

'It's called releasing limiting beliefs, actually,' Tabby said, 'and I wasn't doing that. I was doing my woodland yoga, trying to anyway before I felt those eyes on me.'

'Deer eyes can be scary,' Em said before Sherrie glared her into silence.

'Why don't we go inside, OK, get everyone calmed down,' I said, pointing towards the bifold doors leading into the conservatory.

Sherrie went in first, the others following as I turned to see Roy walking back across the lawn. I cupped one hand over my brow and squinted. 'Anything?' I yelled.

'All clear, I've called off the cavalry. What happened anyway?'

'Depends who you ask. Tabby insists she heard something, Em thinks she's imagining things.'

Roy shrugged. 'Can't blame her, being on high alert, and it is quite creepy out there, to be fair, even gave me the willies.'

I turned at the sound of footsteps behind me, Sherrie standing arms folded. 'Sorry to interrupt this little tête-à-tête, but you coming inside or what?'

'Yes,' I said, 'we were just checking—'

Sherrie's deep sigh interrupted me. 'I wouldn't waste your time. As much as I want to slap her sometimes, Em's probably right. Tabby's likely got herself all het up over nothing; it wouldn't be the first time. She calls it "attuned to nature", I call it "high bloody maintenance". And on that note, she's demanding we get out of here; the current *vibes* are not to her liking. We're gonna go out, get some fresh air, try and calm her down a bit. She's been wanting to go down to take some photos of herself with that bridge in the background; that'll distract her for at least half an hour.'

'I'm not sure that's the best idea. It's quite a popular tourist spot, especially on a nice day like this. If people recognise the band it could—'

'This ain't my first rodeo, Sergeant, I know how to look after my girls. And we'll have Manu and one of the boys with us. We'll be fine. How come you're here anyway? I know Tabby's loud, but surely you didn't hear her all the way from the station? And if you did, that'd be quite the response time.'

In all the palaver, the reason we'd driven out here in the

first place had slipped my mind. 'We came to have a quick word with Em.'

Sherrie squinted. 'Why Em, what's she done now?'

'We'd rather speak to her directly, if you don't mind.'

I got the distinct impression she did mind, but that she also saw the reward her end of not having to drag Em out on their excursion against her will.

Roy and I hovered in the hallway until Nush, Tabby and Sherrie left, taking Manu and another security guard with them. Kit, Em and the third member of the security team stayed behind, watching the others drive away in their black people carrier. I pointed Em towards the kitchen. 'Shall we?'

The three of us walked in, the security guard staying by the front door as Kit slunk off upstairs. I regretted the choice of room immediately, the sloped glass making up half the ceiling turning the place into a giant microwave. I tried to ignore the heat as Roy and I sat down next to each other at the large dining table, expecting Em to sit opposite us, but instead she leant against the wall by the door.

'Take a seat,' I said.

Em tutted and scratched the back of her head as she moved towards us, the action lifting her baggy top and exposing the first few inches of skin above the worn black belt holding up her combat trousers. The first thing I noticed were the scars on her lower midriff: several inch-long lines parallel to each other in a pattern so uniform it looked like an army of snails had marched across her belly leaving their trail behind, the secretions several shades lighter than her tawny brown skin. In reality, I doubted they were caused by such a gentle touch. The second thing that registered was her awkwardness. She was clearly going for nonchalance, but her muscles refused to unclench, giving away a tension in her neck and shoulders.

'Why d'you just want to see me and not the others?' Em said. She sat and folded her arms over her chest.

'We'd like to ask you some questions that have come up since our visit to Dee Dee in prison,' I said.

Em sniffed. 'What's that got to do with me?'

'We were hoping you could tell us,' Roy said.

Contempt radiated from her, the rays stronger than the sun pouring in through the glass ceiling. 'I gotta do your job for you now?'

'Have you spoken to Dee Dee, Em?' I asked.

'Course I've spoken to her, she came on tour with us for a year, I've spoken to her millions of times.'

Usually someone becoming a pedantic teenager when they knew damn well what you'd meant would immediately get my back up, but the scars on Em's body that I presumed were self-inflicted told me to take it easy. She wasn't doing this to wind me up. It was a defence mechanism. Just like her baggy clothes and the arms crossed over her chest. All little pieces of armour. 'I meant, have you spoken to Dee Dee since she's been in prison?'

'No.'

Again, I'd asked the question wrong. She'd managed to avoid the hit second time around. *Technically* she wasn't lying to me. 'Have you had *any* form of communication with her?' I asked.

'Like what?'

'Like sent her any letters.'

'No.' Her chin dropped and she chewed the inside of her lip. She was lying now.

'You sure, Em,' I said, 'or should I call you Rose?'

Em opened her mouth and I could tell she was contemplating trying to pretend she had no idea what I was talking about, but then she closed her eyes and sighed. 'The others *can't* know I wrote to her, they wouldn't understand.'

'I'm sure you have your reasons,' I said, 'so why don't you tell us about them.'

'Do we have to do this? It's got fuck all to do with your investigation.'

'You haven't been honest with us so far,' I said. 'Why should we believe you'll start now?'

Em looked at me, shaking her head. 'I didn't lie, no one *asked* if I'd been in touch with her, and it's got nothing to do with us being threatened, so why would I mention it?'

'If it's all the same to you, we'll decide what's relevant to the investigation,' I said.

'This is a joke. Just read the letter, you'll see there's nothing bad in there.'

'We can't,' I said, 'Dee Dee didn't keep it.'

Whether this was a relief or a worry for Em, I couldn't tell. 'What, she throws them away?'

I shrugged. 'I don't know what she does with her letters, but she doesn't have them any more.'

'Well then, that settles it. It was a private conversation and it's done now.'

'Em,' I said, leaning forward, 'I promise you, the only thing we want to do is keep you all safe. No one is trying to trick anyone into saying anything they shouldn't, we just want the truth. What did you write to her about?'

'I dunno . . . general shit. Told her about the reunion, asked how she was getting on.'

'And?' I prompted.

'And what?'

'You asked her to do something for you.' I made air quotes with my fingers. '"One last time." What's that all about?'

Em pushed her tongue against the back of her lips before she spoke again. 'Thought you hadn't read it.'

'We haven't, but prisoner correspondence is checked.'

She threw out her arms like an aggrieved footballer confronting a referee who'd shown them a red card. 'There you go, then! I told you there was nothing bad in there, someone checked it.'

'What were you asking her to do for you?' I said.

She stood and paced behind her chair, running her hands through her hair. 'When you see this has nothing to do with the threats, it doesn't need to go any further, yeah? You don't need to tell the others?'

'That completely depends on what's going on here,' I said.

'This ain't about any secret plans, it's about songs.'

Roy and I looked at each other in confusion before I responded. 'What d'you mean?'

155

Em stayed standing but leant her weight against the table. 'People think I wrote most of our songs, but I didn't. Dee did.'

I leant forwards on my elbows. 'Dee Dee wrote The Dolls' songs? What – all of them?'

'Ris did a couple of the early ones, but after that most of our hits were Dee's. I mean, we worked on them together, kind of, but it was mostly her, and I've been trying to write some new ones – they want us to do an album off the back of all this – but they're shit, like the ones I tried to write when I went solo. I don't get it. Trauma, tick. Depression, tick. I've got all the hallmarks of a tortured artist but I can't capture it, whatever it was Dee had. That's what I was asking for, "one last time".' I was stunned into silence. This was not where I was expecting this conversation to go. Em carried on talking, 'I know it must seem weird, me writing to her after what she did, but we got on, before . . . we had things in common.'

Running through what I knew about their backgrounds, they couldn't be more different. Dee Dee growing up in a working-class single-parent household with a mother more interested in drugs than raising her, versus Em's privileged upper-middle-class background, not quite up there with Tabby's, but still including private schools and expensive music programmes that must have stood her in good stead, no matter how much she tried to roughen her home counties accent. 'What things?'

She picked at the edge of a small scab on her neck. 'Both of us knew what it felt like to be on the outside looking in.'

'But you weren't on the outside, you were right there on stage with the rest of the band, not watching from the wings like Dee Dee.'

'You never heard the quote "Sometimes the loneliest place to be is in a crowd of people"?' Em said, avoiding eye contact.

Something churned in my stomach. I didn't have to hear the quote. I lived the damn thing. I was distracted from my own discomfort by the movement of Em's hand at her stomach, gently rubbing a finger absentmindedly over the material covering the scars. I swallowed hard as I thought back to the prison visit, to Dee Dee's long-sleeved top despite the high temperatures. I could hazard a guess at what they might have had in common. Pain and a form of release. Given some of the things I'd seen in the job, I should've known better than to assume that financially privileged families were always happy and loving ones. I thought back to the video of the band's homecomings. Had Em really been the difficult bad girl she was made out to be for not having one, or was the sadder truth that she had no one in her life who'd be excited to hear the news?

She started talking again. 'I enjoyed writing the songs with her. And, don't get me wrong, I cannot fathom how she did what she did, but I still miss who she was before, you know?'

Tess's betrayal flashed through my mind. I forced it away, clearing my throat. 'Why isn't Dee Dee credited? Those songs have sold in the millions, made the band a lot of money.'

'Pfft, they made *someone* a lot of money, some la-de-dah music exec, not us. And she didn't want to be credited, anyway – don't ask me why, I never understood it. Most people would give their left tit for that kind of validation. Dee didn't seem to care. Not in the slightest. She was chuffed for us they did well, or at least she seemed to be – none of us had a clue what was going on inside her head, clearly. If you'd asked me if Dee would ever so much as hurt a fly, never mind kill anyone, I'd have laughed in your face, and especially not Ris, so what the fuck do I know.'

Dee Dee really was an odd character. I wasn't a fame whore, certainly didn't do *this* job for the fans, but would I hell sit back and let someone else take all the credit for a job well done if they'd barely played a part in it? 'So whose idea was it to give the names Myra and Rose when you got arrested? Kinda bad taste, isn't it?'

The mild thawing of her icy demeanour reversed like we'd leapt forward in time to a cold, dark winter. 'Don't look at me for bad taste, look at your own workforce. I said it to mess with the officers who arrested us, freak them out, because they were enjoying every second of it a bit too much.'

'What d'you mean?' I said.

'Need it spelling out? They saw two young, admittedly pissed women and instead of checking we were all right, they saw what we were wearing, the emo clothes, the dark make-up, and couldn't get in there fast enough with the piss-taking. Start of the encounter to cuffs getting put on me was about ten seconds, and I didn't even do anything except roll my eyes when one of them started singing "Last Resort" by Papa Roach at us. And don't give me the "banter" excuse, because when one of them cuffed me he made a point of saying he better not do it too tight 'cause us goth girls like it rough and he didn't want me getting too *excited* in case my eyeliner ran.' My throat thickened as she stared into my eyes like she was facing the officer in question, reliving that moment in real time. She sniffed hard and looked down at the table between us. 'I came this close to headbutting the prick,' she said, holding her thumb and forefinger an inch apart. 'But I'm not a fucking idiot, so I screwed with them instead.'

From the corner of my eye I could see Roy fiddling uncomfortably with the edge of the table. 'I'm sorry you experienced that, Em, I really am,' I said.

'Yeah, well. I'd love to say that was a long time ago and things have changed, but we all know that ain't true. Anyway, I swear that was the only reason I was writing to Dee. And she wrote back saying she couldn't help.'

'Do you still have the letter she sent?' I asked.

Em shook her head. 'Binned it. It literally just said, "I can't help you, I'm sorry." That was it. Like some corporation form rejection. After everything we all went through. Cold, man, ice cold.'

'OK, I think that's covered everything for now, all right?' I said, trying not to let the anger I felt at the officers who'd arrested Em and Dee Dee come through in my voice.

'And you won't say anything to the band, yeah? This is all I've got . . . please.' She swallowed hard, her eyes glazing.

'I don't think telling the band will help with anything in terms of our investigation, but maybe you should. They're your friends, aren't they?'

Em opened her mouth to respond but instead her eyes darted towards the closed door. I'd heard it too, boots scuffing on the other side. I marched over and pulled it open to see Kit standing there, her face jolting back as she looked up at me.

'Can I help you?' I asked.

'Sorry, I was . . . I was coming to get myself a drink.'

I pulled the door further open and stepped aside to let her in. 'We're finishing up in here anyway. Help yourself.' She made her way to the fridge. I was sure she would help herself to a nice refreshing drink and whatever juicy titbits she'd overheard listening in on our conversation with Em.

20

Kit retreated to the studio as Em showed the officers out. She hadn't been able to hear what they were talking about, but whatever it was had left Em in a fouler mood than normal, if that was possible. And the others would be back soon, meaning one thing and one thing only: more bickering. Arguments about cancelling the gig. Assurances and dismissals about their safety, even with more police and security on site. They had no clue. As if cancelling this stupid show came close to their biggest problem.

Speaking of problems, the last thing Kit needed right now was *more* police and security lurking about. Even though there'd been no more uncomfortable looks from Manu, she'd have to be extra careful now. Getting herself kicked out of here wasn't an option. Because she was the only one looking for the truth, and if they found out what she was doing, it would never come out. And Kit couldn't let that happen. Not again.

She closed the studio door behind her and reached for the light switch but stopped short, letting the room remain pitch-black. Running her palm across the velvet padded wall, she took tentative steps forward until her hand hit one of the guitars hanging on the rack. The neck of what she presumed must be the vintage Stratocaster was solid and cold as she curled her fingers around it, the thick wire strings compressing against the fret board under her grip as she lifted it from the prongs of the holder.

It was lighter than the one they'd had in her house as a child, her dad's old Epiphone Les Paul he'd taught her to play when she was barely big enough to hold the thing. Not that she was much bigger now in the height department. But she was bigger in other ways, stronger. She'd had to be. Both physically and mentally. It had taken every drop of willpower she'd had to stop herself from smashing the instrument she'd shared with her dad after finding out what happened, seeing with her own eyes how it ended the way it did. Forcing the memory from her mind, she felt around for the thick braided strap, before looping it over her head, the weight of the guitar pulling the material taut across her left shoulder. She didn't need the light to play. Didn't need to see what she was doing. She'd practised Girlschool's version of 'Race with the Devil' so many times she knew instinctively where her hands needed to be. She played the intro riff without a second thought, pressing and bending the strings to her will. Fingers dancing, almost independent from her body. Free.

She was halfway through the second verse when she stopped, a thought entering her mind where the music had made space. These death threats had put the band on edge: Tabby freaking out over what was probably some burrowing woodland creature, Em stomping around upstairs after her encounter with the police. If anything was going to make them crack, give Kit what she needed, surely this was the perfect scenario. Whoever was sending them hadn't ruined anything at all, quite the opposite. Maybe they'd done her a favour.

Pulling out her phone, she dialled her contact. 'It's me. Look, don't get your hopes up, but I think I might have some good news.'

She listened to the voice on the other end before responding.

'. . . no, but I said it was going to take time . . . Wait, what are you on about?'

Kit sat bolt upright as she heard the response, almost dropping her phone. 'What does "getting it sorted yourself" mean . . . no, wait! . . . hello? Hello!' she yelled as the line went dead.

21

Roy and I arrived back at the station just as our shift ended. I sat down at my desk and updated the system as Roy changed into his cycling gear.

'You heading home?' he asked, emerging from the toilets and pulling on his bike helmet.

'In a sec, just finishing up.'

'Don't stay too long, no one'll thank you for it.' He saluted and clomped off across the office, his cleats clicking on the landing and down the stairs as the door swung closed behind him.

I pushed air through my lips like a whinnying horse. I had nothing to rush off for and at least the office was marginally cooler than the cottage. Logging on to my emails, I skimmed what had come in while we'd been out. The first was from Eddie, who'd already left.

Sarge, hi.
Tracked down one of the contestants who went
bonkers and tried to hit people with a guitar. Safe
to cross her off the list. Lives in Japan and is quite

164

big on the rock scene there, so much so she's in the
middle of starring in what looks like their version
of I'm a celeb, except they do it in that forest where
loads of people hang themselves – each to their own,
wouldn't catch me in there for love nor money :-)
Still looking into another girl, will keep you posted.
    Tx,
    Eddie

My shoulders slumped. It wasn't like I'd pinned all my
hopes on that line of enquiry, any hopes at all really, but
I could use a win right now. At least there was a potential
second nutjob in the wings. A yawn took over my face as
I stretched my arms over my head. I should go home. This
was starting to look sad, me hanging around here because
I had bugger all else to do. I was about to pack up when
the phone on my desk rang.

'DS Washington,' I said, answering it.

'Oh, hi there, I didn't think you were still on duty, I was
gonna leave a message.'

'Today's your lucky day,' I said, as if any other day of
the week he'd have missed me due to my playboy lifestyle
of living la vida loca. 'How can I help?'

The caller introduced himself as the constable who'd
been allocated the job of investigating the graffiti on my car
and went on to give me an update, which was much as I'd
suspected. No working CCTV. No witnesses. No nothing.

'We're having a nightmare with that estate,' he said. 'It's
getting worse every week, and we're doing all the things:

NPT work with charities, local authority, the works. I swear the kids there are feral.'

'Thanks for your efforts anyway. Keep fighting the good fight,' I said, not sure who needed the cheerleading more, me or him.

'Will do. Mind, it's getting to the point now even the victims don't wanna get involved. Intervened in an attempted robbery last month by the bus stop out the front of Fenmore House, some journalist trying to talk to the kids on the estate, they nearly ate her alive. But when I went past on patrol and stepped in, well, you'd think I was the one trying to rob her the way she reacted. And would she make a report? Would she heck.'

'Only so much you can do, isn't there? At least you stopped her getting robbed, or worse.'

'Wish she'd seen it the same way, practically snapped me hand off when I tried to give her back the necklace they'd ripped off her – not that they'd have gotten much for it, mind you, it was only one of those cheapy velvet choker things.'

Several thoughts converged in my mind. The address of Judith's estate. A journalist with a dislike of the police. And a velvet choker. 'You didn't happen to get a name for this woman, did you?'

'No, like I say, she wasn't interested in making a report. Best I can do is tell you her name probably started with a K.'

My breath snagged. 'What makes you think that?' I asked, though I was ninety-nine percent sure I already knew the answer.

'The necklace, it was one of those personalised ones, had the letter K on it. I suppose that doesn't mean it was her name – could be a boyfriend, or *girl*friend these days, couldn't it?'

Oh, it was her name all right. Kit bloody Ashton's name.

A chill swept through me. What was Kit doing outside Judith Nolan's block? I made an excuse to hang up and immediately opened the death threat case file, clicking through the tabs and scrolling through the linked persons page. My eyes lingered on the entry for Kaitlyn 'Kit' Ashton, date of birth 27 March 2000. There was no associated intel on her. I searched her name. The first result was the *Louder* magazine website. It seemed legitimate. Kit was listed as a freelancer, and it all looked very on-brand for working with a band like The Dolls. Rainbow-coloured hair, full-sleeve tattoos and micro fringes, thumbnail after thumbnail of people with supposedly bold and individualist style whose societal non-conformity all somehow managed to look exactly the same.

Returning to the main search page, I scrolled through more links and images, pausing on a photo from a few months back, before the reunion had been announced. Kit and Tabby were arm in arm, smiling for the camera. Tabby was smiling anyway, every inch of her held in the perfect position to get the most photogenic angles. Kit's face was stiffer, as was her whole body, like she'd been caught in the middle of the road, feet bolted to the floor, the flash of the camera representing the headlights of a massive truck careering towards her. I read through the associated article, the image taken at some social justice influencer event called *Rock for Change*. I did another search for KIT ASHTON JUDITH NOLAN. Nothing came back, but the unsettled feeling in my stomach stuck fast. I grabbed my car keys. I'd believed Judith when she'd said she hadn't made the threats against the band. But maybe I'd fallen into the same trap I had with Em, not asked the right questions. Maybe she wasn't making the threats, but she had someone on the inside making them for her.

Em looked less than pleased to see me again as she opened the door of Aurora House.

'What d'you want now?'

'Is Kit around?' I asked. 'I need a word.'

Em looked me up and down before stepping back and letting me in. 'She's in her room. Upstairs, end of the corridor. Says *Mockingbird* on the door sign.'

'Thanks.' I climbed the stairs quietly, slowing as I approached the room Em had directed me to. I wanted to see what Kit was doing before she knew I was there.

Her door was ajar. I got my face as close as I could to the architrave before peeking around the frame. Kit was sat at a small desk underneath a porthole-style window, large black headphones over her ears, watching something on her laptop. Slipping through the gap in the door, I walked closer, freezing as I saw what she was watching. There was no doubt I'd seen that footage before. The grainy quality. The amateur movement in the hand of the inexperienced videographer.

Kit turned and flinched at the sight of me standing behind her, throwing her hands to her headphones and yanking them off. 'Jesus! You scared the shit out of me. What you doing here?' A moment of realisation hit her, eyes widening before she slammed the laptop closed.

'What are you watching?' I asked, knowing full well.

'Some old videos of the band, why d'you care?'

That wasn't the band. The only person in that video was Dee Dee. 'Where from?'

Kit folded her headphones up and put them on the desk. 'I get my research from all sorts of places. It's footage from the old documentary that followed them on tour.'

'You sure?'

'Yeah, what's your problem? Why are you back here?'

'Show me,' I snapped.

She looked me up and down. 'Why?'

'Just show me.'

She paused, presumably trying to think of a valid-sounding reason as to why she couldn't. 'You not got access to YouTube or something?'

I folded my arms. 'That's where you got it from, is it, YouTube?'

'Yeah,' she said.

'So Judith Nolan didn't send you it, then?'

'W— no, why would—'

'Don't bullshit me, that's not from YouTube.' I jabbed my finger towards her laptop. 'That's a video Judith Nolan recorded of Dee Dee, so do you wanna tell me how you got hold of it?'

Kit's shoulders slumped. 'OK, Judith sent it to me. Not a crime, is it?'

'No, but death threats are.'

She scrunched up her face. 'I don't know anything about the threats! Neither does Judith.'

'You sure? 'Cause that would make your little magazine spread a whole lot more interesting, wouldn't it, really give the article some oomph. And Judith gets a bit of payback for them taking her daughter away – win–win, right?'

'Are you high or something? You've lost it, absolutely fucking lost it.' Kit stood up from her chair and backed towards the corner of the room.

'Come on then, enlighten me. How do you know Judith? What's she got you doing here?'

Kit's eyes filled with tears. 'It's not what you think. I'm not doing anything wrong.'

'Really? Wheedling your way in here under false pretences just before someone starts threatening the band?'

'I didn't . . . it's not like that . . . Fuck,' Kit laughed through the tears, 'what's the point, asking a cop to listen to what you've got to say? Should have known that was pointless. Here,' she held both hands out towards me, placing her wrists together, palms facing the ceiling. 'Just get on with it and arrest me.'

Something was going on here and I couldn't quite work out what. 'And what exactly should I be arresting you for?' I sat down on the bed to reduce the level of threat posed. What I needed from Kit now was answers, not a scrap.

'Do you even need a reason? Don't you lot do whatever

you want?' I didn't respond, instead waiting for the answer to my original question. Her face softened. 'If you must know, I didn't *wheedle* my way in here. I really did come here to do a piece on them after I met Tabby at an influencer event thing the magazine sent me to. And I *was* a fan of theirs. I was buzzing to be involved, at first. The false pretences came later, when I realised that . . .' Her chest heaved, blocking the rest of the words.

'Whatever's happened, Kit, you can talk to me, it's OK.'

'No, it's not *OK*, nothing about this is O fucking K.'

'If you tell me what's going on here, I'll do everything I can to help you.'

Her eyes fixed on me like she was battling with herself about whether to say anything else. After a few seconds, she spoke. 'Someone here knows more than they're letting on about what really happened the night Ris Angelini died.'

Despite the stuffy air, a chill ran down my spine. 'What d'you mean, what *really* happened?'

'I mean—'

Footsteps pounded along the hallway and both our gazes flew to the open door.

'Everything cool in here?' Em said as she appeared in the doorway.

Kit looked at me, her eyes wide.

I forced my face to stay neutral. 'Almost done, just something I needed to follow up on for paperwork – more paperwork than anything else in policing these days.'

Em looked back and forth between us. 'The others'll

171

be back soon, and you're on dinner duty, remember?' she said to Kit.

'Yeah, course, I'll be down in a sec,' Kit said.

Em nodded and turned, walking back in the direction she'd come from.

We waited in silence until we heard the creak of the stairs as Em descended. I scoured Kit's face, looking for the telltale signs of deception, but all I was getting was desperation radiating from every pore. 'Tell her you're missing an ingredient or something for dinner, and I'm giving you a lift to the shop. We need to talk, in private.' I turned and walked out of the room, my heart thudding so hard in my chest I could hardly breathe.

22

Somehow, I got us to the twenty-four-hour American-style diner by the petrol station without crashing the car. Kit had refused to say anything until we were in a public place, and my head was swirling with theories as we slid into opposite sides of a booth.

A waitress took our order of two coffees as Kit eyeballed the closest person to us: a man fiddling with the lime-green plastic gun attached to a vintage arcade machine and making *pew-pew* noises every time he pulled the little red trigger. The milkshake he was slurping must have been alcoholic, given he kept sliding off his bar stool. Convinced he was in no fit state to hear, let alone process, what she was about to say, Kit finally spoke after the waitress walked back behind the counter.

'Dee Dee's lying about what happened the night Ris died.'

This wasn't a scramble for an excuse to get out of the lie I'd caught her in, she was deadly serious. 'Did Judith put you up to this?'

'No one "put me up" to anything. I'd never even met Judith until *after* I got the job on The Dolls piece.'

'Start from the beginning,' I said.

Kit glanced at the drunk man, who was still *pew-pewing* but had swivelled away from the machine and was aiming the plastic gun around the room. 'I met Tabby at some influencer thing, I was there with *Louder* magazine. We got talking, she was drunk, told me about the reunion. We swapped numbers and she called the next day begging me not to say anything, nothing had been released yet. And then, I dunno, I guess she appreciated my discretion. Next thing I'm getting a call from Sherrie asking me to come do a fly-on-the-wall article.'

'So, what changed?' I asked.

Kit looked at the table, lips pursed as if she was having an internal debate. 'Sherrie gave me a link to a load of digitised files from the production team who did the follow-up TV special off the back of *So You Think You Can Rock?* She wanted me to do some video content for their social channels, pull out some of the old footage, splice it with the new stuff, like a "then and now" sorta thing. And I found this . . .' She pulled a laptop from her bag, unlocked the screen, clicked a few times and turned it to face me.

I leant forward. 'What is it?'

'Transcripts. I spoke to one of the production runners who worked on the show to make sense of what they'd sent over. There's no rhyme or reason to how it's stored, just a folder with random shit dropped into it. There's hundreds of hours' worth of recordings in there, they were filming for six months. The guy said it wasn't unusual for them to set recorders on the tables as part of the interviews and leave them running, let the band get into a flow, and, well, this time I guess someone forgot to turn it off.'

'And?'

'This one's marked up as being from the afternoon of the seventh of September 2013, about eight hours before Ris died.'

I looked at the bold and underlined lettering at the top of the page.

AUDIO TRANSCRIPT NOTES:
MAKE-A-DOLL-OUT-OF-YOU-07092013-00156

I skimmed the first page. The transcription quality was shocking and the notes didn't specify who was speaking, but given the subject was talking about how it was less about the fact the band *made* music and more that they *canalised the ethereal vibrations of the universe*, I presumed it was an interview with Tabby. 'So, Tabby's pretentious, what's new?'

Kit shuffled around to my side of the booth before jabbing a finger at the numbers down the left side of the screen. 'This is the timestamp. If you keep reading, it jumps an hour from twelve to just after one o'clock, presumably the next time any voices are picked up with the tape still running.'

I followed her finger and read.

13:07:20: Its me we needto talk
13:07:26: [inaudible] i cart just leave her like that.
13:07:35: I donknow, maybe it [inaudible] help her. If
         she knows no one else will see them.

13:07:55: yeah, but what if she doesn't get over it, [inaudible]sbin six weeks already.

13:08:11: fine is the last thing she is

13:08:29: Shes getting worse. Maybe [inaudible] just told her the truth.

13:08:52: Wait I no I didn't wait wait

'Who is this?' I said. 'What are they talking about?'

Kit scratched her cheek. 'I don't know. There's no audio recording to go with it – I've checked, but since it's all been digitised every physical recording's been chucked.'

'Surely someone must have listened to it to do the transcription?'

She shook her head. 'The guy said this would have been done using automatic software, and a shitty cheap one by the looks of it, there's so many mistakes.'

I re-read it. 'It doesn't even make any sense.'

'That's what I thought, until I realised, it's only picking up one side of the conversation. Look at the gaps in the timings, the seconds counter at the end there. It doesn't take eighteen seconds to say "fine is the last thing she is", does it? This isn't a back-and-forth between two people in the same room.'

'Sounds like we're getting one half of a phone conversation,' I said.

'Exactly!' Kit's eyes widened as if she was telling me she'd uncovered the identity of Jack the Ripper.

'But what makes you think this has anything to do with Ris's murder?'

She pointed at the screen like I was missing the obvious. '*Something* was going on, something that meant "she" was getting worse, and whoever is doing the talking here did something that contributed to it. And six weeks back from the seventh was the night the band announced their US tour at a gig in Birmingham.'

I still couldn't see exactly what point she was making. 'They could be talking about anything – Ris's behaviour getting worse for one. From everything I've heard, she changed those last few weeks; that doesn't go against what Dee Dee said. Or maybe Dee Dee's the "she" and her animosity towards Ris was getting worse.'

'That doesn't explain "no one else will see them" – see *what*? And what's with all the telling her the truth shit? Dee Dee didn't say anything about anyone else from what I could see from the news stories and speaking to the band. She said what happened was between her and Ris. No one else, so explain that.'

I shifted my weight so I could turn to face her. 'I'm not sure what I'm supposed to be explaining. Any related grievances would have been looked into at the time as part of the investigation.'

She let out a mocking laugh. 'You're sure about that? That's funny, because I asked the runner guy. The police didn't take any of the documentary footage. None of it. No one has even so much as requested this stuff until Sherrie had it sent to me.'

'I can understand why. You said yourself, there's hours of footage here, and as much as we'd like to trawl through every single piece of possible evidence, there isn't the resource, and they had what they needed.'

She made her way back to the other side of the booth. 'You can say that again. A vulnerable young girl to pin everything on? Bingo!'

'That's not fair, and for all you know Dee Dee could be the one talking on that transcript.'

Kit slapped the laptop closed, dragged it towards her and shoved it into her bag. 'I've been doing interviews with the band, asking them stuff about the old days. Dee Dee wasn't with them the afternoon of this recording, they told me that themselves. Her and Ris had already fallen out by that point. They argued a few weeks after the Birmingham gig – though no one claims to know what about – and Dee Dee was basically banished from the entourage until the night she showed up at the Big Top and managed to sneak past security. So that can't be her.'

'Maybe Dee Dee was the one on the other end of the phone?'

'Maybe, and maybe this conversation set in motion what happened later, in which case, something was going on with someone either in the band, or someone hanging around them who was there that afternoon, and no one bothered to look into what.'

The drunk man put the arcade machine gun down as the waitress brought him a plate of something so slicked with oil it made me feel queasy. Or maybe it was the conversation unsettling my stomach. 'So where does Judith come into all this?'

'I tracked her down and went to speak to her after I found the transcript. I wanted to get her take on what happened, and something she said didn't match with some of the evidence I'd read about Dee Dee.'

'Like what?'

'They used a notebook to show Dee Dee's state of mind and her intent to kill Ris, but Judith said Dee Dee didn't keep notebooks. In fact, Judith was always amazed that even when Dee Dee was making up songs she never used to write them down, kept them all in her head. She was really funny about clutter as a kid, kept her room as bare as possible, but when the police came around, this notebook was just lying out on Dee Dee's bed.'

I thought back to Dee Dee's pristine cell and what the prison officer told us, and the anger in her when she told us Judith had sold her guitar. Maybe she'd kept things bare as a child because if she didn't have anything, there was nothing for Judith to sell. 'So, you're suggesting the notebook wasn't hers?'

'Judith's convinced it's not.'

'Then how did it get there?'

'You tell me.'

It was obvious where Kit was going with this, that evidence had been planted. I wasn't sure whether now was the right time to ask if she was aware that Judith wasn't the most attentive mother in the world, so I'd need some convincing she'd paid reliable attention to her daughter's journalling habits. 'Surely Dee Dee would have told the police if it wasn't hers.'

Kit shrugged. 'Maybe she did. Maybe they didn't wanna listen.'

I thought back to my conversation with Gordy. He might have a bullish way about him, but that didn't mean he'd stoop to that level.

'Dee Dee confessed, Kit.'

'Oh, come on.' Kit slapped her palms on to the table. 'She wouldn't be the first to lie about what went down during a crime, you know that better than I do. And how many people have you come across who just straight up confess to murder, no excuses, nothing?'

'People lie all the time. But there's always a reason, and none that fit with Dee Dee. She certainly doesn't seem to want any kind of notoriety – from what I'm aware of, she's done everything she can to stay *out* of the spotlight – and her mental health assessment at the time showed no issues or conditions that would explain a false confession.'

'You're conveniently skipping over the main reason people make false confessions. Police coercion,' Kit said, stony-faced.

The job had its issues to sort out, no one would deny that, but this was all starting to get a bit Hollywood. 'I understand you're not a huge fan of the police, and I get that, I'm not either right now, but the arresting officers had barely walked through the front door of Judith's flat before Dee Dee told them what she'd done, there was no time to coerce her. It was an open and shut case.'

'Course it was.' Kit climbed out of the booth. 'I knew you wouldn't listen, you're all the fucking same.'

'Wait, sit down, please. I *am* listening, I just don't think you've found the silver bullet you think you have here. It's no secret the band had a fraught relationship. What's on those transcripts might be about something completely unrelated to any of this.'

'Yeah, it could be. And maybe what Dee Dee said was true. But it could also mean someone is hiding something. Maybe someone else was involved. Someone she's protecting. But we'll never know, because no one bothered to look into it properly. I'm not claiming to know exactly what happened, but something doesn't add up here. Dee Dee was supposedly jealous of Ris and didn't like the way she'd been acting, but you could say the same about every single one of the band. Let's face it, they were all jealous of her. Ris was the star. So if that's what did it, then they all have motive.'

I thought back to what Em said about Dee Dee not wanting any recognition for the songwriting. Now that I thought about it in this context, it didn't ring true. Surely if she wanted the adoration Ris had, she would have staked her rightful claim. 'So what exactly are you saying?'

She shrugged. 'I haven't got it all figured out yet, but something's not right, and if that means there's been some sort of miscarriage of justice . . .'

I wasn't sure if she ended her sentence because she wanted to or whether she felt there was no other way to hide the wobble in her lower lip. Given the glisten of tears in her eyes, I guessed it was the latter. Was there something more personal about this for Kit? Something else fuelling her mistrust of the police? Now didn't feel like the right time to ask.

'Let's not get ahead of ourselves here. The transcript brings up some questions, but it in no way proves something was missed, certainly not in any way big enough to warrant re-opening the investigation. That your idea too, was it, the letters Judith's been sending to HQ trying to get the case re-opened?'

Kit ran her fingers through her hair in exasperation. 'What a surprise. Looking after your own, 'cause it'll look bad on your buddies if it turns out they didn't investigate properly, if she's innocent or someone coerced her into it. And I don't know anything about any letters. But d'you know what? Maybe she's onto something there, 'cause you lot seem to need a push to do your jobs properly, a bit of public pressure. Maybe I'll join her, and I won't do it in a letter, I'll do it on any socials I can get my hands on, get a bit of a hashtag going, yeah, #FreeDeeDee, got quite the ring to it, I'm sure it'll go viral in no time.'

'Doing that isn't going to help anyone,' I said. 'All it'll achieve is making this a free-for-all for armchair detectives, I promise you. If there's something to this and you do that, then anything you've found will get swamped – is that what you want?'

'No, I want the truth,' Kit said, drilling her index finger into the tabletop.

'Good,' I said, 'then we're on the same page. I'm going to look into this, OK? Maybe some of it was investigated at the time and went nowhere. Not every single police action is reported in the public domain, you know, especially when there's no trial. But don't misunderstand what I'm saying here: this can't be a two-way information exchange, because I don't fancy ending up in front of a gross misconduct panel. I can't tell you about things in the case file that aren't public knowledge, so you're going to have to trust me.' Kit didn't say anything, but gave a reluctant nod. 'And in the meantime, no #FreeDeeDee, and no more letters from Judith riling up HQ. If I'm going to look into this, I need to be able to do it without the bosses up my arse.'

Another single nod from Kit was clearly the only re-assurance I was getting. This trust was going to have to work both ways.

'Thank you, and for what it's worth, I don't think you should stay at Aurora House.'

'Is there anything you can do legally to stop me?' From the look on her face, she clearly already knew the answer. She wasn't doing anything wrong. In theory, I could tell Sherrie why Kit was really there, but part of me was curious to know what more she might find out now she'd built a rapport with the band. I'd never be able to manage that, my badge an immoveable barrier between us. 'You can go,' she said, knowing I had no comeback, 'I can get a taxi.'

'You sure? I can give you a lift back.'

'No, it's fine.'

I pulled a business card out of my purse and gave it to her. 'Call me anytime you need to, OK?' Kit stared at the card for a second before picking it up and shoving it into her pocket. 'And you be careful, because if they find out why you're really there, they probably aren't going to be too pleased about it.'

Kit swung her bag over her shoulder. 'I've been looking after myself since I was thirteen. I know what I'm doing.'

No amount of mini cold plunging as I splashed water on my face the moment I got home was going to wash away what I'd been told. Part of me wanted to believe Kit was just as deluded as Judith, that she'd jumped on this bandwagon because it suited her anti-police rhetoric and added a dash of spice to her article on the band. But there was no denying the hum of doubt rumbling through my mind.

I finished up in the bathroom, flopped on to my bed, and ran through everything I knew about Dee Dee's conviction. First and foremost, there'd been the confession. But Kit had a point: people *did* confess to crimes they didn't commit, probably much more frequently than the general public would imagine, even to crimes so abhorrent it seemed unfathomable anyone would falsely admit to them. And it was for exactly that reason the investigative team would still have had to build a case around it, the confession alone not enough to secure a conviction. I didn't know the job in great detail, but I knew they'd had witnesses, people in the crowd that night who saw Dee Dee on the stage roof. But there was no denying that while eyewitness testimony had its place, it was well documented that it could also be as unreliable as the weather forecast.

Rolling on to my side, I grabbed a glass of tepid water from my bedside table, downing half of it before moving on to the next piece of evidence I could remember being a factor: Dee Dee's DNA found on the lapels of the jacket Ris had been wearing that night. If I was to play devil's advocate, all that told us was that Dee Dee had likely had contact with the item in some way, at some point, so given Dee Dee and Ris had been close friends, I was surprised they'd bothered submitting it for examination in the first place.

A positive result didn't prove that contact came from Dee Dee pushing her. In fact, if any of my previous jobs involving touch DNA were anything to go by, getting a useable profile from anything other than prolonged and vigorous contact when there were no bodily fluids in play was rare. I made a mental note to check the full report for an explanation before moving on to another key item recovered as part of the investigation: the notebook. Dee Dee said it was hers, so there would have been no reason for handwriting analysis to confirm whether it was or not.

My mind whirred like clunky machinery, its maintenance check-up long overdue. This guesswork was getting me nowhere; I needed to have a thorough look at the case file, get my head around what happened. Because surely there must be an explanation for what Kit had found. Mustn't there? The hum of unease continued between my ears. I would have loved to pass it off as the beginnings of an oncoming headache, the heat of the day and my lack of water consumption leaving my body parched. But I knew that wasn't what this was. It was the old Washington instincts firing on all cylinders.

Danger, danger, right ahead!

I turned off the lamp and forced myself to sleep, my mind insisting on revisiting a thought I'd had at the start of the death threat investigation, an initial assumption I'd made that maybe Dee Dee had been in contact with someone outside the prison, getting them to do her dirty work. Now I couldn't help but wonder if it was the other way around: Dee Dee the puppet, the master still out there wandering free. Waiting. Watching.

23

I could have covered every inch of my face with cucumber slices and it would have done nothing to reduce the puffiness and grey bags under my eyes brought on by getting only an hour of sleep. But at least all that fretting had led to something. I had a plan. And I was about to put it in motion.

Terry was behind the front desk eating what looked like a plum, juice dripping on to his white shirt. 'Morning, morning,' he said, wiping his chin with the back of his hand. ''Scuse the mess, this little sod appears to be getting away from me.'

Ignoring Terry's sloppy eating habits, I prepared to put on my best calm and collected expression to make my request sound like one I was totally chill about and not remotely worried would land me in a massive pile of stinking shit. 'I need a favour. Can you arrange to get some exhibits from the pit for me, please?' I handed him a torn piece of paper with the case reference number scribbled on it. 'Everything under this.'

Terry's eyes widened at the mention of the pit: the

nickname for the facility housing all items kept long term in line with retention guidelines, usually relating to murder and other major offences. It was where exhibits went to collect dust, rarely ever seeing the light of day again unless they were the subject of an appeal or cold case review.

'You're after a pit, you say? This one do ya?' Terry held up the gnarled, saliva-coated brown stone he'd sucked the plum flesh from. He clearly saw my lip twitch, no longer able to hide the disgust, and regretted his attempt at a skit, throwing the pit into the metal bin with a resounding clang. 'Not a problem, I can sort that for you, tout suite.'

Now I'd officially initiated Operation Look Into This on the Down-low, I felt sick. And not because of the blob of fruit clinging to the side of Terry's chin for dear life. For a second, I considered letting this whole thing go. Surely the team investigating back then would have gone through everything relevant. And while Dad hadn't been the SIO, he'd still have been micromanaging the crap out of Gordy Scott, hovering over his shoulder and keeping a close eye on what was going on, so what the hell was I expecting to find? Something churned in my stomach. In any other instance I'd have every confidence that would be true, but I couldn't discount Dad's comment at dinner the other night about the timing, him not being at his best with everything that had been going on with Mum.

What if . . .

I flinched as Terry's hand waved across my face.

'You all right, Sarge?' he asked.

I needed to calm down. Commit to the damn plan and

stop worrying. This was the right thing to do. My concerns stuck in my throat despite my best efforts to swallow them. 'Yeah, fine, was just thinking about something.'

'Now then, quid pro quo,' Terry said as he picked up the yellow plastic bucket displayed on one side of the front desk. 'I couldn't tempt you for a donation, could I? The community centre are raising money for a new roof after some little buggers nicked the lead flashing off it. It's lucky we're having such a nice summer, otherwise the place'd be flooded.'

'Erm, yeah, sure.' I rummaged in my bag for my purse, but it wasn't there. I'd gotten it out at the diner to give Kit my card. I must have left it. 'Shit. Can I take a rain check? I'll get you some tomorrow.'

'No problemo, Sarge.'

Jane appeared in my periphery, her loafers tapping briskly down the stairs.

Terry shook the bucket in her direction. 'How about you, ma'am? Spare a few pennies for—'

She held up a palm to silence him. 'Not now, Terry. Alice, get yourself up to HQ.'

Oh God, what Judith-shaped slop did Gordy Scott want me cleaning up for him now? 'What's the matter?'

'It's Tabby Falstead.'

'Tabby? What's she done?'

'Gone missing, that's what.'

Tabby's tear-streaked face looking up at me from Sherrie's embrace outside the back of Aurora House yesterday, and the others' dismissal of her claims about what she'd seen in the woods, hit me like a wrecking ball and my blood ran cold.

The body heat from the numerous people packed into the briefing room at HQ did its best to override the impact of the air con. I gulped down the bottle of water I'd brought with me as I looked for an empty seat before nabbing one at the back and sitting down. Bret was standing at the front forming one corner of a small huddle, accompanied by Gordy, DCI Simon Carver, and Head of Comms, Pru Bishop, the four of them consorting like a gang of drug dealers working a street corner with tilted heads and hushed whispers.

They broke from their pre-briefing chat, Pru and Bret leaning against a desk off to one side of the room, Carver remaining front and centre beneath a large screen on the wall behind him as Gordy made for the door.

'Right, pipe down, you lot,' Carver said as Gordy exited, the chatter amongst attendees stopping instantly. 'OK.' He leant over to the laptop plugged into the screen, rubbing a finger over the control pad before an enlarged headshot of Tabby appeared.

'Tabitha Arabella Falstead, goes by Tabby, bass guitarist for The Dolls, thirty-three years old. Last seen at around eight o'clock last night doing a photoshoot by the bridge over the back of Oakham Reservoir.'

I jotted down notes on the rest of Carver's overview which had been established from the first accounts of the last people to see her, that being Nush, Sherrie and the security guard who'd gone out with them, and a handful of other people who'd been in the vicinity. There'd been some sort of altercation, Nush kicking off at a bunch of schoolboys who asked for autographs before slapping her arse. According to Sherrie and the guard, one minute Tabby was beside them, giving the boys a lecture on male allyship, but by the time they'd stopped Nush from kicking the boys' heads in, Tabby was gone. CCTV in the area was limited, some new kit installed in the car park but not much else.

Carver handed over to Bernie for an overview of the crime scene report. He rose from his seat at the front and spun around to address his audience. 'OK, the most exciting thing I have for you today issssss . . .' He held the last consonant until Carver moved the slides on the screen along from the image of Tabby to one of some writing scrawled across what looked like a path fringed with grass. I swallowed hard as I made out the text.

TWO DOLLS DOWN, THREE TO GO.

Fuck.

I'd done everything possible on the drive here to convince myself this had nothing to do with the threats or what Tabby had thought she'd seen in the woods at Aurora House yesterday. That this was all a misunderstanding somehow, Tabby having simply wandered off and gotten lost. But there was no kidding myself now. Tabby hadn't gone missing of her own accord. She'd been taken, whoever had made those threats making good on their promise.

Bernie continued as I shifted uncomfortably in the stiff plastic chair, 'It's pretty slim pickings forensics wise. The only physical item we found at the scene was a mobile phone, which has been identified as Tabby's, annnnndddd—' he said, leaning over and zooming in on the image to focus on the red writing, '—I'm pretty sure that's been done wi' a lipstick.'

'*Lipstick?*' said one of the DCs in the front row. 'Do we know what brand?'

The glare emanating from Bernie's eyes told me the Scottish accent was about to be dialled up a notch. 'Do I look like I work the counter at Boots in my spare time? I dinnae know the brand, and what use would that be anyway? They probably pump these things out in the millions.' I could have sworn I heard him murmur 'eejit' under his breath before he carried on. 'No, what I'm thinking is, if this is a used lipstick, rather than a brand new one, there *could* be a chance of DNA, here,' he said, pointing towards where the horizontal and vertical lines that made up the T at the start of the word TWO met each other.

'Why there?' the DC asked.

Bernie lifted his hand and held it in front of his face. He rubbed his index finger across his mouth like he was applying lipstick, then drew a T shape in the air with the same finger.

I said the words out loud as I realised what his re-enactment was getting at. 'That's the spot where most people would start when writing the letter T, the place where the top layer of lipstick will be, so if it's been used before, that's where there could possibly be traces of saliva, if there was any on there to start with.'

Bernie pointed his fake lipstick finger at me. 'A star, Miss Washington, go to the top of the class, collect a lollipop on your way out.'

'Could be Falstead's own lipstick,' said another officer to my right. 'There's clearly been a struggle, with her phone being dropped; maybe she had lipstick on her too, and whoever's grabbed her has used it to write the words when it's fallen out of her bag or pocket or something.'

'Very possible,' Bernie said, 'but my guess would be this person planned on leaving a message behind to add to their little collection of *odes to a death threat*, so odds are they'd have brought something along to write it out with, not just waited to see if she happened to have anything on her they could use, and for the price of getting a couple of swabs looked at it's worth a punt, I'd say. We can get a sample of her DNA easy enough to rule her out before loading anything to the database, just need her toothbrush or something.' Bernie carried on talking the group through some other images of the general scene, layout of the area and possible access points.

'Thanks, Bernie,' Carver said. 'Right, OK, over to Bret, who's going to be leading this one for us.'

What the hell? Why would the intel bureau be leading the job? Bret pushed himself from the desk he'd been leaning on and joined Carver, who slapped his back to pass on the proverbial baton.

'No pressure, eh,' Carver said. 'Don't say we didn't give

you anything to do on your first day in the MCU.' He guf-
fawed before standing off to one side as Bret started dishing
out instructions about area searches and vehicle registration
checks like the OIC he'd clearly been appointed as.

Since when had there been a new vacancy in the MCU?
I hadn't seen anything advertised. No wonder Bret wanted
to keep his lips zipped about work at kickboxing, keep
his entry to the literal backslapping boys' club under the
radar. Was that why he'd been interested to know why
Gordy had summonsed me the other day? Not actually
giving a shit if everything was OK, more to see if he was
going to have any competition? I was dragged from my
thoughts as Bret said my name, the sea of heads swivelling
to face me.

'You can give us a run-through of yesterday's event,
yeah?' he asked.

Shit. I'd missed the start of what he'd said, which was
clearly visible on my face as he paused, probably thinking
of the best quip he could use to shame me in front of the
whole team, show once and for all why he deserved to be
in the MCU instead of me. Thankfully my brain kicked in
before he had the chance. Yesterday. He must have been
talking about Tabby thinking she'd seen someone in the
woods. 'We turned up just as it happened. One of my DCs
and the band's security team checked the area. There was
no sign of anyone. And from her own account, she wasn't
sure she'd actually seen someone; there was a suggestion
she may have just heard something and got freaked out –
they're all very understandably on edge at the moment.'

194

'Well, Bret said we know for sure someone was doing more than watching at the reservoir, and it seems unlikely this person just stumbled across them down there. Most likely bet is they've followed them there from the retreat, maybe our mystery woodland lurker, which means they know where the rest of them are staying. We need to get them out of there before another one gets picked off.'

Was he implying this was my fault? Hindsight was a fine thing indeed, but there wasn't much more Roy and I could have done based on the information presented to us. I opened my mouth to defend myself but Bret beat me to it.

'You've already got the rapport with them, so it makes sense for you to liaise with the band, talk to them about relocating, yeah?' There was no point arguing. Bret was in charge here. And there was nothing I could do about that. I nodded, retracting my claws slightly at the small acknowledgement of my victim communication skills. 'And Ryan Hope and Tabby's family, they'll need to be kept informed too,' he said.

I nodded.

'OK,' Bret said, clapping his hands together. 'Let's get to work.'

Chairs scraped as the crowd shuffled from the room. I waited for everyone to leave and took a deep breath before approaching Bret, who was in the process of unplugging the laptop from the screen. There was no way I could keep what I'd learned from Kit to myself with Tabby's life potentially on the line. If what was happening now was linked to what happened to Ris, Bret needed to know about it. I'd just have to get creative about how I put that information across. I couldn't blurt out my suspicions about the original investigation, especially not now it was clear Bret had officially signed up to the MCU club, somehow getting in there without the job even being advertised. Surely he'd tell tales to Gordy Scott faster than I could get the words out. And what I had was flimsy at best. There was no doubt questions needed to be answered, but that and a gut feeling didn't prove anything.

Bret looked up as he noticed me hovering beside him. 'Problem?' he said.

'Those first threats on socials referred to Dee Dee, and Ris's death is included in this sick countdown. Maybe it's worth me having a look back through the old case file, see if there's anything in there, someone involved in the original investigation who could be linked.'

He thought for a while before responding. 'Can't hurt. Keep me updated, yeah?'

I nodded and left, hoping no one would notice I'd put in my request for exhibits from the pit before getting the green light.

24

The headache that had brewed in the car was in full swing by the time I got back to Fortbridge. I climbed the stairs to the CID office, massaging my temples and praying it would be empty and therefore quiet, giving me time to think. Luck clearly wasn't on my side: as I opened the door, I saw Roy sitting at his desk eating a banana and Eddie on the other side of the room on the phone.

'All fun and games up at HQ, then?' Roy said. He took a final mouthful of banana and rubbed its skin on his face like it was the most normal action in the world.

I stopped mid-stride. 'What in God's name are you doing?'

'Natural moisturiser, this,' he said, holding the floppy yellow skin out towards me. 'Trudy says it's got some shit in it that gets rid of puffiness and wrinkles. I'll be as smooth as a baby's backside in no time. You wanna turn? No offence, but you look like you've gone twelve rounds with Mohammed Ali.'

First Terry with his half-chewed plum, then the lowdown on Tabby's disappearance, now this, as if I didn't have enough going on to knock me sick. 'I'll stick with good old soap and water. Eddie, can you round everyone up, please, I've got some jobs to dish out.'

Five minutes later I conducted a mini briefing in the CID office and sent the team off on various local tasks to support the MCU in the hunt for Tabby. 'Roy, you take updating Ryan, please; I'll speak to the band about getting them moved out of Aurora House; Bernie's already been in touch directly about picking up Tabby's toothbrush.'

Eddie piped up, 'You seen this, Sarge?' He held his phone out. 'They've just posted on The Dolls' Instagram account.'

I took the handset from him to get a closer look. It was the same promotion photograph I'd seen announcing their performance now re-posted with the word CANCELLED across the middle. I scanned the caption, asking people to respect the band's privacy at this difficult time and requesting everyone join them with their thoughts and prayers for Tabby's safe return.

At least no more festival appearance gave me one less thing to worry about. With Em and Nush out of the spotlight, there would be less opportunity for them to be picked off next. 'Thanks, Eddie.' I handed him back his mobile and reached for the phone on my desk so I could call the band.

'Wait,' Eddie said, 'there's more.' He tapped a couple of times on his screen and turned the phone around again as a reel began to play. It was Tabby Falstead.

'What the—?' I snatched the phone back, the video pausing as I accidentally hit the screen. 'Is this thing live?'

'No, no,' Eddie said, re-starting the video as Roy joined our little viewing party. 'Posted yesterday morning before she went missing but it's gone viral, 'cause everyone's commenting on it now.'

Tabby was sat against a plain white wall in the footage, recording herself in what I'd heard was referred to as 'the golden hour', either immediately after sunrise or sunset when natural light was at its most flattering. Her blonde curls were pulled to one side of her head, the perfect combination of 'just got out of bed mess' with a 'this is my natural look' amount of zhooshing. She pouted her lips before she started talking.

'People and things come into our lives for a reason, even when those things seem negative at first, and I very much feel these threats have come into our lives with purpose. To show that we are strong and powerful souls who will not cower. We will self-heal. We will revive. So I'd like to thank whoever is doing this. Because you have taught us that we are stronger than you'll ever know, and we could not be more excited to come and share that strength with you at next week's festival. The event is sold out, hashtag blessed, but we'll be live-streaming via our drone so you can catch all the action by subscribing to my page.'

'Bold move, isn't it?' Roy said. 'Thanking someone for wanting you dead? Might as well be waving a red flag to a bull!'

'D'you think the person who took her saw it?' Eddie said. 'Wanted to prove a point?'

Comments popped up along the bottom of the screen as the video replayed. 'Keep an eye on that commentary, yeah?' I said. 'Whoever's doing this clearly doesn't like to be challenged. Maybe they won't be able to resist a jab at all these well-wishers. What with the social threats and what they left behind at the reservoir, they clearly like to put on a show.'

My two supposedly simple tasks of contacting Tabby's parents and getting the band out of Aurora House ended up being more difficult than I'd hoped. After being told by Sherrie point blank they weren't leaving the retreat until Tabby was found, as if she was clinging to the hope Tabby would find her way back there like some sort of homing pigeon, I'd finally managed to track Lord and Lady Falstead down to a yacht somewhere in the South Pacific after everyone else had left for the day. They assured me they'd be on the next available flight to London, though given their location, that'd be at least a few days. While they sounded concerned, I couldn't help but notice the tinge of annoyance at the inconvenience of having to cut their trip short. I thought back to my discussion with Em and her suggestion that rich in money didn't equate to rich in love. Had any of these people had normal upbringings?

Once I'd completed my tasks, I called the diner to check if anyone had handed in my purse. They had, so I grabbed my keys and made my way over there to collect it. Pausing in the car outside before going in, I made a quick call.

'All right, kid, how's things?' Dad said.

I filled him in on Tabby's disappearance.

A light *woomph* sound puffed down the phone, like he'd flopped on to the sofa. 'Shit. I've been out in the garden all day, I haven't seen the news. Poor lass – any leads?'

'Nothing yet. There's a theory I'm working on, though. The threats make reference to Ris's murder, so maybe it's someone who knew them back then, knew Dee Dee, thinks they're carrying on what she started. Can you remember if there was anyone else in the picture for Ris's job, you know, before everything pointed to Dee Dee? Anyone on the periphery?'

He whistled. 'Not that I remember. There was never any other official suspects, no one else who the team were worried about. Like you say, every single thing pointed towards Dee Dee; nothing pointed in any other direction.'

'Right, course.'

'You should ask Gordy, he'd know better than anyone.'

'Yeah, yeah, I will.' I absolutely would not. Because if Kit's theory was true, Gordy would be the last person who'd want to hear about it. 'Never mind, bit of a silly gut-feel thought anyway, that's all I was calling for.'

'You're not still at work, are you?'

'No, I'm in a much more glamorous location sat in a diner car park.'

'Oh, right, dinner plans, eh? Anyone special?' he said, a hint of cautious hope in his voice.

'Erm, yeah, maybe, I dunno.' What the hell? Why on earth had I lied? I scrunched my eyes as if the action would wind back the last couple of seconds.

'Maybe you will have someone to bring to that barbecue after all.'

I jabbed at my forehead with the heel of my palm. 'Maybe

a bit too soon for that yet.' *Yeah, and don't forget your imaginary friend has a very busy schedule; they're probably not available at such short notice.*

'Well, the offer's there.'

I made my excuses to go before I dug myself deeper into my pointless lie.

'OK, you take care, kid, bye.'

I didn't have the energy to dissect whatever the hell that was, so I shoved my phone into my pocket, deciding to pretend the entire exchange hadn't happened.

Inside the diner, the man behind the counter nodded in recognition as I repeated our earlier phone conversation about my purse before he disappeared out back to retrieve it. I turned and leant against the bar, scanning the room. Thankfully, there was no sign of Pewy McPewface from the other night, and the arcade game was left in peace, but the place was full. Every booth and table filled with a variety of people. Parents and children. Friend groups. Couples. A few solo diners who—

My eyes fixed on the table in the back corner, on one solo diner in particular whose table was full of food. Burger and chips on a plate with several napkin-filled baskets surrounding it, enough to be an indulgent meal for a party of four. I marched over to the table and stood beside it, arms folded, coughing to make my presence known.

Roy looked up, his mouth agape, about to bite into his burger. He froze like an animal hoping the predator stalking it wouldn't notice it if it stayed still long enough. I slid into the booth opposite him and scanned the table. The baskets bulged with chicken wings, potato wedges, and mac and cheese.

'This isn't what it looks like,' Roy said, putting the burger down and staring at me like I was his wife who'd caught him in bed with another woman.

'It looks like you're eating some proper food for the first time in months while Trudy is distracted by her sister visiting.'

'All right, I guess it's exactly what it looks like.' Roy picked up a potato wedge and stuffed it in his mouth, chewing slowly. 'I'm trying, I really am, and the things Trudy makes *are* lovely, but I'm bleedin' starving. *All* the time. Almost ate the dog in me sleep the other night, dreamt she was a literal hotdog.'

'I'm not surprised. I mean, you could do with eating a bit healthier, but the way Trudy's got you going you'll disappear if you're not careful. You don't have to bend to everything she asks, you know, you're a grown man who can have a bacon sarnie every once in a while.'

'It's not her fault, she's not forcing me or anything, just suggested it with the whole "starting afresh" thing, and she's got really into it and I . . .' He looked away from me, picking at the edge of a napkin as his cheeks reddened. 'I didn't wanna be a disappointment, not *again*.' My heart broke a little for him but I didn't know what to say, so instead I picked up a potato wedge in the hope that my eating it would indicate solidarity. He followed suit, licking the salty coating off his fingers before he started talking again. 'After everything I put Karen through, I want things to be different with Trudy.'

'The Trudy who turned up to your hospital room last year did so because of the old Roy, not this new kale-munching one. She loves you for you, for some reason. Talk to her. I'm sure the fact you're not quite as into her home-made hummus as she is isn't going to be a deal breaker.'

'Thanks, Sarge,' he said, picking up the basket of chicken wings and holding it out towards me. 'Want one?'

'I should probably have more than one, help you be at least a little bit healthy still.'

I picked up a wing and was about to take a bite as my phone rang. This better not be Irma following up on the lie I'd told Dad, wanting to know every detail about my non-existent date. 'Sorry, one sec.' I wiped the buffalo sauce off my fingertips and went outside. The call was from a number I didn't have stored in my contacts. 'DS Alice Washington.'

'Hi, erm, it's Kit. Kit Ashton.'

The hairs on my arms stood on end despite the muggy heat. 'Is everything OK?'

'Yeah, fine. Sorry, I was going to call when we realised Tabby was gone but Sherrie had already called 999 and I didn't want to ... you know ... I dunno what the protocol is for this. Then we all got interviewed and, I dunno, this is the first time I've had a moment to myself. I didn't want to say the wrong thing, mess anything up.'

'Kit, you tell the police anything you feel you need to, OK? Don't hold anything back you think might be useful, you won't be in any trouble.'

'I didn't tell them about the transcript. I didn't see how it would help anything, given we don't know who it is or what it really means.'

'That's completely up to you, but I happen to agree. I haven't mentioned it either, but that's only because I'm not convinced it actually tells us anything. I'm still looking into it, in case it can help us find Tabby, but of course if I find anything more substantial then I'll have to report it, d'you understand?'

'Yeah, I get it, I'm not stupid. And with everything that's gone on, I haven't been able to speak to Judith yet, about reining it in with her letters, but I will.'

'OK, thanks. You take care of yourself, yeah?' I said, going to hang up.

'Wait,' Kit said, 'don't go, there was something I wanted to ask.'

I peered through the window, checking Roy was still out of earshot. 'Go on.'

'Are you free tomorrow night? I need to show you something.'

'What? Why can't you just tell me now?'

'No, it's something you need to see with your own eyes, it might help. There's a band on at the Big Top Ballroom up in town, where Ris died.'

What could Kit possibly think would be useful to show me at the venue ten years after the fact? 'And?'

'You asked me to trust you to look into this, now I'm asking you to trust me.'

'Can't you tell me what it is and I can go look for myself?

If Sherrie is going to insist you all stay at Aurora House with the increased security, d'you really think it's a good idea for you to be swanning off on your own?'

'No one's actually threatening *me*, remember? No one even knows who I am, and I'm gonna go crazy if I don't get a break from the band. You saw how much they were at each other before – how d'you think they are now, worrying and with none of them sleeping properly?'

She had me there. 'Fine, what time does it start?'

'Nine thirty. Doors open at nine.'

'Do you need me to come get you?'

'No, I'll meet you outside. Nine o'clock,' she said before hanging up.

What the hell are you doing? I almost screamed at myself before taking a deep breath and going back into the diner.

'Everything all right?' Roy asked.

I thought about telling him what Kit had told me, but Roy had enough problems of his own, he didn't need dragging into this quagmire with me. I'd tell him if I found something more solid, but the best thing I could do for him right now was give him plausible deniability.

'Fine. You got room for dessert?'

25

A wolf in sheep's clothing. How early they teach us. Look out for the kindly stranger, look out for the mask, look out for the real face, not the one they want you to see. Do not be fooled by the wolf in sheep's clothing.

But who is the wolf here and who is the sheep?

Your clothing is your skin, a permanent suit you never take off to hide what's inside. Keep it in until I force it out. Because I will. I'll claw and scratch and peel it away until it's gone. Slowly, slowly now, slip yours off to wear like it was my own. Would they notice then? Would they see? You wear mine and I wear yours – now who is the wolf and who is the sheep?

26

Day two of the investigation into Tabby's disappearance had gotten us nowhere, not one bit of positive news in either the morning or afternoon briefing calls. No sightings, no contact from whoever had taken her and nothing significant found in the subsequent area searches. Part of me wanted to call Kit and cancel our meet-up. It felt wrong, clocking off when Tabby was still missing, but given the bulk of the work was being done by the MCU, there wasn't much else I could do other than sit here and twiddle my thumbs. And technically, this *was* work if it helped me figure out whether there was anything to Kit's theory or not, maybe give us another line of enquiry to interrogate.

I was outside the Big Top Ballroom by nine, surrounded by a gaggle of gurning twenty-year-olds who I was pretty sure would all have baggies of coke in their socks if I had the inclination to check. Vape clouds and drunken chatter filled the air, underscored by the *thump, thump, thump* of the bassline drifting out through the door, past the bouncers, before dispersing into the balmy night air.

Jesus Christ, you're too old for this.

I heard Kit before I saw her, purple Doc Martens with bright yellow laces clomping down the pavement.

'You're here,' she said.

'Said I'd come, didn't I?'

She snorted. 'I tend not to believe everything someone says just because they're a police officer.'

I couldn't really argue with that at the moment. 'Kept my word so far, haven't I?'

'S'pose,' she said, walking past me into the venue.

I'd never been in the Big Top Ballroom but could see where its name came from as I followed her inside, emerging from a short hallway into the main space. It was like being in some bohemian circus for giants, the domed ceiling a good fifty feet above our heads lined with materials of different colours and fabrics. I gawked upwards like a kid seeing a blanket of twinkling stars against a jet-black sky for the first time.

'It used to be a railway shed,' Kit said, 'where they fixed trains.' Clearly she was nothing if not thorough in her research. 'It's weird to think the people here that night would've been standing around just like this, getting drinks, waiting for The Dolls with no idea what was about to happen, and then to see that . . .'

'I can't imagine what that must've been like,' I said, looking at Kit, the glassiness I'd seen in her eyes at Aurora House the other night returning as if she'd been transported back to an equally horrific memory she'd rather forget. A thought struck me. *Had* she witnessed it, been in the crowd that night? Was that what was personal about this case for her? She'd have been in her early teens at the time, but it wasn't unusual for kids to get into over-eighteen venues, especially girls, capitalising on a mask of make-up to age them. 'Is that why you've brought me here, to see what you saw?'

Her face scrunched in confusion. 'What d'you mean?'

'Were you here the night Ris died?'

'What? No, what I came to show you, was this.' She took hold of my forearm and tugged me towards the steps leading down from the raised perimeter flooring on to the sunken dancefloor. We weaved between the people already gathered in small clusters, bagging the spots with the best vantage points for when the band came on. She stopped about two metres back from the stage off to the right-hand side. 'Look up there.' She pointed to the ledge above the stage, where Ris must have been pushed from. A chill ran through me as my gaze followed the route her body would have taken before smashing on to the stage. I forced the thought of her broken neck from my mind. 'What exactly am I looking at here?'

'Line of sight,' she said. She nodded towards where we'd stood when we first came in, up on the raised area that went around the outside of the room. 'From back up there, with the angle, you can see the stage roof clearly, but the view of the stage itself isn't great because of the pillars.' She pointed at several thick black posts holding up the ceiling. 'Everyone comes down here to get a better view of the stage, but from down here,' she said, craning her neck to look up at the ledge, 'you can barely see shit up there.

You'd see someone on the edge of the platform, looking over, but anyone even a step behind them would be out of most people's line of sight.'

I looked up at the obscured view. She wasn't wrong. 'Hmm.'

'Hmm indeed, and . . .' She pulled my arm again and we were off to the other side of the dancefloor, repeating the process in three different locations in total, all with the same restricted view, before we made our way back to the raised area around the dancefloor.

'All right, I get the point,' I said. 'But that's three people. There were almost three *thousand* people here that night. And even if someone else had been up there with Ris and Dee Dee, who are you suggesting it was? Because from what I can remember, all key people were accounted for. They were either in their dressing rooms or backstage.'

'So they *say*, but the band are fussy twats, they had their own individual dressing rooms. Very handy, no one to corroborate. And backstage is so busy before a show, how can they prove exact timings for being in particular places? There's no CCTV back there, I've already checked. And the witness statements weren't from thousands of people,' Kit said. 'Fans of The Dolls aren't exactly known for their love of the cops. Most people didn't want to get involved. And those who did, how many of them just *happened* to be looking up at the stage roof at exactly the right time? Look around us – most people are chatting, drinking, they aren't staring up at the ceiling. According to the few articles I've read, the police had three significant witness statements:

two from people who said they looked up straight away and saw Dee Dee glaring down, and one who swears blind they saw Dee Dee push her. But come on, there are studies that tell us eyewitness testimony is wrong all the time.'

'How do you know what the witnesses said they saw? And how do you know where they were standing?'

'Because,' she said, shrugging, 'I asked them.'

Who was this girl, Wessex's very own Lisbeth Salander? Though less girl with the dragon tattoo, more girl with the lower back ACAB tattoo. 'How do you know who they are?'

'You'd be amazed what you can find on the internet if you know where to ask, and people trip over themselves to be associated with things like this. One of them shared a video he'd taken just before it happened; it doesn't show anything juicy – only him and his mates "cheersing". He's stood right here. Nice bloke, but I'm sorry, there's no way he saw what he said he did.'

'Why lie though?' I asked.

'I don't think they're lying. I'm sure they think that's what they saw, and if you were to ask them again now they'd say the same. They saw Dee Dee, there's no denying she was up there. Then Ris hit the stage. I think their brain filled the gap in between. And I'm not brimming with confidence that whoever took their statements would have literally come and stood here to check.'

I certainly would have. It was common practice to ask about things like lighting conditions and how far away witnesses were from whatever it was they were giving a statement about. But how sure could I be that some overworked or under-caring DC back then hadn't just checked the general line of sight from the main area by the entrance?

An invisible fist punched me. What if someone else had been up there that night, influenced what Dee Dee did? Or what if Dee Dee didn't push Ris at all? What if someone else did and Dee Dee was covering for them?

'D'you believe me now?' Kit said.

I swallowed hard, my mouth getting dryer by the second.

'It's OK, you don't have to admit it out loud. Baby steps and all that.'

Before I had the chance to respond, a man appeared beside us and stroked Kit's arm.

'Hey, hey!' he said. 'You're too pretty to be standing still, come dance with me.' He held his hand out towards her in the hope she'd take it, but Kit didn't move.

He reached closer as if he was going to grab hold of her anyway and my instincts kicked in. Sliding myself between them, I mimicked his tone, 'Hey, hey, let's not touch people we don't know, OK? Why don't you go and dance by yourself, we're having a conversation.' I turned back towards Kit. 'You OK?'

She nodded as a firm finger tapped three times on my shoulder.

Fuck's sake.

I turned around again, old handsy still standing behind me, leaning forward, scanning me from head to toe.

'Do I know you?' he said, hot beer-tinged breath hitting my face.

'Doubt it.'

He wagged a finger at me. 'I do, I do know you. Name's Alice, right? The cop.' I scanned his face but didn't recognise him, which he could clearly tell from my expression. 'Jake, from WeMatch. I definitely remember you, 'cause I was thinking I'd love to see you in your uniform.' He winked and I almost vomited right in his sweaty face.

Now that he'd said the name, and if I squinted really hard, I could kind of see the resemblance to his profile photo. 'Right, Jake. Unless you didn't notice, I didn't reply to your message and I can't say your behaviour tonight has changed my mind on that front, so off you go, have a good night, yeah?'

Jake muttered under his breath, 'Fucking cock tease.'

I stepped towards him. 'Excuse me?'

He squared up to me, a cold smirk breaking out across his face. 'Nothing important, *officer*,' he practically spat at me before sloping off down the stairs to the dancefloor.

'Quite the catch,' Kit said.

Something crawled across my skin. I wasn't sure if it was fury or droplets of sweat. A woman in leather shorts and a crop top appeared next to me with a tray of shot glasses, their golden contents sloshing over the rims as she held them out towards us.

'Free shot, ladies? Best tequila in town,' she said.

My hand grabbed one and the liquid was already burning my throat before I even had time to think.

*   *   *

214

Was drinking with someone who'd be a witness in whatever review might be initiated off the back of all this a good idea? Nope. Was it the worst thing police officers seemed to be doing to bring the service into disrepute? Not even close.

I downed another shot. What was that? The sixth? Seventh? Who the fuck knew. I couldn't remember the last time I'd had spirits, and they were going straight to my head. 'We're not all bad, you know,' I said, the salt and lemon stinging a small ulcer on the inside of my lip. 'Most cops are bloody good people, bloody, bloody good people, s'just the ones that're bad or shit seem to be working overtime at the minute.'

Kit took another shot and winced. 'Urgh,' she said, shaking away the tang. 'Are you *not all men-ing* me right now?'

''Scuse me?' I stifled a burp with the back of my hand.

'*Not all cops*, like *not all men* when it comes to sexual harassment stuff. I'm not an idiot, I know every police officer doesn't turn into an arsehole the second they get their badge. But there are enough arseholes around that, when you're dealing with one, you have no idea if they're one of the good ones or one of these supposed "bad apples" your bosses seem to use as an excuse to dismiss every single one of the cases that hit the news, as if it's not a systemic issue. So, if it's all the same to you, I'll be on guard every time I see a uniform.'

She had that look on her face again, the glassy-eyed one. Something was going through her mind. Something painful.

'Look, I know I'm the last pershon you wanna talk to,' I slurred, my tongue failing to comply with my instructions to keep its shit together, 'but if there's shomething that's, you know, happened to you, involving police, you can tell me.'

'Why, so you can help cover it up?'

Her hand stayed on the table but the words sobered me like a cold, hard slap. 'Hey, I'm here, aren't I, came to see what you had to show me when I had no idea what it was. If something's wrong, I wanna make it right.'

Tears filled her eyes, more than glassy this time, pooling and overflowing her lower lashes. 'You can't. Unless you can go back in time and stop what happened to my dad.'

I *knew* it. I knew there was something. 'What happened?' I asked.

The story poured out as she fiddled with the K on her choker. About how letchy officers had turned up at her house and arrested her dad on suspicion of the murder of a woman he'd been seeing, a family friend. 'He was struggling after my mum left. Me and my sister weren't exactly the easiest kids, and the woman he was seeing, she was having problems with her husband too, and I guess they, I dunno, connected or whatever. They were discreet, but me and my sister knew there was something going on: secret phone calls, Dad coming home late, that sorta stuff. We didn't even know she was dead until the police came to the door. They'd found her in the boot of her car at the train station, her ... her throat had been slit. I knew there was no way my dad would do anything like that, he was the most gentle person, but the police didn't seem to give a shit about that, just hauled him in for no other reason than because he was seeing her.'

She paused, momentarily taking her hand away from her necklace to wipe tears from her cheeks before going straight back to it like she was clutching a comfort blanket. 'Long story short, it was her husband. He'd guessed something was going on, followed her and waited for my dad to leave after they'd met up, then killed her. But some idiot who worked in the custody suite and knew my family thought it was acceptable to get drunk and mouth off in the local about how Dad had been arrested, that they'd been having an affair, and you know what people are like. No smoke without fire. Some people still thought he'd done it even with the husband getting charged. And even the ones who didn't were still yapping shit about him being partly to blame for having the affair, like, what the fuck?' She paused, trying to collect herself, but the tears refused to stop. 'Dad threw himself off the top of a multi-storey car park, and I found out on social media because some vultures recorded it and put the video and pictures online. I saw everything, like, *everything*. I had to change my name, started using my grandma's maiden name because I couldn't get away from it all.'

That explained why no associated intel had come up on Kit's name check. And why she was hellbent on uncovering police failings. Now didn't seem the time to point out that of course the police would need to question the person a victim of murder was having an affair with, and if the shoe had been on the other foot and Kit was the dead woman's

SAM FRANCES

daughter, she'd be furious at the police if they *hadn't* investigated him. Regardless, her father's identity should never have been released in that way, and what she needed to see now was that I was listening. And seeing. Her almost constant contact with the letter on her choker while she'd been talking wasn't lost on me. 'I'm sorry, Kit. That should never have happened. What was his name, your dad?'

Kit wiped her cheek again, catching some stray tears. 'Ken.'

'That what the necklace is for?'

'Yeah, I like to keep it close to me, see it every time I look in the mirror.' Her face flushed like she'd shared more than she wanted to. She picked up her phone and checked the screen. 'Anyway, this isn't about me, and, well, I've done what I came here to do, so I better be getting back.'

'Sure. I might stay for a bit, catch the band.' I had no interest in the band, but the desire to keep drinking had hit me like I'd been caught in a fishing net, its weights pulling me down and trapping me in my seat.

Kit pushed herself off the stool and slung her bag over her shoulder. 'See you later then.' Walking past me towards the exit, she paused. 'And, er, thanks, yeah? For listening.'

A bubble filled my throat. 'Course.'

I wasn't sure how long I'd sat alone after Kit left, but it was long enough that I struggled to count the empty glasses on my table. Were there really that many or was I seeing double . . . triple? I rubbed my eyes as the twang of guitars and whomp of a bass drum vibrated through my bones and the next thing I knew I was on the dancefloor, as if the chair I'd been on had disintegrated beneath me, no longer holding me up, other people doing that now as the crowd crushed against me. Their collective force took control of my movement, swaying me back and forth, back and forth.

One song played. Then another. And another. Until I wasn't sure how many there'd been. Arms waved above my head. Their arms? My arms? No, not mine. Mine were pinned to my sides. I couldn't lift them. Blocked by the bulk of sweaty bodies, hot and sticky against me. More arms now, not flailing this time, but pulling, tugging at my waist. My head lolled as I followed the movement, stumbling, my feet separate to the rest of my body as I watched them tip over each other, willing them to listen to my instructions. But they carried on regardless. Across the dirty brown carpet, different coloured lights flashing across it. Before pavement, a gush of fresh air, then darkness.

27

Calling one of the security team for a lift back from town was the last thing Kit had wanted to do, but she'd missed the last train and four Ubers in a row had cancelled on her. She thanked the stars that at least it wasn't Manu who'd come to get her. Despite being as sure as she could be he didn't recognise her, she was still avoiding one on one time with him like the plague, just in case.

It was gone midnight by the time they got back to Aurora House, Em and Nush's voices wafting into the atrium from the kitchen. *Fuck.* She'd hoped they would either be in bed or in the studio taking out their frustrations on their instruments. Kit made for the stairs, her short spell of luck expiring as Manu stepped out from the office. He nodded towards the voices.

'Said they wanted to see you when you got back,' he murmured.

'I'll talk to them in the morning, I'm knackered,' Kit said, letting her hair fall across the side of her face closest to Manu as she made to move past him and carry on up to her room.

The combination of movements that came next happened in such rapid succession that she wasn't a hundred percent sure the pair of them hadn't just skipped forward in time. His wide frame, well over a foot taller than her and at least seventy pounds heavier, lurching forward to block her path as he took hold of her forearm. Her instinctively stepping back to gain stability, relaxing her wrist before rotating it with force towards Manu's thumb, whipping it back away from him so he couldn't grab it again. Just like she'd done a million times before and would have done earlier with the creep at the club if DS Washington hadn't felt the need to play the role of dame in shining armour.

She knew it had looked like an overreaction from his point of view the second she saw the confusion on his face, his head cocked to one side. Wait, was that confusion, or recognition? *Shit*. So much for keeping a low fucking profile with this guy. He opened his mouth to speak, but it wasn't his voice that flowed into her ears, it was Nush's as she appeared in the kitchen doorway.

'Alreet, kitty cat,' Nush said, 'ya dirty little stop-out. Get your arse in here.'

Manu was still squinting at her, but he closed his mouth and walked back into the office without any follow-up. Whatever he had to say would have to wait.

Kit forced the anxiety from her body and did her best to adopt a casual swagger as she followed Nush into the kitchen, entering to see Em sat at the dining table. Several wine bottles and food bowls were strewn in front of her, the only light coming from a standing lamp in one corner casting an elongated shadow version of Em's head across the tabletop.

Nush sat down opposite Em and pulled out the chair beside her, patting its seat. 'Come and sit down, have a drink.' She picked up empty wine bottle after empty wine bottle before shrugging when she realised there wasn't a drop left in any of them. 'Soz, here, have a . . . a . . .' Nush grabbed the nearest thing to her and presented it like a sacred offering from one of the three wise men. 'Will a bag of Quavers do ya?'

Em reached across the table and snatched them. 'Oi, they're mine.'

'You've already had about four bags, man, ya greedy bint,' Nush said.

Bursting the packet open, Em shoved a handful of crisps into her mouth, crumbs falling out as she talked. 'I think we've got bigger problems right now than too many E numbers.'

'Any news on Tabby?' Kit asked as she sat down next to Nush.

Em shook her head.

'Nar, nowt yet,' Nush said, picking up one of the wine bottles and going to take a swig before remembering it was empty.

Em looked up. 'Yet? You need to stop kidding yourself, mate, she's been gone over forty-eight hours. Have you ever seen a single cop show? The first twenty-four hours are—'

'How many times have I gotta say?' Nush interjected. 'Wind ya neck in, will ya? Nee one asked for an encore from the talking fuckin' clock. Have some faith for once

222

in ya life.' She stood and went over to the digital radio on the breakfast counter. 'Here, let's cheer ourselves up a bit, can't go wrong with a boogie.' She turned it on, her eyes lighting up as soon as she recognised the song playing, 'Gypsy' by Fleetwood Mac. 'Howay, man, how's that for giving ya some faith, this is Tabby's favourite song. It's a sign, I'm tellin' ya.'

Em sat back in her chair and folded her arms. 'No, it's not. She just *tells* people it's her favourite song because it sounds cooler than her telling the truth and admitting it's really "Moves Like Jagger".'

Nush fiddled with the hem of her striped T-shirt as tears rushed her eyes. 'She did like singing them Christina Aguilera bits. Her and Ryan deein' them stupid duets on the tour bus, d'ya remember?' She leant back against the kitchen cabinet and slid down it to the floor.

'Are you OK?' Kit said, getting up and kneeling beside Nush.

'Do I look OK? What if Em's right? What if Tabby's dead? And we're next?'

Em's chair legs scraped against the tiles as she got up and marched over, squatting on her haunches in front of Nush. 'Hey, whatever might've happened to Tabs, we are *not* gonna be next. I won't let it happen, all right?' she said, before manoeuvring herself until she was sat beside Nush, draping an arm across her shoulder.

For a second, there was a glimpse of the friendship Kit recalled seeing in the band's early days, and she saw an opportunity. Taking advantage of the fact that the wine

223

and their worries might make them more likely to let their guards down didn't feel good. But this was bigger than her, bigger than them; this was about finding the truth about Ris's death. She was still considering the best way to gently steer the conversation when the main lights flicked on and they all turned to face the door, a tired-looking Sherrie standing by the switch.

'Dora finished exploring, has she?' Sherrie said, looking at Kit, her eyes widening as she saw Nush and Em huddled on the floor. 'What's going on, what's happened?'

Nush wiped tears from her cheeks. 'Nowt, we're just worried about Tabby.'

Sherrie walked over and stuck a hand in front of them both, pulling them to their feet in one swift movement before bringing them in for a hug, Nush returning the gesture, Em's arms dangling by her sides like a child forced to give an aunt a goodbye kiss at Christmas. 'I know, but come on, we've gotta stay positive. She's more robust than she looks, that one; she's a fighter, under all that hair. You all are, all right? Trust me, my dad trained some of the best boxers in North London in the seventies, I know my fighters when I see 'em. Now, go on, get yourselves off to bed, yeah? Some shut-eye'll do you good,' she said.

They nodded, slowly making for the door. Kit watched the two of them go before Sherrie's gaze swung to her. 'D'you need a hand clearing this lot up?' Kit asked.

'No, you get yourself up to bed as well,' Sherrie said. 'Trust me, I'm used to cleaning up this lot's mess.'

* * *

In her room, Kit pulled out her phone and called Judith. The ringing lasted far longer than usual and Kit was on the verge of hanging up when Judith finally answered, her voice muffled.

'Yeah?'

The small talk was reducing every time they spoke, Judith too desperate for a sliver of good news to bother with niceties. 'Everything OK?' Kit asked.

'I'm fine. Look, I'm in the middle of something here, what's wrong?'

'Nothing's wrong, well, not really, but you need to stop writing letters, Judith, to the police – it's not helping anything.'

'How d'you know about my letters?' Judith said, the volume of her voice coming in and out as if she wasn't holding the phone a consistent distance from her face, moving it away then back again.

'That cop told me, DS Washington.'

The shift in tone from curiosity to anger was instant. 'Oh right, you and her in cahoots now, are you – that how it's gonna be?'

'Calm down. She's listening to me, at least, looking into stuff, which is more than they seem to be doing with your letters. You're giving them fuel to dismiss you as a crazy person. Just leave it to me, like we agreed. I think I'm getting somewhere. You need to give it time, yeah?'

Judith practically spat her next words down the phone. 'Time? Me and my Dee Dee've lost enough time already! I want my girl outta that place. No more waiting around, no more letters.' The rage melted to tears as Judith sobbed.

Kit had reminded Judith numerous times that finding the truth might not mean total exoneration for Dee Dee. She'd still been involved in Ris's death somehow, that was clear. And Judith had seemed to understand that, so what had changed? Kit's mind replayed the last few minutes of their conversation, the rollercoaster of Judith's mood. 'You haven't, you know, taken anything, have you?' A noise came down the line from the back of Judith's throat that started as a derisive snort but turned into a violent cough. 'Judith, are you OK?'

'I'm fine, and no, I haven't taken anything. Look, I've gotta go, yeah?'

'Wait, I believe you, and I didn't mean to accuse you, it's just . . . I get it, this is a stressful time, so if you need to talk, you know I'm here.' Kit couldn't help but feel sorry for Judith. She knew all about Dee Dee's childhood, but at least Judith had stuck around, given mothering a go, even if she had been crap at it. Having had her own mother walk out on her and her sister when she was still in primary school meant Kit knew first-hand she'd have given anything to have a shit mum compared to none at all.

'Talking,' Judith scoffed. 'Let's see how far that gets us.'

Kit went to reply but Judith had already hung up.

28

Slowly coming to after a fitful, alcohol-fuelled sleep, I winced at the sunlight streaming in through the thin white curtains. If someone told me a family of rats had taken up residency under my tongue during the night before curling into a ball and dying, the taste in my mouth would have made me believe them without hesitation. The head-spinning started the instant I dragged myself off the pillow. 'Jesus Christ.'

I took a second to find my bearings, blinking repeatedly in the hope that re-setting my vision would help me recognise my surroundings. The bedding I was wrapped in was white. I didn't own white bedding. I'd learned a long time ago that trying to keep anything white with Vince's dirty little paws rampaging everywhere was a lost cause. This wasn't my bed.

Where the hell are you?

Nausea stirred as I scanned the rest of the room. It was plain. Beige walls. A white wooden wardrobe. White bedside table. No décor on the walls. No shelves. No trinkets or property giving any telltale signs of the owner.

Oh God, oh God, oh God, oh God.

Hazy memories shifted in and out of focus. Kit. The dickhead from the dating app. Drinking. More drinking. Then dancing. Then ... nothing. Had I been so desperate to have something going on in my life other than work that I'd gone home with some random? It couldn't be Jake. I wouldn't have stooped *that* low, would I?

I was about to throw myself out of the bed and find a way to shimmy down the drainpipe when the sound of people talking seeped through the floor from downstairs. The first voice was deep. I strained my ears, listening. The second voice was speaking now. Quieter. Higher pitched. The hairs on the back of my neck rose. Because the second voice was female.

Was someone chatting to their missus while I festered upstairs? *Oh, good morning, rock bottom, I hear you've been expecting me in your VIP lounge.* I stayed still, praying that if I did so long enough I'd be transported back to my own room, wiping sweat from my brow after a nightmare. But no matter how hard I willed myself to, I didn't disappear. And worse than that, the high-pitched voice was getting louder, closer, accompanied by footsteps on the stairs.

Fuuuuck!

The door burst open before I had a chance to think. I yanked the covers over my head.

For several seconds, there was silence.

'Hello under there.' It wasn't the voice of a woman, it was a child. I stayed stock-still. 'Hellooo?' she said again, quietly, before raising her voice and shouting, 'Uncle Bret, I think she might be dead.'

My hand flew to my mouth, quelling both a 'FUCK MY FUCKING LIFE' and the puke that was refusing to take no for an answer simultaneously. *Bret? You went home with Bret?* I pressed my knuckles into my eye sockets and wondered what the next rung down the ladder from the rock bottom VIP area was.

The voice had gone quiet but I could still sense her presence. I tugged the duvet down, scrunching it tightly around my neck. A little girl was standing in the doorway. Thin, tousled waves of long, mousey-blonde hair cascaded across a baggy white T-shirt, almost touching the waistband of her black cycling shorts, the only pop of colour coming from the pair of red glasses that looked too big for her small, round face. 'Er, hello,' I croaked.

More footsteps bounded up the stairs and Bret filled the doorframe behind the girl. He placed his hands on her shoulders. 'Pips, why don't you go downstairs and pour out some orange juice? I'll be down in a sec, OK?'

My stomach clenched and threatened a mutiny. 'No juice for me.' *No, nothing for you. No food, no drink, no more shall pass your lips again, you're joining a monastery.*

The girl pushed the bridge of her glasses up her nose. 'I'll pour you a glass in case you change your mind. Orange juice has lots of electrolytes and vitamin C. It's good for rehydration.'

My mouth gaped in confusion as I scanned her again, rubbing my eyes to check it was actually a child stood in front of me and not a really short fifty-year-old pharmacist. The girl turned and walked away, her small feet pitter-pattering down the stairs.

'What the hell was *that* and, more importantly, what the fuck am I doing here?' I said.

'That,' Bret said, pointing over his shoulder towards the stairs, 'would be my niece, Pippa. Ten going on a hundred and ten. And you're here because when I bumped into you outside the Big Top Ballroom last night you could barely walk, let alone get yourself home. Mind you, you were doing a half-decent job of trying to fight the bouncer who'd chucked you out. I tried putting you in a cab but you couldn't remember your address, and I don't know it, so I didn't really have much choice but to bring you back here. And I didn't want to leave you on your own in case you choked to death, so I slept down there.' He pointed past me towards a pillow and camping mattress on the floor, peeking out past the end of the bed.

I suddenly felt extremely sheepish, even more so when I looked under the duvet and saw the shirt I was wearing wasn't mine. 'What were you even *doing* there anyway?' I said, deflecting harder than a politician caught up in a sex scandal as I pulled the duvet tighter around myself.

'Picking up a takeaway after my shift. It's been a long couple of days.'

The embarrassment was almost burning now, the fact I was treating this, albeit mortifying, situation as the worst thing in the world while Tabby Falstead was at best being held by some lunatic, at worst . . . 'Any news yet?' I asked.

230

'Nothing useful. Stayed late last night waiting for the DNA results on those lipstick swabs. Got a full profile from it, but it was Tabby's, checked it against a sample from her toothbrush. Clearly Bernie gave whoever's taken her too much credit to come prepared, or maybe they had no intention of writing the message until they saw her drop the lipstick and took an opportunity, I dunno, anyway, it's not getting us anywhere. And on that note,' he said, checking his watch, 'I need to get back into work.' He pulled the bedroom door towards him and nodded at my jeans that were hanging on the back of it. 'Your clothes are there, except your top, that's in the tumble dryer. It should be dry by now – not sure I got the stain out though.'

'Oh God, did I throw up on myself?'

'No. You found a spaghetti carbonara when you were rummaging around in the fridge and insisted I made it for you, but then you spilt the whole thing down your front.' I wasn't sure which was worse, to be honest. 'And don't worry, I didn't undress you, you did that yourself while singing a rather interesting version of "You Can Leave Your Hat On". I've never heard anyone do a rap version, it was quite something.'

The cringe burned so hard someone might as well have dipped me in a vat of acid. 'Was there dancing?'

Bret studied his nails. 'Not sure what you were doing classifies as dancing, but there was certainly . . . movement.'

Someone kill me. Kill me now. 'I am *so* sorry, hope I haven't scarred your niece for life.'

231

'I'm sure she'll be fine. She wasn't here last night, only got dropped off this morning.'

'Still, pass my apologies to her parents. I'm sure seeing the aftermath was bad enough. I'll pay for her therapy.' Bret scratched his head but didn't respond. 'Sorry, have I said something wrong?'

'No, nothing, just her parents aren't around, that's all. She lives with my mum.'

'Oh, right. Sorry.'

'It's fine. Look, erm, I'm dropping her down to Fortbridge actually, before I go into the office. D'you wanna lift back there or do you want taking into town? You said something last night about your car being there.'

Given how fast my head was spinning, I probably shouldn't be driving for at least a few hours. 'Fortbridge would be great, thanks, if you're sure. What's your niece doing going there?'

'There's something on at the bridge museum she wants to go to, a kids' club they're doing over the summer, and it's free childcare for the day until my mum can get her later.'

'Really? Are bridges that exciting to a ten-year-old?'

One side of Bret's mouth curved into a faint smile. 'Pips isn't your average ten-year-old. She's either going to grow up to be the leader of the free world or a crime kingpin. You can ask her about it in the car.'

I should have known Bret was setting me up as revenge for wasting a perfectly good carbonara when he told me to ask Pippa about why she wanted to learn more about the bridge. As if my headache wasn't bad enough already, she spent most of the thirty-minute drive giving me more information on eighteenth-century architecture than anyone should know. Ever.

'Is she running this open day thing or just attending it?' I said to Bret, before Pippa carried on.

'I'm making my way through the top ten,' she said. 'I've already been to the one in Ironbridge. That was the world's first single-span cast-iron bridge.'

'Right,' I said, doing my best to look interested, 'and was it, erm, good?'

She did a 'so-so' gesture with her hand. 'It was OK, I've got ideas for a better one.'

I nodded, impressed with her gumption. 'I'm sure you have.'

'I'm going to be an engineer,' she said proudly.

Bret shifted his head to look at her in the rear-view mirror. 'You've changed your tune, last month it was a doctor.'

'Yeah, but we were learning about other countries at school and that some of the poorest ones haven't got proper roads, so I read about what would help all the poor people in the world the most, and being a doctor is good because you can help people who are poorly, but it said maybe people wouldn't be as poorly in the first place if there were better roads and transport because my teacher said that makes people's quality of life better, so I'm going to do that instead.'

I was impressed. Normally I couldn't get away from

kids fast enough, but there was something intriguing about Pippa. She was like a little old lady in the body of a child, and it was confusing because I loved old ladies but generally didn't care for people under the age of thirty.

'And,' Pippa continued, 'Nana likes that idea better, 'cause she doesn't like doctors.'

Bret visibly clenched his hands tighter around the steering wheel. 'Pips, why don't you tell Alice about—'

Pippa carried on as if Bret hadn't spoken, 'She didn't like it when I said I wanted to be a doctor 'cause she blames doctors for my mum dying. It wasn't the doctors' fault, Nana just needed someone to be angry at, it's called deflection.'

'Oh, erm, I'm sorry to hear that,' I said, my gaze swinging from Pippa to Bret, his facial expression unchanged. 'I didn't know you had a sister.' I wasn't sure if it was the hangover confusing my senses, or how taken aback I was by Pippa's openness, but for some reason I had an overwhelming urge to tell them about my brother. I stopped myself before I opened the Fortbridge faction of the dead siblings society.

'He doesn't like to talk about it,' Pippa interjected. 'I think he's got alexithymia.'

Bret shook his head as if this was a debate he was used to rebuffing. 'I don't have— Right, that's it, no more medical journals for you. Just because I don't talk about my emotions every five minutes doesn't mean I don't have any.' The relief on Bret's face was clear as we pulled to an abrupt halt outside my driveway. 'Last week she convinced herself I had lupus because I took an afternoon nap,' he said in a clear attempt to brush off a nerve Pippa might as well have hit with a hammer.

'Right, well,' I said, pushing the door open, 'it was nice to meet you, Pippa.'

'You too,' she said, pushing her glasses back up her nose. 'Don't forget to replenish your electrolytes.'

I nodded a silent thanks towards Bret and pushed the door closed, before he revved the engine and drove off.

29

Neither the power nap nor the half loaf of bread I toasted and ate dry before walking into the office did anything to stave off my hangover.

'Morning,' Roy said as I trudged towards my desk. I wanted to take the attention off myself and ask if he'd had the food conversation with Trudy yet, but Eddie and one of the other DCs were hanging around so I held the thought. 'Those boxes are for you,' he continued, nodding towards three plastic containers stacked behind my desk. 'Terry brought them up this morning.'

'Thanks.' I slumped into my chair and took a swig of the Lucozade I'd picked up on my way in, the cold fizz burning my throat.

'What they for?' Roy said, still looking at the boxes.

'Just some stuff from Ris's murder investigation – wanted to get more of a feel for what happened with the band before. Dot i's, cross t's.'

'You wanna hope you find something in there, 'cause Bernie called this morning and there's bugger all of use fingerprint-wise from the dolls left at the festival ground.

236

He's sending a few swabs off to the lab this afternoon but he didn't sound hopeful of getting any DNA off 'em. And I've been ringing Ryan Hope for two days now, can't get hold of him.'

'Can't get hold of him as in you've spoken to Leigh and he's not been around, or . . .'

'As in no one's answering their phone.'

My stomach clenched, and it had nothing to do with my hangover. 'Get on to Devon and Cornwall, ask them to do a welfare check. They may just be holed up in there waiting for all this to blow over, but we can't be too careful.'

Roy nodded. 'Right, couple of other things. Intel have been on, there's nothing identifiable on that account that sent the original threats, not even with the handle spelt right this time, and I've had the checks back on the site workers and spoken to them all now, nothing of use. And Eddie's been through all the comments on Tabby's "Thanks for wanting to kill me" video: no more threats, just people either taking the piss, or other middle-class white girls namaste-ing her and congratulating her on her *journey*. Eddie's keeping an eye on the rest for us, ain't you, Ed?'

Eddie looked up from his screen and nodded. 'All over it.'

The NPT sergeant wouldn't be happy about Eddie spending all this time helping CID, but I had bigger worries right now. I nodded at Eddie, directing my next comment to Roy quietly under my breath, 'Careful, he'll be after your job next. Do you have *any* good news for me?'

'They haven't found a body yet,' he said, shrugging.

237

'Wow, the job's really coming to something if that's the most positive thing we've got. How about you, Eddie, anything back on the production company or any of the other jilted contestants?'

'Still looking, Sarge,' Eddie said.

'Right.' I turned my attention to the boxes from the pit. 'Let's see if this box of dusty crap gives me anything to work with.'

I made a note of the reference numbers on the zip ties holding the packing crates closed at each end before snipping them off. There were several exhibits inside, but I already knew what I was most interested in seeing: the notebook. Pulling on a pair of latex gloves, I rummaged before finding it at the bottom of the box. I made an incision in the exhibit bag wide enough to slide the A5 notebook through, before tipping it on to the desk and thumbing through it. I was amazed the pages were still intact, given the ink coating them looked like it had been gouged into the surface with such force the author had been at risk of shredding the paper.

A shudder ran through me as I read, every page filled with darker and darker thoughts. I could see why they'd used it as part of their evidence into Dee Dee's state of mind, if it was hers, vitriol bursting from the pages. Though I was still none the wiser as to whether it *was* hers, since no names or identifying factors were mentioned.

I finished reading and went back to the digital case file. Scrolling through the attachment list, I started with the forensics documents. The first toxicology report showed a small amount of alcohol in Ris's system and low levels of LSD. I tutted – so much for Ryan's claims about drugs not being the band's thing outside of a few spliffs. What had he thought we were going to do, arrest him for some recreational drug use ten years after the fact? Like I didn't have enough paperwork already. I opened another report about segmented hair analysis. I'd never fail to be amazed at how lengths of hair could tell part of a person's life story, how roughly each centimetre gave a history of drug use, catching out many a supposed reformed addict. Analysis of Ris's hair suggested she'd been taking LSD for between one to two months before she was killed. I checked the DNA reports next: nothing but her own found underneath her fingernails. Dee Dee's custody report showed no injuries noted when she was arrested, no scratches. So it was unlikely Ris had used her nails to defend herself.

Another result told me that a mixed DNA profile with two clear contributors, matching samples taken from Ris and Dee Dee, had been found on the lapels of Ris's jacket. Usually mixed DNA profiles were a nightmare, an unhelpful swamp of genetic gunk, especially since the more sensitive the analysis techniques became, the more they detected. But reading the full report now, it made a little more sense why they'd submitted it; the jacket was brand new, a gift from the record label and worn for the first time that night, so transference from previous encounters with Dee Dee was unlikely. A brand-new jacket would also explain the cleaner result – no other DNA to confuse the interpretation of the mixture. Still, that didn't change the fact that finding Dee Dee's skin cells on the lapels didn't prove either way whether Dee Dee had pushed Ris.

I scanned through several other documents. Witness statements, including the accounts of the band, a breakdown of the venue CCTV, every single one of them telling me what I already knew. No smoking guns. No overlooked anomalies. Just the story as it had been told back then. I opened the transcript of one of Dee Dee's interviews, surprised to see Simon Carver's name as the one conducting it back in his DS days. I skimmed past the introductory formalities. Thankfully, it was of much better quality than the transcript Kit had found.

DS CARVER: Had you and Ris had any kind of falling-out?

D. NOLAN: [inaudible sound]

DS CARVER: Would you mind speaking up a little bit, for the benefit of the tape recording, Dee Dee?

D. NOLAN: I really did it I . . . I did it.

DS CARVER: Right, and now we just need you to help us understand what happened. Did you have any arguments, disagreements, that kind of thing?

D. NOLAN: I killed her.

DS CARVER: Yes, you've told us that, we have it recorded that you've said that, ok, what we are doing now is trying to get more information on how this has come to happen. So we just want to talk about what's happened from the start, in your own words. Can you talk me through that?

D. NOLAN: [inaudible] I did it I killed her.

DS CARVER: Why don't you have a drink of your water, all right, take a deep breath. Take as much time as you need, try to calm down and then we can go through what happened, ok? Tell us your side of it.

D. NOLAN: She's been a different person, like she's turned into someone else, someone I don't know and I [crying]

DS CARVER: Right, ok, that's good, Dee Dee, can you tell us a bit more about what you mean by that, how she's been different?

D. NOLAN: I [inaudible] I did that, I just, god I killed her I killed her.

I wasn't sure how many times Dee Dee would have repeated the damning words if there hadn't been an interruption to the interview, the transcript noting that a solicitor had turned up at the front desk demanding to see Dee Dee, some heavy hitter sent by the record label. From what I could tell, she'd initially refused legal representation, but given the next transcript recording was the solicitor reading out Dee Dee's prepared statement admitting the whole thing, she must have changed her mind.

The statement continued to reinforce what I already knew. That Dee Dee said she went to the Big Top to try and make up with Ris, to get back into the fold, Ris said some cruel things about her being a hanger-on and Dee Dee, realising her time with the band was over, made excuses to get Ris up on to the roof, then pushed her off it. There was no way anyone could say Carver had conducted the interview inappropriately, applied pressure to her in any way to coerce anything out of her. But even though I couldn't put my finger on what, something didn't seem right. I googled the name of Dee Dee's solicitor, tracking down a contact for his firm. I probably wouldn't get much out of him from behind his shield of legal privilege, but at least I could gauge a reaction to some cleverly worded questions. I'd leave the clever part to future me who wasn't hanging out their arse. *You're welcome, future Alice!*

I thought back to what Kit said about the gig that coincided with the change in Ris, their show at the Bull Ring Academy in Birmingham, the night they announced their US tour, six weeks before Ris's death. Six weeks, according to whoever the voice was in the transcript, during which someone, presumably Ris, had been trying to 'get over' something. I reopened the hair analysis report. Ris's LSD use had started approximately one to two months before she was killed. Had that been the night she'd started taking it? Celebrating the announcement? A step up in their careers equating to a step up in their rock-and-roll lifestyle? Something niggled in the pit of my stomach.

Googling THE DOLLS and BULL RING ACADEMY brought up several images. Most were of Ris on stage performing from various angles, her tiny body barely a blip on the stage, but somehow still obviously commanding it even in a static image. I kept scrolling until I got to a group photo of the band, plus Dee Dee and a few young men I didn't recognise. I clicked the link and it took me to an old Facebook post from Legends Nightclub. BANDS THAT PARTY TOGETHER, STAY TOGETHER! the caption said. I clicked the tags, one directing towards The Dolls' official Facebook page, the other now greyed out, like the page it led to was defunct. THE SAXONS – OFFICIAL, the text read. I opened another tab and googled The Saxons alongside the date of the Birmingham gig. They were listed as having been The Dolls' opening act that night, before clearly staying with them for what seemed like quite the after party. But what did any of this have to do with Ris and Dee Dee going cold towards each other? I scrolled through the comments on the group photo, mostly syco-phantic drivel, until one caught my eye.

ADZY LOADER: AYE AYE @OLIVERCAMPBELL
REMEMBER THIS? WHAT A NIGHT ;-) OLLIE OLLIE OLLIE,
OY OY OY!!!

I clicked on the poster's profile first. Adzy Loader was a little greyer around the edges in his current picture, but he was clearly the guy at the back of the group photo, peeking up between Em and Dee Dee's shoulders, both hands doing rock fingers, his stuck-out tongue practically touching the bottom of his chin. There weren't any recent posts, so I switched to the profile of Oliver Campbell, quickly matching the much neater, family-man version of him in his latest picture to the younger Oliver in the band photo. His head rested on the shoulder of a smiling but slightly stoned-looking Ris, arms wrapped firmly around her waist as she raised hers in the air, a can of lager in one hand and a half-smoked cigarette in the other.

It was only now I noticed Dee Dee was looking over at Ris and Oliver. Ryan was also staring at them. Oh, please don't let that be the reason this all started. Over a boy. Really? Dee Dee and Ris had been best friends since they were kids. I'd give them the benefit of the doubt that surely it would take more to end a lifetime of friendship in such a dramatic way.

I spent the next hour scanning every page of the case file looking for any references to the Birmingham gig, as well as anything that might hint towards any other possible suspects in the crates from the pit, finding nothing. But something *had* happened that night, I could feel it, and I was becoming more and more convinced that whatever it was had set off a chain of events that resulted in Ris's death. And for Dee Dee's sake – and Tabby's if this was linked to what was happening to the band now – I had to find out what.

30

After picking up my car from the street behind the Big Top Ballroom, I'd spent my rest days either glued to the news, never more than a few feet from my phone in case there was an update about Tabby, or doing various searches on both Oliver Campbell and The Saxons, as well as Dee Dee's solicitor.

Oliver had left his musician days behind him and was now the managing director of an insurance firm. Despite his company having several offices across the UK, I'd narrowed his workplace down to the Canary Wharf site after comparing street views of all the office fronts to the one behind him in his LinkedIn profile picture. A call to the law firm Dee Dee's solicitor worked at dashed my hopes of killing two birds with one stone on my trip to the Big Smoke; I could visit Oliver, but the man who'd represented Dee Dee had apparently given up law and emigrated to the Cayman Islands. A trip to London I could blag as part of this investigation. The Caribbean? Not so much.

I got an early train to Paddington then the Elizabeth line, my phone ringing as I emerged from the station at

Canary Wharf. I stood off to one side to avoid the throng of commuters and answered Roy's call. 'Yeah?'

'Morning, just wanted— Hello? Can you hear me? Where are you? Piccadilly Circus or something?'

I turned to face the wall, cupping my hand around the receiver to block out the background noise. 'Close but no cigar, Canary Wharf.'

'What you doing all the way over there?'

'I'll explain later, what's up?'

'Had an update from Devon and Cornwall this morning – they've been to Ryan's farm a couple of times this weekend, no sign of any of 'em. No Ryan. No Leigh. No little girl. No dog. Finally managed to speak to someone from the neighbouring property; apparently Leigh asked them to keep an eye on the place, said they were having a last-minute getaway.'

'They didn't mention they were thinking of going any-where when we were there.'

'Maybe he's swept her and the little 'un off somewhere. What's happened with Tabby's been all over the news, and they have got televisions in rural Devon, you know.'

Roy was probably right, but 'maybe' wasn't good enough to quieten my concern. 'Get a mobile number for one of them, we need to make sure they're all right.'

'Will do. What time you back? Jane's looking for you.'

Fuck's sake. I looked at my watch. 'Mid-afternoon, I reckon. Keep her busy until then.'

'Will do, see you later,' he said.

Pushing my worries about the Hope family away, I

brought up the map on my phone, typing in the address of the insurance broker office.

Given that Oliver Campbell didn't know why someone from the police was there to see him, twenty minutes seemed like a long time for him to leave me waiting in the plush reception of Abercrombie Towers. Finally, the lift opened with a *ping* and a woman in what looked like her early twenties called my name. She took me up four floors and swiped us through two sets of doors before we ended up outside an office.

She knocked once but didn't wait for a response before pushing the door open. 'Mr Campbell, I have a visitor for you.'

I hovered in the doorway as the man stood from behind a small desk. 'Thanks, Holly. Could you grab us a couple of drinks?' He looked at me. 'Tea? Coffee?'

'Just water's fine, thanks,' I said.

Holly scuttled away and closed the door behind her. Campbell pointed towards an empty chair. 'I didn't know you were coming today; I thought someone would've called first. I'll need to get the footage ready.'

'Sorry,' I said, lowering myself into the seat. 'What footage?'

'The CCTV.' The look on my face clearly spelled out confusion. 'Of the cleaner, helping himself to the laptops. You can see the whole thing clear as day, absolute moron.'

'I think there's been some confusion. I'm not here about stolen laptops.'

Panic rushed his face. 'Then why *are* you here? What's happened? Is it my wife? Or the girls? Has—'

I held up a palm. 'No, no, I'm not here about anything to do with your family, Mr Campbell. I'm investigating some threats made towards The Dolls, and the disappearance of one of their band members, Tabby Falstead. I believe you know them, or knew them, anyway, and I'd like to ask you a few questions.'

Discovering I wasn't here as the bringer of bad news about his family only half relaxed him. '*Me?* I'm not sure what use I can be. I saw on the news about Tabby, but I barely knew her, spoke to her for a total of about two minutes over ten years ago. What's this got to do with me?'

'My questions aren't about Tabby; they're about Ris Angelini.'

'Ris? I don't understand.'

I explained the case and my tentative link between what happened to Ris and the threats, but his face remained clouded in bewilderment.

'But ... that was ages ago. What's that got to do with threats being made now?'

'It might be nothing, but given the person making them has referenced Ris's death, and Dee Dee, it's a line of enquiry we're exploring, covering all bases.'

Beads of sweat bubbled on his top lip before he wiped them away, and I wasn't convinced it was caused solely by the warm temperature. 'I don't know what to tell you, I barely knew her. Met her once, that was it.'

I pulled my phone out of my pocket and held up the picture I'd found of them. 'You seem pretty close here.'

He ran his tongue across his top teeth. He knew something, I could feel it. 'It was a party, we were drinking, having a laugh.'

'What was your relationship to Ris?'

'There *was* no relationship. Look, what's this got to do with anything?'

I didn't have time for games and semantics. I'd be damned if the next note we found said THREE DOLLS DOWN TWO TO GO. 'Let's not mess around. I think something happened that night that could be relevant to my investigation. And if another member of that band gets hurt, and you know something that might've helped me stop it . . .'

He let out a deep breath and dropped his head into his hands. 'I wish we'd never done that bloody show now. I didn't even want to do it in the first place. It was everyone else that wanted to, I was outvoted.'

'Why wouldn't you want to do it? The Dolls were huge, and no offence, but The Saxons weren't exactly a household name.'

'No, but at least we had a bit of credibility.' He lifted his head and shook it with regret. 'We started out with some, at least. Their crowds were massive, but they didn't have much respect in the industry, got booed off stage a few months earlier at the NME awards.'

'Why?' I asked.

He paused as Holly came back with the drinks, only starting again once she'd closed the door. 'Because most people don't get handed a record deal on a plate after a five-minute audition, especially not in the rock world. They practise in dirty garages, come up the hard way playing late-night gigs to single-figure crowds in venues where you're lucky if you get out of the place without catching legionnaires' disease.'

'So how did you end up opening for them?'

'Like I said, the others wanted in.' He sat back and clasped his hands around the back of his neck. 'We weren't their usual warm-up act, got drafted in about an hour before the show when the band they'd booked pulled out. We didn't even have time to meet them before we went on stage. They invited us to an after party they were throwing at some club as a thank you for stepping in.'

'And Ris?' I prompted.

He shrugged. 'She was nice. Chilled, you know? The rest of them were a bit much, but she was all right. And I understand what people mean about them not paying their dues, but there was no getting around the fact they were actually good, especially Ris. I mean, Christ, she opened the show that night with a Black Sabbath cover. Doing "Paranoid" in the hometown of Ozzy Osbourne takes some balls, especially in the Bull Ring. Everyone knew it was a tough crowd. And they only added it to the set that afternoon, first time she'd ever sung it. And she smashed it, made that song her own, wrapped herself around every syllable. You'd think it'd been written for her. I was impressed.' He looked past rather than at me, like he'd jumped back in time, before pulling himself from the memory and getting back to the point. 'We, erm, got chatting after the gig, then at the after party, and then . . . well, one thing led to another. We had a bit of a one-night stand.'

I bristled at the memory of the half-closed eyes of Ris in the photo. 'You said you'd all been drinking – how much?'

His eyes widened at the realisation of what I was getting at. 'No, it wasn't like that. We'd both had a drink, but we weren't out of it or anything.'

The toxicology report flashed behind my eyes, Ris's LSD use starting around the time of the Birmingham gig. 'Was alcohol all she'd had that night?'

'As far as I know, yeah.'

'No drugs? No going on a nice little acid trip together first, hmm? Heighten the experience?'

'I don't do drugs, never have, neither did she. That was actually one of the things that got us talking, about how we made pretty lame rock stars with our cans of Stella.'

'Mr Campbell, I'm not interested in your drug use, I've got bigger fish to fry. I know drugs on that scene go around like packets of After Eight mints and I also know Ris started taking LSD around the time of the Birmingham gig. Stop wasting my time, please.'

'I'm not—' He forced a loud exhale through his nose like he was trying to calm himself down. 'Look, officer, you have whatever preconceptions you want about the rock scene, all right, but all I can tell you is that when you've had to learn how to resuscitate your own dad because he'd over-dosed three times before you'd even made it to secondary school, I can promise you you're not exactly rushing to start tripping out anytime soon, even if you have got any drug you could ask for at your fingertips, trust me.'

My shoulders sagged. I'd officially overstepped the line with my attempt at a one-man show of good cop, bad cop. 'I'm sorry, Mr Campbell.'

'Ris, she'd had a similar experience with Dee Dee Nolan's mum; the pair of them had found her one time, when they were little, thought she was dead. That's why I'm as sure as I can be she wasn't on anything the night I spent with her.'

My mind whirred. Given her aversion to them, if something had happened to make Ris turn to drugs, it must have been something bad. 'Is there anything else you can tell me about that night, Mr Campbell?'

'We talked for ages before anything happened. And she was fine the next morning, she asked for my number, said she wanted to see me again.'

'And did you, see her again?'

He shook his head.

'Why?'

'She called me the next day, but before I had a chance to say hello she started having a go, asking me about photos.'

'What photos?'

He let out a deep breath. 'She said someone had photos of us, you know, in the middle of it.'

The hairs on my arms prickled like I'd stepped inside a fridge. 'Photos of you having sex?'

'Yeah.'

The text from the transcript re-played in my mind. The person on the phone saying something about Ris possibly being comforted to know 'no one else will see them'. Had they been talking about photos? 'Who had them? How did she know about them?'

He pushed his fingers through his hair. 'I don't know, honestly, she didn't say, just asked if I'd got one of my mates to do it as a joke. When I told her I didn't have a clue what she was talking about, she hung up.'

'So you don't think it could have been one of your band-mates?'

'No way, we weren't those kind of blokes.'

And hadn't I heard that a million times before. Unfortunately, in my experience, a worrying number of *those kind of blokes* had no idea they were *those kind of blokes*, not seeing the true impact of some of their so-called 'banter'. 'And did you hear from her again after that?'

'No, the next thing I knew was when I saw on the news what happened to her.'

I shifted in my seat. There was nothing about any of this in the case file. 'Did you contact the police?'

'Why would I?'

'You knew someone had done that, then you found out she'd been murdered, and you didn't think to tell the police?'

'No, 'cause it was Dee Dee who said she'd pushed her, and she'd gone off with Adzy already that night before me and Ris, you know, so I didn't think it had anything to do with any photos, and I'm not being funny but I'm in those pictures too. It's not like I wanted them dug through by a load of police officers, maybe even released to the public.'

'Someone took those photos, Mr Campbell, someone

who has never come to light. I know it was a long time ago, but I need you to tell me everyone who came back to the hotel after the party that night.'

He scratched his head. 'I dunno, there was the bands, both bands, our managers, a few roadies, the odd groupie, you know, the hangers-on, and security. I think that was it but I'm not sure.'

A knot formed in my stomach as he wrote down a list on to the notepad beside him. Ris knew the person who'd violated her privacy and their name was somewhere on this list. Did Dee Dee know? If she did, why hadn't she mentioned it? Who was she covering for? 'And if you have any contact details for your former band members, write those on there too, please.'

He shook his head as he handed me the piece of paper. 'I haven't, sorry, I didn't stay in touch with any of them. Adzy was travelling the world – in Australia, last I heard, but that was years ago. I'm sorry I can't be of more help, I really am.'

An hour later I was on the train and Kit answered on the second ring.

'Hello?' she said.

'That theory you had about something happening at The Dolls' gig in Birmingham, is there anything else you know about it?'

'No, why?'

'I can't tell you why, but don't discount it, particularly anything that might have happened at the after party, and anything about the hotel afterwards.'

There was a pause and I braced for an onslaught of questions.

'Yeah, OK. Oh, and I spoke to Judith. She's not happy about it, but I think she got the point, about the letters.'

'Great. Thanks, Kit, I appreciate it.'

We hung up and I was about to put my phone away when it started ringing. It was the CID office. Shit, probably Jane, Roy having run out of excuses to keep her occupied. Every fibre of my being wanted to let it go to voicemail, but with Tabby's disappearance hanging over me, I couldn't risk it.

'DS Washington.'

'Sarge, it's Eddie. You got a second?'

My shoulders slumped with relief that it wasn't Jane, and if anything important about Tabby's case had come in then Eddie wouldn't be the one telling me. 'Yeah, what is it?'

'Bit of an interesting one, thought you'd want to know. I found the clip of that other contestant who kicked off when they didn't make the band, and you'll never guess who it is?'

Eddie had a habit of making things sound more dramatic than they actually were, so I played along. 'I dunno, Elvis Costello? Aretha Franklin?'

'Nope,' he said as if my guesses were serious.

'I'm about to go through a tunnel on the train, Ed. Put me out of my misery, will you?' I said, rubbing my brow.

'Ashleigh-Marie Curtis.'

'OK, and am I supposed to know who that is?'

'You should do, you've met her.'

'I've met her? What are you on ab—' The train went

under a bridge and the change from bright sunshine to dark then back to bright again kickstarted my brain. Ash*leigh*.

'Let me guess, Miss Curtis now goes by her married name of Mrs Hope?'

'Bingo,' Eddie said.

My mind re-played the call with Roy I'd had on the way up here. Where the fuck were Ryan and Leigh?

31

Kit made her excuses to leave Em and Nush in the studio. They'd likely be in there for hours, oblivious to what was going on outside those soundproof doors. Sherrie was out and the security team were keeping eyes on various entrances; the upstairs of Aurora House was empty, an opportunity she couldn't waste. She pulled the spare set of keys out from under her mattress and took a steadying breath.

Going out on to the landing, she scanned the other bedrooms, re-reading the names etched into the small wooden plaques on the doors as if that would give her a clue which one to start with. She'd been so distracted by her own possible association with the mockingbird, thinking she'd been assigned it deliberately as some underhanded *We know why you're really here*, she hadn't really thought about the others. But as she went to stick the key into the lock of Em's room, aptly named Raven, she began to wonder.

If any bird could be classed as the ultimate emo kid of the avian world it would be the raven with its jet-black plumage, not dissimilar to Em's short hair which was always slicked over to one side to expose her undercut. Kit had learned about ravens on a school trip to the Tower of London before she dropped out when her dad died. The man giving the talk had done his utmost to redeem the birds' fearsome reputation, informing the class that these harbingers of doom with a taste for carrion were technically songbirds. Kit pictured Em and a raven side by side: misunderstood, gentle creatures, or heartless scavengers who'd pick through the remnants of a corpse on a battlefield without a second thought?

Hmm.

Keys still hovering in the lock, she looked at the signs on the other rooms. Nush the Grasshopper. The drummers of the insect world with little pegs on the inside of their hind legs that they rubbed together to give them their very own percussion instrument. How apt. In fact, now that she thought about it, Tabby's door sign was just as fitting. Dormouse. She couldn't remember where she'd heard the fact, but she knew one thing about dormice: they weren't mice at all – one rodent masquerading as another. That was Tabby all right, her new wellness-guru persona a far cry from the party-girl socialite she'd been in the pre-band days.

There was a crash of metal as the bunch of keys she'd forgotten she was holding fell to the hard wood floor, the sound dragging her back to the task at hand. What was she doing standing there gawping? She wasn't going to get the information she needed by pondering which personality traits Sherrie might share with a fucking dragonfly. She picked the keys up, unlocked the door and slipped into Em's room.

The place wasn't exactly brimming with clues given there was barely anything to look through, just piles of dark clothing, some unused notebooks in the drawers, and the most basic of toiletries. Kit searched as quietly as she could, careful to put everything back in its place, not that she thought Em would notice if she didn't – nothing was tidy anyway. She felt around under the bed but there was nothing except a pair of trainers and an empty suitcase.

Padding quietly across the floor, she slipped back out and re-locked the door. She was about to go into Nush's room when the stairs to the ground floor creaked under the weight of someone climbing them, someone heavy.

'What you doing up here, eh?' Manu said as he reached the landing, his strong fingers gripping the curved banister.

They hadn't been alone together since their encounter at the bottom of the stairs when she'd come back from the Big Top, whatever suspicions he may have had about her put to one side. For now, anyway. And Kit wanted to keep it that way. She scanned her surroundings looking for an excuse to explain why she was loitering. 'I was just looking at, erm . . . this painting,' she said, pointing at a large canvas adorned with the image of a naked man standing in the position of David. 'Cool, isn't it?'

Manu looked at the picture, his face devoid of any visible reaction. 'Not my taste. Shouldn't you be in the studio with the others?'

'Taking a break – my eardrums can only cope with so

much every day, you know.' A thought popped into her mind. Maybe she'd been going about this all wrong, trying to avoid Manu when really she should have been trying to ingratiate herself with him. He was the eyes and ears of this place, a fact that she'd seen as a negative, always watching, always listening, but it also meant there probably wasn't much he didn't know about any goings-on with the band. And without meaning to, she'd given herself a natural opening. 'You *do* actually know, better than me. I'm surprised you're not deaf doing security duty. I mean, you're so close, the speakers might as well be playing directly into your ears,' she said, in an attempt to build some camaraderie. Clearly it hadn't worked as Manu just stared at her. She changed tack. 'Still, it's a good outlet to have, music. I'm glad they've got something to keep them going through all this. My thing's writing. Happy, sad, bored, scared, whatever I'm feeling, I like to write it out. Get whatever it is down on the page. What about you?'

His face remained stony. 'What about me?'

'Come on,' she said, reaching out and nudging his arm, trying to be playful, but merely jarring her wrist as he stood planted to the spot. Why anyone would want to threaten the band with this absolute behemoth in their corner was beyond her. 'Doing what you do must be stressful – surely you've gotta do something to release the tension? And you've been doing this a long time, right? You worked with them the first time around, so that's at least a decade. Surely you've gotta let all that stress out somewhere.'

His small eyes narrowed, making them practically

disappear into his round cheeks. 'I'm here to do my job. Nothing else.'

The term *getting blood from a stone* didn't come close to what it was like talking to this dude, but she had to at least try. 'I get it, a job like yours, you've gotta be switched on, can't take your eye off the ball for a second, or . . .' His jaw clenched and her mind leapt to Tabby. *Shit.* Implying her going missing on his watch was somehow his fault would do the opposite of getting him to open up to her. 'You're from New Zealand, right?'

A curt nod was all she got in response.

'What did you do back there, before this?'

'Same thing, security.'

'For bands?'

'Bands, celebrities, whoever needed it.'

At least he was actually answering her now, which was an improvement.

'You must see a lot of stuff, doing what you do, and no offence to your homeland or anything, but surely getting to go backstage at somewhere like the Bull Ring Academy in Birmingham must be a career highlight? It's an iconic venue. The biggest bands in the world have said it was one of their favourite crowds to play. Stones. Zeppelin. Queen. Admit it, even you must have been at least a little impressed when you got to go there with the band. You were there with them then, right, at the Birmingham gig?'

Kit wasn't certain, but she could have sworn a muscle in his veiny upper arm twitched.

'Birmingham. Manchester. Glasgow. Edinburgh. I did most of their shows.'

'Cool, cool. Must have been tough, though, I heard they had some pretty, erm . . . interesting after parties; they must have been a right handful. I heard that after the gig in Birmingham they invited loads of people back, things got a bit out of control.'

For the first time his face of stone became animated, the mask slipping. 'Nothing happened in Birmingham.' He collected himself before speaking again. 'I don't let things get out of control. I keep what needs to stay in, in. What needs to stay out, out. And you should know that better than anyone.' His glare made her insides feel like they were going to drop out.

Manu turned and stomped off down the stairs, leaving Kit certain of two things: he knew exactly what had happened in Birmingham, and he *did* remember her.

32

Roy had already kicked off enquiries into the whereabouts of Ryan and Leigh and updated Bret by the time I got back to the office. Phone clutched between his chin and shoulder, he held up a piece of paper as I made for my desk. SEE JANE, it said.

I let out a groan, yearning to drop on to my chair instead of carrying on to her office.

'Yeah,' Jane yelled from the other side of her door as I knocked. I pushed it open a crack and stuck my head in. 'What seems to be the problem today, Alice? Cat ate your homework?'

My phone buzzed in my pocket. I pulled it out, Kit's name flashing across the screen. *Shit*. I'd call her back as soon as I was finished with Jane. I turned it off and shoved it into my jeans. 'You wanted to see me?'

'Ah, yes, Judith Nolan, can I tell HQ they can cross her off their list of problems?'

I debated being completely honest with her for about two seconds before realising how dumb that would be. I still didn't fully trust her to understand where I was coming from with this whole Kit situation. 'I think we're good on that front, they shouldn't be receiving any more correspondence from her.' Correspondence from me, on the other hand, if I found something substantial enough that convinced me once and for all the case should be re-opened, was another matter. But that was a bridge I'd cross if I came to it. Yet another absolute zinger for future Alice to deal with.

'Good, I'll let them know you've spoken to her.'

I opened my mouth to correct her. Technically, *I* hadn't spoken to her. Kit had. But what did it matter? They wanted the letters to stop. They were going to stop. I ignored the pang of guilt, coughing it away before replying. 'All sorted. Was that everything?'

'No, give me a rundown on where we are on helping to find Tabby Falstead. I've got a seniors call in half an hour and no doubt it's going to come up.'

'It may be a coincidence, but we're looking into the whereabouts of Ryan and Leigh Hope.' I gave her an overview of who they were and their connection to the band. 'They seem to have left their property in a rush around the same time Tabby went missing, which is odd given they run a working farm, and none of their neighbours seem to know where they've gone. They didn't mention anything when we went down there about going away and there was a weird vibe between them; he seemed quite nervous of us still being there when his wife came back. And we've also found out Leigh was a contestant on the show – seems a bit off neither of them mentioned it, especially when she had quite the exit.'

Eddie had sent me the clip he'd found and I'd watched it

on the train. An almost unrecognisable Leigh, face covered in thick make-up, her long brown hair chopped short and bleached blond with pink streaks. She'd cried and clung to one of the judge's legs when they'd said she hadn't made it through to the next round of the competition and she had to be physically removed by security. 'I don't know what's going on, but it's certainly not sitting right. And I've been working on a theory since Tabby went missing, that maybe this is connected to someone who knew them back in the old days. I've got some items down from the pit to go through, see where it gets me.'

Jane's eyes narrowed, her gaze so sharp it was like she was trying to penetrate my skull and see inside my brain. I was beginning to sweat when she opened her mouth, holding her thought as the phone on her desk rang. She looked at the caller ID panel and answered. 'Terry, I'm in the middle of something, can you—'

Oh, thank fuck for that, a get-out clause. *Should I . . .?* I mouthed, nodding my head towards the door, ready to make my escape. She shook her head and jabbed a finger at the chair I was standing next to: *You're not going anywhere. Sit.*

I sunk slowly on to the seat as Terry's voice leaked from the phone, but it was so faint I couldn't hear what he was saying before Jane cut him off. 'Not now, Terry!' she yelled before banging the phone back on to its holder.

'Something up, ma'am?' I said, suddenly hotter under the collar than I'd been in the last few weeks of almost constant sunshine.

She stood and walked to my side of the desk, perching her bony arse on the corner of it. 'When you said something about Tabby's disappearance sparked this little theory of yours, made you request items from the pit, was that a mistake or a lie?' Jane didn't give herself the usual pleasure of watching me flounder as she jumped straight back in. 'I heard Terry on the phone organising the collection when you were up at HQ for that first briefing, so you must have asked him before you went up there, no?'

While her being a dog with a bone usually caused annoyance amongst her subordinates, it was also why she was a bloody good cop. She knew something was up. And there wasn't a delicate way to put it. I just blurted it out. What Kit had told me. What I'd discovered myself. Every last drop of it. For a few seconds after I'd finished all I could hear was my own breath before Jane broke the silence.

'So,' she said, pressing her fingers into her temples, 'what exactly are you saying here? That someone else made Dee Dee Nolan do what she did, or that she didn't even do it in the first place?'

My honest answer came out. 'I don't know, ma'am, but I think Dee Dee is definitely lying, covering *something* up, and it's connected to all this. I just haven't figured out how yet.'

'The woman's been in prison for a decade with no attempt at freedom. Why on earth would she do that?'

'I know it sounds crazy, and I don't know, but I'll find out, I just need more time.'

Jane stared at me, neither of us speaking for a moment. She let out a deep sigh. 'I'm sorry, Alice, this is on me. I should've encouraged you to have more time off after last year. I know it's made trusting people difficult for you, and with everything going on in the service at the minute I understand, it's hard to trust it even when you're inside the damn thing, see how the sausage is made, so to speak, but—'

I didn't recall pushing to my feet, but I must have, because all of a sudden I was up and Jane was leaning away from me. 'That's not what this is, I swear to God. I wish I *didn't* trust my gut on this, I really do, and I'm not surprised you don't believe me, but every single fibre of my being is telling me something's wrong here. And I'm trusting you now, telling you this. Now I need you to trust *me*!'

The phone on Jane's desk rang again. She ignored it. 'May I suggest that you find out very strong answers to the questions who, why and what in the heavens you think it is you know, because now both of our necks are on the line, understand?'

A fire lit in my stomach. She believed me. *Jane.* I almost grabbed her by the cheeks and kissed her but thought better of it. I needed to live long enough to find the evidence either to prove this thing or put it to bed for good. 'Thank you, I won't let you down, ma'am.'

Her phone stopped ringing then immediately started again. She picked it up this time, not taking her eyes off me.

'Terry, how many times— Oh, Mr Scott, afternoon, sir.'

I looked for a twitch, any indication in her face that she

was about to have a change of heart, the sound of Gordy's voice making her realise indulging my theory wouldn't end in anything good. I watched and waited for the betrayal.

'Mm-hmm ... yes, I understand ... yes ... absolutely, thanks, sir.' Jane put the phone down.

'Everything all right, ma'am?' I said.

She leant back in her chair and ran her fingers through her hair. 'Better than all right, they've found Tabby Falstead. Alive.'

I'd dialled into the follow-up call about Tabby but there wasn't much left for us to do here in Fortbridge. Bret and his new team were all over it: scouring the CCTV along the dual carriageway where she'd been found stumbling around the grass verge, setting search teams and SOCO off to figure out which way she'd most likely come from to get there, as well as cordoning off and picking through every inch of some nearby abandoned warehouses for any evidence of where she'd been and what had happened to her in the previous five and a half days.

I needed liquid and caffeine. Chilled liquid, not the practically boiling water from the bottle on my desk.

'How is she?' Roy asked as he followed me down to the mess room.

'Physically, not much more than cuts, bruises and dehydration. She's in shock, of course; Bret said they only managed to get so much out of her before the doctors called time on it, said she's not fit to be questioned.' I grabbed a can of Coke from the small fridge by the till.

'That's something, I s'pose,' Roy said before reaching in after me and taking a bottle of water.

We paid for our drinks and sat down. 'All they know so far is, someone pulled her back during the argument with those schoolboys at the reservoir,' I said, opening the can and taking a swig. 'She went with it, thinking it was one of the security team, and by the time she realised it wasn't and tried to scream there was a hand over her mouth and something over her head. She doesn't know who took her, only that there were two of them, they didn't speak and had their faces covered.'

'I can tell you who it wasn't,' Roy said. 'Ryan and Leigh Hope. Managed to track them down, that's who I was on the phone to when you came in. They're at Leigh's parents' house in France. Apparently they had some paps turn up, taking pictures of their kid over the fence, so they packed up straight away. Leigh was fuming.'

'I bet she was. What was her excuse for keeping quiet about her little performance on the show?'

'Doesn't like to talk about it, said she's still mortified about how she went on. Eddie showed me the video an' all – not really surprising.'

I'd avoided telling Roy my theory about Ris's murder for as long as I could, but there was no point keeping it to myself now Jane knew.

He looked at me as I finished explaining, eyes wide. 'Are you mad?'

'I wish I was. I mean, from what I've seen so far it doesn't look like there's misconduct or anything going on, but the investigation does seem to have missed a whole chunk of something that's seeming more and more relevant every time I find out anything new about it.'

'Blimey, you really don't make things easy for yourself, do you? You know when the next MCU job comes up, Gordy Scott'll very likely be on the interview panel.'

I shrugged. 'Don't think my ability to climb the professional ladder or not is a good enough excuse to leave this one alone.'

'So what you thinking? How we gonna play this thing?' Roy asked.

'I need to speak to Bret, because we need to properly interview the band about what happened in Birmingham. In their original interviews when Ris died, they all said that she'd been acting unusually for the last few weeks before she was killed, but none of them said anything about her being blackmailed or whatever the hell those photos were supposed to achieve. And surely there's no way Ris wouldn't have said anything about it to anyone. Oliver Campbell has given me a list of who he remembers being around after the gig at the hotel, the bands, their entourages and some others; someone amongst them must have taken the photos. Bret will be up to his eyeballs right now, probably no point trying to speak to him today. I'll give him a call tomorrow, hope he doesn't slam the phone down on me.'

'Nah, he's got a good head on his shoulders, that one.'

'Since when did you join the Bret Seaborn fan club?' I said.

'I'm hardly his cheerleader, but I don't know why you've pegged the lad as Satan himself. He's not a bad bloke.'

'How would you know?' I asked. 'He never bloody talked to anyone when he was here.'

Roy shrugged. 'Nothing wrong with being quiet, is there? He seems decent enough, and from what I can tell, isn't too bad-looking either. Maybe you should ask him out.'

I looked at him scornfully, the same way I used to when he did big spicy meat burps in the office after a greasy lunch. 'Out where? To the moors for a duel? To Marks and Spencer for a new jumper then on to the haberdashery to pick up some elbow patches?'

Roy held his palms up. 'I'm only saying, good genes, keeps to himself, steady pay cheque, and he's in the job so he gets it. There's a reason policing is so incestuous – makes it easier being with someone who knows what it's like.'

'Yeah, well, policing can carry on its little incest party without me, thank you very much. And on that note, that's our shift done and I'm exhausted. I'm going home to try and get a decent night's sleep now we know Tabby's safe.'

Two hours later I was true to my promise after making myself a random dinner of whatever the hell I could find in my cupboards, before going to bed. And I actually did manage a semi-decent sleep until my phone ringing just after 6 o'clock the following morning woke me with a start. 'H'lo?' I said.

It was the control room and my brain took a moment to tune in to what they were talking about. Aurora House.

I sat bolt upright. 'What's happened?'

The phone slipped from my hand as I heard the response.

33

The sun was up by the time I got to the retreat, its low rays skimming the surface of the pond. An ambulance sat under the willow tree, the back of it open with Em, Nush and Kit standing looking into the vehicle. I could hear Sherrie's raised voice before I'd opened my car door.

'Should we try Spanish? Or how about some Mandarin? How many languages d'you need me to say it in? I'm *not* going to the fucking hospital, all right?' she bellowed.

Part of me felt relieved it wasn't just the thin blue line of the emergency services Sherrie didn't have the time of day for this morning, having already refused to speak to the first officers on scene. I stood in the gap between Nush and Kit. Sherrie was sitting on the step leading into the ambulance with a blanket draped across her shoulders, a harried-looking paramedic squatting in front of her.

'What's going on?' I said.

Nush gestured at Sherrie. 'Here, see if you can talk some sense into this muppet, man, will ya?'

Sherrie had an egg-sized lump in the middle of her forehead, a zigzag of dried blood at its crest. The paramedic stood up and faced me. I introduced myself before she turned her attention back to Sherrie for one more try.

'Honestly, love, it really is the best thing to do.' The paramedic's tone of voice made it sound like she was trying to get an only child to share their toys, which probably did nothing to help Sherrie's mood. 'We need to get you properly checked out, OK? We don't know how long you were unconscious for. You've taken a serious knock to the head, you could have bleeding on the brain.'

Sherrie glared, shrugging off the blanket as she stood, the paramedic's gaze rising with her. 'Sherrie Anne Pearce is my name. Wednesday the twenty-third of August 2023 is today's date. The Prime Minister is Rishi Sunak, unfortunately, though given the state of this government that could have changed twice in the time I've been sparked out. Four times seven is twenty-eight and three is the number of seconds you have to give it a rest before you have to worry about bleeding on your own brain.'

'That's enough,' I said, stepping between Sherrie and the paramedic, who looked like she was about to cry. 'She's just doing her job.'

Sherrie slumped back on to the step. 'Yeah? And I'm doing mine. Those girls are my responsibility and I ain't leaving them.'

Nush and Em threw out varying protests about being able to look after themselves before I interjected. 'Sherrie,' I said, calmly, looking up as Roy's car pulled into the driveway, 'DC Briar, who you met the other day, is going

273

to make sure everyone gets taken to the hospital with you. They can visit Tabby while you get yourself sorted, then you'll all be together in one place. And in the meantime, I need to know what happened to you. So why don't we go take a seat in my car, and you can tell me, OK?'

Sherrie let out a resigned sigh. 'If anything happens to them on the way, I'm holding you personally responsible,' she said, jabbing a finger at me.

She hugged Nush, Em and Kit in turn and then headed for my car. I stopped Kit as the others walked towards Roy's. Seeing her reminded me that I'd forgotten to call her back after all of yesterday's commotion with Tabby being found. 'You OK?'

'Yeah. The first I knew of it, Sherrie was waking us all up, blood running down her face, telling us to get into the studio. It was like a scene out of *Carrie* or something.'

'Listen to DC Briar, you can trust him, I promise. Everything's going to be fine. And look, I'm sorry I didn't call you back yesterday; I was in with my boss and then everything kicked off. What did you need?'

Kit chewed the inside of her mouth like she'd changed her mind about telling me.

'What is it?'

'Look,' she said, 'it sounds worse than it is . . .'

Oh God. 'What does?'

'I was calling to tell you that I met Dee Dee, years ago.'

Every muscle in my face tightened. I tried to keep my expression neutral, since I could see in my periphery that Sherrie was looking over from inside my car. 'Are you kidding me? You've known her this whole time and you didn't tell me?'

'I don't "know her" and I honestly *didn't* think it was worth mentioning. It was literally for a few seconds after I got chucked out of one of their London shows. I told you I'd been a fan of theirs, I just didn't tell you me and my mate snuck into their gig once. And we got in fine, but then we pushed our luck, tried to get served for drinks, and the barman was like "no chance", and fair dos, we were only thirteen, so security booted us out. I was upset. Dee Dee was out back. She saw the whole thing; I think she felt sorry for us. She gave us some band T-shirts.'

I tried to stay calm. 'She gave you some free merch when you were thirteen, that's it?'

'Yeah, well, kind of, except for the tweets.'

Oh, Jesus fucking Christ. 'What tweets?'

'She was so nice to us, and we'd just joined Twitter, so we sent Dee Dee a message. She had her own account where she posted stuff about band life, we followed it, it seemed so cool. We sent her a photo of us wearing the T-shirts, she replied a few times, she was really nice. And we wanted to start our own band one day, she encouraged us. That was *it*, I swear.'

'A *few* times? How long did this budding little friendship go on for, eh?'

'Not long at all. I deleted all my socials a few months later after what happened with my dad – I was getting messages, abuse and stuff about him.'

I'd closed off my worries about Kit having a personal

connection to this case when she'd told me about her dad, satisfied that her own negative police experience was the only thing fuelling it. Now I wasn't so sure. 'Please tell me some long-standing loyalty to Dee Dee isn't what started you off digging into the band?'

'No! I swear, everything I told you at the diner was the truth, and I don't have any *loyalty* towards her. You're making it sound like I'm one of those psychos from that documentary. I mean, yeah, it was a shock when I saw the news about Ris and Dee Dee, I was surprised she'd do something so awful. But I didn't have any reason to think she hadn't done what she said she did until I saw those transcripts. And I know they aren't conclusive, I'm not stupid. I just ... she was so nice to me for no reason, and I don't know a lot of people like that. And I could be wrong, she could be this vindictive person everyone painted her as, but something in my gut is telling me those two things just don't go together. I haven't messed this up, have I?'

I wanted so badly to walk away from this whole situation right now. What the hell had I done? And where was this 'I could be wrong' caveat in our discussion at the diner? She'd seemed so sure she was on to something. This doubt would have been useful to know about before I'd told Jane and Roy, making them accessories to this mess alongside me. 'Why the hell didn't you tell me this from the start like everything else, given me all the information?'

'I honestly didn't think it was important.'

'So why tell me now if it's all so insignificant?'

She took a deep breath before answering. 'Because Manu

was the security guard who sent me packing back then, and I'm pretty sure he recognises me now.'

'Oh, this just gets better and better. *Manu* was the one who threw you out of their gig? And he hasn't said anything about it until now?'

'Technically he hasn't said anything now, but I was talking to him yesterday, trying to get something out of him about the Birmingham gig – which he was definitely twitchy about, by the way – and it was just something he said, like he wanted me to know he'd recognised me.'

This was an absolute shambles. One I'd helped create by suggesting Kit find out more about what happened in Birmingham. 'Why wouldn't he just say he recognised you? I mean, you were a kid who snuck into a concert – what's the big deal?'

Kit winced. 'That's the thing, we didn't *just* sneak into the concert.'

I pinched the bridge of my nose then stopped myself. Sherrie had turned away from us but Roy was looking over now. 'Jesus, how many more little surprises have you got up your sleeve? What else did you do?'

'After he threw us out, we may or may not have slashed the tyres on their tour bus.'

'Oh my ... Christ, Kit, what the hell are you trying to do to me here?'

'I'm sorry, Dee Dee was nice to us, but Manu was a right dick, and we were kids! We were stupid. If he tells Sherrie, she'll kick me out for sure. And then that's it, no more exposing what really happened.'

'What really— Look, this needs to stop, OK? If there's something to find, I'll find it. You stay out of things from now on. This situation is already messed up enough as it is without you adding to it. Now, go with the others. I'll deal with Sherrie and Manu. Where is he anyway?' I said, realising I hadn't seen him, or any other members of the security team for that matter, amongst the throng of people milling around on the driveway.

'I don't know, I—'

Footsteps crunched across the gravel towards us and Kit fell silent as Roy appeared by my side.

'We ready to go?' he asked.

I painted on a smile as if my entire career wasn't flashing before my eyes and nodded.

'Come on then,' Roy said to Kit. 'Let's be getting you in the car.' She gave me an apologetic look before she slunk off.

I filled him in on the little I knew so far about Sherrie's attack – leaving out Kit's newest revelations – before heading towards my car. I pushed thoughts of Manu from my mind, I'd deal with him later. Right now I had to find out what had happened to Sherrie, who was still sitting in my passenger seat, tentatively tapping the skin around the lump on her head with one hand and fiddling with the air con vent with the other.

'Get the engine on, will you? It's roasting in here, and me nut's throbbing,' she said.

'Sorry, air con doesn't work, and even if it did, I'm not sure cold air is gonna be enough to soothe that.'

Sherrie sat back and tutted. 'D'you wanna know what

happened or not?' I nodded and pulled the tablet out of my bag to note down the details. 'So I come down to get some water, right, it must've been, I dunno, fourish or something. Anyway, I come down and I can hear him talking.'

'Who?'

'Fucking Manu!'

So much for pushing him from my mind. What the hell was this guy up to? '*Manu* attacked you?'

'Yeah, he was on the phone, and at first I thought he must be talking to someone back in New Zealand – you know, with the time difference – but then I heard what he was saying, how they were screwed now Tabby had been found, that just because she hadn't named them yet didn't mean she wouldn't, that she might still make the connection. And I know the first thing I should've done was call you lot, but I lost it. I thought I could trust the bastard. Right under my nose he's been scheming. I wanted him out, away from the girls, I went upstairs, got me bat and came down, told him to get out. And I got a few good hits in before he grabbed the end of it and yanked it off me, and . . .' She pointed to her head. 'I don't remember much after that. Next thing I know I'm waking up on the floor and Manu's gone. First thing I did was run and check the girls, thought he might have done something to 'em, then his other security lot turned up and started making a fuss, so I thought fuck this and got the girls down into the studio, locked us all in there until the old bill arrived.'

That explained why Manu was nowhere to be seen, my plan to talk to him about why he was messing with Kit going clean out the window. But then a different thought struck me, a piece of the puzzle slotting into place about the transcript Kit had found. From what I could remember, the voice of the person on the phone had several inaudible gaps in their speech. That would make sense if Manu had been the one making the call; he spoke quietly, and with his strong kiwi accent, the crappy transcription software would be more likely to struggle capturing accurately what he'd said. There was no doubt Kit had added layers of complexity to this situation with her omissions, but maybe I shouldn't discount her gut feeling. Especially when my gut was telling me that Manu had been the one on the phone that day. But who had been on the other end? And was it the same person he'd been talking to last night? 'Did he say anything to you, make any excuses, or hint at who he was talking to?'

She shook her head. 'Didn't really give him the chance. Like I said, I just wanted him out of there, before ... look, there's something you need to know about Manu. And you've gotta understand, I had it on good authority that he was a decent kid who'd got himself caught up with a bad crowd, that's why his family had had him sent over here. And he's been no bother over the years, he really hasn't. If I even so much as thought he'd be a danger to the girls I wouldn't have let him anywhere near them, d'you understand?'

I wasn't sure how many more Manu-related pieces of information I could process right now. But I needed to know who on earth this man was. 'What about Manu, Sherrie?'

She let out a deep sigh. 'His real name isn't Manu Tuala,

it's Manu Matafeo. He came here on one of his cousin's passports – stabbed someone to death in an initiation thing back in Auckland, always told me it was a him-or-them-type situation, that he never wanted all that stuff and just wanted a new life here. Fuck!' She slammed her hand into the dashboard.

This thing was getting murkier by the minute. I needed to stay focussed. 'OK, that's really useful, Sherrie. Now we need to get people out there looking for him, to make sure he can't do any harm to the band, and find whoever he was talking to. Can you type his phone number in here for me?' I leant over so she could reach my tablet.

Sherrie looked confused. 'Not trying to teach you how to suck eggs, but I'm not sure he's going to be taking calls right now, Sergeant.'

'Probably not, but we can still get access to his phone records, find out who he called this morning.'

She jutted out her bottom lip. 'Fancy. How long will that take?'

'It depends, but I'll do everything I can to get it pushed through as a priority, and once we're all finished at the hospital, we'll get you and the band somewhere safe. As far as you're aware, did any other people in the security team know about this?'

'They were all off duty last night, only Manu was on. What if he was on the phone to one of them?'

'Don't worry, they'll all be brought in for questioning.'

Sherrie traced the lump on her head with her finger as I relayed the information she'd given me to the control room.

I finished and turned my attention back to her. 'Now, to the hospital, yes?'

She nodded and I let out a sigh of relief.

The nurse took Sherrie into one of the consultation rooms, and I made my way back to the main reception. The waiting area hummed with impatience, filled with the tired faces of people who were either waiting to be seen themselves, or were friends and relatives waiting for loved ones. They all looked up at me as I passed through the double doors, the sniff of hope in their eyes replaced by immediate disappointment when they realised I wasn't a doctor coming to call their name.

Roy stood up from a row of metal chairs. 'How's Sherrie?'

'Just a concussion so far; they want to do a few more checks, keep her in overnight. How are the others doing?'

'Left 'em in Tabby's room,' he said. 'She's a lot calmer than she was yesterday apparently, just waiting to be discharged. Still don't know where I'm supposed to be taking them, mind you – they sure as shit can't go back to Aurora House.'

'No, course. We need to get them all back home in one piece.'

'That's the mental thing. They're adamant they ain't going home, not yet, not until they've done the festival.'

I resisted the urge to yell. 'The *festival*? But they've cancelled their slot. Surely after everything Tabby's been through she's in no state to be the frontwoman at a bloody music show – they can't make her do that.'

'Make her?' Roy said. 'She's the one insisting on it! She's convinced that whoever took her only wanted to scare her, and that if they give in they're letting these bastards win. Em's right up for it, too. Mind, I think that one just wants any excuse to fight someone; I don't think she gives a monkey's about proving a point. Nush is the only one playing devil's advocate, but she might as well have been talking to a bedpan; the other two ain't having any of it.'

'Wait, the people who took Tabby just *let* her go?'

'Yeah, she said one of them made a phone call – she couldn't hear what they were saying – then they took her out in a car, dumped her in a field and left her there. That's when she made her way to the road.'

'Who does that?' I said. 'Who kidnaps someone, holds them for the best part of a week, then lets them go?'

Roy shrugged. 'You say that like we're talking about rational people here.'

'Fair point. Still, there's no way we can let them perform now. Surely there's enough risk for us to shut this thing down whether they like it or not, especially with Manu on the loose, and given we know he's working with other people. We have no idea who we're trying to protect them from.'

'It's not me that needs convincing,' Roy said, 'it's the ivory tower lot. I don't think they're gonna need too much arm-twisting. Surely anyone can see the band'll be sitting ducks on that stage.'

Usually I'd agree with Roy, that this credible threat to life would be taken seriously, the appropriate steps activated to protect both the band and those in attendance from serious harm, but given the person who'd need to make that call was Gordy Scott, I could feel in my bones that things weren't going to be quite so straightforward.

34

I thought things would be different, everything out in the open, raw and exposed like a fresh wound. But it will never be different again, I see that now. This is it. My forever state. Exposed as I wait for a scab that does not form. Every day I wait. For the clotting and hardening to create the bloody shell that should protect me from this, from you, keep the bad things out until I am healed.

But I realise now.

Even if the scab comes, it will not last. You will make sure of that. You will scrape and scrape and scrape until it is gone, inviting infection in like you always do.

I have waited long enough. Let you do this long enough. I promised you your time would come. And that time is now.

35

The search for Manu had HQ bubbling with activity as I arrived and made my way to Gordy's office, his door opening after the first knock this time. He didn't say anything, simply stepping to one side and waving me in. Carver and Bret were already there, the DCI seated, with Bret standing beside him.

'Alice,' Carver said, 'didn't get a chance to catch up the other day in the briefing – how's things?'

Oh, trust me, you don't wanna know. 'Erm, fine, thanks,' I said, sitting in the seat beside him.

'How's old Washington senior?' he added with a nostalgic smile. 'He hasn't been down the golf club for the last few months – everything all right?'

What a surprise. Dad had a girlfriend, ergo, he must give up everything about himself and change his entire personality like Roy had with Trudy. 'Yeah, he's—'

Gordy butted in as he dropped back into his chair. 'Save the gossip for the ladies' powder room. In case you hadn't noticed, we've got a murderer on the loose and I presume there's an actual reason you're here, so shoot.'

I looked to Carver in the hope that, given his seniority to me, he'd push back on the sexist tinge to Gordy's comment, but all he did was readjust his tie and swivel in his seat so he was facing the boss's desk. Bret didn't so much as squeak either.

Gordy leant on his elbows and interlaced his fingers, staring at me.

'The Dolls want to perform at the festival again, sir,' I said. 'I think it's far too risky. We need to shut it down.'

He just sat there looking at me. What was he doing? Deliberately trying to make me feel uncomfortable? Well, two could play that game. I matched his silence, keeping my face neutral.

After a few awkward seconds, Carver squirming in his chair beside me, Bret shifting his weight from one foot to the other, Gordy finally spoke. 'I've got a manhunt on my hands, Interpol up my arse, and quite frankly the last thing I need is some WI march picketing the building because I won't "let women's voices be heard".'

It was obvious he had no interest in letting the band maintain their sense of agency. All he cared about was avoiding a PR disaster. 'This isn't about silencing them, sir, it's about keeping them alive.'

He shrugged. 'They know the risks, and it's not like security are gonna let Manu Matafeo waltz in there tooled up to the nines, are they? And we'll have boots on the ground. If he tries, we'll be on him. They get to do their little show, we get to hand over a wanted man, win–win.'

I baulked. 'You're using them as *bait*?'

'Did I say that?' His gaze moved from me, to Carver, then to Bret, asking each in turn the same question.

'No, sir,' Carver said.

'No, sir, but to be fair, Alice has—' Bret said before Gordy cut him off.

'Well then, there's nothing I can see that suggests festival-goers in general will be targeted, and shutting this thing down will be a nightmare. You saw what happened with the vigil for Stanmore's victims the other day, turned into an absolute clusterfuck.'

I'd deliberately avoided coverage of the heavy-handed approach that'd been used to police the gathering, knowing it would fill me with a rage that would be no use to anyone. Gordy wanted me to bite. I ground my teeth instead. 'With all due respect, we have a responsibility, *sir*.' The way his title crossed my lips, slow and pronounced, reminded me of the way Roy used to say mine when I'd pissed him off.

'And all due respect to you,' he said in a tone so contemptuous there'd be no mistaking anything he was about to say as remotely akin to respect, 'as Gold Commander, that responsibility to protect individuals from harm *and* maintain public order is mine. And my assessment is that cancelling, in the current climate, will do more harm than good.'

My skin prickled at the realisation of what I had to do. Maybe Gordy was being a dick because he wasn't armed with all the information, didn't have the same concerns I did because he didn't know there was potentially someone out there who'd killed before, or certainly orchestrated Ris's murder. I couldn't keep this from him any more, even if Kit had dented my trust in her by keeping her prior contact with Dee Dee and Manu from me. If The Dolls' lives depended on it, I couldn't take the risk. 'Sir, there's something else I think you should know that might impact your decision.'

He leant back and clasped his hands behind his head, kicking his feet up on to the corner of the desk. 'Do enlighten me.'

'I think this may all be linked to Ris Angelini's murder somehow, sir.'

Gordy's top lip curled, eyes narrowing. 'What's that got to do with anything?'

'I've been looking through the case file as part of the investigation into the threats, given they referenced Dee Dee, and Ris's death. I wanted to see if there was anyone involved with the band who might've held a grudge.'

He stared at me. 'And you don't think I would've looked into anyone with a grudge against the band at the time? Don't you think that would have crossed my mind as an experienced SIO? Or Simon's, as an experienced detective? Or are you saying we missed something?'

What I wanted to say was I thought it possible that despite being an experienced SIO, he might have become blinkered and not investigated as thoroughly as he would've done if he hadn't had a viable suspect handing themselves to him on a plate. And that most people at HQ seemed a little afraid of him, so would likely avoid pushing in any other direction to the one he was following – including Carver and Bret, it seemed. But I didn't see how saying that out loud would get me anywhere. I refused to give him ammunition to make this about anything other than finding the truth and keeping the band safe. 'I'm saying, I think there may be more to it than originally thought, sir. I don't believe Dee Dee's confession was entirely truthful and I think that someone else may have been involved somehow.'

He blinked as if I'd shone a laser in his eyes. '"Someone", "somehow", that's what you're bringing to the table here?'

I was about to list the reasons fuelling my suspicions, but realised it was pointless. Gordy Scott clearly wasn't going to entertain for a second the possibility he might have gotten something wrong, Bret was playing a blinder in his mission to be crowned Musical Statues Champion of the year, and Carver had done little more than grip his weak chin like a wet fucking lettuce.

Gordy started talking again before I had a chance to. 'Dee Dee Nolan killed Ris Angelini and now she's paying the price. End of story. So I strongly suggest you stop wasting your time going over old ground. The festival goes ahead as planned, unless you can use your womanly charm to convince the band to pull out of their own accord?'

The words snapped out of my mouth before I could stop them. 'Womanly charm?'

Neither Carver nor Bret could look me in the eye.

Gordy dragged his feet off the desk, stood and adjusted the waistband on his trousers. 'Victim rapport, whatever you wanna call it. You think the risk is too high, you convince them. I've every faith in you, Alison.'

'It's Alice, *sir*.'

'Course it is, are we done here?' he said, checking his watch.

I didn't want to do Gordy Scott any favours. But I also didn't want the band up there on Saturday to give either Manu or whoever he'd been speaking to the ability to pick them off one by one like neatly lined-up targets at a shooting range. 'Sir,' I said in as neutral a tone as I could muster.

'Off you go then,' he said, shooing me away with his words. I stood and turned to leave as he spoke again. 'You'd do well to remember that policing isn't a one-man— I beg your pardon, *person* show. It's about teamwork, and fitting into the team is important around here.'

He might as well have pulled out any future MCU applications I might make and held a lit match under them, teasing the edges of the paper with flames.

You can stick your teamwork up your arse, sir, I thought, saying nothing in return and walking out the door, suppressing the urge to slam it so hard the entire building rattled.

I jabbed the lift button until my finger hurt, desperate to get out of this stupid place and away from the politics. Before it opened, a shadow fell across the metal doors from behind me. I turned to see Bret about to tap me on the shoulder.

'Are you OK?' he asked.

'Why wouldn't I be?'

He nodded in the direction of Gordy's office. 'What were you talking about in there?'

'Oh, so you did hear me, then?' I said. 'Presumed you'd turned into a waxwork. And I assume you also noticed how much of a dick the boss was being? Well, thanks for making the effort to skulk on over here afterwards. Don't worry, I don't think he's seen you.'

'I didn't know what to—'

The lift opened and I stopped listening as I got in. I wasn't interested in hearing him trip over himself and pretend he wasn't yet another in the long line of people who'd caught HQitis: the overwhelming personality transplant that turned good cops into people-pleasing yes-men with one eye permanently fixed on the next round of promotion boards. I really *was* turning into Roy. Well, sod it, even Roy didn't seem to be Roy any more, so there was a vacancy. And this place could use a healthy dose of cynicism. Someone hand me a tumbler of whisky and a doner kebab.

36

The kitchen of the discreet Airbnb where the label had paid to move the band was roughly half the size of the one they'd become accustomed to, Aurora House's expensive industrial-themed fixtures replaced with budget white gloss fittings and the smell of horse manure wafting through the open window from the stables next door. Roy had dropped them off and gone back to the station by the time I arrived, his presence replaced by officers tasked with guarding the premises until a new security team was arranged.

Tabby, Nush and Em grumbled at the small breakfast bar while Kit made drinks. I scanned Tabby's bare arms. The cuts and bruises I'd heard about from where she'd scrambled through undergrowth to get to the road must have been confined to her legs, currently hidden under a pair of white linen trousers. 'How are you all holding up?' I asked, directing my question towards her, but Nush answered instead.

'I cannit believe it about Manu.' Nush's usually melodic voice was flat and husky.

Kit's eyes caught mine at the mention of his name. Her

secret link to the band was safe. For now. And even if it did come out, in the grand scheme of things, it felt rather small fry.

Tabby's follow-up distracted me from my thoughts. '*I can* believe it,' she said. 'Told you we should have pushed for an all-female entourage. Men are incapable of not encroaching on women's spaces, it's like, a fact, and looking back, I mean, his energy was all, like . . .' She did a weird fluttering movement with her fingers, '. . . you know?'

Em rolled her eyes. 'No, I don't know, 'cause you're talking absolute fucking shit as usual, mate. If you knew so much about his *aura*, or whatever, why didn't your crystal ball tell you he was a psychopath?'

Given Sherrie wasn't there to play referee, I interjected before they got carried away. 'Look, I'm sorry to be doing this, but I wanted to talk to you about performing at the festival. I really don't think it's a good idea. You've all had a big shock, your head of security is God knows where, and the rest of his team are being interviewed as we speak.'

'Like we've already told your colleagues,' Tabby said, 'we're doing the performance. Now more than ever we need to show we won't be scared away. And you don't need to worry about security. My parents have arranged for a new team to come and take over – they're ex-forces, Daddy uses them when he takes business trips in South America.'

It didn't go unnoticed that Tabby's parents hadn't exactly rushed home at the news of her disappearance, nor when she was found, for that matter. Apparently gifts of private security were a sufficient expression of their relief.

'Ex-forces or not,' I said, 'you're gonna be standing in the open on a spotlit stage, with thousands of people around you.'

Tabby folded her arms defiantly. 'We appreciate your concern, Sergeant,' she said, 'but we're going out there, we've already agreed, haven't we, Em?'

'Fuck, yeah,' Em said.

'Nush?' Tabby said.

Nush looked up at the sound of her name. She nodded, but the action didn't look filled to the brim with confidence, more like someone was holding an invisible gun to her head as well as the threat of a real one.

'We're doing the show. End of,' Em said.

I thought Nush might have bucked up the courage to protest as she stood from the breakfast bar stool, but instead she pulled a box of cigarettes and a lighter from her pocket. 'I'm gannin for a tab,' she said before disappearing out the door.

I'd done all I could here. And The Dolls were grown adults. All that was left now was to hope I was wrong. I got up and made to leave.

'Actually, Sergeant,' Tabby said, reaching for my arm. 'There is something you can do. They whipped everyone out of the retreat so fast they had to leave all our things behind, and I still don't have any of my belongings, what with me coming straight here from the hospital. Will you be allowed to pick up some items for us?'

'Once the crime scene has been cleared, sure.'

I waited while they wrote a list and handed it to me.

SAM FRANCES

'Please don't forget my lockbox,' Tabby said. 'It's a very, *very* important part of my vocal warm-up process. Oh, and Sherrie will want her blue folder from her top left bedside drawer. It's got her day planner in it; she'll be lost without it when she gets out of hospital.'

'No problem,' I said.

'And *do not* forget my lucky pick from my bedside table, yeah?' Em said, as if she was asking me to rescue her only child from a fast-flowing river.

'Pick, got it,' I said on my way out.

Nush was sitting on the front step as I left, and I took the opportunity to catch her on her own, sitting down beside her. 'You OK with all this, still doing the show?'

She blew out a series of smoke rings. 'I don't know what I am at the minute, like. I just want me drums. Smashing the shit out of them always sorts everything out.'

I thought back to the catharsis of smashing up the computers with Terry. 'I can imagine they're a good form of stress relief.'

She smiled and shook her head. 'It's more than that. It's the one thing in this world that . . . I dunno how to describe it, it like, takes ya to a different place and everythin' gannin' on up here,' she said, poking her temple, 'just disappears, and literally the only thing I'm thinking about are the sticks in me hands and the vibrations and the beat. Honestly, man, I can sit there for hours, days probably, and think about nowt else. Might sound pure wanky, but it's the best feeling in the world.'

I thought back to the time I'd worked the Fortbridge Flasher case. Over twenty incidents of girls approached by some sicko. I'd trawled the reports for hours, hunched at my desk pawing over every detail, looking for patterns and clues, not noticing the sun had gone down and risen again until Jane arrived the next morning and asked what the hell I was doing there on my rest day. 'They call it flow, that state.'

'Wey, whatever it is, it's fuckin' mint, man.'

'But surely you don't need to be doing it specifically on stage at *this* festival. You can drum anywhere; there'll be other gigs, Nush.'

'Not if we pull out of this one. Once you get branded "difficult" in this business you've done yasel up like a kipper. And aye, I've got a drum kit in me garage I could play to me heart's content, but being the drummer in a defunct rock band isn't exactly lucrative. Me family are relying on this money. I'm not stupid, I know I get paid less than the others, but it's something at least. I haven't got a nice little trust fund like Tabby and Em. And believe me, I've already checked the contract. If the entire band pulls out for safety reasons, they still have to pay us, but if I pull out and Tabby and Em still gan up there, and they will, 'cause if ya haven't noticed they're belligerent little fannies, then I get nowt, and if this gig doesn't gan ahead to launch the album off the back of, I'll be doubly fucked.'

She took another long drag on her cigarette before stubbing it out on the step.

A combination of thoughts rattled through my brain: the news article about Nush working in a supermarket and what

Ryan had said about the paparazzi knowing what the band were doing before they did. Exactly how strapped for cash was Nush? 'There were a lot of stories released back in the day, supposed "insider scoops" on the band,' I said. 'I've heard people pay good money for them. You wouldn't happen to know where they got those stories from, would you?'

Nush's head spun towards me. 'What ya implying, like?'

'I'm not implying anything, I'm asking a question. I saw in an article you'd been working on a check-out before coming back to the band.'

'And? What's wrong with working at a check-out?' She flicked the crinkled cigarette butt into a nearby flower pot. 'People have memories shorter than Tom Cruise these days. During the pandemic people couldn't be thankful enough for supermarkets, practically wankin' over bags of pasta and bottles of Dettol. And how d'ya think they got them? Because supermarket workers put up with the coughs and splutters and the absolute wobblies thrown when the loo roll supplies ran out to keep those shelves stacked. Deserve flippin' medals if ya ask me, like.'

I held up my hands in apology. 'I'm not knocking shop workers, not at all, but I doubt it pays anywhere near what it should, and that maybe there's a temptation to top it up.'

'I'm poor in money, not self-respect. If someone was feeding stories to the rags, it wasn't me. Sherrie would've had our guts for garters if we'd done owt like that.'

'Were there no connections to the stories that you can remember? Something that might suggest where they were getting them from?' I asked.

'What do I look like, fuckin' Rain Man? Isn't figuring that out meant to be your job?' She let out a sigh. 'Soz, I don't mean to be such a stroppy bitch, it's ... I wasn't expecting all this. I just wanna play me drums.'

'It's OK. Look, I'll leave you to get some rest.'

I walked to my car parked out by the main entrance, my phone ringing as I was about to get in: Roy. I leant against the door and answered. 'Yeah.'

'Gig off yet?' Roy said.

'Nope. Gordy doesn't want the bad PR, and my negotiation skills to convince them to pull out on their own are clearly not up to standard.'

'You're shitting me?'

'I shit you not, Roy.'

'Well then, let's hope your gut's wrong about this one.'

'I guess we'll find out in three days' time.'

37

News of the attack on Sherrie and the hunt for Manu had made it to France before I'd gotten back to my desk, a message to return a call from Ryan Hope waiting for me. He answered after a few rings of an international dial tone. 'Ryan, hi, DS Washington, sorry no one's updated you yet. I'm sure you can imagine it's all systems go here at the minute.' I explained what had happened and the fact the case had been handed over to the MCU.

'I can't believe Manu'd do something like that,' Ryan said. 'He seemed like such a solid bloke. Not much in the personality department, but dependable. We always felt safe with him, did whatever was asked of him, no questions.'

My thoughts about what had happened in Birmingham pushed their way to the surface. 'Can I ask about a gig you did about six weeks before Ris died, at the Bull Ring Academy in Birmingham?'

'Sure, what about it?'

'What d'you remember about the after party? A load of people went back to your hotel with the band, I'm trying to find out who was there.'

'Erm ... I'm not sure exactly, that was the night I met Leigh so I was kinda wrapped up in her. But I presume it would be the usual crowd. Manu kept things tight. He didn't let just anyone come back, but there were always people hanging with us.'

'So who would the usual crowd have been?'

He reeled off a similar list to the one Oliver Campbell had. 'That's all I can think of for now, I'll let you know if anyone else comes to mind.'

'That'd be really helpful. One other thing, did Ris say anything to you about that night, afterwards?'

'No, I mean, I know she had a fling with The Saxons bloke, and I think Dee Dee copped off with one of them, too, the others were all gossiping about it the next morning.'

'What kind of gossip?'

'Just the usual, you know, poking fun, that sorta thing.'

'And Riz and Dee Dee were all right with that, were they?'

'Dee Dee was a bit moody about it, probably not used to the ribbing – no shade on her, but it wasn't usually the roadies people were after hooking up with – and Ris didn't seem bothered at first, just ignored them, but then Tabby brought it up again the next day, asking Ris if she was gonna see her bloke again, and Ris kicked off. And it's not like they were the best of friends, but they got on, usually, she'd never had a go at any of us like that before. And it went downhill from there, to the point where Tabby always used to braid Ris's hair before we went on stage, put these little feathers in it, it was a bit of a ritual, but a

301

few weeks later Tabby went to do it and Ris smacked her one. It was weird; she'd barely even touched her. But Ris'd gotten totally out of hand by that point.'

I thought back to one of the tabloid stories I'd read about Ris hitting Tabby. It had fitted with the general moody behaviour at first. But as I thought about it now, factoring in what I knew about Birmingham, the photos someone had taken and possibly blackmailed her with, as well as remembering what Ryan had said when we'd first spoken to him about the change in Ris's behaviour, how she'd thrown herself at him a couple of weeks after he met Leigh, I saw the whole situation in a new light.

I'd seen it time and time again working on cases involving sexual offences, both in the physical and non-contact form: dramatic changes in the victim's behaviour as they tried to deal with what had happened to them. Everyone had assumed Ris's diva-like conduct started when the US tour was announced, her ego also supposedly bruised when she lost Ryan's affection to Leigh. But I was starting to think it wasn't those things at all. It was the photos. The blackmail. The unknown perpetrator amongst the group of people closest to her. Her trust in everyone evaporating before her eyes. Pulling away from up-close-and-personal time with fans. Lashing out at Tabby because even her once familiar contact had become a violation of her personal space. What if she hadn't been trying to regain Ryan's attention when she came on to him? What if instead, she'd been trying to regain control of her bodily autonomy after someone snatched it away, wanting to feel safe with someone she trusted? 'How convinced are you that it was finding out about the US tour that kick-started Ris's change in behaviour?'

'What else could it've been?' Ryan replied.

'If something,' I thought about my words carefully, '*bad* had happened to Ris, would she have told someone, asked for help?'

'Bad? What d'you mean, bad?'

'I'm still trying to figure that out, but if something had happened after the Birmingham gig, something that upset her, who would she have told?'

'I dunno, before we fell out I'd have said me and Dee Dee were the closest to her. But if it was about Birmingham, then like I said, we didn't really speak much after that.'

'So she would have told Dee Dee?'

'I reckon so, yeah; they didn't fall out until a couple of weeks after that. She would have told Dee Dee if anything happened, I'm sure of it, or written it down at the very least.'

'What d'you mean, "written it down"? Written it where?'

'Anywhere, scrap paper, notebook, on the back of a fag packet if needs be.' *Notebook.* My heart leapt into my throat, barely registering as Ryan carried on talking. 'Ris used to write songs, kinda like therapy on the page, I mean, we all did, at least we tried to, anyway. Em's seemed to be the only ones that were any good, though Ris did write a couple of bangers back at the start. One of the benefits of being a creative, I guess – something shitty happens to you, at least you have the silver lining of being able to put it into your art.'

My mind whirred. *What if . . .*

'Hello? You still there?' Ryan said.

'Yes, sorry, I was . . .' The plastic crates from the pit still piled behind my desk caught my eye. 'Thanks, Ryan, that's been a big help. Sorry, something's come up, I've gotta go.'

Information buzzed around my head like a fuse box about to overheat as I pulled open the crate containing the notebook. I skimmed the pages once more, seeing the same nonsensical ramblings about dolls, snakes, tumours, wolves in sheep's clothing and scabs that I'd read through before, but seeing them in a new light as the words pulsed from the page.

Dolls: small models of human figures, made to look real with all the right parts. Bodies and arms and legs with pretty little heads . . . Play nice now, like a good little toy . . . Sharp and slick as I slice you, proving you are more than flesh-coloured plastic, filled with bone and tissue and fat and blood and lies . . .

My chest tightened as I carried on reading, looking for the paragraph that had flashed through my memory as Ryan had been talking. Skimming my finger across the dents in the page, I stopped at the final entry.

And then I remember, the choice is mine, no longer yours to own. Whatever I decide is how this will end. I am in control. This is the only way. The only option left to get what I want. To make it stop. And it will stop. When I say so. It will all be over soon.

Taking back control. Making it stop. Words filled with so much pain the author could no longer bear. 'Holy sh—' Doubt stopped me mid-sentence, my mind refusing to contemplate the theory that had formed like a thick, heavy raincloud in a thunderstorm. I took a deep breath to calm the pounding in my chest as I picked up the phone, held it to my cheek and called the prison liaison team. I had a question only Dee Dee could answer.

38

No doubt wind of me visiting the prison again would make
its way to HQ, but I didn't care. I sat across from Dee Dee,
her arms still covered in a long-sleeved T-shirt despite the
fact it was even warmer than it had been at last week's
visit. Her gaze remained fixed to the table as I told her
about Manu.

'Right,' she said, as if I'd given her an update on the
weather.

'Does that surprise you, what he did?'

She shrugged.

This would likely be my last shot at talking to her if
Gordy had anything to do with it. There was no time for
games. I needed her to open up to me, because the theory
I wanted to ask her about required much more than a
one-word answer. 'You know better than anyone, Dee Dee,
about people doing things no one expects them to. From
what I've been told, Manu ran a pretty tight ship, but I've
also heard there were exceptions. Like the night of the
band's gig at the Bull Ring Academy in Birmingham.' The
tour Dee Dee had joined them on involved thirty-six dates

across ten cities, but the way her eyes widened as the rest of her face clearly fought the reaction, told me she remembered the significance of that particular gig. It didn't take long to see she had no intention of filling the silence so I carried on. 'Do you remember that night?'

She tried to keep her breath settled, but the heavy rise and fall of her chest under her baggy top was unmistakeable. 'What about it?'

Something told me not to mention the photos just yet. 'That was the night they announced their US tour, right?'

Dee Dee visibly unclenched a little. 'Yeah, so?'

'Was the plan for you to go with them?'

She nodded. 'I was the only one they trusted to set up their kit.'

'Must have been exciting, twenty-one years old, going off to America, all expenses paid. Gotta be a dream come true for someone from your neck of the woods.'

All I got in response was another nod. This chit-chat approach was only going to get me so far; I needed to hit a nerve. I thought back to the only topic eliciting real emotion last time we'd spoken: Judith. 'And your mum was all right with it, you going off like that?'

Dee Dee bristled. 'She wouldn't have noticed I'd gone.'

'America was your big ticket away from your mum, wasn't it?'

'Would've helped, yeah.'

'So you wouldn't have wanted anything to get in the way of that, right?'

'What does all this matter?'

'You wanted to go to America,' I said, 'to get away from your mum, get off that estate.'

'And?'

'So why sabotage it?' I asked. 'Surely you knew pushing Ris wouldn't just kill her; it'd kill the tour, the band, the whole lifestyle you'd been living vicariously through them. She was the big ticket item. There was no band without Ris.'

Her whole body clenched. 'I wasn't thinking about that when I pushed her.'

'No, you were thinking about how much she'd changed, yeah? Wasn't the person you'd grown up with any more. How jealous you were of her, for all the attention she was getting – that's right, isn't it? You wanted revenge, to get back at her after you had a big blow-out a few weeks before she died – that's what you told the police, right?'

'Yeah.'

'See, there's something that doesn't sit right about that with me, Dee Dee. Because then what?'

'What d'you mean, "then what?"' she asked.

'What was the plan after you killed Ris? Are you honestly telling me you didn't stop to think about what would happen next? Where you'd go? You'd have had no other option if you'd gotten away with it than to go back to living at your mum's. And I don't think there's a chance in hell you'd want that.'

The veil of disinterest she'd clung to slipped and I could tell by the look on her face she'd never been asked that question before.

'And another thing I can't get my head around,' I said,

'is the jealousy. I get why people bought it as a motive. You didn't make the band; she did, after she didn't even want to audition. She got all the adoration on stage while you stood on the sidelines. Most people *would* be jealous of that. But I know something most people don't. I know about Em's letters. About the songs. I know you wrote most of them.' Her nostrils flared and she cleared her throat. I waited but she didn't speak. 'If you wanted validation, a little slice of the glory, you could've taken it. There was nothing Em could've done if you'd said you'd only write the songs if you got the credit you deserved for them. So why didn't you? If you were so desperate for attention you'd kill your best friend over your jealousy? It doesn't track.'

Again, she said nothing.

'OK, if you're not going to tell me, I'll tell you what I think happened. I think that, yeah, you probably were a bit miffed at first, that Ris got the spot in the band you wanted, but then she made sure you got to come along for the ride anyway. And I think you realised you'd landed a pretty sweet deal after all. You got the rock and roll lifestyle, got to write your songs, had a front row view watching them be performed in front of thousands of fans night after night, but without any of the other shit that goes along with it: the stories in the tabloids the others had to put up with, having their lives and outfits and every second of their itinerary dictated by the label. You got all the fun with none of the pressure. I don't think you were jealous of Ris at all, and I don't think you wanted to give any of that up for a second. So there goes half the motive you gave as part of your confession.'

Tears filled Dee Dee's eyes but still she didn't confirm or deny anything.

'Now, the other half,' I continued. 'I don't think that's an outright fabrication. Ris *did* change, there's no doubt about that; in fact, from what I've seen, she had quite the spiral in those last six weeks. I've learned a lot about that time, things that if looked at in isolation don't mean much, fit with the caricature of her that the tabloids started and you finished off, the "good girl turned diva". But it's not my job to look at things one by one. It's to put them all together, look at the bigger picture. And that bigger picture is making me see things differently, telling me Ris wasn't being a drama queen. She was going through something. Something bad. Now you don't know me and I don't know you, well, not the real you anyway, but the one thing you should know about me is when I get a sense something is going on, that something isn't right, I don't let go of it until I figure out what. D'you understand?'

She attempted a laugh. 'I don't ... I don't know what you're on about. There is no bigger picture. There's *the* picture. The one I've talked about a million times. I don't know what else you want me to say.' The conviction she was going for crumbled with each word.

'From what I can see, there's a significant part missing from that bigger picture that no one seems to have talked about. I know about the photos someone took of Ris, after the Birmingham gig. Intimate photos,' I said.

Her mouth gaped like she was struggling to find her next words. 'W— what photos?' she managed to get out, but her eyes told me she knew exactly what I was talking about. She'd done well in our first interaction to keep that shield up, stop me seeing the emotions swimming around in there, but there was one coming through loud and clear now. Panic.

'Come on, Dee Dee. You've kept this lie up far too long now, and I'm not going to stop digging until I find out why.'

A large tear escaped over her lashes before she could stop it. 'I'm not lying, I don't know what you're talking about.'

'I think you do. And I already know you went off and spent the night with Adzy Loader, and Ris stayed at the hotel with Oliver Campbell, and the next morning someone told Ris they'd taken intimate photos of the two of them together. What I don't know is how this was communicated to her, as no one else in the band seems to have mentioned it, and she called Campbell asking if he knew who took them, so I can only assume someone contacted her anonymously. You were her best friend, Dee Dee, and Ryan is positive if she was going through something she would have told you about it. So what I need to know is what she said about those photos. Did she find out who took them? How did they send them to her?'

She was clearly trying to keep her face neutral, but her lips were trembling. 'I don't know anything about any photos. I can't help you. Can I go?' She gestured to the door. The officer waiting outside looked at me through the window and I held a finger up to request another minute.

'Just a few more things. Since I found out about the photos, I've been re-evaluating the other evidence as well as what you said in your statement – through this new lens.' I reached into my bag and pulled out the notebook. It was safely sealed back inside its exhibit bag, but I'd left it open, the page with the last entry on clear display through the plastic.

Dee Dee leant forward slowly, before the recognition hit and she recoiled as if the notebook was on fire and the flames had lashed out at her face. 'I can't, please, I can't look at that. Put it away.'

I didn't want to put her through this, but I needed the truth and I was running out of options. 'Whose notebook is this, Dee Dee?'

She swallowed. 'It's ... it's mine.'

'Are you sure about that? Because from what I've been told, you're not really a notebook person. Even when you write songs, you hold everything up here.' I tapped the side of my head. 'I've had a read-through, and knowing what I know about Ris now, what she was going through, I think this belonged to her, not you.'

Dee Dee fixed her gaze on me, though it didn't feel like she was trying to intimidate me, more that she wanted to focus on what was in front of her to stop her eyes being drawn to the words on the page.

Nudging the notebook towards her, I tried again. 'I can see how the officers who found it might think it was yours and why they were concerned about what was inside it. There's a lot of anger in those pages, Dee Dee. A lot of suspicion, losing trust in everyone around them. Whoever wrote it was clearly in a terrible amount of pain and felt completely alone and helpless, with no one to support them.'

Dee Dee's hand flew to her mouth and she shook her head as though she was trying to shake away the visible emotion she'd done everything in her power to hold in.

Come on, Dee Dee, tell me what happened! I forced myself to stick to the facts, hoping they'd convince her she had nowhere else to go but towards the truth. 'I read about the DNA tests they did, on the lapels of Ris's jacket. In my experience, you generally only get decent results like that from touch DNA when there's been prolonged and vigorous contact, which got me thinking, they aren't usually words people would associate with a simple push.'

Dee Dee wiped her face with the back of her hand, her voice wobbling as she spoke. 'I dunno, I . . . I might have grabbed her or something, it all happened quickly, I can't remember exactly.'

'That's right, I think it did all happen quickly, and you did grab her. I think you grabbed her really tightly and clung on for dear life, but she got away from you, didn't she?' I picked up the notebook and read the last couple of lines aloud. '*This is the only way. The only option left to get what I want. To make it stop. And it will stop. When I say so. It will all be over soon.*' I dragged my eyes from the page to meet Dee Dee's. 'She wanted her pain to stop – that's what she was talking about, wasn't it?'

Dee Dee shoved the heels of her palms against her eye sockets, fingers clenched, knuckles so white it looked like the bone might tear through the skin. 'Stop! Please!'

'Why were you hanging on so tightly, Dee Dee? Why so desperate to hold on to her?'

313

No words came back in response, just a whimper from behind the hands still covering her face.

'Was it because you knew if you let go she'd jump? Is that what happened, Dee Dee? Did Ris jump?'

She may not have said the words of confirmation, but the way she flew from the chair told me I was right.

'*That's* why your DNA was on her jacket,' I said, 'isn't it?'

'Please, just stop. I deserve to be here, I should've . . . Just stop, I don't wanna do this any more. Leave me alone!' The last three words came out in a shriek so loud the guard who'd been watching from the window pushed the door open.

'Wait, please, one minute,' I said to him before turning my attention back to Dee Dee, who was now slumped against the wall, sobbing into her hands. 'I promise you, all I want is to make this right. Why would you say you did it when she did it to herself? Why lie? Who are you protecting, Dee Dee?'

The guard hooked his hands under her armpits and pulled her to her feet. 'All right, I think that's enough. Come on, up you get.'

'But—' I stopped myself, knowing there was no point protesting while Dee Dee was in this state. All I could do was stand there and watch as the guard took her back to her cell, her cries echoing down the hallway, before being replaced by the sounds of keys against locks, clunking and clattering. Then silence.

39

All night Kit had been calling Judith. All fucking night. At first it had rung before going to voicemail, but then it had started going straight to the recorded message. Wherever Judith was, either her battery had run out, or she'd deliberately turned the phone off. It had been around four by the time Kit finally fell asleep, so *appreciative* was the last word she'd use to describe how she felt when a knock on her door woke her just as the sun was coming up.

'What the—?' Kit had enough on her plate; the last thing she needed was more band drama. Dragging herself out of bed, she unlocked her door to find Tabby on the other side, her hand lifted, ready to rap again. 'Ah, please, I've told you, I'm not interested in sunrise yoga, OK?' Tabby barged through the door anyway, knocking against Kit's shoulder. 'Ow! Come on in, why don't you?'

'Can I come in?' It was as if Tabby hadn't heard a word Kit had said, already halfway across the room, looking around.

Kit blinked, trying to wake her tired eyes. 'You're already *in*. Are you all right?'

'Yes. Great. Totally fine,' Tabby said, wrapping one of her thick curls around her finger and yanking on it. 'Have you heard from the sergeant? She said she was getting our things.'

Kit eyed Tabby warily. 'No, I haven't heard anything.'

'Do you think she's forgotten?'

Kit shrugged. 'I'm sure she'll sort it as soon as she can. She's probably busy, you know, trying to find Manu.'

'How sure?' Tabby said, nibbling on her fingernails. What the hell was wrong with her? She hadn't even been this on edge when they'd first gone to see her in the hospital.

'I dunno, I mean, pretty sure, I guess. What's the big deal anyway?'

Tabby darted across the room and ripped the curtains open, looking out across the paddock at the back of the Airbnb. 'The festival. The festival is tomorrow.'

'Yeah, and? The instruments and everything are sorted; all ready to go.'

'I need something from my room at Aurora House.'

'What's so important it's got you in this state?' Kit said, frowning.

Tabby turned around and shook her head. 'I'm not in a state. Who said I was in a state? I just need my things, OK, is that so much to ask? It's not like I'm demanding some ridiculous rider with insane orders like a tub of M&Ms with all the brown ones picked out, or special water that's been shipped in from some exclusive highland spring. I just – want – my box! Why can't I get what I want for once?'

Kit had never seen Tabby this worked up before.

Instinctively, she pulled back. 'It'll be fine,' she said soothingly, 'we can get you what you need. If it's that important, I'm sure Sherrie'll get someone on it straight away when she's back.'

Tabby stepped forward, away from the window. Her voice was suddenly flat and emotionless. 'Don't think that just because you've been here a few weeks you know anything about us. You have no idea, absolutely none at all.'

Kit backed away towards the bed. 'I didn't claim to— Look, why don't I go get one of the others, Nush, or Em? They'll know what to do.'

'I don't need them. Or anyone. I need my things. Call the sergeant, I know you have her number,' Tabby said, her voice still flat but now tinged with accusation.

Kit wasn't sure what she was dealing with here. Did Tabby know what she was up to with DS Washington? Or had Manu told her something before he'd fled? No, that couldn't be it, Tabby had been fine with her until now. 'OK, but it's still early. Let's give her until later this morning – if we haven't heard anything by lunchtime, we'll call her, all right?'

Tabby nodded, her body relaxing a little. 'Thank you, and sorry, I didn't mean to … Sometimes I get like this, before a show, and it's been a while, so …'

Kit stepped towards her, relaxing a little as she realised Tabby was just being Tabby. Overly dramatic, as usual. She placed what she hoped would be a comforting hand on Tabby's arm, almost gasping as she felt Tabby trembling.

40

The excuse I'd given Roy about why I wasn't coming back to the office after leaving the prison yesterday hadn't been a lie. A headache had mushroomed as I'd waited for the guard to come back and escort me out, and it was still pounding now as I woke up on the sofa, my mouth dry, after a broken night's sleep.

I hadn't been able to speak to Dee Dee again. There was no way they were dragging her back out of her cell so I could ask her why she'd lied, not in the state I'd gotten her into. I was almost positive I was right about how Ris had died that night, but what I still couldn't figure out was *why* Dee Dee had made up a whole other version of events. Why didn't she say Ris had jumped and that she'd tried to stop her? Whatever had happened between the two of them, Dee Dee was clearly racked with guilt; shame had practically dripped off her face alongside the tears. Was she punishing herself? She clearly had form. I hadn't seen them, but I was convinced the long-sleeved T-shirts Dee Dee wore despite the sweltering heat were hiding self-harm scars like the ones I'd seen on Em's stomach.

But I still didn't know what she was punishing herself for. Where was guilt this extreme coming from? Nothing seemed big enough. The fact she'd gone off with Adzy that night instead of staying with Ris at the hotel? Maybe she hadn't been supportive when Ris told her about the photos, had been judgemental even, going so far as to blame Ris somehow for what happened to her. Could that be what they'd really argued over? And why hadn't Dee Dee told the police about any of this? Whatever the answers to all these questions were, surely there wasn't enough guilt in the world for one human to absorb so much of it they'd let themselves rot in prison when they'd done nothing wrong? There must be more to it, I just wasn't seeing it. And there was no point updating Jane until I had the full picture, something irrefutable.

Think!

I swung my legs off the sofa and sat forward, massaging my sweaty scalp with my fingers in the hope it would spark an idea, but all it seemed to achieve was to summon a phone call as a buzzing started from somewhere between the cushions.

'DS Washington,' I said after scooping it out.

'Finally!' said a high-pitched female voice, the squeaking enough to make me pull the phone away from the side of my face to protect my eardrums.

'Sorry, who is this?'

'It's Tabby, Tabby Falstead. Are you bringing our things – remember you said you would – from Aurora House?' With everything I'd found out in the last twenty-four hours, the promise had slipped my mind. I was trying to think of a polite way to tell her I had the rather more important problem of a potentially innocent woman languishing in prison weighing on my mind, but she jumped back in before I had the chance. 'I really need my lockbox, Sergeant, it's like, really important to me.'

'I understand, I'll go over there now.'

'*Please* do, the festival is tomorrow.'

Don't I bloody know it, I thought, not welcoming the reminder. 'I know. I'll pop by later this afternoon, you'll have your stuff for tomorrow.'

The atrium of Aurora House was eerily quiet as I entered, the only sounds being my footsteps echoing off the walls and high ceilings and water trickling from the Buddha fountain. I climbed the stairs, stopping at the room I'd been told was Em's. I grabbed her beloved guitar pick from her bedside table before moving on to the next room where Tabby had been staying.

Sunlight poured in through three aspect windows, every surface covered with Tabby's personal effects which largely consisted of a mishmash of stuff that looked like someone had wandered around a car boot sale and scooped up anything looking remotely quirky or spiritual. On one side of the vanity mirror sat two small figurines: a green one of a naked pregnant woman with a Mother Earth vibe, a globe representing her swollen stomach, and a second that looked like some sort of Hindu God. On the other side of the mirror was a smaller version of the Buddha statue that sat in the water feature downstairs. This woman needed to pick a bloody lane. Surely praying to God didn't work if you were doing it to all of them. Wasn't that the first rule of most religions, a bit of exclusivity?

Propped up behind Tabby's vanity mirror, a large frame containing a matrix of small photographs caught my eye, each slot filled with an image of the band. They appeared to be in chronological order. The first one looked like a party on the set of the TV show that had brought them together, smiling and laughing, a far cry from the photo at the opposite end of the frame, clearly much later in their time together. Less embracing. Faces more serious. So much had changed for them in a relatively short space of time. I wouldn't have put rock star up there on the list of jobs being more thankless than being a cop, but what the hell did I know?

I homed in on Ris's face in the last picture. I wouldn't say she looked sad, per se, she just looked . . . empty. *Jesus*. I still hadn't figured out how I was going to explain all this to Jane, to Gordy, that a woman had spent a decade in prison for a murder that had very possibly never even happened in the first place. The term *shit hitting the fan* didn't feel strong enough to describe the storm I was about to unleash at HQ if I found proof, more like molten diarrhoea hitting the Hadron fucking Collider. But that sounded like yet another problem to add to future Alice's list. I had however long it took me to finish up here, drop the items off at the Airbnb, and the twenty-minute drive back to the station to live in blissful ignorance before I potentially became Fortbridge's very own Edward Snowden.

Pushing away the melancholy, I made for the four-poster bed Tabby said her box was kept under and knelt on the carpet to grope around underneath it, knuckles knocking against a smooth, hard surface. I slid out a dark brown wooden box. What was in here that was so important that the panic of not having it for the festival had hiked Tabby's voice up two octaves on the phone?

Curiosity clouded my mind as I examined the box. Two thick metal clasps straddled the lid and the bottom half of it, a flimsy padlock holding them together. My hands moved to one of the grips holding back my hair before I realised what I was doing. I pulled the sliver of metal away from my scalp and used it to pick the lock. Flipping back the lid, I held my breath, before my shoulders dropped in relief when I saw the contents. Nothing exciting, just a stash of newspaper and magazine cuttings and packets of what looked like medication. What had I been expecting to find in there?

I picked up one of the packets and read the prescription label. 'Propranolol,' I said, pulling my phone from my pocket and googling the name. Scrolling through the results listing its different uses, I could guess why Tabby was so desperate to have it back before the festival: performance anxiety and stage fright. I put the pills down and rifled through the cuttings. They were all photos of Tabby, both on stage and at events. A little box marking out her achievements.

Light flashed in the corner of my eye and I flinched, my gaze flicking towards the open bedroom door. 'Hello?'

No response.

'Hello? Police. DS Alice Washington. Is anyone out there?'

Still silence. But somehow the air felt different, like I wasn't the only one breathing it. There was another flash of light, from the other side of me this time. I jerked my head towards the window at the same time as a crow settled on the outside ledge, the source of the flash of light, no doubt, or more accurately the momentary absence of light as its body must have flown past the window, blocking the sun.

'Fuck's sake. What's it gonna do? Peck me to death?' I relocked Tabby's box, put it into a carrier bag along with Em's pick, and made my way next door to Sherrie's room to find the folder the band had said she'd want.

Sherrie's room was sparse, neat and orderly in complete contrast to Em's mess and Tabby's clutter. The light blue semi-opaque folder was where they'd said it would be in her top bedside table drawer. I pulled it out, pausing as something creaked behind me. I spun, holding the folder out like a shield, but there was no one there, just a half-open window and another bloody crow trying to stick its beak through the gap. Since when had I agreed to star in a remake of *The Birds*? 'Go away!' I said, flapping the folder at the window to scare it off, swiping a jewellery box off the sill in the process. 'Shit!' I knelt down, putting the folder on the floor before scooping the spilled contents, which seemed to consist of Sherrie's power suit jewellery accompaniments, into my palm.

'You got a warrant for that?' said a voice from behind me.

A muscle in my neck spasmed as I looked up in the direction it came from to see Sherrie towering over me. I gasped. 'Bloody hell, you nearly gave me a heart attack.'

'Only pulling your leg,' she said, a flat smile appearing for only a couple of seconds.

'They finally let you out of the hospital, then?' I asked.

'Wanted to keep me in another day, but, well, it might not surprise you to know I'm not a fan of being told what to do.'

I didn't doubt that for a second. 'Can't be too careful with head injuries, though. Don't rush it, yeah?'

'I'm a big girl, Sergeant, more than capable of looking after myself. Speaking of looking after,' she said, nodding at the carrier bag hooked over my arm, 'you get everything they need?'

'Yeah, Tabby seemed rather desperate to get this box back.'

Sherrie rolled her eyes. 'Thought she'd be having a meltdown without it. It's her *sunshine box*,' she said, her tone mocking. 'You'd never know it to look at her, Miss Social Media Queen 2023, but she's got the constitution of a Victorian orphan, that one. The clippings are supposed to help with confidence, apparently, remind her how great she is, and with the amount of pills she's on for her nerves I'm surprised she don't rattle. Honestly, this generation drives me mad, the lengths I have to go to keep them facing in the right direction, wrap them in cotton wool. Bring back corporal punishment, I say.'

I pushed to stand as my phone rang. 'Sorry, one sec.' I turned away from Sherrie to answer it.

'Sarge, it's Eddie.'

'I'm in the middle of something, can I give you a call back?'

'It's only a quickie. I've bottomed out looking into that production company who did *The Dee Dee Dolls* documentary. No wonder they went bust – that was the only thing they ever did! Hardly a money maker.'

'Yeah, OK, I'm not sure it really matters any more; thanks for looking into it, though.'

'Ah, OK then, that's good, because SP Productions are clearly nowhere to be found. I'll catch you later then, Sarge.'

I wasn't sure if the word 'bye' actually crossed my lips before Eddie hung up, or if it had remained frozen in my throat, too distracted by two things that had clashed in my mind at the same time: the name of the production company he'd mentioned and the realisation of what it was I was holding in my hand. I hadn't paid too much attention as I'd scooped up the clutter that had fallen out of the jewellery box, but two identical items stuck out like beacons now amongst the earrings and brooches in my palm. I struggled to swallow as I looked at them: two small glass eyeballs. Exactly like the ones from the dolls that had been left hanging on the main stage. Exactly like the ones that would have belonged in the head of the fifth doll. The ones we'd assumed had been eaten. But now I wasn't so sure they'd even been in that fifth doll's head when the goat had walked off with it in the first place, someone having already removed them.

My eyes flicked to the blue folder, still on the carpet

where I'd left it by my feet. I could see something else in there alongside Sherrie's day planner, a gold coat of arms symbol against a navy backdrop. Her passport. *SP Productions*, I mouthed silently. Sherrie Pearce?

It was only now I realised, a split second too late, that Sherrie had been standing with her hands behind her back. I spun around, something heavy and hard smashing into the side of my head before everything went black.

41

I couldn't work out if I was dead or having an out-of-body experience. My senses were returning, a blue blur clouding my vision, echoed sounds of footsteps and metal clanging against metal ringing in my ears, but my body felt like it was floating on air. No, wait, not air. Warm liquid encased me, lapping at the sides of my face. Where was I?

The blue light transitioned to green and I blinked repeatedly. There was a searing pain in my head. I'd been hit. Hard. Had it affected my sight? Knocked something loose? I strained to focus, the light transitioning again, from green to purple this time. My lips stung, salt shocking my tongue as I licked them. Wait . . . what? Why were they salty? And what was that smell? It was equal parts strong and familiar, but I was so disorientated it took me a second to realise. *Chlorine.* The realisation kicked me back to reality. I was still in Aurora House, but in the basement's pool room. And my sight wasn't playing tricks on me. The coloured light *was* changing, and it was coming from tiny pinprick bulbs embedded in the smooth plastic flotation therapy pod surrounding me.

Water sprayed in all directions as I thrashed my limbs, the noise of rattling metal chiming again as I realised my arm was restrained. Running my gaze along the length of it, I stopped at my wrist, seeing now what was causing the sound. I was handcuffed, tethered to the thick pole connecting the base of the pod with its lid.

'You're heavier than you look for a lanky thing. Must have dense bones.'

My head jerked back and forth as I hoicked myself up to sitting, looking for the source of the voice. Sherrie was sat on the edge of one of the loungers dotted around the side of the pool, one of her hands moving strangely. It took me a second to compute what she was doing, what the faint noise was, like she was rolling marbles around in her palm. Except I knew they weren't marbles. They had to be the doll's eyes I'd found upstairs.

She tipped them into her pocket before letting out a deep sigh. 'Gorgeous, ain't they? Thought they might make a nice pair of earrings, a little keepsake to remind me of my girls.'

'What the fuck is going on?' I managed to mumble. 'Sherrie, what have you done?'

She leant forward, elbows resting on her knees. 'What I had to, darlin', just like I always have.' I opened my mouth to speak, but all that came out was a groan of pain as Sherrie carried on. 'You must know what it's like, being a woman in a man's world. It's no different in entertainment. Everything's controlled by the same power-hungry, middle-aged, dick-swinging men. So when you ain't got a dick to

328

swing, you've gotta find something else if you wanna be taken seriously, d'you know what I mean?'

I touched the side of my head, matted hair rough and sticky under my fingertips. My hand was coated in fresh blood, the pool of water around me tinged pink. 'So what exactly did you *swing* to get what you wanted? Your baseball bat? At Manu? Was anything you said about the attack true?'

'The part about him being wanted for murder in New Zealand was,' she said. 'I just, shall we say, embellished the rest. And believe me, I didn't want to, it was no picnic headbutting the wall to get this bad boy.' She pointed at the prominent bump in the middle of her forehead, now adorned with three stitches and surrounded by a deep bruise. 'Trust me, I'd have done what I promised, kept his secret, helped him turn his life around. He's the one who fucked it up, couldn't stick to his side of the agreement.'

'What agreement?'

Sherrie smiled. 'This ain't a James Bond film, love. I ain't got time to fill you in on every inch of rationale before I get sharks with laser beams on their heads to finish you off.'

I thought back to what Ryan had said when I'd told him about Manu. *Manu did whatever was asked of him, no questions.* Sherrie didn't like being told what to do, but she certainly liked dishing out orders. And I'd hazard a guess Manu had made the perfect puppet, her personal life-sized toy soldier with a secret to keep, bending to her will to make sure it never saw the light of day. I was already convinced Manu was the one talking on the phone in the transcript

Kit had found, the one worrying about Ris's spiralling behaviour. And now I knew who he'd been talking to, the one arguing with him, trying to maintain control and keep things under wraps. He'd been talking to Sherrie. She knew damn well about the photos. And I had a pretty good idea why. 'How about I have a stab at your rationale?' I said.

Sherrie checked her watch before sitting back and crossing her legs at the ankles. 'Go on then, colour me intrigued.'

'I know someone took intimate photos of Ris after their gig in Birmingham. I think that someone was Manu. And I think he did it because you told him to, because he knew if he didn't do everything you ordered, you'd expose him, for what happened back in New Zealand. That was your *agreement*, right? Why you took him on in the first place? It's not like you needed the muscle – clearly you can use force perfectly well all by yourself.' I pointed to the gash on my head from where Sherrie had smacked me. 'And I'm guessing you had him keep an eye on the band for you, feed you any juicy snippets worth selling to the tabloids, alongside the ones you were making up yourself. Just like the threats, another little fabrication you got him to sort for you: the social posts, getting someone to sneak around the retreat grounds, rope his mates into masking up and grabbing Tabby to scare the living shit out of her. Drum up some free attention for the festival, really kickstart that new album, eh? The teams looking for Manu are looking in the wrong place, because my guess is you never let him leave this retreat.' Sherrie squinted but didn't reply. 'You use violence as a last resort, that's not how you like to operate. You prefer holding things over people, and you needed something over Ris. The only thing I'm not sure about is why.'

A grin spread across Sherrie's face as she gave me a round of applause. 'Impressive, not far off full marks there, a solid eight out of ten. I should have known you were gonna be a problem the minute I saw you with your bag man, what's his name, Reg?'

'Roy.'

She snapped her fingers. 'Roy, that's the fella. Looks about as much use as a chocolate fireguard, that one. But you?' She clicked her tongue against the side of her mouth. 'I should have kept a closer eye on you.'

'But why? Is a few extra record sales really worth ruining people's lives?'

Sherrie pointed at me like I was a naughty child. 'I don't ruin lives, I make them. And if you wanna go viral these days, you've gotta have something to play off, a sob story or freak factor. It's not like it was back in the day. There's so much bloody content out there, the usual tabloid fodder doesn't cut it any more; even that documentary barely touched the sides for some people, and those girls I rounded up for it were off their heads. No, this day and age you gotta think bigger, really spice things up. Take the Velvet Banshees, for example,' Sherrie said, as if all of a sudden we'd been transported to a casual drink in the pub.

I heard the words but they took a second to compute, the randomness of the segue throwing me. 'The what?'

'The Velvet Banshees, "Haunt You", "Waster". Appreciate they were before your time, but those songs are classics, and d'you know why that is, hmm?' She didn't wait for an answer. 'They had *me*, that's why. They were a good band, good singers, musicians, songwriters, but so are thousands of people. Talent isn't enough. You've gotta stand out from the crowd.' She opened her arms out wide like Christ on the cross. 'And that, Sergeant, is where I come in. I make them big. The Velvet Banshees did everything I told them to, and look where it got them.' She counted on her fingers. 'Gold records, Grammys, Hall of Fame, everything. But this lot,' she said, 'they've had it handed to them on a plate.' She practically spat the last word. 'Em can't deal with her emotions without slicing herself open; the one thing Tabby wanted most in this world was to be lead bloody singer, but now she's got the part she can't even walk on stage without pills, absolutely pathetic! And Ris, that girl could have been the real deal, got on those lists in twenty years' time alongside Stevie Nicks, Joan Jett, Debbie Harry, the lot. I knew it the second I laid eyes on her. And the ungrateful little shit didn't even want it.'

I wondered if Sherrie truly believed this was about what she could do for other people's careers, or if, deep down, she knew she was just stroking her own ego and using Ris as a cash cow. 'What did you do to Ris, Sherrie?'

'I tried to help her, that's what!' she said. 'And she fought me every step of the way. She wrote "Not Your Doll" about me, you know?' The anger spewing from Ris's notebook flashed behind my eyes. Had that been about Sherrie too?

332

She carried on her rant before I had a chance to process. 'And I can deal with that, a bit of spunk, but d'you know what she did when I told her about the US tour? *Cried!* And not tears of joy, not tears of "thank you for making me a star, Sherrie", no. Actual bloody tears. Told me she wasn't gonna do it, that she wanted out of the band altogether. "Not for her", apparently,' she said, clawing her fingers into air quotes with such exaggeration it was like she was trying to gouge out the eyes of an invisible presence in front of her to add to her grotesque collection. 'Can you imagine? After the dirty old arses I had to lick to get them that tour in the first place. I could have slapped her right there on the spot.'

'But you blackmailed her instead. What was the threat this time – that if she left, you'd release the photos to the press, just like you did with all the other stories?'

She stood up and came across to crouch beside the pod. 'Tenacious little bastard, aren't you? We've got that in common, you and me. Dedicated. Do what we gotta do to get the job done.'

My stomach churned. 'I'm *nothing* like you, Sherrie. For me, getting the job done means keeping other people safe, not getting myself ahead.'

She leant away from the edge of the pod, her fingers gripping the side. 'It would never have come to doing anything with those photos, I knew Ris better than that. I saw an opportunity, all right: let her know they existed, create the problem, they come to me with it, like they always do, and I fix it for them. Then, *poof*, I'm the fairy godmother they can't be without. You see how that works? I'd never have released anything like that to the press, I'm not a monster. I needed her to play ball with the tour, that's all. She said she'd do it for me after I rubbed the boo boo, made all the bad pictures go away.'

'You made her suicidal!' My words didn't land like the verbal slap I'd intended. Sherrie's expression remained neutral: she knew Ris had jumped. And she'd let Dee Dee take the blame. 'You knew, didn't you? How could you let a completely innocent person go to prison for doing nothing wrong?'

'I wouldn't put all your eggs in Dee Dee's basket, Sergeant, if you catch my drift.'

'She didn't push Ris and you know it.'

'No, but she's not *completely* innocent either, that's why I marked you down earlier – Manu didn't take the photos, he caught Dee Dee taking them, so let's not canonise her just yet, eh?'

The water was warm yet still I shivered uncontrollably. 'But she wasn't even there, she'd gone off with someone else from the other band.'

'For a bit, yeah, till they came back. I thought she'd come to her senses and left that absolute muppet out to dry, but he was with her. Dunno what the hell she found so appealing about him. Red flag city when someone called Adam goes around calling themselves "Adzy" if you ask me. Fucking loser, and clearly I was right if he thought getting someone to take sneaky shots of his best mate hooking up made for a good time.'

A screenshot of the comment Adam 'Adzy' Loader had left on the post I'd found flashed behind my eyes ... REMEMBER THIS? WHAT A NIGHT ;-) OLLIE OLLIE OLLIE, OY OY OY!!! Oh God. 'She ... why would she do that?'

Sherrie shrugged. 'Dee Dee didn't exactly have admirers queuing at her door. I guess boys will be boys, and pissed girls will do stupid things when encouraged to impress said boys. I confiscated them, of course. Taught them both a lesson there, didn't I? And she could have told Ris the truth, come clean about taking them, but she didn't, and that's on her, not me.'

Did this woman really think she'd done nothing wrong? That she'd simply done what she needed and let the chips fall where they may? That accounted for at least some of Dee Dee's guilt, but I still couldn't see how this was enough for her to stay in prison all this time, then a thought hit me. When we'd first met, Sherrie had mentioned a visit to Dee Dee. 'How did you do it, get Dee Dee to stay quiet so none of this would blow back on you? What did you threaten her with?'

'I think we've had quite enough of the villain's monologue for now, don't you?' she said. 'And I best be getting on my way.' She got up and walked off to one side, my view of her obscured by the lid of the pod.

'Where are you going? Sherrie?' My voice got louder with each question.

'Don't you worry about that,' she said, reappearing alongside me with a bag slung over her shoulder. She rested her hand on the lid. 'I didn't want it to end like this, I really didn't, but I can't have you rushing off, now can I? Your little mates will know soon enough when they get access to Manu's call logs that there was no phone call. And I've got some loose ends to tie up before getting as far away as possible before they do.' She paused, looking at me like we were two old mates sharing gossip over a glass of Pinot Grigio. 'D'you know, the greedy little shit wanted out, said he was done playing ball, couldn't do it no more. But don't think too highly of Manu. The bastard wanted hush money – can you believe the cheek of it? Anyway, he left me with no choice, I hope you tell 'em that when they find you.'

'Find me? You can't just leave me here!'

'You should be thanking me. The other option is for you to join Manu at the bottom of the pond, but like I told you, I'm not a monster, Sergeant.'

With both hands now braced against the lid of the pod, she watched as I yanked against my restraint. 'You won't get away with this, I won't let you.'

'In case you hadn't noticed, Sergeant, this ain't your show. It's been a pleasure,' she said before closing the lid.

'Sherrie! Sherrie, you don't have to—' Footsteps echoed around the room before I heard a door open and close, then silence. 'Sherrie!' I screamed, my voice hoarse, but she was gone. 'Fuuuuck!' I growled, writhing against the handcuffs, grabbing the chain and pulling and pulling and pulling as my brain rattled around inside my head.

I froze, the sudden realisation I needed to conserve as much energy as I could hitting me like a battering ram.

Sherrie may have left me alive, but she'd also left me with a gaping head injury in a pool of water. What if I fell asleep? Slid down the inside of this cocoon and slipped under the surface before anyone found me. *Would* anyone even find me? How long would it take for someone to think to check inside the pods? My job had been to cover planning in the run-up to the festival and investigate the death threats. The festival was planned, and the MCU had taken over my case. There was nothing left for me to officially do and I wasn't due back on shift for another three days. The only other person in my life who might notice I was missing before then was Dad, but he'd assume I was overworking myself and had forgotten to call him back, like I'd done a million times before. And by the time he realised something was wrong, it'd be too late.

42

I'd have slapped myself if I wasn't already worried enough about having concussion. *Get yourself together!* Sitting and wallowing in this blood-stained water certainly wasn't going to get me anywhere. And even if I was going to die here, I sure as shit wasn't going to simply wait for it to happen.

I tried squeezing out of the handcuffs again, the skin around the bottom of my thumb scraped raw from where I'd contorted my arm into every available position, looking for an angle that would give me those extra millimetres needed to get my hand free, but it was no use. 'Come onnnnn!' I growled through gritted teeth, rattling the handcuffs against the solid pole for what felt like the hundredth time.

My head throbbed, feeling worse and worse by the minute. I wriggled from one position to another, desperate to find one that propped me up and would keep my head above the waterline if my injury made me lose consciousness. Nothing worked, my back sliding down the smooth, white surface of the inner walls, barely bigger than a coffin. I turned widthways, pushing my feet against the side of the pod, using my handcuffed arm like a makeshift hammock for my head. Something stabbed into the crease at the top of my thigh as I manoeuvred myself, something sharp in the pocket of my trousers. *What the* ...

Adrenaline rushed me as I realised what it was. Small and pointy. The hairgrip I'd used to break into Tabby's box. I pulled it out, holding it in front of my face, and cried with sheer joy, the tears mixing with splashes of salt water as I heaved myself on to my knees. The sudden movement made my vision blur. I shook my head to refocus, sticking my fingers into the narrow gap between the hairgrip's two metal prongs and prising them apart. These weren't police-issue handcuffs, but the mechanism was similar. Jamming the grip's end into the keyway, I bent it back to form a small L shape before shimmying it into position in the bottom of the hole and rotating it one way to undo the double lock, then shifted it around to the top of the hole and rotated it the opposite way. The ratchets clicked open, freeing my swollen wrist, and a gasp of relief flew from my mouth.

I shoved the hairgrip back into my pocket, unclipped the inside of the pod's lid and pushed upwards, standing with it as it lifted. Black spots swirled across my eyes and I fell back into the water. I reset and dragged myself to the edge of the pod before flopping over it, landing flat on my back on the hard tile flooring surrounding the pool. 'Ugh!' I yelped, the sound practically punched out of me along with every ounce of air in my lungs. I lay there for a minute or two, trying to catch my breath, but the dizziness persisted. Not trusting my balance, I crawled, knees bruised by the time I got to the other side of the room.

Reaching over my head, I tried the handle of the door leading to the corridor. Locked. *Shit!* My eyes were heavy now, my whole skull feeling like it was clamped in a vice. I pulled the hairgrip back out of my pocket, but I was seeing four prongs now, not two. 'Come on!' I said, willing myself to keep going. The lock mechanism was stiff, not budging an inch with the little leverage I could get with the hairgrip. 'Come on, come on, come on, come on, come on.' The thin metal dug into my hand as I twisted and pushed. The prongs, and my hope, snapped simultaneously.

I used the last of my energy to launch the broken hairgrip across the room before I fell back on to the floor, closing my eyes in the hope it would stop the pain engulfing my head.

43

The VIP tent at Fortbridge Rocks was so hot Kit couldn't breathe. She'd been calling DS Washington since last night after Tabby's freak-out had started the second the sun started setting and her stuff from Aurora House hadn't arrived. And from the way Tabby was making a beeline for her now, it didn't look like she was about to calm down anytime soon.

Tabby grabbed Kit by the arm. 'Where is she?' she squawked, her zen-like demeanour a distant memory. 'You said she'd be here. I need my box! And where's Sherrie? She said she'd be back by now too!'

'I don't know, I'm not their keepers.' Kit looked to Em and Nush for help.

Em stubbed her cigarette out on a crushed beer can and Nush dragged herself up off the deck chair she'd been sitting in.

'Calm down, you fucking lunatic,' Em said. 'Why do *you* need an ego box to tell you how good you are? Just look in the mirror.'

'It's a *sunshine* box!' Tabby screeched.

Em rolled her eyes. 'Whatever it is, you don't need it, it'll be fine.' She looked back at Kit. 'Call that cop back, yeah. Tell her we don't need her, or my lucky pick, or this one's stupid box. We're a rock band and we're gonna act like one.'

As if on cue, the roar of the crowd burst through the opening to the tent as the band performing before The Dolls took to the stage. Kit's hand went to her stomach instinctively, nausea bubbling, just like it had the day her dad hadn't come home. Part of her had known something was wrong when he wasn't back on time, that he wouldn't be coming home again. 'I think something's happened, she said she'd come.' Kit's voice was barely audible over the noise of the crowd.

Em scoffed. 'Cops say a lot of things. She ain't coming, get over it.'

Tabby wailed at the realisation she wasn't getting her box in time for the performance.

'Oh my days, will you shut up for one second? Wait ...' Em said before marching off to the pop-up bar on the other side of the tent. She whispered to the guy behind it, and after a minute, came back with four shots. Golden brown liquid sloshed over the rim of the glasses as she put them on to a small table next to Kit. 'Here,' Em said, before picking the shots up and giving one to each of them. 'Drink this.'

Em was the only one who actually drank it straight off, the others just eyeballing theirs. Kit sniffed it; spicy fruit flavours tinged with smoke filled her nose.

'What's this when it's at home like?' Nush said.

'It looks like dishwater,' Tabby said.

'Like you've ever washed a fucking dish,' Em replied. 'It's Havana Club rum. Can't go wrong. And look, Tabs, I know I didn't buy into your little pre-show shot ritual back in the day, but I'll do it now, OK? For you, *if* it'll calm you the fuck down. And yes, I'm switching up the choice of beverage, but I promise you, this tastes a million times better than that wheatgrass shit you used to try and throw down our necks every night. Now, drink.'

Tabby looked touched. 'Em, I—'

'Don't make this weird, all right? Just drink,' Em said, cutting her off.

Nush and Tabby admitted defeat and shotted what was in their glasses. Kit flinched as Em poked her in the ribs.

'Oi, that includes you – you're part of this now,' Em said.

The rest applauded as Kit threw back the shot. She hadn't done it for their approval, more to quell her own panic.

DS Washington was AWOL.

Sherrie was late.

Judith was still ignoring her calls.

Manu was on the loose.

Something was wrong. Very wrong.

She left the band in the tent as they went to the pop-up bar for a second round of shots. Walking to the barriers separating the VIP area from the main crowd, Kit scanned for a police uniform. It didn't take long before she spotted one, standing on the other side of the barriers, dancing with the crowd. She swung her legs over the hoarding and marched towards him, reading the badge on his shoulder as she got closer and seeing he was a PCSO. *OK, part cop, part civilian, a halfway house*, she thought, trying to reassure herself. 'Hi, erm, 'scuse me,' she said, tapping him on the arm.

He turned, still bopping his head to the music. 'What can I do for you?' he said.

'I need to speak to someone, about DS Alice Washington.'

'She's not on duty today, can I help you with something?'

'No, I mean, I know she's not, I need to talk to someone *about* her. Is DC Briar here?'

'Come with me,' the PCSO said. 'I'll take you to him.'

She followed him towards a large gazebo at the back, trying to ignore the panic taking over her body. Spotting the man she was looking for, she broke into a run.

DC Briar turned to face her. 'Kit, what you doing over here? Shouldn't you be living it up backstage?'

The PCSO caught up with her. 'Roy, this lady—' he started to say before Kit cut him off. There wasn't time for introductions.

'I need your help,' she blurted out.

DC Briar waved the PCSO away. 'It's OK, Eddie, I've got it. What's wrong?'

She tried to keep her voice calm so he wouldn't instantly dismiss her. 'Have you heard from DS Washington since yesterday?'

He shook his head. 'No, she's rest days this weekend.'

'I think something's wrong,' Kit said, her chest tightening. The roar of the crowd was deafening and she couldn't hear herself think, let alone articulate what she was trying to say. 'She was supposed to pick some stuff up for the band

344

yesterday and she promised and . . . and now Sherrie's gone and . . . something's not right and I don't know what to—'

He held his palms up in front of her. 'OK, OK, just take a breath, all right? Slow down. Come over here, sit down and tell me what you know, OK?'

The panic of planning what she was going to say, how to make him see she wasn't being dramatic and stupid, ebbed away as she scanned DC Briar's face. He was already taking her seriously.

44

It felt as though only moments had passed since my eyes had closed, but according to the clock above the pool, it'd been hours. Saturday. Festival day. 'Fck,' I mumbled, the whole word not making it out as my cracked lips stuck together, throat so raw it was as if someone had gone hard at it with coarse sandpaper. I pushed on to my hands and knees, head still banging, but I was less disorientated than before I'd passed out.

Slowly, I rose to my feet, steadying myself before staggering to the water cooler in the corner. I snatched a conical paper cup and filled it, again and again, gulping down the liquid. Discarding the cup, I caught the water in my palms and splashed it on to my face, shocking my brain into action.

The door between me and freedom was solid, no glass to break and squeeze through. I scanned the rest of the room, the majority of it taken up by the swimming pool, its shimmering surface casting a bluey-green, rippling glow off the white walls and ceiling. There were no windows. The only other door on the opposite side was wide open, and I could see from here it was just a large cupboard used to house stuff for the pool.

There was no way out.

I threw my head back in frustration, instantly regretting the move as the pain multiplied, offshoots slicing down my neck and across my shoulders. On the plus side, it had put the ceiling vent a few metres from the pool's raised lifeguard chair into my line of sight.

Wait . . . could I . . .?

Who did I think I was? Bruce Willis in *Die Hard*? I probably wouldn't even fit inside. And if I did, what was the likelihood of it leading somewhere useful, somewhere I could get out of at the other end instead of getting stuck, face pressed against a filter blocking my path? No. I might as well have stayed in the pod and let myself slowly drift off, drowning peacefully in my sleep and unaware of my passing instead of suffocating to death in a small metal pipe. *Someone will find you in here eventually. And you've got a water cooler, for Christ's sake! Just make yourself comfortable, wait it out.* I knew as soon as the instruction finished playing in my mind that I couldn't follow it. The longer Sherrie was on the run, the less likely we'd be to find her. And what loose ends had she been talking about? The band? How much did they know? I probably hadn't learned the half of what Sherrie was capable of, how far her twisted mind would go, but I had no doubt she'd do whatever it took to come out on top. 'I'm not a monster' my arse. I couldn't sit here and do nothing.

The feet of the lifeguard chair scraped across the floor

as I dragged it into position under the vent before climbing on it and standing on the seat. The cover was just above my head, held in its frame with two small clips. I undid them, but the mesh panel stayed in place. I braced one hand against the ceiling and stuck the fingers of my free hand through the holes, gripping, then yanking downwards. It broke free with a clunk and fell past me, clattering on to the floor before bouncing into the water. I watched as it sank to the bottom of the pool, praying I wasn't about to follow suit.

Hooking my hands over the side of the hole in the ceiling the cover had left behind, I was profoundly grateful for the pull-up bar I'd installed in the back garden, and that I'd forced myself to use it. Not that this would be anything close to a normal pull-up, but hopefully I'd built enough upper body strength to execute the only option available to me, which seemed to be putting my palms flat on to the sheet metal inside the vent and jumping, before straightening my arms and dragging myself inside.

I circled my wrists, opening and closing my fingers to warm them up before reaching inside the vent. Taking a deep breath, I counted myself in, 'Three . . . two . . . one . . .' I pushed into my splayed fingers as I sprang off my toes, the movement sending the lifeguard chair toppling on to the solid surface below. 'Shit!' I spat. I was halfway up. Head inside the vent. Everything below the middle of my chest was outside, hanging in mid-air, no momentum left to lift my body weight and straighten my elbows. The muscles in my arms burned as I pushed, torso trembling, summoning

every ounce of energy I had and channelling it to my arms.
All I needed was an inch or two. Get my elbows past the
midway point and I was there. But a millimetre in the other
direction and I was going down, all the way down on to
the metal structure of the lifeguard chair, straight on to the
floor, or into the pool.

My scream ricocheted down the vent as I squeezed
everything I had left out of me, my arms finally straightening, pulling my upper body inside the ceiling cavity. 'Oh
thank God, thank God, thank God, thank God.' I flopped
forward on to the sheet metal and braced my hands against
the sides so I could shimmy forward and drag my legs up
behind me.

Once I'd gotten fully prone, I stopped, letting myself
recuperate for a second. It wasn't until this point I'd even
noticed there was complete darkness ahead of me. This was
a terrible fucking idea. What was I thinking? At least John
McClane had a bloody lighter with him to guide his way. I
had no choice but to keep going now. And surely the hard
part was getting up here. Any able-bodied person could
crawl forward in a straight line through a tube.

I pushed on to my forearms, trying to wriggle into a com-
mando crawl position, my head banging against the metal
sheeting above me. 'Ow!' The vent must have narrowed
from the section above the opening as I'd shimmied forward
to pull my legs in. How narrow was this thing going to get?
I forced myself to ignore the suffocating sensation closing
in around me like melted wax slowly firming. I lowered
my head so it was just above my forearms and crawled

forwards, if you could even call what I was doing crawling, the space too narrow to properly bring my knees up, most of the movement coming from me dragging forward with my forearms and shuffling on my toes to provide some propulsion from the rear.

The metal squeaked as I slid across it, walls brushing my shoulders, tugging at my clothes, fabric tearing as protruding bolt heads and rogue edges of sheeting lining the vent grabbed at it. Jesus, this was narrow. I made myself as small as possible, tucking my elbows into my ribs as tight as I could while still being able to use them to pull me forward. Was this thing getting narrower? It was. Tighter. Smaller. *Shut up!* I almost yelled aloud at my intrusive thoughts. I focussed on anything else. The metal squeaking. My feet shuffling.

Squeak-squeak-squeak

Shuffle-shuffle-shuffle

What if I was right, what if it was getting narrower? What if I got stuck?

Squeak-shuffle-shuffle-shuffle-squeak

God, this was a bad idea.

Squeak-shuffle-squeak-shuffle

No matter how hard I tried to stay narrow, it didn't work. Because the deeper I got into the darkness, the wider my lungs and ribcage expanded with each breath, like I wasn't controlling them any more. It was as if some puppeteer with a tube down my throat was pumping in more air than I could take, until it felt like I was going to expand so much I'd burst through the walls. But I couldn't. Because the walls were solid sheets of metal. Bolted together. Enveloping me.

A stab of pain snapped me from my panic. For a moment, anyway, before a brand-new one set in as something yanked at my scalp, holding me back as I tried to pull forward. *What the . . .?* It took a second to realise what it was. My hair was caught. A bolt or some other stray edge had latched on and refused to let go. I couldn't see above me or move my hands to feel around and unhook it. My eyes filled with tears as I manoeuvred myself, left, right, forwards, back, desperate to dislodge my head from the grip of the vent. But nothing worked, the sizeable portion of hair wrenched harder with every movement. I tried going backwards but reversing made my chest tighten.

Can't go back. Have to go forward. Have to get out. Out. Now.

I jerked my head as hard as I could, pain tearing through me as the hair was ripped from my scalp. 'Fuuuuck!' I roared, my cry echoing down the vent. I shuffled again, inch by inch, nothing stopping my forward movement this time, until my forearms hit mesh. Another vent cover. Though whichever room it opened into was also in total darkness. I didn't care where it led. I needed to get out.

My left forearm took my weight as I balled my right hand into a fist and punched down in a short, sharp motion with everything I could muster, the mesh shearing the skin from my knuckles as I punched again and again before the vent finally disappeared into the darkness below. The relief lasted barely a second before I wondered how the hell I was going to get out. Shuffling myself across the gap and getting my legs out first would work if I was lying on my back, allowing my knees to bend. But there was nowhere near enough room for me to flip myself over from being on my front. If I wanted out of this vent, there was only one way I was doing it. Head first.

Jesus Christ.

I already had a probable concussion. And the alternative was lying here until I either suffocated or dehydrated to death. I hung my upper body out through the hole, whirling my arms around to the sides, taking a second to stretch them out and savour the sensation of not having walls closing in around me. I still had no idea where I was, but it felt spacious, not some utility cupboard at least. 'Here goes nothing.'

Rocking my hips from side to side, moving them off the metal sheeting and over the hole, I positioned my legs to make sure they wouldn't get caught against the top of the vent, bending them as much as the small space would allow, until more of me was out of the ceiling than in and gravity finished the job for me.

Then I was falling.

Braced.

Eyes closed as I waited for impact.

A *pfft* of air blew past my face as I landed rather than the dull thud I was expecting when my body hit the floor. Because I wasn't on the floor, I was on something soft. I lay there for a second as my eyes adjusted to the darkness. Relief burst out as I realised I was in the studio, Tabby's floor bags breaking my fall.

Running to the door, I yanked it open before stumbling

down the corridor and dragging myself up the spiral staircase to the hallway. Sun poured in through the glass ceiling,
shocking my pupils which had grown accustomed to the
dark. I scanned the hallway for a phone but there was
nothing; the room I knew to be the office was locked. I
needed to get the word out. Quickly.

Bursting through the front doors on to the driveway, my
hand flew to my pocket, instinctively reaching for my car
keys at the sight of my Volvo parked where I'd left it under
the willow tree, but of course they weren't there. Sherrie
must have taken them. Along with my phone. And even if
she hadn't, I could see they'd be useless given Sherrie had
slashed all of my tyres. I wasn't sure I could even drive
without crashing head first into the mounds of mud flanking
the narrow roads, the state I was in. I forced one foot in
front of the other down the driveway, pushed the button to
open the gates and practically fell on to the road. I wanted
to run. To sprint. But I was moving so slowly I wasn't even
sure if I was moving at all.

45

By the time I reached the entrance to the festival, I'd have sworn to a jury I'd been walking for days, but given it was only about two miles from Aurora House, it couldn't have been much more than an hour, even at my bumbling pace. Spotting the security checkpoint up ahead, I pushed on towards it, scanning for someone with a phone or a radio. Eddie was standing alongside several security officers who were checking the bags of some late arrivals. 'Eddie,' I yelled – tried to yell anyway, but it came out as nothing more than a croak.

His eyes widened as he did a double take. 'Holy shhh—' Clearly realising I was toppling before I did, Eddie lurched forwards and grabbed my arm. 'What's happened, Sarge?'

'Just ... just give me your radio.' Yanking it from his vest, he handed it to me. I barked instructions at the control room. About Sherrie. About Manu. About everything. Eddie's jaw dropped further and further with every word. I directed my next instruction to him rather than the radio. 'Give me your phone.'

He pulled it from his pocket without question and handed

it to me. I fumbled my words, trying to speak at the same time as I googled Sherrie's name. 'They're here, yeah? The Dolls, I mean, they're . . . the band are here, aren't they?'

Eddie looked confused. 'Yeah, they're due up next on the main stage, I think.'

A sliver of relief released some of the pressure in my head. Surely if the band were the loose ends Sherrie was referring to, she'd have gone straight for them, did what she needed to and be miles from here by now. But that was the rationale of a normal person. And nothing about what Sherrie Pearce had been doing was normal. God knows what went on in that warped mind of hers. I found an image of her and held it up towards Eddie. 'Have you seen this woman today?'

Eddie leant forward, peering at the screen. 'Not that I remember, no. Why, who is she?'

I blurted out the fastest explanation I could muster to Eddie and the security officers, along with a warning: if Sherrie was here and we caught her, there was no way in hell she was going down without a fight.

'Help me over to the main stage.' Eddie was still holding one of my arms and I gripped his in return as a wave of dizziness tried to take over.

'The stage?' Eddie said, perplexed. 'You need to go to hospital!'

'I *need* to get to the band, make sure they're OK.'

'Sarge, come on, y—'

'There's no time for this, Eddie! Take me, now.'

He shook his head to compose himself, my tone obviously

conveying that I was going whether he helped me or not. 'Come on then,' he said, letting me put some of my weight into the hand that he'd cupped under my elbow, the other resting gently across the back of my shoulders to steady me. Together, we battled through the crowd, the people around us dancing to a song I didn't recognise but knew couldn't be The Dolls as the singing voice was male.

I scoured the heads bobbing all around, looking for a flash of Sherrie's bright red hair, but all I could see were varying shades of neutral tones attached to bodies swaying like rippling water, everyone moving in unison as arms and flags waved in the air like detritus floating on the surface. My eyes flicked from person to person, scanning each of them in turn, trying to take in every detail, ignoring the throbbing in my head and forcing myself to concentrate so I didn't miss anything. And I didn't miss them, the person in the navy polka dot mac, their stillness in sharp contrast to everyone else, like a statue had been dropped into the middle of the field about ten metres back from the stage.

There wasn't a wisp of a rain cloud in sight, so why was their hood up? What were they hiding under there? *Sherrie?* Foreboding swallowed me whole as the figure took off towards the stage, surging forward and slicing through the crowd like the hull of a boat through choppy waves. Their hood caught on the flailing hand of another festival-goer, pulled back to reveal not the burst of red I'd expected, but a nest of mousey blonde hair, the static from the material making it look even more dishevelled than when I'd last seen it.

'Judith.' What the fuck was she doing here? Her words replayed in my mind. *If I wanted to threaten them, I wouldn't be a coward about it, I'd do it to their faces.* Judith was here for answers. And she was going to get them. One way or another.

I flinched as cheers and applause rang out like thunder, only now noticing the last song had finished and there was movement on the stage. The changeover of the bands. Tabby, Nush and Em striding out, arms aloft waving at the crowd.

'Hello, Fortbridge, are you living your best lives out there?' Tabby said into the microphone as she reached the front of the stage.

I could see from here Judith's eyes were fixed on her. 'Oh fuck ... Judith!' I yelled, my words sucked into the noise of the crowd like I was screaming into a jet engine. In the short time I'd been stood watching, more people had appeared behind me and Eddie, hemming us in as they tried to get as close as possible to the stage. Em's guitar shrieked through the speakers, piercing the air like a siren, before dropping down into the roaring intro riff of 'Not Your Doll', laced with what I now knew to be Ris's rage. Someone knocked the gash on my head with their elbow and I cried out.

'Sarge!' Eddie yelled as he was eaten up by the swarm that had forced its way around and between us. I didn't have time to be in pain, didn't have time to think. I needed to get to Judith. But as the music screeched to a halt as quickly as it had started, I knew I was already too late. I used the shoulders of the people around me to push on to my tiptoes to see the stage again. Kit was up there now, front and centre, standing between Judith and Tabby.

Judith's arm was raised straight out in front of her, the crowd splitting as people noticed what was in her hand. The small, dark object clutched in her palm, held out like an extension of her. A gun.

Oh God.

'Kit, get down!' I yelled. 'Everybody get down!'

Everyone saw it now. And everything went into overdrive. Like when you accidentally sit on a remote control and the film you're watching flits forward in double time. My hand clenched. As if I had a remote I could press. A button to stop what was happening. To give me more time.

But there was no button.

No time.

I forced my way closer, only metres from Judith now as she yelled frantically towards the stage, the gun flailing at the end of her arm.

'Tell me the truth! Tell everyone the truth!' Judith cried.

Kit was clearly doing all she could to snap Judith from her trance-like state, screaming her name, but the only words it seemed she was going to allow through were the ones she'd come to hear.

'Please, put the gun down, let's talk about this, OK?' Kit begged.

Judith ignored every word. 'My Dee Dee's a good girl, she didn't deserve any of this. What did you do to her?'

'Judith!' I shouted as loudly as my hoarse voice would

allow, trying to push closer as people fled around me. 'Judith, listen to me!'

I wasn't sure of the exact order things happened in next, but there was a loud crack, screams, and the sight of a figure throwing itself at Judith, the pair of them crumpling to the floor. Unsure how I was actually still on my feet, I pushed forward again. But I was the only one trying to move towards the chaos; everyone else was running away from it. I shoved. Clawed. Shouted. Used everything I had left in me until I reached the mound of bodies on the floor, trying to get a proper look at the person who'd thrown themselves at Judith.

I edged closer, but hands were on me in seconds, dragging me away. Police and security guards swarmed and pulled the two bodies apart.

The words I heard next rang loud in my ears.

'Officer down! Officer down.'

46

I fingered the fresh bandage fixed to my head as I walked down the hospital corridor. Despite their best efforts to get me to go home and get some rest after discharging me early that morning, I couldn't leave. Not until I knew everything was going to be all right. And I had at least twenty minutes until Eddie was coming to give me a lift home anyway. I approached the room the nurse had directed me towards. Reaching out to knock on the door, my hand hovered inches away instead as I heard Pippa's voice.

'... multisystemic traumatic injury. Mortality and morbidity rates are high. It says practitioners should recognise that emergent surgical evaluation is warranted when haemodynamic instability persists and evidence of peritonitis is present.' She paused for a second. 'Do you have any of those?'

Bret chuckled in a way that sounded painful. 'I have no earthly idea. I don't even know what they are.'

'The first one is to do with your blood pressure,' she informed him, 'and I think it said the second one is an infection in the lining of your stomach.'

'What said – who've you been talking to?' Bret asked.

'National Library of Medicine,' Pippa said proudly.

'Of course you have. I think you can stand down now, I'm sure my doctors have access to that too.'

Their voices stopped for a second and I took the break in conversation as an opportunity to knock gently before pushing the door open.

'Hey,' I said, 'OK to come in?' I expected to see Pippa holding the phone or iPad she'd been reading the medical jargon from, but her small hands held nothing but each other in her lap as she swung her legs back and forth, kicking the air in front of her chair.

'Come on in, we're having a real party in here, aren't we?' Bret said, smiling at Pippa.

I pushed the door closed behind me and walked to the bed. 'How you feeling?'

'Like I've been shot in the stomach,' Bret replied.

Pippa swivelled to look up at me. 'He has a multisystemic traumatic injury.'

'So I heard, you're quite the Doogie Howser. He was a . . .' The kid had memorised the entirety of the National Library of Medicine; it was unlikely she needed the follow-up explanation, even though the show I'd referenced was taken off air twenty years before she was born. 'You already know who that is, don't you?'

She nodded. 'Neil Patrick Harris.'

I looked back at Bret. 'You should hire her out for pub quizzes, you'd make an absolute mint.'

'Be my guest. I don't think I'll be going to the pub anytime soon.'

'You hardly go to the pub anyway,' Pippa said. 'You've only got two friends, and they're busy half the time.'

Ouch! I couldn't help but laugh. Mind you, that was two more than I had, so who was I to judge?

'I have more than two friends,' Bret said. 'There's Pete and Joe, and . . . and Alice is my friend, kind of.'

'Swinging a bit fast and loose there,' I replied.

Bret put on an exaggerated hurt puppy-dog face. 'Do you not count as my friend, Pips?'

'Yeah, but I'm not old enough to go to the pub. And Alice doesn't count, she's your work colleague, that's what you said when Nana asked.'

Heat tickled my cheeks. 'You've been talking to your mum about me? Bit weird.'

Bret opened his mouth but Pippa beat him to it. 'Uncle Bret's been talking about you quite a lot actually.'

My face fully flushed and I looked at my nails. 'Only good things, I hope.'

'Some good things. Some areas for improvement.' Areas for improvement? When did this become an end of year performance review? 'That's OK though,' Pippa continued, oblivious to my discomfort, 'Nana says you shouldn't trust people who only say good things about you. No one's all good, so if they say you are, it means they're probably not being honest.'

I opened my mouth to make a challenge before realising her theory actually made a lot of sense. 'OK then, so what areas do I need to improve on?'

Bret interjected, 'Pips, come on now, let's not.'

I leant over and placed my hand across his mouth, muffling his words. 'Go on, Pippa. I'm pretty sure we can overpower him between the two of us.'

She shuffled in her seat, like she had to be totally comfortable before spilling the metaphorical tea. 'That you're stubborn and can be a bit of a pain in the arse, but so's he, Nana says, so I wouldn't worry about that one too much.'

'All right, that's a fair shout.' I looked down at Bret and removed my hand from his mouth. Having his lips pressed against me felt a bit too intimate.

He opened his mouth as soon as I'd freed it. 'Pips, why don't you—'

She was still looking up at me and not paying any attention to his pleas. 'Should I do a good one now?'

I sat on the spare chair. 'Go on then.'

'He said you've got courage.'

I wasn't sure what I thought she was going to say, but I wasn't expecting that. '*Courage?* What exactly have I been courageous about?'

'Pips, why don't you go and ask the nurse if she'll give you another one of those jelly pots?'

'If I eat too many of those my teeth will rot,' she replied.

'I'm sure one more won't hurt,' Bret said.

She shrugged. 'Do you want one?'

'No, thanks,' Bret said.

She looked at me with a questioning stare.

'I'm good, already had my jelly quota for the day,' I said.

Pippa nodded and headed for the door.

I waited until her footsteps disappeared down the corridor. 'Did she conduct your surgery herself or . . .?'

'Probably would have been in safer hands if she had. So, what have they said, am I dying or what?'

I sucked air through my teeth like a mechanic assessing a car, knowing full well they were going to fleece the owner for everything they had. 'Touch and go. They've managed to stitch you up but your T-shirt's well and truly fucked. Maybe if you'd been wearing your horrendous green jumper they could have used the elbow patches to fix the hole like a polyester skin graft.'

'Thank God for the heatwave then, that's all I can say. My sister made me that jumper, she'd be rolling in her grave if I ruined it.'

Every snide remark I'd made about his jumper replayed like a tasteless sitcom, shame scorching my neck and chest. 'Sorry, I didn't realise.'

'Why would you? You didn't even know I had a sister until a week ago. I keep my work and home life separate, remember? Not to be difficult, and not because I don't care; it's just the only way I can keep doing this job without it dragging me under. If you don't turn off the system every once in a while, it short-circuits, you know what it's like.'

To be dragged under, absolutely. To find an effective way of keeping my head above water? Not so much. 'I don't think anyone could argue you don't care enough; you've just literally jumped in front of a bullet for a complete stranger – one who is actually rather anti-police, you might be interested to know. If that's not courageous, I don't know what is.'

He shook his head, wincing as he adjusted his position on the bed. 'There's a difference between bravery and courage. I think so, anyway. It's easier to do the right thing when you've a split-second decision to make, not enough time to think of the fallout or feel the fear. But courage,' he shook his head, 'courage is something else. My sister had courage. Jessie, she found out she had cancer the same day she got the news she was pregnant with Pips, and she was terrified, of both things. Didn't think she was ready to be a mother, wasn't anywhere close to being ready for it to be the end.' He stared down at his hand as he picked at the bedsheet. 'They really made her think about it, the choice to have treatment or not. Her only options were aggressive and experimental, too much for the baby. She had to make a choice. And she made it. She felt the fear when she refused treatment, for sure she did, but she did it anyway. *That's* courage.' His face flushed and he glanced at the tube running from a cannula in his arm up to the drip it was hanging from. 'What the hell are they pumping into me here, some kind of truth serum?'

'Wow, erm . . .' I wiped tears from my cheeks that I hadn't noticed had been falling. For a moment, I thought of telling him about my brother, but now didn't seem the time. 'There you go then, that proves it. I definitely don't have courage.'

'You stood up to Gordy Scott; most people would think that was courageous. He was out of order. Me and Carver, we should have said something.'

'I wouldn't say that's *quite* up there with "saving the life of your unborn child over your own".'

Bret shrugged. 'Not saying you're at Jessie levels of courage or anything; she's, I dunno, Meryl Streep level, you're more of an up-and-comer, like a . . . I don't actually know the name of any young actors.'

'Florence Pugh?' I offered.

Bret shook his head. 'She's been in some big stuff, surely she's already up and come. Whatever,' he said, 'the point being, you don't just sit there and take things. And I know it must've been hard for you to come back, after last year. But you did it anyway. I'm not sure I'd've been able to.'

'Why, too embarrassed?'

He sighed. 'I'm *trying* to pay you a compliment here, which clearly you're never going to let me do. How about we talk about your favourite thing instead, work. What's the latest?'

I almost protested. Almost told him it wasn't that I didn't want the compliment, I just didn't feel it was deserved. And that even though he didn't think what he'd done was special, it was. That he had no idea how much I'd needed that bit of faith restoring in the job, reminding me that as long as people in this world kept firing bullets at each other, we needed people who'd be willing to jump in front of them. But none of those words came out of my mouth. 'Obviously they have Judith in custody and everyone and their aunty is on the look-out for Sherrie. I called Jane, but the only thing she would tell me was that they'd found Manu's body in the pond at Aurora House, then she ordered me to rest and hung up.'

'All that stuff Judith was yelling, I'm guessing that has

366

something to do with what you said in Gordy's office, about Ris Angelini's death?'

I still hadn't figured out how I was going to present what I'd discovered without getting Kit into trouble. She'd done nothing wrong other than try to find the truth. 'I think that's probably a story for another day, unless you want your stitches to burst.'

He opened his mouth, no doubt to protest, but Pippa saved my bacon, appearing in the doorway with a jelly pot in one hand and a wooden teaspoon in the other.

'I better leave you to it then.' I patted Pippa's shoulder. 'You promise you'll look after him, OK? We need cops like your uncle Bret back on duty as soon as possible, 'cause he's a good one, and, you know, we're also very, very under-resourced.'

'I will,' she said, pushing her glasses further up her nose.

My heart did a weird throbby thing as she put her dessert down on his bedside table and straightened his bedsheet.

47

The glass reception doors slid open as they sensed my presence, sterile hospital air replaced with the smell of damp soil as I stepped outside. An overnight downpour had broken the heatwave's hold, the sky's offerings greedily sucked up by the parched residents of the flower beds lining the walkway towards the car park. I was about to head for the bench by the taxi rank to wait for Eddie when a voice stopped me.

'How's he doing, that cop?'

I turned to see Kit on the other end of the question, leaning against the wall rolling a cigarette.

'Those things'll kill you, you know,' I said.

'Could be worse,' she said, shrugging. 'I could've been shot.'

I walked over and stood beside her as she stuck the rollie between her lips. 'He's gonna be fine,' I said. 'How come you're here anyway? You didn't get hurt yesterday, did you?'

Kit shook her head. 'Nah, they brought us all in to check us over, for shock or whatever, offered us sedatives, the lot. The others have all gone back to the Airbnb, but I'm not leaving until I know Judith's OK.'

'Judith? What's she doing here?'

Kit took a short, sharp drag of her cigarette before answering, 'Collapsed in custody, apparently, saw them bringing her in last night.'

'What's wrong with her?'

'Dunno,' Kit said. 'I was worried she might be back on the gear. She's not been thinking straight, that's what I told the cops who came to speak to us last night. I told them everything, sorry if that gets you in the shit.' She held the partially smoked rollie out towards me in what I presumed was her version of an olive branch.

I didn't smoke, but at this point, what was the worst that could happen? I took it from her. 'You did the right thing, telling them the truth. I'll sort it from here, with Dee Dee. And for the record, what you did yesterday, getting up there, was brave,' I said, 'standing in front of the band like that. Stupid, but brave.'

She shrugged. 'Your mate did the same thing, and he didn't even know them.'

I sucked the smoke in, the sensation burning but not enough to make me cough, instantly going to my head. 'Yeah, but at least he gets paid for it. You did that shit pro bono.'

'Not really why he did it though, is it?'

I thought of what I'd really wanted to say to Bret just now, about him helping restore my faith in the job. 'No, it's not.'

'It was more stupid than brave,' Kit said. 'I didn't think she was gonna pull the trigger.'

'If I've learned one thing in this job, it's that people can surprise you, no matter how well you think you know them.'

'Judith's a good person, deep down; she just, I dunno, she hasn't had it easy her whole life.' From the little I knew about Kit, I guessed she knew exactly how that felt. 'What'll happen to her now?' she asked.

I shrugged and put the cigarette out in the designated bin next to me, the smoke already clinging to my fingers and reminding me why I didn't take up the habit in the first place. 'Depends what she says, how she fares on any assessments they do of her mental state once she's out of here.'

'She needs help, she's been through a lot.'

I nodded.

'They'll get her some help, won't they?'

'I'll make sure of it,' I said. 'I know you haven't got a lot of faith in the system, for understandable reasons, but there are some decent people in the job, I promise you. And hey, we could always use more. It's tough at the minute; we're losing some of the good ones because they can only take it in the neck for the bad ones for so long. And if they go, that'll only leave the shit, apathetic and outright criminal ones who got into it for all the wrong reasons.'

'Maybe you should do something about it then,' Kit said as she pushed herself away from the wall.

'Believe me, we're trying.'

'Good luck with that.'

The Chief's project about recruiting more women to policing flashed through my mind, and the thought didn't anger me as much as it had before. 'You should think about it.'

She paused and looked at me like I was speaking another language. 'About what?'

'Joining the job.'

Kit let out a manic laugh and clasped her fingers over the top of her head. 'That smoke gone straight to your head or what?'

'Doesn't have to be on the frontline, there's plenty of civvy roles. Analysts, researchers, loads of stuff. But for what it's worth, I think you'd make a great cop.'

'Why?'

I couldn't tell her the full extent of what her findings had led me to discover, not until I'd officially fed it up the chain. 'Call it gut instinct,' I said. She opened her mouth to speak but then stopped, tilting her head to one side like a confused dog. 'It's easy to criticise things from the outside, and I'm not complaining about the criticism – there's more than enough officers I've wanted to throttle myself – but very few people are willing to be part of the change. Think about it.'

'I'll get right on that once I've finished sticking pins in my eyes,' she said, her tone of voice not matching the words. Was that a hint of intrigue I noticed or was it just wishful thinking on my part? Who the hell knew. 'Hey,' she said with a shrug, 'stranger things have happened. I actually witnessed Em being *nice* to Tabby yesterday – it was like watching a newborn foal try and walk for the first time – so who knows, maybe one day you'll see me donning a cap and truncheon.'

'Em? *Nice?*' I said, my eyebrows jumping up my forehead. 'Wow, well, at least there's a silver lining to all this if it brings them all a little closer together, like the good old days before they got eaten alive by the music industry.'

'Think she might be regretting it this morning though,' Kit said. 'Now Tabby thinks they're besties she's roped them all into a "group healing" session – glad I have an excuse to miss it, to be honest. She's making smoothies. God knows what in the Holland and Barrett will be going in them.'

A laugh snorted from my nose. 'I'm sure they'll be thanking her when their digestive tracts are as clean as a whistle.'

'Yeah, it's so weird to think what Tabby used to be like versus what she's like now.'

'What d'you mean?'

'Oh, she's gone full circle,' Kit said. 'She was an acid-queen raver girl before she turned into the rock circuit's version of the Dalai Lama.'

Something buzzed in my brain, and it wasn't the remnants of the nicotine hit. 'She what?'

'Yep, you better believe it, less CBD oil, more LSD dots. I found some absolutely classic pics of her in the party-girl days when I was digging into them, gurning her tits off dressed head to toe in neon, I barely recognised her. She was mortified when I showed her, assured me she gave all that up when she got serious about becoming a "*star performer*",' Kit said, mocking Tabby's posh accent, ''cause that stuff messed her up, on and off stage.'

A tightness clawed at my chest, the text on Ris's toxicology report flashing behind my eyes. *Positive for low levels of LSD.* 'Messed her up how?'

Kit shrugged. '"Dulled her shine", apparently, made her forget her words and stuff, 'cause she was a singer before she joined the band as the bassist. And she said there were other side-effects too, like anxiety, depression, all kinds of stuff. I tried acid once and never touched the stuff again. I was tripping my balls off for weeks afterwards, the flash-backs were crazy, felt like I was going mad.'

My assumption had been that Ris took the LSD herself, turning to drugs to ease her pain, but instead triggering dark distortions of her perceptions of reality. But now several thoughts collided in my mind at once: Sherrie's pool room rant about how Tabby wanted nothing more than to be the lead singer, a dream that could only be achieved with Ris out of the picture; Em mocking the wheatgrass shots Tabby used to force down everyone's necks before their shows; and the words Roy spoke when the security guard took his ginger shot at the prison, *How's anyone gonna use a health drink as a bleeding weapon?*

Tabby had gotten what she'd wanted, in the end. Had she manifested that? Or had she taken action? I'd had a wheatgrass shot before, the taste so strong you'd never know if someone added something to it. Had the pre-show shots been the perfect Trojan horse for Tabby to slip Ris her own special ingredient, something Tabby knew from experience might throw Ris off her game? As if the picture I was painting wasn't disturbing enough, another realisation almost knocked me off my feet. There was no way Sherrie in all her omnipotent glory wouldn't have known about this, and now her cover was blown, surely Tabby was more than aware of the risk of hers following suit.

Kit had carried on talking, completely oblivious to the panic mushrooming out from the pit of my stomach, but the circle back to 'group healing' and 'smoothies' dragged me back to the conversation.

'. . . anyway, I'm sure whatever she's got them doing this morning will end up in an Insta live. Maybe we should watch it, get some tips on healthier living,' Kit said.

I grabbed her upper arms. 'Tabby hasn't given you anything to drink, has she?'

'What? No, w—'

Eddie still wasn't here and I didn't have time to wait.

'Where are you going?' Kit yelled after me as I sprinted to the taxi rank, praying I was wrong about exactly how far Tabby would go to keep her moment in the spotlight.

48

Two PCs sat in a patrol car outside the band's Airbnb, one of them calling from the open window as I dashed past.

'All right, Sarge, what you doing he—'

'Are they in there?' I said, cutting him off.

'We'd hardly be sat watching the place if they weren't,' he said with a chuckle.

I ran through the gate, slamming my balled-up fist against the front door. 'Em? Nush?' I banged again, harder this time. 'Tabby? It's DS Washington. Hello?' No response. *Shit.* A car door shut behind me and boots clomped up the short path to the thatched cottage as I jiggled the handle, checking to see if it was locked.

'Something the matter?' the PC said.

I turned to face him. 'You're sure they haven't gone out somewhere?'

'Hundred percent, the blonde one brought us out a little tipple to cool the old cockles not long ago,' he said, pointing back towards the car where his colleague still sat.

I grabbed his shoulders, looking from one eye to the other for pupil dilation before scanning his face for any other signs he might have been spiked. 'Did you drink it?'

'Not yet, no. It's in the car. Why, you want some?'

'Do *not*, under any circumstances, drink that. There might be something in it,' I said, before yelling over his shoulder, repeating the warning louder so the other PC could hear me.

Not waiting for a follow-up question, I ran off around the side of the building, looking for another way in. There was an open window at the back. Plates and glasses crashed to the floor as I knocked a drainer full of crockery from the side of the sink on my way in. 'Em? Nush?' I paused, listening for any responses or sounds that might suggest where they were. But there was nothing, no one rushing to the kitchen to find the source of all the smashing.

Bolting for the hallway, my hip slammed into a large swing bin, knocking it over. 'Argh!' I yelped before bracing myself to push through the pain so I could search the rest of the property, but stopped when I noticed what was on the floor. Nestled amongst the rubbish that had fallen out of the bin sat several brown plastic pill bottles, each one empty. There was something odd about them but I couldn't pinpoint what. I didn't have time to figure it out now. If Tabby had emptied those pills into smoothies and given them to Em and Nush, I needed to find them. Fast.

The pain radiated down my leg as I limped into the first room off the hallway. It was a small library, and it was empty. I dragged myself to the next one, heart spasming at the sight of Em and Nush sprawled on the floor in the living room. 'Oh, shi—' Banging coming from the other side of the front door cut me short. I unlocked it and yanked it open, the two PCs looking frantically at me from the doorstep.

'Get in here,' I said. 'I've got two adult females, unconscious, I think they've been drugged, I—' It hit me what had been odd about the pill bottles: they didn't have prescription labels on them. I forced myself to replay what Kit had said outside the hospital, something about them being offered sedatives. Had Tabby helped herself somehow? Taken way more than anyone would have prescribed? I barked instructions about ambulances and back-up before leaving the officers to start first aid. I had to find Tabby.

Adrenaline took over as I hobbled around the house, but there was no sign of her. I unlocked the back door and went into the garden, scanning for movement. There was a paddock spanning the rear of the property and a large barn off to one side. If she was still on the grounds, that was the only other place she could be.

I made my way towards it, quietly, holding my breath. Reaching the door, I pressed my ear against it. I couldn't hear anything but shuffling, like socked feet sliding across a hard floor. Grabbing hold of the large metal handle, I yanked it open, rusted runners grinding as I forced the door open bit by bit, exposing a dusty concrete floor littered with farming equipment, then sacks of what looked like horse feed, then—

Oh God.

It was like someone had stuck a giant needle into both

my lungs, deflating them as I looked up at the mezzanine level set at least ten feet above the ground and taking up the back half of the barn. Tabby was standing on it, jagged streaks of sunlight shining down on her through broken laths in the gabled roof. In one hand she held a glass bottle containing a few inches of clear liquid, in the other, the end of a thick piece of rope that hung from a heavy-duty pulley, its rail running the length of the barn's apex. A metal hook was fixed to the part of the rope she was holding, looped to form a noose. 'Oh my—'

She swayed from side to side, head lolling. Was she *dancing*? Using the rope like it was the arm of a dance partner, she twirled under it as if she sensed my need for confirmation. A chill rushed my body as I realised she was singing quietly to herself. 'Tabby?' I said with caution.

She carried on her song as if I wasn't there. '*You can dress me how you like, do my hair and make-up nice . . .*'

I recognised the lyrics. She was singing 'Not Your Doll', Ris's angry ode to Sherrie. The reference, coupled with what I was seeing, reminded me of the venom etched into the pages of that notebook, one particular section branded on to my brain. *You do not strike. You are slow and steady as you coil your body around my neck, tighter and tighter. Choking, squeezing until only one drop of life is left . . .* Had that been about Sherrie, too? About how she used these people to get everything she could out of them, dangling their greatest hopes and dreams in front of them and threatening to snatch them away at any minute? What had she done to them, twisting their young minds like clay?

While I couldn't go back in time to change any of that, I could at least limit the fallout. There'd be nothing squeezing tight around Tabby's neck today if I could help it. I had to either talk her down, or figure out how to get on to that mezzanine level quick enough that she wouldn't have time to get the noose around her neck and step off the ledge, because once she'd done that there'd be no way of me reaching out to grab her, the pulley system swinging her too far out into the centre of the full height area of the barn. The only set of access stairs I could see were right at the back, at least thirty metres from me. *Get her talking, fast!*

'Tabby, it's DS Washington, or Alice if you prefer. I've got your box, I'm sorry there was a delay in getting it. I can give it to you when you come down from there.'

She looked at me for a split second but then turned back to the direction she'd been facing when I came in just off to the left side of the mezzanine, still singing. '*But you don't get what's down inside, never yours, always mine.*'

'Ta—' My words caught in my throat as I followed her gaze. I hadn't noticed at first, too distracted by Tabby, but I saw it now: the tripod on the edge of the platform, a mobile phone attached to the top of it pointing up at her.

Tabby stopped moving, slowly, like she was battery powered and the energy had drained of its last drop, before she finally looked at me and spoke. 'Smile for the camera, Sergeant,' she slurred. 'We're live on Instagram.'

Oh Jesus Christ, an audience was the last thing this situation needed. I inched forward. 'You don't have to do this, Tabby. Come down from there and—'

'Don't come any closer,' she said, cutting me off with a sharper voice. She gulped down the last dregs of liquid in the bottle and dropped it off the edge of the mezzanine, the glass smashing as it hit the concrete floor.

'What was in the bottle, Tabby?'

Slapping her free hand against her face, she started to cry. 'Sambuca. It's Em's. She gave it to me. Can you believe that? Em's never given me anything before. But now it's . . . now it's too late.' Her face crumpled. 'I didn't want to hurt anybody,' she wailed.

'Can you tell me what you've given to Nush and Em, Tabby?'

She wiped the tears from her cheeks. 'Are they all right? I needed them to stay away, just for a little bit, just while I . . .' She looked down at the rope in her hand, resignation washing across her face.

'They're being looked after right now by my colleagues and an ambulance is on its way, it's probably already here. If you tell me what you've given them that would be a big help for the paramedics so they know what they're dealing with – can you do that for me, Tabby? Then we can get you down and they can check you too, make sure you're OK.'

Her head rolled forward, a mass of blonde curls hiding her face for a second before she flung it back, exposing her throat as she took a deep breath. 'It won't ever be OK now, it's all ruined, everything is ruined,' she said.

'Trust me, Tabby, in my line of work I see lots of people in very dark places who've made a lot of bad decisions. You'd be amazed what people can come back from. Let go of the rope, come down the stairs, and we can talk about this properly.'

She shook her head. 'There's no coming back, not when you find Sherrie. You'll know it all, everyone will find out the things ... the things ...' She forced her words out as she visibly struggled to catch her breath between sobs. '... the things I've done. And everyone, everyone will hate me. Em will hate me, Nush will hate me, even all of my ... of my—' She cupped both hands over her face for a second before dragging her nails down her cheeks. 'My followers, my wonderful followers.'

There was no way Tabby's spiking episodes would go unpunished if I managed to get her out of this situation alive, the drugs no doubt having contributed to Ris's spiralling behaviour, never mind what she'd done to Em and Nush, but it would do no good to highlight that now. I needed to get her to believe none of this would be as bad as she was imagining.

'We all make mistakes. Nush and Em, me, everyone watching this right now, we all have. Now, I'm going to be honest with you, OK? I know about the LSD, and I believe you didn't mean to hurt Ris by giving her some, maybe make her mess up a little, which is a shitty thing to do but it's not worth all this, Tabby. It's really not.'

'How did y—' She wiped her face with the back of her hand. 'It doesn't even matter. Nothing else matters now. And I really didn't mean to hurt Ris, and ... and if you think about it, really, I was helping her, helping her get out. She didn't even want to be in the band, I heard her telling

Sherrie she wanted to leave, but they wouldn't let her. I just wanted them to see, to see it was *my* time, *my* turn.' I could tell by the look on her face she'd completely convinced herself that was the truth. 'And, and Sherrie, Sherrie said it was my turn now, and that it would all work out. Just five days, she said, just five days I had to stay there, and then it'd make everything even bigger and better and, and I'd be an inspiration to people and—'

Her words were replaced by more sobs, but I was still stuck on the ones she'd just said. *Five days*. The kidnapping. I'd afforded Tabby too much grace, thinking Sherrie had staged it to scare her and the others, but clearly she was in on it too. Anger pulsed beneath my cheeks at the deception, but I had to keep it hidden, not let Tabby see the trouble she was in. Because despite everything, I couldn't help but feel sorry for her. What kind of life had she had if this was where it had brought her? Made her feel that her paid partnerships and the band were the only things she had, so desperate for the attention she got from them that she thought dying was the better option rather than be ostracised by them. I swallowed my emotions as Tabby carried on rambling.

'I know Dee Dee pushing her like that was terrible, truly terrible, but ... but look at her now – no one will ever forget the name Ris Angelini,' she said, a trace of the defiance I'd heard before when she'd refused to cancel the gig returning to her voice.

The realisation I was fighting a losing battle trying to make her think she could come out the other side of this hit me like a vicious wind. If there was one thing that would get her the attention she so desperately craved, make her infamous, it would be pulling off a stunt like this. This *was* her time, her turn, and she had no intention of letting her fans down.

I jerked my head to the ceiling, following the length of rope along the rail, trying to find the part that the operator would use on the ground level to raise and lower the lifting mechanism. Tabby began talking again as I spotted the large wall-mounted cleat off to my right, the other end of the rope to the one Tabby was holding looped around it multiple times in a figure-of-eight pattern.

'They'll remember me now, won't they, Sergeant?' she said, her words coated in a peculiar pride as she composed herself.

I needed to untie that rope from its anchor, making her attempt at using it to hang herself useless.

Her next words were directed towards the camera. 'Your support has meant the absolute world to me . . .'

I took off towards the wall, reaching it in seconds, but now that I was closer to the contraption I saw the full extent of the tangled mess. The old rope was practically fused with rust to the metal it was looped around, held in place by several other ropes and bits of twine that had been piled on top in the numerous years since the last time this thing had been undone. 'Fuck!' I growled, before turning to look back at Tabby to see how much time I had left.

'. . . and I'm sorry, I truly am,' she said, placing the noose over her head and tightening it around her neck. 'Know everything I do, have done, is filled with love and light.'

Fuck, fuck, fuck. 'Tabby, don't do this!' I said, trying to keep the panic from my voice as I dug my fingers into the knots, testing one after the other, fingernails bending back as I tried to yank them apart with nothing budging, not even a centimetre. 'Tabby? You stay with me now, d'you hear?' I said, my eyes focussed on the knots.

She spoke again, but not in answer to my question. '. . . and . . . and I . . . I hope you at least enjoyed the show.'

A second later, metal groaned above my head, a *whoosh* moving through the air behind me. I spun, Tabby's feet swinging just out of reach. 'Tabby! No!' I knew there was no point reaching for her, I'd barely skim her toes even if I jumped. Finding something to stand on would be pointless as it'd be nowhere near stable enough for me to lift her and stop the rope crushing her windpipe. I scoured the equipment strewn around the edges of the room for something of use, trying to tune out Tabby's spluttering and gurgling as her feet kicked desperately in my peripheral vision.

I gasped as I saw it, an axe as rusty as the wall cleat, but it would have to do. Grabbing it, I ran back to the end of the rope, swinging the axe up over my head before sending it crashing down on to the mesh of knots. Only the back edge of the blade hit its target, the rest embedding itself into the wall. 'Shit!' I yelled, yanking it back out before swinging it over my head again. *You're in the station car park, just smashing up computers with Terry, easy breezy*, I thought, trying to calm myself and forget about the pressure of the woman's life literally hanging in the balance behind me. I swung again, strands of fibre splitting and fraying this time. I hacked at it twice more before finally cutting through, the remaining rope hanging limp from the cleat while the rest of it shot off into the air like a firework, squealing like a fisherman's reel as Tabby's weight dragged it through the pulley system and her body thudded to the floor behind me.

49

It had been almost two weeks to the day since Sherrie caved the side of my head in. The concussion had gone, the gash scabbed over, but the painkillers had done nothing to stop the nightmares; the constant loop in my mind replaying the festival shooting and images of Tabby's best attempt at a macabre swansong in the barn. My therapist would no doubt have an absolute field day at our next session. And I'm sure she'd do a fabulous job fixing my brain, but the one thing she couldn't do, to help me fully feel healed, was find Sherrie: a prospect that felt less and less possible every day that passed. I pushed the thought away with a deep inhale of crisp pre-autumnal air. Wooden slats creaked under my bum as Roy sat down on the bench next to me.

'Cemeteries usually give me the creeps,' he said, taking in the whole view around us as we sat in St Mary's churchyard. 'This one's actually quite nice, peaceful.'

'Not sure I'd go quite as far as saying it feels *peaceful*, but they certainly keep it well maintained.' I checked my watch, wondering how much longer we'd have to wait. Roy pulled a packet of Doritos from his pocket and prised it open. He took a mouthful for himself before offering some to me. 'Ew, Roy! You're not meant to eat in a graveyard.'

He shoved another batch of crisps into his mouth. 'Says who?'

'Don't you think it feels, I dunno, disrespectful or something?'

Roy shrugged. 'I'm sure these fine people wouldn't begrudge me a snack.'

'At least it's not hummus, that's all I can say.'

'I'll have you know I take my cheat days more seriously than Milli Vanilli. Me and Trudy are off to that new Chinese buffet in Kinton later.'

I was glad he'd finally had the conversation with Trudy about their food situation, even though, as it turned out, she was only doing it because she thought *he* was enjoying it. *Couples, urgh.*

'Have at it, Roy. You only live once, so you might as well enjoy it.'

We both took an impromptu moment of silence and I imagined we were thinking the same thing. Tabby's parents would be visiting their daughter at a psychiatric hospital instead of a grave, for now, providing they didn't have more pressing yachting matters to attend to, of course. But I couldn't help but wonder if by cutting her down that day in the barn I'd simply delayed the inevitable, rather than prevented it. Physically, the damage she'd done to herself had been minimal, but her mental scars were a whole other matter. Pursuing charges for theft of medication from the hospital, drugging Em and Nush and faking her kidnapping didn't seem to be in anyone's best interests.

Roy broke the silence. 'I quite fancy one of these when I pop me clogs,' he said, swivelling and pointing to the weathered metal plaque between us on the bench's backrest.

The sign had clearly been there a while, the engraved text barely visible, unlike the inscription on Ris's well-kept head-stone we'd paid our respects to on the way in, the bright white words standing out from the black marble like it had been put there yesterday instead of ten years ago. I licked my finger and rubbed away the plaque's grime, reading as it became legible. 'Sandra Mc . . . Mc-something . . . sister . . . mother . . . wife . . . daughter . . . loved by all, always missed.' My throat swelled, voice cracking. What was wrong with me? I didn't even know this Sandra woman. Maybe she was a terrible person who didn't like dogs and drop-kicked babies.

Thankfully Roy was concentrating on getting the scraps of crisp dust from the bottom of the packet and not on my face. 'It's nice, isn't it? Nice to have somewhere to come, somewhere to think about people and have a seat at the same time. Take stock,' he said.

My thoughts came out without my even meaning them to. 'Not sure there'd be any point me getting one, not enough people to come sit on it.'

Roy reached out and nudged my arm in an awkward but well-intentioned gesture. 'I'd come, bring the dog. Can't promise she won't do a wee on your bench leg though.'

I cleared the lump in my throat. 'No offence, but I hope

I live long enough that you'll already be a good six feet under by the time I'm gone.'

I'd thought a lot about some of the things Sherrie had said in the pool room, highlighting our supposed similarities. Part of me worried maybe she'd been right, that if I had another twenty years on me I'd be just as bitter and twisted, resigned to the inevitability that things are the way they are. End of. And you either played the game or got trampled by it. But that's where Sherrie and I couldn't be more different. Because every time I felt the weight of wearing the metaphorical uniform, the sins of the worst of us dragging at my shoulders, there was always something to remind me of the best of us, that things could get better. Bret had thrown himself in front of complete strangers because he felt it was his duty to do so. And when I'd told Dad how Ris really died, his guilt had broken my heart. Even though it wasn't his case, he'd still insisted this was on him, that he should have kept a tighter grip on things despite what he'd been going through with Mum. That was the difference between cops like Gordy and Dad. Gordy was still blaming everyone but himself.

Roy's voice pulled me from my thoughts. 'Maybe Bret'll come and sit on it,' he said, nudging me in the side, 'now you and him are *BFFs*, doing him favours.'

'Will you piss off. I'm not doing *him* a favour, I'm doing his niece a favour.'

'You say tomato . . .' Roy said with a knowing smile.

'Yeah, and so do you because we're both fucking English, you idiot.'

I was about to carry on my verbal assault when something out the corner of my eye distracted me, the movement we'd finally been waiting for at the door of the church as Nush, Em and Ris Angelini's family filed out of the anniversary service.

'You keep your tomatoes to yourself,' I said, standing and straightening my suit. 'How do I look?'

'Very dapper, but I don't think it's gonna be your outfit that makes Ris's mother tell you to do one.'

'I wasn't going for dapper, I was going for respectful.' I turned and walked off towards the car park where the group were headed.

'Good luck,' Roy called after me.

And boy was I going to need it. Because this was the only thing left I could think of to get Dee Dee to finally admit that the facts I'd laid out in front of her, based on what Kit and I had found and what Sherrie and Tabby had told me, were the truth. She was still scared of something, but I couldn't figure out what hold Sherrie still had over her. And if Santina Angelini – the only other person who Dee Dee had cared about in her life – couldn't get it out of her, then I didn't know who could.

The relief I'd felt at getting Santina to at least agree to visit Dee Dee in prison had evaporated the second I passed through the gates of Blackberry Grove Primary School two hours later. As I parked up and made my way towards the entrance, I wondered whether Bret's heroic act had really stemmed from the overwhelming desire to protect, or if he'd seen the date marked in his calendar for the careers day at Pippa's school and thrown himself in front of the bullet so he wouldn't have to give the presentation about being a police officer he'd been roped into. I hadn't been quick enough to think of an acceptable excuse when he'd called with Pippa on speakerphone and asked me to step in. *Jammy bastard*. I half wished Sherrie had whacked me a bit harder.

Butterflies danced in my stomach as I walked into reception and told the woman behind the desk I was there for Mr Logan's class. Why was I so nervous? Surely they weren't all like Pippa, smart enough to make you feel like you were undergoing the Spanish Inquisition. Even though I hadn't spent a lot of – well, actually, any – time around children since I was one, I knew she was the exception, not the rule. And I'd dealt with worse crowds. Far-right protesters. Football hooligans. How bad could a classroom of ten-year-olds really be?

I got my answer when a frazzled-looking man I presumed was Mr Logan burst through the double swing doors, waving at me with one hand and scrubbing some sort of brown stain from his baby-blue tie with the other. 'Detective Sergeant Washington?' he said.

'Please, just Alice is fine, hi,' I said, shaking his hand.

He gestured towards the stain. 'Nothing to worry about, one of the Year Threes had a little accident. Stashed a whole packet of Penguin biscuits in their bag and thought eating them before PE would be a good idea. The gym floor took the brunt of it.' He smiled in a way that meant I couldn't tell if he genuinely thought it was funny or if he was forcing himself to pretend it was so that he didn't scream and walk straight into the head teacher's office and hand in his notice. 'Honestly,' he said, 'don't worry, the Year Sixes are more chilled out, and they've just done PE too, really knackered them out for you so they should be good as gold.'

'I'm sure falling asleep will be more fun than listening to anything I have to say.'

'Don't be daft, they're really looking forward to your talk. So far they've had an accountant and an IT Project Manager, so let's just say their potentials haven't exactly been set on fire,' he said, eyes – the same baby-blue colour as his tie – scrunching as he smiled, definitely a genuine one this time.

I followed him down the corridor to his classroom. He pushed open the door and simultaneously a chorus of voices rang out.

'GOOOOOOD MORNIIIIIIING, DETECTIVE SERGEANT WASHINGTOOOOOOOON,' the children said in mostly synchronised melody, some of them tripping over the middle syllables.

Pippa waved from the front row. Seeing their hope-filled faces made me feel a little bit like Freddie Mercury at Live Aid. I resisted the urge to really get them going with a back and forth of 'Ay Ohs'. 'Wow, that's quite the welcome! Good morning, everyone,' I said.

Mr Logan pointed towards a small podium that had been haphazardly decorated with bits of paper containing hand-drawn words, produced by the children, I assumed.

DREAMS. AMBITION. WHEN I GROW UP, they said.
Oh Jesus, no pressure.

'If you could pop yourself over there for us, Alice,' Mr
Logan said, pointing in the direction of the podium, 'and
Pippa, could you come up and introduce your guest, please?'

I walked over to my spot as Pippa got up, turning and
pushing her glasses up her nose before she spoke. 'My guest
is Detective Sergeant Alice Washington.' She turned and
pointed at me like we were at Crufts. 'And she's here to
talk about being a police officer, which is a really important
job because police officers keep everyone safe, and make
sure bad people can't hurt us.' I half expected her to carry
on, reeling off the Peelian principles, but she didn't, and I
realised she didn't need to; she'd put it so perfectly already.
'And being a police officer is really hard. I know, because
my uncle Bret is one and he was supposed to come today
but he can't because he got shot in the stomach.'

I winced as a collective gasp filled the room. I wasn't
going to get a single question about policing now, was I?

Mr Logan interjected, 'Thank you, Pippa, you can sit
down. OK, who wants to go first?' Every hand in the room
went up. *Oh God.* 'Feel free to call on whoever you like,'
he said.

'Erm . . .' I picked a girl with pigtails, hoping she might
be less likely to ask about blood and guts than some of the
boys, because I'd been reliably informed by Jane that little
boys were gross. 'How about you there, in the green dress.'

'If you get shot in the tummy, do you have to poo out the
bullets?' she asked, head cocked to one side in fascination.

393

I made a mental note to never, ever rely on gender stereotypes again. Little girls can be just as gross as boys. Should have stuck to my initial assessment that all children are disgusting.

'Abigail!' Mr Logan said. 'That's not a question about being a police officer, is it? Fiona, how about you? And no more shooting questions, please.'

Three quarters of the hands in the room went down.

The little girl he'd pointed at spoke through the fingers that were in her mouth. 'Is it fun being a police officer?'

All of a sudden I was desperate for more questions about shooting and guts and poo. I scanned the room, their faces all new and shiny, no time to have become cynical about the world. Then I caught Pippa's eyes, which were exactly like Bret's, and I remembered. 'Sometimes it's fun, and there's lots of times it isn't fun. But policing isn't a job you should do because you want to have fun. It's a job you do because you can't think of yourself doing anything else. You have to love it, even when it's not fun. Even when it makes you angry and makes you cry sometimes. But you do it because, if you do it well, you can stop people from doing bad things, help to keep people safe, like Pippa said.'

They asked questions for another twenty minutes, thankfully nothing too taxing, before we all posed for a group photo. I squatted down so I was on their level, but then I noticed they'd all copied me and were also squatting, so I still stuck out like a sore thumb. 'What are you doing, I'm ... never mind,' I said.

'Cheese!' Mr Logan said before the children repeated the word and he walked me back out to reception.

'Nice to see them excited about something – maybe we've got the next generation's thin blue line in there.'

'We could do with some fresh blood.'

He shoved his hands into the pockets of his trousers. 'I didn't wanna say, must be hard at the moment.'

'Not ideal, but I imagine teaching isn't exactly a walk in the park either.'

'No, well, if you ever want to cry into a pint over it, you know where to find me.' He looked instantly panicked. 'God, that sounds like I've asked you out, doesn't it? Sorry, I just meant . . . I don't know what I meant, actually.'

'It's fine, don't worry about it . . . Mr . . .' I paused; it felt weird calling him Mr now.

'Sal, sorry, I should have said when I introduced myself. It's short for Salvatore. Mum's Italian, Dad's Scottish, ergo, Salvatore Logan. Sorry, you only asked my name, not my life story.'

'That's OK, sounds like an interesting one. Maybe I'll take you up on that drink sometime, you can tell me more about it.' Bloody hell, where did that come from? Am I making a *move* – is that what's happening here? I forced my face to stay neutral as he grabbed a leaflet from the shelf beside us and a pen from his shirt pocket and wrote down his number. I took it from him, the paper almost fizzing between my fingers. 'Look, erm, full disclosure, I've kinda got some stuff going on right now that means I probably shouldn't use this for a while,' I said.

He held his palms up to face me. 'Don't plan on changing it anytime soon.'

A warmth blossomed in my stomach. 'Thanks. Nice to meet you, Sal.'

'And you,' he said with a smile before turning and walking back towards the corridor.

I waited for the door to swing closed behind him then smiled myself, folded the piece of paper and put it into my purse. I was fully aware I'd probably never use it, that getting a 'someone' wouldn't come close to solving my problems. But I had to admit, there was something nice about having the option.

Epilogue

It made a change to be sat opposite Dee Dee without a prison table between us, her perched on a sofa in Santina Angelini's new home on the outskirts of Oxford, me occupying the large armchair on the other side of the room.

'I can't believe it's here already,' Dee Dee said. The hair she tucked behind her ears was half the length it had been in prison; the weight of her conviction and split ends left behind in one fell swoop. 'When they first set the date it felt like ages away.'

'Tell me about it,' I said. 'You think you've got ages to get everything ready for trial, then boom, it's the first day of court and you're scrabbling around for things last minute.' I wouldn't normally have said something like that to a member of the public, but given Dee Dee's experience, I figured she was already more clued up on the shitshow that was the criminal justice system than most people would be in a lifetime. 'But not to worry, we're all prepared for Monday, good to go, finally,' I said, alluding to the fact Sherrie's legal team had run out of excuses to orchestrate yet another postponement.

For someone with such a set of balls on her, they seemed to be withering and dying the closer Sherrie got to facing justice for what she'd done. She wasn't stupid, she knew she wasn't going to have a long leg to stand on. The evidence against her was overwhelming, especially with Tabby being well enough to be a witness for the prosecution, and Dee Dee's account of the threats Sherrie had made when she'd visited her in prison would be the final nail in the coffin. Sherrie had promised to ruin the only two things left that mattered to Dee Dee if she'd told the truth and upset her operation: Ris's memory and Santina. I'd never know if Santina's forgiveness alone had been enough to get Dee Dee to reveal the truth in the end, or whether the spell on her had been broken by the fact we'd arrested Sherrie two days later after Tabby's parents finally contributed something positive to this mess, utilising her father's rather questionable contacts to trace Sherrie to South America. Quite frankly, I didn't care. We had her. And the truth was out now. Those were the only things that mattered.

As if she was responding to the presence of her name in my thoughts, Santina entered the living room, placing a tray of tea and biscuits on the low coffee table.

'Here we are,' she said, before sitting next to Dee Dee on the sofa, grasping her hands until they were balled up in hers like they had been on the video I'd watched of Ris telling them she'd made it into the band. They were sat on a different sofa, in a different house, in a very different time, but the same affection had returned, even after everything they'd been through.

'Thank you,' I said, picking up a biscuit. 'I just wanted to check in, I know giving evidence can be daunting.'

Dee Dee smiled softly. 'I spent a decade in prison, I think my "daunting" threshold is probably a bit higher than most people's.'

'How are you settling in ... or out, I suppose?'

'I'm fine,' Dee Dee said with a shrug. 'All feels a bit weird. I know this might sound strange, but I actually didn't mind prison, once I got used to it – better than where I spent the first two decades of my life anyway.'

Usually that would sound very strange indeed, but I'd seen the home Dee Dee had grown up in.

'Don't worry,' Santina interjected, 'I'll get her back on her feet in no time. I've missed having someone to look after.'

She placed an arm around Dee Dee's shoulders and pulled her closer. Dee Dee went with the motion, but pain dulled her smile. She may have been released from prison, officially exonerated, but I had the feeling she'd never fully forgive herself for what happened to Ris and what Santina had gone through as a result.

The transcript I'd read of Dee Dee's initial police interview, the one where she'd kept repeating the words *I killed her*, had been recorded when Dee Dee was still in shock, before the record label had sent their solicitor in to mess with her head even more, tie her up in knots made from a rope of lies laced with threads of her own culpability, convincing her she was better off entering an early guilty plea to get a reduced sentence and not put Santina through the excruciating pain of a lengthy trial. If only Dee Dee's mouth had translated the words aloud exactly as she'd thought them in her head, *I may as well have killed her*, then maybe things could have been different, not taken so easily as fact.

Kit and I may have got the ball rolling on piecing things together, but it had been the review resulting in Dee Dee's conviction being overturned that completed the puzzle. Ris had sent her notebook to Dee Dee's flat in the post, though it still wasn't clear why. Dee Dee was convinced she was the subject of the rage-filled ramblings, and that Ris wanted her to know how angry she was that Dee Dee hadn't supported her, wanted her to see the pain she'd caused by encouraging Ris to remain part of the band she'd never wanted to be involved with in the first place so Dee Dee could come along for the ride and get away from Judith. But I didn't buy it. It was obvious to me the notebook was about Sherrie. And even if some of the anger was directed at Dee Dee, Ris may have been in a dark place, but nothing I'd learned about her suggested she was cruel. My best guess was that Ris had sent the notebook either as a cry for help or to act as her suicide note. Not that Dee Dee would ever be convinced either way, refusing to let go of this last thing she could continue to flog herself with.

Dee Dee had turned up at the Big Top Ballroom to apologise to Ris. Finding her alone in her dressing room with a razor blade to her wrist, she'd managed to wrestle it from her, before Ris ran for the stage roof as an alternative, Dee Dee in pursuit, trying and failing to stop her from jumping. The real gut punch had been Dee Dee's account of what happened with the photographs. Dee Dee had admitted taking them, a combination of her drunken haze and being egged on by Adzy Loader's claims it was 'just a bit of a laugh', but she'd refused to make excuses for herself. She took full responsibility for the fact that when Ris came to her a few weeks later to tell her she thought she was being blackmailed, Dee Dee had been too ashamed to take the opportunity to admit the part she'd played, and hadn't stuck up for Ris when Sherrie had talked her out of going to the police by scaring her with whispers of the questions she'd likely be asked. *How much had you had to drink? Are you sure you didn't know they were being taken? Have one-night stands with people you don't know often, do you?*

Sherrie's desire to keep the photographs private was for her own benefit, not Ris's, but there was a reason her scare tactic had worked. Because it was probably exactly how it would have played out back then. And while things were getting better, I certainly couldn't guarantee that sort of thing wouldn't happen again now. I pushed the thought away, reminding myself of the commitment I'd made to cling to the hope that things in the job would improve; it'd just take time. I distracted myself with something positive, scoffing down the biscuit in one go. 'Anyway,' I said after swallowing it, 'I'm glad the two of you have each other.'

Dee Dee nodded and squeezed Santina's hand.

'And on that note,' I continued, 'please don't shoot the messenger, but have you given any more thought to going to see your mum?'

Dee Dee looked towards the window. 'No.'

'To clarify, I'm not sticking up for her; she made your childhood hell, I can see that, but she's still your mum. And they don't think she has much time left. If there was anything you wanted to get off your chest – for your benefit, I mean, not hers – then now's the time.'

Judith had been in and out of hospital since her collapse in custody turned out to be related to lung cancer, which had now been diagnosed as stage four, the coughing into the towel at her flat and her sudden desperation to make everything right with Dee Dee all making more sense when I'd heard the news.

A tear rolled down Dee Dee's cheek and she tried to wipe it away before I saw it. 'What would I even say to her?'

'Whatever you want, scream at her, call her every name under the sun.'

Dee Dee got up and walked to the window.

Santina gave me an *I'll talk to her* nod and I let out a relieved breath. Dee Dee couldn't have a better guide for helping her reconnect with Judith. Ris's mother had clearly mastered the art of forgiveness in a way I'd never seen before. A thought of Tess blew through my mind like a leaf on a gentle breeze, before leaving again as quickly as it had entered.

I'd barely been back home ten minutes when the delivery driver pulled up outside.

'All right, love, where d'you want this stuff?' he said.

'In the garage, but if you can just get them off the back then I can take it from there.'

My dad, who I'd roped in as my helper for the afternoon, pulled up and parked alongside the van.

'No problem,' the driver said before climbing out of the cab and pulling up the large roller shutter.

The smell of vinegar and deep-fried batter filled the air as Dad opened his car door and got out carrying a rustling plastic bag full of fish and chips.

'How much have you bought?' I said. 'There's only two of us!' I had invited Irma, but she'd suggested maybe it'd be a good idea for us to have a bit of father and daughter time. Any excuse to get out of manual labour.

'We're gonna need it,' Dad said, 'if we've gotta carry all that.' He nodded towards the pile of boxes. 'I hope you're not relying on me to set this lot up, mind, you know I'm not musical.'

'Oh, believe me, I do know. My vivid memory of you trying to sing Meatloaf on the karaoke at Mum's fortieth gives me another box to tick in the childhood trauma test.'

'Not my fault I can't carry a tune in a bucket.'

'Here,' I said, handing him one of the boxes, 'carry this instead.'

We set up the drum kit based on some poorly written instructions and several YouTube videos. Whether or not we'd done it correctly was a whole other matter, but given I had no idea how to even play the damn things, I didn't think it would matter. It had been Nush and Terry combined that had given me the idea; her description of what it felt like playing them, the flow state, combined with the release I got from the pressures of the job from smashing things up. Putting the two together seemed like the perfect hobby. And who knew, maybe my bony arms were hiding the next John Bonham. And even if the online drum lessons I'd paid for did no good and I ended up just bashing the shit out of these things as my own form of rage reduction, no one would ever hear it, so what did it matter?

I pulled the plastic and cardboard packaging off my new set of drumsticks, holding them in the palm of my hands. 'Apparently, I have to give these things names.' I held them up and appraised them one at a time. 'I have a feeling you're going to need a hell of a lot of stamina, because if the job carries on the way it is much longer, you're gonna be getting a lot of use, and you're going to have to be tough as nails, because while my musical prowess might not amount to much, I do back myself on my ability to hit things. Hard. So,' I cleared my throat as if I was about to announce the winner of the next Nobel Peace Prize, 'I christen thee, Dench and Mirren.'

'Come on then,' Dad said from his seat on a crate in the corner of my garage, dipping a chunky chip into a pot of mushy peas. 'Show me what you've got.'

I squeezed the two pieces of pine in my hands and adjusted my position on the small stool before planting my feet firmly on the ground. The kick pedal would have to wait. Trying to figure out what to do with my hands was going to be difficult enough; I'd give it a while before bringing my feet into the equation. I hit the sticks together and counted myself in, 'One, two, three, four . . .'

Acknowledgements

First and foremost, I'd like to thank Lucy Dauman for being the best editorial chef I could ask for. I handed you a bag of random ingredients, and it was your astute insights that helped me turn them into a tasty meal that I'm truly proud to serve to readers. Sticking to the food theme for a moment, a big thank you to Isabel Martin for your feedback and enthusiasm in the early stages of stirring my messy bookish pot, along with the whole team at Headline for the hard work you all do in the publishing kitchen.

To my amazing agent Sabhbh Curran at Curtis Brown, for helping me on this journey and for the energy with which you talk about Alice and Roy in our catch-ups. It warms my heart that it feels like we're talking about real people.

My mam and dad, Sue and Frank, provide an endless supply of unfaltering encouragement and for that I will always be grateful. An additional thank you goes to my dad for initiating the love of music that provides the backdrop to this story (sorry, Mam, but your musical taste is canny crap). I may have moaned at the time when you made me listen to the likes of Bob Dylan and Van Morrison on our long drives to Liverpool, but if you hadn't persisted, I'm not sure my taste would have broadened beyond Take That, and the references threaded throughout this book would have been all the cheesier for it. So thank you for the music.

I cannot express strongly enough my eternal gratitude to the friends, family and writing/reading community who supported book one in this series, *All Eyes on You*. I'm not going to list names as there are so many of you I'm terrified of missing people out, but whether you attended my event to celebrate publication, bought the book, borrowed it, shouted about it online, or helped spread word of mouth, a huge thank you to each and every one of you. Your encouragement made me all the more excited to dive back into the world of Fortbridge and write this second book. Extra special shout-outs go to my besties, Shell and Nicki, for their unwavering support and excellent bartending skills at the launch party (despite 'losing' three bottles of Prosecco), as well as everyone in the Bookish Buddies WhatsApp group – the insights into the world of dating apps were very useful for this book!

To the authors who read proofs of my last book and gave me my first ever endorsements – Lisa Timoney, Daniel Aubrey, Chris Bridges and Ciar Byrne – your time is extremely precious writing and promoting your own fabulous books so I could not be more grateful to you for giving some of that up to read and support my work. An extra thank you must go to Lisa for taking me under her wing at my first visit to Harrogate and doing a sterling job as my unofficial publicist. Without you introducing me to people, I would never have spoken to anyone and would have just sat in the corner of the beer tent like an anti-social goblin.

A big thanks to my former policing colleagues, particularly Greenie for answering lots more random procedural questions and Mark S for giving me the low-down on digital investigations (and tips on how to drag out getting results back!). Any inaccuracies are once again either my own errors, or liberties I've taken for the sake of dramatic effect.

To my partner, Tom. We don't do PDAs, but I'd like it on record that your knowledge of air vents and barn lifting equipment mechanics really made this book what it is. Thanks again for keeping Matilda, Beatrice, Douglas, Olive, Maggie and Molly occupied long enough for me to type this.

And finally, to the readers of this book. I hope you enjoyed it. If you did, I'd be so grateful if you'd consider leaving a review. Not only do they make my day, they'll also help Alice and Roy reach new readers. And God knows Alice could do with all the friends she can get her hands on.

Credits

Sam Frances would like to thank everyone involved in the production of One by One:

Editorial
Lucy Dauman
Isabel Martin
Ayana Playle

Copy-editor
Sarah Bance

Proofreader
Jill Cole

Audio
Ellie Wheeldon
Jessica Callaghan

Design
Lisa Horton

Production
Victoria Lord

Marketing
Hannah Whittaker

Publicity
Lily Birch

Sales
Rebecca Bader
Sinead White

Contracts
Helen Windrath
Rosalind Rustom

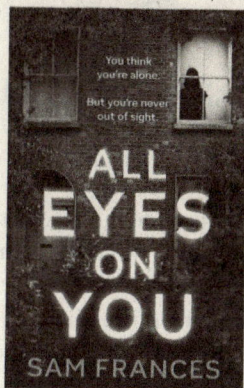

RAISING READERS
Books Build Bright Futures

Dear Reader,

We'd love your attention for one more page to tell you about the crisis in children's reading, and what we can all do.

Studies have shown that reading for fun is the **single biggest predictor of a child's future life chances** – more than family circumstance, parents' educational background or income. It improves academic results, mental health, wealth, communication skills, ambition and happiness.[1]

The number of children reading for fun is in rapid decline. Young people have a lot of competition for their time. In 2024, 1 in 10 children and young people in the UK aged 5 to 18 did not own a single book at home.[2]

Hachette works extensively with schools, libraries and literacy charities, but here are some ways we can all raise more readers:

- Reading to children for just 10 minutes a day makes a difference
- Don't give up if children aren't regular readers – there will be books for them!
- Visit bookshops and libraries to get recommendations
- Encourage them to listen to audiobooks
- Support school libraries
- Give books as gifts

There's a lot more information about how to encourage children to read on our website: **www.RaisingReaders.co.uk**

Thank you for reading.

hachette
UK

[1] OECD, '21st-Century Readers: Developing Literacy Skills in a Digital World', 2021, https://www.oecd.org/en/publications/21st-century-readers_a83d84cb-en.html

[2] National Literacy Trust, 'Book Ownership in 2024', November 2024, https://literacytrust.org.uk/research-services/research-reports/book-ownership-in-2024